DEUS-X

Also by Joseph A. Citro

Curious New England (with Diane E. Foulds), 2003

Vermont Air (edited with Philip Baruth), 2002

Lake Monsters, 2001

The Gore, 2000

The Vermont Ghost Guide, 2000

Guardian Angels, 1999

Green Mountains, Dark Tales, 1999

Shadow Child, 1998

Passing Strange, 1996

Green Mountain Ghosts, 1994

Vermont Lifer (writer/editor), 1986

Dorothy Canfield Fisher (Mark J. Madigan, ed.),
Seasoned Timber

Dorothy Canfield Fisher, *Understood Betsy*

Joseph Freda, *Suburban Guerrillas*

Castle Freeman, Jr., *Judgment Hill*

Frank Gaspar, *Leaving Pico*

Robert Harnum, *Exile in the Kingdom*

Ernest Hebert, *The Dogs of March*

Ernest Hebert, *Live Free or Die*

Ernest Hebert, *The Old American*

Sarah Orne Jewett (Sarah Way Sherman, ed.), *The Country of the Pointed Firs and Other Stories*

Raymond Kennedy, *Ride a Cockhorse*

Raymond Kennedy, *The Romance of Eleanor Gray*

Lisa MacFarlane, ed., *This World Is Not Conclusion: Faith in Nineteenth-Century New England Fiction*

G. F. Michelsen, *Hard Bottom*

Anne Whitney Pierce, *Rain Line*

Kit Reed, *J. Eden*

Rowland E. Robinson (David Budbill, ed.), *Danvis Tales: Selected Stories*

Roxana Robinson, *Summer Light*

Rebecca Rule, *The Best Revenge: Short Stories*

Catharine Maria Sedgwick (Maria Karafilis, ed.), *The Linwoods; or, "Sixty Years Since" in America*

R. D. Skillings, *How Many Die*

R. D. Skillings, *Where the Time Goes*

Lynn Stegner, *Pipers at the Gates of Dawn: A Triptych*

Theodore Weesner, *Novemberfest*

W. D. Wetherell, *The Wisest Man in America*

Edith Wharton (Barbara A. White, ed.), *Wharton's New England: Seven Stories and* Ethan Frome

Thomas Williams, *The Hair of Harold Roux*

Suzi Wizowaty, *The Round Barn*

DEUS-X

The Reality Conspiracy

Joseph A. Citro

University Press of New England
Hanover and London

University Press of New England
37 Lafayette St., Lebanon, NH 03766

Originally published in 1994 by Twilight Publishing, Sparta, NJ

ISBN 1–58465–339–6
Library of Congress Control Number: 2003110897

Acknowledgments

To properly thank everyone who helped me with *DEUS-X: The Reality Conspiracy* would require another volume this size. Scores of individuals made contributions, whether they realize it or not. However, I owe a substantial debt to the following: Michael Johnson, Pat Whitman, Craig Goden, John Keel, Steve Bissette, Diane E. Foulds, Wayne and Darlene Decker, Phil Pochoda and Sarah Welsch. Thanks, too, to everyone who, by request or oversight, is not listed above.

"The only thing I will say with complete confidence about the mystic and invisible power is that it tells lies."

— G. K. Chesterton

Contents

PART ONE

In the Beginning...

"God laughed, and begat the Son. Together they laughed, and begat the Holy Spirit. And from the laughter of the three, the universe was born."

—Meister Eckhart

"Then we who are alive, who are left, shall be caught up together with them in the clouds to meet the Lord in the air; and so we shall always be with the Lord."

—Thessalonians 4:17

Excerpt from
The Reality Conspiracy:
An Anecdotal Reconstruction of the Events at Hobston, Vermont

We are born into a tiny room without windows and doors. Docilely, through unspoken consensus, we name the six planes that surround us; we call them *reality*.

Four walls, the floor, the ceiling, they define our limits and our aspirations.

Yet, there are some among us who say there is more. They place an ear against the wall and swear they hear a whisper on the other side. Some hear footsteps. A scratch. A gentle, rhythmic tap.

Others say they hear a chorus of voices chanting the unfamiliar words to an unfamiliar song.

While all the time our priests and politicians, our cynics and our scientists, testify that we are alone in the room, that its sturdy walls, infinitely thick, extend into eternity.

But wait! Now, from the far side of the wall, the gentle scratch becomes a tap.

And the tapper starts to pound.

Our wall trembles, begins to split. And now—oh God—something is coming through!

1

Tribulation

Boston, Massachusetts
Thursday, November 12
08:05 hours

Dr. Ian "Skipp" McCurdy led the man from the Pentagon along the narrow, neon-lit corridor.

The man, who had introduced himself only as *Rex*, carried a small leather attaché case and wore dark glasses, even in the basement rooms. His suit was obviously expensive, cut to complement his health-club physique. It seemed perfectly pressed, brand-new. McCurdy couldn't figure it: the man had flown in from Washington much earlier that morning; he had no doubt been jostled at the airport, bumped on the streets, and cramped in the cabs, yet he looked as if his suit had just come freshly from the closet.

For a moment McCurdy thought perhaps he himself should have dressed better for the occasion. Maybe his corduroys and sweater vest were not the most well-chosen attire. After all, there was a lot of money hanging on this demonstration, almost a billion dollars, another two years of generous research funding. McCurdy thought how horrible it would be if the whole project were shot down because there was no dress code at the Academy.

Absently, McCurdy clicked his tongue, "Tch, tch, tch."

"What's that, Doctor?" Rex asked.

"Oh, ah . . . nothing."

McCurdy stopped before a locked metal door. "Right in here, sir," he said as he punched in a numerical code that released the lock. He pulled the door open. The man nodded and preceded McCurdy into the dim, indirectly lighted chamber. The door locked behind them with a metallic thud.

The room was nearly bare. At its center, two canvas director's chairs faced two forty-five-inch Mitsubishi television screens about ten feet away. Without waiting for formalities, the man took a seat, placed the attaché case on his lap, as McCurdy walked over to an electronic control panel on the wall by the television screens.

"Are you satisfied with the briefing to this point?" McCurdy asked. "If I can answer any more questions . . . ?" His voice seemed weak and hollow to his own ears. He hoped his nervousness didn't show.

"Quite satisfied, Dr. McCurdy. I'm not here for more explanations. I'm here for a demonstration. If you'd be good enough to proceed."

McCurdy clicked his tongue. It was hard for him to come to grips with the fact that the entire demonstration was for the benefit of a single individual. He had expected some kind of committee. Three people, at least. He was uncomfortable that so much seemed to rest on the opinion of just one man. But as Rex had explained in military jargon, the fewer people who were "cognizant" of this, the better for all of us.

Well, if this was how it had to be, then so be it.

McCurdy turned the switches. The screen on the left began to glow red. A golden circle formed at its center. The circle expanded until it nearly filled the screen. White lines began to intersect the circle.

McCurdy said, "I'll turn up the volume so you can hear the sounds that accompany this. They'll continue throughout the demonstration, but we won't have to listen to them. I just want to give you the idea. . . ."

The man nodded impatiently.

McCurdy pressed the volume control and a guttural, synthetically produced dirge filled the room. McCurdy could pick out a word now and then, but his mastery of Latin had never been what it should be, and the electronically articulated syllables were really not that easy to understand, anyway.

For a moment he stared, almost hypnotized by the flowing, shifting patterns on the huge screen.

"Dr. McCurdy . . . ?" Rex urged.

McCurdy turned down the volume, and the dirge faded slowly into silence. Here goes, McCurdy thought.

He flicked on the second TV.

The video image was in black and white. The background was featureless, just a flat, white, nondescript wall.

In the foreground stood an empty chair. It was wooden. Square and solid-looking. McCurdy knew it was bolted to the floor. He had seen such chairs in Vietnam. No one sat in them willingly; they were for interrogation.

At the bottom of the screen electronic letters flashed on and off, reading: November 12 / 05:18 hrs.

McCurdy picked up a microphone and spoke into it. "Please stand by," he said. "We're almost ready to begin."

McCurdy turned to Rex. "This picture is coming to us via satellite all the way from California. The signal is thoroughly scrambled, indecipherable. That's all I know. Your people picked the location. It is unknown to anyone at this facility. You and I will see everything in real-time, exactly as it happens. We'll hear everything just as it is being said. The important thing to remember is that what we'll watch is happening four thousand miles away at an undisclosed location. And the only thing connecting us with them is the television signal."

"Yes, yes, I understand, Dr. McCurdy. Now if we could begin . . ."

McCurdy picked up the microphone again. "You're on," he said. This time his voice cracked like fragile ice.

On the screen two men in black suits, with ski masks over their heads, led a third man into the frame. The man was naked. He didn't struggle. There was a vapid glaze to his eyes. His mouth hung open.

McCurdy noted how skinny he was, took in the filthy, dark hair tied back in a ponytail. A ring in his left ear caught the light; a homemade tattoo blemished his left shoulder. Some kind of scar was visible on his abdomen. Surgery or knife wound, McCurdy couldn't tell.

The men in black worked like a well-practiced team. They pushed the naked man into the wooden chair and efficiently bound his arms at the wrists and elbows with nearly invisible monofilament ties. Then they bound each of his legs at the ankle and at the knee. One of them tied a final loop around his throat. It held his spine tightly against the chair.

With a terrified expression on his face, the seated man watched the men in black. When he made as if to say something, the man to his left jerked a flattened hand to chest level, poised for a karate blow. The naked man fell silent, eyes downward. There was no further struggle or protest. No further attempt to communicate.

The monofilament held his legs so that they were slightly apart, butted against the frame of the chair. McCurdy could see the man's penis, a hairy gray knob of putty between skinny thighs.

Without taking his eyes from the screen, McCurdy sat in the director's chair beside Rex.

He watched the two men in black leave the frame, abandoning the tethered man to the TV camera. The man looked imploringly into the lens, then looked away. McCurdy looked away, too.

A fourth man, dressed in a white smock, entered the frame. He wore a surgeon's mask and a tied cap that covered his face and hair. He taped sensors on thin wires to the man's skin. McCurdy could hear him muttering to the man, "This won't hurt at all. We're just going to track your vital signs. It's no more painful than a lie detector test."

The man nodded. Tried to smile.

The doctor worked rapidly, then left the screen.

In a monotone, an electronically altered voice spoke clearly through the speaker between the two TV screens, "Can you hear us, gentlemen?"

McCurdy cleared his throat, "Perfectly."

"Then we'll begin. I'd like to introduce you to Mr. Denton Rene LaChance, age forty-seven. Denny, his friends call him."

Denny's eyes flicked back and forth. He shifted his weight in the wooden chair. A light rime of sweat glistened on his forehead. McCurdy could see how the invisible monofilament made grooves in his arms and legs.

The voice continued, "Denny's in excellent health for a smoker and frequent drug-user, our medical assures us. But Denny's not a very nice guy. Got kicked out of the army for playing with heroin. It was planted on him, he says. Might be true, I might add. Like everybody else, the army was anxious to get rid of him. Overwhelming evidence suggests he put a bullet through his lieutenant's head. We had enough trouble with the Cong without Denny blowing our officers away."

"Tch, tch, tch," McCurdy said.

"Stateside, he's got an arrest record that oughtta go platinum. Armed robbery, assault, rape, kidnapping, drug trafficking. All low personal risk occupations, 'cause that's the way Denny likes it. Not enough convictions, though; he's been lucky. In fact, he likes to brag that his name, LaChance, means 'luck'. But his luck ran out the day he picked up a ten-year-old on Ventura Boulevard, brought her out to the canyon, where he had some fun with her. Then, to keep her from identifying him, he punctured both her eyes with a screwdriver. To make sure she wouldn't talk he cut out her tongue with tin snips. And so nobody could identify *her*, he sliced the skin off her hands and face, using a knife for the rough work and sandpaper for the finish. When a couple of campers found her they discovered the worst crime of all: the poor kid was still alive. The police got him though; someone saw him pick her up. The D.A. proved he took her all right, but couldn't prove he did her. He got off. Nice guy, Denny LaChance."

"Soulless," McCurdy whispered. His stomach heaved. Acrid gas bubbled into his mouth. He blew it out silently and looked over at Rex who stared stone-faced at the screen.

"So, gentlemen," the electronic voice said, "if you're tempted to feel badly about anything that follows, save your pity for someone who needs it. Our friend Denny's a real scum-bag . . . a perfect candidate for the garbage disposal. That's it for us, I guess. Your move, gentlemen."

McCurdy moved to the control panel and turned a button. "I've just activated the computer link," he told Rex. Again he sat in the director's chair facing the twin screens. He crossed his legs, trying to look comfortable.

The patterns on the left-hand screen began to undulate and twirl. The background flashed red, neon green, blaze-orange. White spark-images jumped and danced.

What seemed to be a length of white cord, almost like an animated drawing, appeared, crossed and uncrossed, looped about itself, changing patterns as it seemed to tie itself in knots. It became a square, a star, a rectangle. When it turned into a circle, a 3-D computer graphic replication of Denny's face materialized in its center. The circle blinked like an eye and the face was gone.

On the other screen Denny fidgeted a bit. He pressed his lips together. His eyes darted back and forth. The wires taped to his skin swayed slightly.

Numbers at the bottom of the screen blinked and vanished: 05:29 hrs.

Nervously, McCurdy clicked his tongue. He wanted to watch; he wanted to look away. He had a pretty good idea what was coming.

He detected a faint smell, like incense, in the room. Everything was working perfectly.

05:30 hrs.

All of a sudden Denny's eyes widened. His surprised expression was almost comic, as if he'd been goosed or shocked. Then his spine stiffened. He sat up ramrod-straight. He bucked once, again. His arms and legs strained against their invisible bonds. The fetters seemed like deep black furrows in his skin.

He let out a startled cry. "Uuh—!" It was clipped short as his tongue squirmed from between his lips, sealing his mouth like a cork in a bottle. McCurdy could see perspiration pouring from the man.

Denny began to jump and twitch as if he were being jolted by electrical current.

The monitoring wires moved like a spiderweb with a fly trapped in it.

"The wires are just for monitoring equipment," McCurdy whispered. "There's no juice hitting the subject."

Rex said nothing.

Pellets of sweat shot from Denny's forehead. He bucked and heaved. Black blood spread from the grooves in his arms and legs. The embedded monofilament tie made his neck look as if an invisible knife were pushing deeper and deeper into its flesh.

A magnificent seizure jerked him forward. His jaw clamped. Teeth broke. A good three inches of severed tongue dropped from his mouth and plopped onto his throbbing erection.

His skin seemed to shine. Black blood from his wounds looked like motor oil. His mouth was a bloody black hole. Garbled, blunted syllables barked from his slick lips. His eyes bulged like overripe fruit about to burst.

He ejaculated.

He puked.

Somehow, he screamed.

McCurdy averted his eyes, then thought better of it. This was no time to appear squeamish.

He looked back at the screen in time to see Denny LaChance in the midst of a violent convulsion. He bucked and bounded like a prisoner in the throes of electrocution. The monofilament sliced the flesh from his arms and legs. White bone peeked from meaty folds of skin.

Denny jerked toward the camera again. His eyes exploded. Viscous liquid flowed down his cheeks.

His body sagged. Convulsed again.

A huge gaping mouth opened in his neck. No blood gushed from the wound.

2

Rapture

Hobston, Vermont
Thursday, November 12
7:30 A.M.

Alton Barnes followed his friend Stuart Dubois across the snow-covered meadow, making toward the woods. The men kicked tides of powdery whiteness from their path as their Sorrel boots sliced through patches of the brown brittle grasses.

Again Alton slowed down, allowing Stuart to remain in the lead. Glancing over his shoulder, he saw their meandering four-footed trail that marked their route all the way back to the Dubois farmhouse.

Alton looked at his own footprints; their line was so much straighter than Stu's. And Stu's stride wasn't as long, though the men were approximately the same height. Stu's trail was punctuated by frequent rest stops where he'd stood, deep breathing, shifting his weight from foot to foot, pretending to look around.

He's getting old, Alton thought, he's slowing down.

Facing forward again, an undisturbed carpet of white offered the men a royal welcome to the wilderness.

"Couldn't've got a more perfect day for trackin'," said Alton.

Stu stopped, turned around, spat a black wad of tobacco juice into the snow. "Praise the Lord," he agreed with an emphatic nod.

Alton wrinkled his nose at the black blemish on the pure white snow. "You back to that creosote chewin' gum again, are you?"

"You betcha." Stu spat again. "This blessed Red Man's the secret of my success. I buys me a two-week supply every year same time I pick up my huntin' license."

Normally, Al knew, Stu didn't chew tobacco. But today was special; it was the first day of hunting season. Stu made a point never to smoke his pipe in the woods. Pipe smoke, the old man explained year after year, would scare the deer away. One whiff of Prince Albert and they'd head for the high country, thinking a forest fire was chasing them.

Maybe Stu was on to something with the chewing tobacco; he got his buck every season, no arguing that.

When the men stopped again they had reached the top of the rise. They leaned their rifles against the stone wall and waited a moment before entering the forest.

"You want high or low ground?" Alton asked. He spat, too, but his colorless saliva left no stain on the virgin ground cover.

Stu looked up, then down at the earth between his boots, giving the question ample consideration. "You take the high ground, Al," he said. "Anything I can do to get you closer to the Heavenly Land is gonna work to my credit when I get the Call."

Alton laughed. "You're gonna get 'the Call' all right, and sooner than you think if you don't stop harpin' at me with all your high holy rollin'."

Stu smiled toothlessly and chuckled as he always did. "Heh, heh, heh-heh-heh." He took off a buckskin glove and massaged his craggy cheeks. Al could hear the scratch of chin whiskers beneath Stu's arthritic fingers. "I'm doin' it for your own good, Alton. I just hate the idea of havin' to talk to you long distance when I'm up there on the righteous side of them Pearly Gates."

Al held up his hands in resignation. "I surrender. I'll mend my ways, just lay off this Oral Roberts stuff."

"Zat mean you'll come to church with Daisy and me on Sundee?"

"Well, I don't want to get fanatical about this—"

"It's settled then. Let's shake on it." Stu held out his gloveless hand. Alton pushed a silver flask into it.

Stu drank, smacked his lips, then passed the flask back. "Nothin'll cement a bargain better'n a bit of ay-pricot brandy."

"Nothin'll shut you up faster'n a bottle in your mouth."

"Praise the Lord," Stu said.

* * *

The fading crunch of Alton's boots vanished into the distance.

Stuart was alone.

To his right a short row of evergreen trees, their branches heavy with snow, bent toward—sometimes touched—the ground.

The snow weighed on Stuart, too. He was winded. His heart thumped. He could hear the muted roar of blood pulsing past his ears as he stood sweating in the cold wind. That climb from the house to the forest got steeper every year.

Now, with Al out of sight, Stu permitted himself to stop and rest for a while. After placing his rifle against a hickory tree, he reached into his coat pocket and pulled out the plug of Red Man. He chomped some off between his gums. A stinging sweetness bit back at him and he smacked his lips.

"Lordy," he whispered, "Lordy, Lordy."

Not far away he saw evidence that a rabbit had passed by, and not long ago. As sunlight found each cluster of four tiny paw prints, they were transformed by the melting snow. They blended, ran together, formed the strange tracks of some large, unfamiliar animal. Stuart smiled. The woods'll play tricks on you if you let it, he chuckled. Yessir, Mother Nature can be a great deceiver.

He rested his hand against the peeling bark of a white birch trunk, gently, as if touching a lover who would soon depart.

He closed his eyes, the rubbery smile still broad on his face. How grand it would be if a man could grow tall and old like the trees. He could keep an eye on everything from above, he could study the mysterious shifting of seasons, look down upon the beautiful ever-changing patterns of sunshine and shadow on the Green Mountains. And at night he could fall asleep to the lullaby of the stream and the soft secret whisper of the wind.

Stuart opened his eyes and looked around.

A cloud must have passed the sun for suddenly it was colder. Trees rustled slightly, depositing tiny falls of snow that scattered in the breeze.

Something was nearby.

Snatching up his pa's ancient 32-40 Winchester, Stu tuned his ears to the forest sounds.

Reflexes ready, he scanned the snowy ground, the black tree trunks, the roll of earth where it dipped sharply before angling upward to become the eastern slope of Stattler Mountain.

Lord God it was all so beautiful.

His mind drifted from the thought of game to the wilderness itself. From where he stood, he could see no reminder of civilization: not a road, not a telephone line, not even a church steeple in the distance. The silence was unpolluted by chainsaws or automobiles, or even the barking of dogs.

He breathed deeply and tipped his head back. No jet exhaust discolored the crystal-blue winter sky.

This is the way the forest was meant to be. This is how it must have looked when the first white men came. And this is how it had looked to the Indians, a thousand—or a thousand thousand—years ago.

The thought pleased him, made him feel as if he were part of the ages.

Whatever had caught his attention was gone now.

Stuart lowered the barrel of the rifle. Soundlessly he stepped up onto a little rise of moss-covered bedrock, protected from the snow by a ledge. From there he could look across a shallow depression, past a shelf of shale, and up at the mountainside.

Then he saw it.

No more than twenty feet in front of him.

White light.

Stuart took an involuntary step backward.

Bright as a flashbulb.

He blinked several times, expecting the strange vision to tighten into some recognizable focus.

The light, it doesn't go out!

The hovering circle of brilliance seemed to pulse as it grew more intense. Stuart squinted, lifting his right hand to shade his eyes. He let the rifle slip from his left.

And the angel of the Lord appeared to him in a flame of fire out of the midst of a bush . . .

Part of his bewildered mind registered something about the shadows. Juniper bushes. Thick tree trunks. Their shadows should spread out around the glowing thing like the spokes of a wheel. But—

. . . and lo, the bush was burning, yet it was not consumed . . . !

Stuart turned his head away, trying to protect his eyes from the piercing white light.

When the Lord saw that he turned aside to see, God called to him out of the bush . . .

"STUART, STUART!"

"Here I am, Lord," he whispered, taking a cautious step forward.

"Do not come near; put off your shoes from your feet, for the place on which you are standing is holy ground."

Stuart dropped to his knees. He was closer to the fire. But he felt no heat.

He sat down. Cold wet snow darkened his woolen pants. His frantic fingers worked numbly with the laces of his boots. Before he could pull them free of his feet the brilliant white circle began to rise from the ground.

Stuart followed it with his eyes as it floated upward, passing like smoke through interwoven branches of towering evergreens.

Somehow, he found he was standing. His arms reached out, groping for the vision as it withdrew.

He took a step. "Oh my Lord, I have been a sinner. . . ."

Another step.

It was above him now, like a white-hot sun directly overhead.

"Deliver us from evil, oh my Lord. . . ."

* * *

It was then that his feet left the ground.

* * *

Stuart felt himself rising into the air. He was weightless, a feather, a lost balloon.

Up. Faster and faster. Cold air streaming past his face, sliding under his collar, chilling his back. He looked down at his feet as they peddled for purchase in the empty air. Clumps of packed snow fell from the soles of his boots, vanishing far below.

Boot laces hung in midair like dead worms dangling from a fishhook.

It's the Rapture, he thought. The Rapture's come!

Stuart continued to pray until fear seized him. In a flash elation turned to terror. This wasn't right. None of it was right. He didn't feel at peace, he wasn't—

"Hey leggo! Good God Awmighty, put me down!"

His numb fingers clutched at frozen branches as he drifted higher and faster into the air. Each time his hand locked around a pine bow snow cascaded toward the receding earth now so very far below.

A warm sensation crawled down his legs, coiling around them like warm-blooded snakes. Christ, he thought, disgust glaring through his terror.

He shot through the stiff covering of pine branches, their needles sharp as miniature daggers. Face bleeding, hands torn, Stuart floated above the treetops. Greedily, he sucked in a lungful of air so he could . . .

* * *

Scream!

Alton Barnes froze. Long unused military reflexes kicked in; his rifle jumped to the alert position. Adrenaline surged. Standing absolutely still, his eyes darted back and forth.

Another scream. The terror in that rising call was almost tangible.

"Stuart!" Alton cried. "STUART!"

Al ran through the woods, moving in the direction of the cry. Bushes whipped at him, sharp green needles clawed at his face.

A snow-covered root caught his Sorrel and he pitched forward, somersaulting in the snow. He came up in a crouch, soldier style.

Rising slowly, he looked around before entering the little clearing ahead of him. He saw footprints in the snow.

"Stuart!"

That was Stuart's weapon, half-covered with snow. And that wasn't right. The antique rifle was Stuart's pride and joy.

From there the footprints led off toward . . .

Toward . . .

Alton traced the progress of the tracks as they made their way uphill, to where they . . .

Stopped.

The tracks just ended.

Careful not to disturb the trail of footprints, Alton walked along beside them.

There could be no doubt about what he was seeing. It was crazy, but there it was, right in front of him like an open book. The snow was packed down near the spot where Stuart had dropped his rifle. Apparently he had fallen, or perhaps—for some reason—he'd sat down in the snow.

Then, the tracks said, Stuart had stood up and walked another eight feet, until his trail ended. Just ended. As if Stuart had somehow . . .

Vanished!

Alton looked around at the shadow-filled woodland.

Then—with a great effort of will—he dared to look up.

PART TWO

The Next Year...

"We inhabit a strange cosmos where nothing is absolute, final,
or conclusive. Truth is an actor who dons one mask after
another, and then vanishes through a secret door in
the stage scenery when we reach out to grab him.
All he leaves behind is a sardonic chuckle
which we record, take away,
analyze and debate.
Be we never see his face."

—Ted Holiday
The Goblin Universe

3

Mr. Splitfoot

Boston, Massachusetts
Friday, June 17

Karen Bradley stood at the Tremont and Park Street corner of Boston Common. Still waiting for the light to change, she had watched it go through its green, yellow, and red cycle three times already.

You gotta do it, she thought. But she simply was not prepared to cross the busy intersection. To Karen it was a moving barrier that separated her from State Street and from Dr. Gudhausen's office.

"Come on, come on, move it, will ya!" an exasperated driver shouted.

She hugged her briefcase to her chest, trying to make herself as two-dimensional as possible as once again her will warred with her timidity.

Do it.

A man with an oversize artist's portfolio scurried around her.

Now the light said "Go." She saw the green WALK signal flashing insistently. Following a cautious step into the street, she jumped back, almost tripping over the curb. She let out a startled cry as a cab screeched to a halt just inches in front of her.

Relax, she told herself. Relax, relax.

She was hyperventilating. Her eyes burned. Dizziness unsteadied her, making her legs feel like Jell-O.

This is stupid, she thought. I just have to—

But she couldn't move. Couldn't risk another step. Didn't dare go back.

"Move it or lose it, lady," a cabdriver shouted, a trace of an oriental accent clinging to the L's. He blasted his horn.

Karen squeezed her briefcase tighter. God, now she was sweating. She couldn't force her feet to move. People brushed against her, jostled her as they flooded the crosswalk. The taxi's horn maintained its unrelenting blare. Others joined it. A cacophonous symphony for horns sandpapered her nerves.

The cabby backed up, screeching rubber in reverse. Then he floored it, executing a wide arc around her, almost wiping out a young woman pushing twin toddlers in a tandem stroller.

Paralyzed.

With eyes tightly closed, Karen bit her lower lip and tried to force calming images into her mind: a warm fragrant breeze; green sunlit grasses swaying, swaying.

"Here, let me help." It was a man's voice, deep and confident.

A hand touched her upper arm. She felt a gentle tug urging her toward the traffic.

"It's okay," the man whispered.

Her feet balked at first, but she allowed herself to be led. As though she were blind, the stranger assisted her all the way across the street.

Safe now on the opposite sidewalk, she summoned the courage to look up at her rescuer. The man's smile was disarming, wide and sincere. His black curly hair and meticulously trimmed beard were graying a bit where they merged at the temples. His brown cotton suit appeared tailor-made.

"Are you all right?" he asked. His voice was gentle, caring.

Karen felt herself blushing. "Yes . . . sure . . . I'm . . . Oh gosh, I feel so foolish."

"No need on my account. I'm just happy I was there to lend a hand." His unfaltering good nature went a long way toward putting her at ease.

"Me, too." She giggled and hated herself for it. "I"—clearing her throat—"I should remember my manners and thank you . . . ."

"Not at all. No need." He raised a quizzical eyebrow. "You're from out of town, aren't you?"

"Ah, yes . . . I mean, is it that obvious?"

He tossed his head to the side, his eyes twinkling. "Just a wild guess."

"I'm from Vermont. Burlington, Vermont."

"Vermont? Where's that? Up by the Arctic Circle?"

She could tell he was kidding, and she was grateful he didn't make any cracks about some naive farm girl's first time in the big city. But she had no snappy comeback. Instead, she felt compelled to explain. "Sometimes I freeze up. I don't know why I do it. If something startles me, I . . . I just freeze up."

"That's what you get for living in the Arctic Circle." He was still grinning.

Still, she couldn't stop the rush of words. "It's a neurological condition. Something like epilepsy. Something like a panic disorder. They don't know exactly what—"

His smile softened. "It's okay. Really."

Karen grinned, too.

Then the man seemed unsure of himself for a moment, as if he didn't know what to say next. "Listen," he said, "how about letting me buy you a cup of coffee? You can thaw out while you catch your breath?"

Again he took her arm and stepped in the direction of a Pewter Pot Restaurant. She felt herself holding back. "I'd love a cup of coffee, really. It'd be just the thing right now. But I'm late for an appointment." She looked at her watch as if that would prove it to him.

"In town on business, eh? I bet you're with the government?"

Karen laughed, she couldn't help it. "The government? Why on earth would you say that?"

"Another wild guess. Government Center is just down that way; the State House's up there. And you're dressed so . . . professionally, with your gray suit and briefcase and all. I just thought . . . Aw, it was just a guess."

She detected his embarrassment, identified with it. Somehow it made her feel more at ease. "I've got to admit, you got all the clues exactly right, you just came to the wrong conclusion. Actually, I'm a . . ."—she faltered here, not wanting to say it—"I'm a doctor."

Was he impressed? Men usually were when she named her profession. It slowed them down, pushed them away. But she didn't want to push this man away; she did it by reflex.

But he was raising his eyebrows in mock-astonishment.

"Oh, are you now? Why, so am I!"

They both laughed and shook hands. "I'm Jeff Chandler, Ph.D.," he said with exaggerated importance.

"And, I'm Karen Bradley."

"Listen, Karen, let me retract that coffee offer. How about if I walk you to wherever you're going while I try to talk you into having dinner with me tonight. What say?"

"Well, I'll take it under advisement." She couldn't hold her pretend-frown. "I could go for some seafood?"

"I know just the place."

* * *

Karen found herself alone in Dr. Gudhausen's waiting room.

Sure, she'd expected it to be a bit more plush than her tiny office at Lakeview Health Center in Burlington, but this was positively regal! Bright watercolors adorned white plaster walls, cut flowers exploded from hand-painted vases, green-leafed plants dangled from ceramic hooks in the fourteen-foot ceiling. In the room's darkest corner, tiny tropical fish darted and spun in a glowing aquarium.

Karen found she was clutching the handle of her briefcase in a white-knuckled wrestler's grip. She was always uncomfortable in the presence of conspicuous wealth, a throwback to her childhood, when her nearly impoverished parents had worked so hard to maintain a paying farm in Vermont's dying agricultural economy.

Fighting the reaction, she tried to concentrate on the unobtrusive classical music playing faintly in the background. What was it? Sure. Easy. Beethoven's Seventh. The beginning of the . . . second movement! Perhaps a bit melancholy for a psychiatrist's office . . .

When Karen heard high heels tapping on the hardwood floor, the enormity of her errand flashed into her mind like a spotlight switched on in a dark room. She had to force herself not to turn around to leave. She could head back to the hotel, phone Dr. Gudhausen. Tell him she'd suddenly become ill, that she'd—

No! Stop it! Hadn't she embarrassed herself enough for one day? Meeting Jeff Chandler should have been a pleasure, but instead she'd stood there like a dumb farm girl, babbling and blushing.

A tall, trim woman in a dark, coldly sophisticated suit entered the room, walking toward the mahogany receptionist's desk. When she looked at Karen, a warm smile brightened her entire aspect. Stepping forward, the woman offered her hand. "Dr. Bradley, how good to see you. I'm Gloria Cook; we spoke on the phone. Dr. Gudhausen is expecting you."

The women shook hands.

"Maybe 'expecting you' is too much of a euphemism; I should say he's eager to see you." She raised her eyebrows conspiratorially. "He'll be with you in a minute. He's on the phone just now."

"Oh, okay, thanks."

"May I get you some coffee? Decaf? Or we have tea or mineral water . . . ?"

"Oh, no thanks, I'm fine." Fine? No way! She was perspiring like a lumberjack. "I'll just sit down. I want to organize my notes."

"Surely. Make yourself comfortable. I'll let Dr. G know you're here."

Gloria left the room.

Alone again, Karen walked to the large spotless window that offered a fantastic view of Quincy Markets and Boston Harbor. Then she scanned the titles on a teak floor-to-ceiling bookcase. The complete works of Freud, leather-bound and embossed. Bass and Davis's *The Courage to Heal, The Handbook of Psychological Assessment*—pretty standard fare, she thought.

She perused the shelf above. Books on gardening, a cookbook, Brooks and Evans's *Thoughts That Kill*, a couple of novels . . .

Strange, Karen thought. Are these just for show?

Then she noticed a curious title: *Mania, Magic and Religion* by William J. Sullivan. She picked up the book, flipped through it, examined the author's photo on the dust jacket. She was surprised to see that the man was wearing a collar. He was a Catholic priest!

A Catholic priest . . . ?

When she saw that the book was inscribed to Dr. Gudhausen, she realized she was trembling. *Oh my goodness,* she thought, *what am I getting myself into?*

* * *

Jeffrey Chandler pressed the seven-digit number sequence on the telephone. He waited till he heard a single ring, then punched in his access code. The line remained dead. No messages. He disconnected, then hit the redial button. This time he let it ring four times. His own voice answered, "Hi, this is Jeff. Please leave a message of any duration right after the double beep."

Beep-beep.

"Casey? Hi, babe. I'm just calling to let you know I won't be home for dinner. Sorry, hon. Don't wait on me, okay? You go ahead and eat. I'll grab something down here. I've got . . . well, I've got some things to take care of . . . work-related stuff, you know? I'll try not to be late. Love you. Bye."

* * *

"Dr. Bradley, how very good to meet you! I must confess I've been wondering about the mysterious woman behind so . . . enticing a letter."

Seeing Dr. Gudhausen again after more than a year, Karen was reminded of how poorly his name matched his appearance. Gudhausen: the name suggested some laid-back, balding Freudian with horn-rimmed glasses and a pencil-sharp goatee. Instead, Stanley Gudhausen looked like anything but a psychiatrist: a dock worker, maybe, a bartender? Perhaps a retired catcher from a baseball team? Mostly, Karen decided, he looked just like the stereotypical Irish cop. His thick silver hair needed combing; his beefy, florid-cheeked face crowded sharp blue eyes into wrinkly little crevasses where they twinkled mischievously. One shirttail had escaped his belt, emphasizing what may well have been an ample beer belly. He had a tooth-pocked Bic pen behind his ear, and looked as if he should be wearing a police revolver in his belt.

"Y-yes, Dr. Gudhausen, thank you for seeing me."

"For seeing you! Why, the pleasure's all mine. Let me congratulate you on an effectively cryptic letter. My curiosity has been aroused ever since I got it."

"Oh, I can write a mean letter. It's the interpersonal stuff that slows me down."

"Nervous about seeing me? Come on now. You're not in school anymore, Doctor. You and I are colleagues, professionals, kith and kin and all that, for heaven's sake. Please, relax, Dr. Bradley, come in and sit down."

As he led her into what must have been his consulting room, Karen was surprised when she didn't see a desk. Instead, two comfortable-looking leather chairs faced a brick fireplace, two more stood on either side of an antique table. Nearby, beneath a framed mirror, there was a six-foot couch. Cheerful artwork was everywhere.

"Let's sit by the fire," said Dr. Gudhausen, with a wink and a wave of the hand. "Oh! And may I get you something to drink? Some tea? Or better, some white wine? I can even offer you a beer."

"Oh, no. No thank you. Nothing." Karen sat down, looking at the dark fireplace. Gudhausen crossed the room and pressed a hidden button on the corner of the mantel. Logs appeared. Sparks jumped up among them. By the time he took his seat next to her, the fireplace was burning merrily.

Karen discovered she was smiling. "I've never seen anything like that."

"It's an illusion, my dear. A hologram. No need of a fire this time of year. But it's relaxing. The fire has a calming effect, don't you agree."

"I'll let you know."

"What's all this? Nervous around an old man with a boy's taste for gadgets? Honestly, Dr. Bradley."

"Please call me Karen." Smiling, she took a deep, calming breath—in, one-two-three; out, one-two-three—it was a relaxation technique she had suggested to many of her patients. She hoped it would work for her.

Karen squared her shoulders. Here goes nothing, she thought. This was the moment of truth. Hoping not to make a fool of herself, she began, "Dr. Gudhausen, last year I attended your lecture on Multiple Personality Disorder at the conference in Toronto. Back then . . . at that time . . . well, I was just starting out, I hadn't had any hands-on experience with that particular disorder, and . . . and . . ."

"And now you have," he finished the sentence for her.

She looked him in the eyes. "Yes, now I have."

He leaned back, lifted a foot off the carpet, took his knee in his hands. "I remember my first time," he said. "There was nothing—I should say not much of anything—in the literature back then. The disorder was still hovering somewhere between witchcraft and scientific respectability. No one knew how to diagnose it. Many thought the whole thing was a sham, didn't believe it existed. And many still don't, I might add, parenthetically. In fact, back then we didn't call it MPD. Different therapists had different names for it. I recall how . . . startled . . . I was. I'd never seen anything quite like it. It was—what would be a good word?—eerie?"

Karen nodded. "Eerie is a perfect word."

"But you've come all the way from Burlington, Vermont, to tell me about your patient, haven't you? You didn't come to endure one of my interminable history lessons."

"Oh, but I did. At the conference you showed us a videotape of"— Karen looked at her notes—"a Mr. Herbert Gold."

"Yes, of course, Herb Gold. He's an automobile mechanic from Andover, just a few miles north of here. A good man, solid, a salt-of-the-earth type. Before he discontinued therapy we had identified at least six separate and distinct personalities."

"I remember. Some male, some female. One was just a little kid, as I recall."

"Right, little Betsy Bottom, she called herself."

"One of the things I remember, Dr. Gudhausen, is that you had tested several—maybe all—of the personalities. Correct me if I'm wrong, but didn't you say that the IQ tests you administered showed one personality to be a dull-normal, and another to test around 160? That's genius!"

"Yes, exactly. That particular pattern, though not unusual among multiples, continues to fascinate me. Whatever the test score, high or low, they all come from the same brain."

"Dr. Gudhausen, I still have the photos of Mr. Gold that you handed out. It's—I hope this doesn't sound unprofessional—but it's just plain weird the way his face, the actual features of his face, seems to change so very much."

"Weird? Yes it is." He chuckled, sat back in his chair, and smiled at her. "I used to call that phenomenon 'personation,' meaning to temporarily take on another person's physical characteristics, habits, symptoms of illness, whatever. It's a term, I'm embarrassed to admit, I borrowed from turn-of-the-century spiritualists. A decision I soon regretted. It should be my job to demystify this vastly misunderstood illness. I should be the last one to drive it further in the direction of demon possession, returns from the dead, and all the other claptrap and high-weirdness."

Karen passed the photocopied page to Dr. Gudhausen. It showed five full-face photographs of Herbert Gold, each very different from the one beside it. They were labeled Homely Herbert, Betsy Bottom, Sasha, Thornton, and—

"This is the one that interests me, Dr. Gudhausen." She pointed at a scowling face that looked darker and far more ugly than the rest.

"Ah yes, that's Mr. Splitfoot. He was always a bit of a mystery. Very bright. Very cagey. Totally sociopathic, as far as I could tell. When he was 'onstage'— that was the term used by all Gold's personalities. The displayed personality was 'onstage,' the rest were 'backstage.' I recall how difficult it was to get Mr. Splitfoot onstage. He liked to hide in the wings, I suppose you could say. But when he was out he was evasive, insulting, and downright mean, just as you saw him on the videotape."

"Yes, I remember. He was horrible, abusive. A hard one to forget."

"I suspect Mr. Splitfoot was Herbert Gold's raw libido, his carnal self, the sociopathic side that Gold himself couldn't tolerate, wouldn't even admit to." Gudhausen stared at the photograph and chuckled. "An ugly brute, isn't he?"

"Yes, ugly," Karen said absently. She looked—perhaps for the hundredth time—at the photograph of smiling, gap-toothed, crew-cut Herbert Gold. His good-natured face reminded her of Uncle Benny, who used to drive a milk truck and who would come to the farm almost every Sunday for dinner.

Below Gold's grinning portrait, she saw the same face, twisted into the sneering countenance known as Mr. Splitfoot. It was the "Hyde" part of Gold's "Dr. Jekyll." Here the normally cherubic eyes were narrowed so much they appeared as black horizontal slits beneath his furrowed forehead. The muscle tension of Mr. Splitfoot's jaw stretched Gold's fleshy cheeks far too tightly over his cheekbones. The jutting jaw made his chin oddly shaped, almost pointed. The mouth stretched too widely, exposing long teeth and a grossly protruding tongue.

At this point Karen knew she had tiptoed to the end of the diving board and was about to take the plunge. She cleared her throat. Here goes, she thought, determined not to apologize for anything she was about to say, no matter how far out it might sound. "Dr. Gudhausen, if I may, I'd like to talk about my patient now."

"Of course, Doctor. Yes. Please, take your time."

He assumed a practiced listening posture, professional attending behavior that on Gudhausen looked perfectly natural, totally sincere.

Karen reached into her briefcase and removed a videotape. "Do you have a player, Doctor?"

"It just so happens . . ." said Dr. Gudhausen, pushing against the arms of the chair to assist himself to his feet. He took the cassette from Karen and pressed another button on the mantel of the fireplace. A landscape painting rose in its frame like a theater curtain, exposing the television screen beneath it. Gudhausen pushed the tape into a hinged slot below the screen. He handed Karen a remote control.

"Hit PLAY when you're ready," he said and he took a seat beside her.

Karen pressed the button; a picture filled the TV screen. It showed a young girl slouched in a recliner. She wore jeans and a plaid blouse. With eyes closed and body relaxed, she appeared to be sleeping. Karen was aware of the washed-out quality of this third-generation video image. Too little light, subject poorly centered, background dark, almost invisible.

"This is my office," she explained, perhaps unnecessarily. Karen gave a little start when she heard her own voice coming from the hidden speaker. "This is a portion of a recorded interview with Lucine Washburn, known as Lucy. She is twelve years of age, the daughter of Ed and Winona Washburn of St. Albans, Vermont. She has a younger brother, Randy.

"This excerpt is taken from a videotaping of our seventh session together. The recording was made with the permission of the child and with the consent of both parents. In the previous two sessions, using hypnosis, I have leaned toward a diagnosis of MPD. However, I note for the record that the Washburns seem to be a close, happy, well-functioning family. I can detect no evidence of the parental abuse patterns that are almost invariably present in cases of MPD."

"Hmmmm," said Dr. Gudhausen.

Karen's taped voice continued. "Today's session is an attempt to record those personalities which have so far made themselves known to me."

Karen hit the PAUSE button and said to Dr. Gudhausen, "She has been in the trance for about thirty minutes at this point. She has been resistant to showing her other alters."

"Yes, of course, please go on." He was leaning forward in his chair, watching the screen with great concentration.

Karen tapped the PLAY button and the girl began to squirm in the chair. On the tape's soundtrack, Karen's voice said: "Okay, Lucy, are you ready, sweetie?"

"Mmmm. No. Afraid."

"There's no reason to be afraid, hon. You're safe here. Your mom and dad are right in the next room, and I'm right here with you. No one can hurt you. There's nothing to be afraid of. I just want to take your picture, okay?"

"He doesn't want it."

"Who doesn't want it, Lucy? P-Man? Is it P-Man who doesn't want it?"

"No. Mmmm. P-Man's asleep."

"Is everyone asleep now?"

"Yes, except not . . ."

"Except who, Lucy?"

"Except . . . except me."

"Can I talk to P-Man now?"

"No. Asleep."

"Is Noonie awake? Can I talk to Noonie?"

The little girl squirmed in the recliner. She balled up her fists, brought them to her closed eyes. Vigorously, she rubbed her eyes and yawned deeply.

From off-camera Karen's voice said, "Is that Noonie waking up? Now can I talk to Noonie?"

Lucy said, "No, no, Noonie's not asleep, Noonie's"—here Lucy's voice lowered; it sounded flat and deep—"Noonie's not asleep. Noonie's dead." The child smirked and giggled. Spit sprayed from her pursed lips.

Karen heard the discomfort, the startled reaction in her own recorded voice. The tape would always remind her how she had lost her composure. This is where it all started to go bad, she thought, fighting the impulse to stop the tape and offer excuses to Dr. Gudhausen. Yet, she couldn't help tensing, gripping the leather arm of the chair, knowing the worst was still to come.

She whispered to Dr. Gudhausen, "I had never heard that deep voice before."

"You're doing a fine job, Karen. Just fine," he whispered without taking his eyes from the screen. "Now, ssshhh."

"Who am I talking to?" Karen's voice came from the television.

The little girl's hands were on the collar of her blouse. She pulled it away from her throat as if it were choking her. The strange voice deepened more, almost to a growl, "Noonie's dead, and P-Man's dead, and Brussel's dead. Now there's me; there's just me. I'm in here all alone."

Again the coarse giggle came from the child's throat, but her face was not smiling, her lips didn't move.

Karen saw herself enter the frame of the video screen. She knelt down in front of the little girl, who was now thrashing in the chair, pulling at her collar until the button popped open at the top.

Karen tried to take Lucy's hand. "You're all right, Lucy, you're all right. You can calm down now, honey, you—"

Abruptly the child pulled her hand away. "Lucy's dead; now I'm in her head."

"No, I don't want to talk to you. Let me talk to Lucy!"

"Lucy's done and you're no fun." Again the half growl, half giggle. Lucy's body thrashed and squirmed.

Karen watched herself on the screen; clearly agitated, approaching panic. Now she had grabbed the little girl and was shaking her, holding her by the upper arms! "Lucy, listen to me: you're okay. You're fine and safe. It's me, Lucy, Dr. Karen. Please come and see me."

The muscles of Lucy's face contorted, rippled. It looked as if fat worms were crawling beneath her skin. The flesh actually stretched. The lips rolled back over her teeth, appearing to retract into her gums.

"Lucy, can you hear me?"

"Dr. Karen . . . ?"

"Yes, Lucy, it's me." Karen's voice was eager, expectant. "Come out, honey. You'll be safe out here with me."

Lucy straight-armed Karen, shoved her mightily. She toppled backward and sat on the floor just outside the video frame. Karen watched herself scrambling to get back up, trying to stop Lucy from ripping open the front of her blouse.

Too late! The child's hands, now gnarled, looking almost like claws, grabbed her small, newly developing breasts, their tiny hard nipples tumid with bright blood.

"You want my tit," the child rasped, "you eat my shit."

Lucy's talonlike hands scraped her chest and stomach. Bright welts, some of them bleeding, crisscrossed her torso.

Karen's image froze. Now red-faced, nearly frantic, she had locked up. She sat there on the screen immobile and useless.

Lucy stood up on the chair, her face out of camera range, screaming.

The recording of Karen's speech was almost inaudible. "Lucy, listen to me. I'm going to clap my hands three times and you're going to wake up. Do you hear me Lucy? Do you understand? Answer me."

The sweet, frightened voice of a child: "Yes, I hear."

Karen clapped her hands, once, twice, three times.

Lucy flopped back into the seat, again within range of the camera. Now clapping her own hands as if applauding, she laughed crazily.

"Wake up, Lucy."

Her eyes were still closed.

Then more softly, "Wake up, honey."

"No, noooo, he won't let me. He's holding me."

"Who is? Who's holding you?"

"He is, he won't let me wake up."

"Who, Lucy? P-Man?"

"No, it's . . ."

Again, Lucy began to squirm. Her fingernails bit into the arms of the recliner, puncturing, tearing the material. Then, after a moment, her body became still. Only her head moved. It rolled around as if her neck muscles had turned to rubber. Slowly, deliberately, her slack mouth twisted into a sneering grin. Her tongue squeezed from between taut lips like foul organic waste extruding from a fleshy orifice. Her eyes widened, then her pale cheeks seemed to shift upward as, impossibly, her brow descended, pinching her eye sockets into narrow black slits.

The cheeks flattened; the jaw thrust forward.

Now the growling seemed to come from far away, getting louder, as if some dreadful beast within her were coming closer and closer, almost in view.

"Who are you?" Karen demanded, her voice cracking. "Tell me your name."

"Nahumich."

"Who?"

"Estheruth."

"Darn it, what are you talking about? Let me speak to Lucy. I want to speak to Lucy. *Now.*"

With slow, precisely enunciated syllables, the twisted, sneering face said in Lucy's faint voice, "Lucy is dead. I'm here instead."

"*Who's* here? Who are you?"

Karen looked away from the TV screen, embarrassed to see herself lose control. Her video image screamed at the frightened little girl, "WHO?"

"Malachisaiah."

"Tell me—"

"EZRAMOS!" The child-thing exploded into a roar of belligerent bawdy laughter—

"Who!" Karen was shaking the child. "*Who? WHO?*"

"You know me, you whore. We've met before." The squinting eyes looked into the video lens. As if speaking directly to Karen and Gudhausen, the voice growled, "My name is Splitfoot."

4

The Ancient Priest

Montreal, Quebec

Father William J. Sullivan looked down at the tiny man in the hospital bed.

He looks like a corpse, Sullivan thought as an unfamiliar tremor of dread coursed along his spine. But no, that wasn't exactly right; the man wasn't exactly . . . dead.

A more apt but equally horrific image crystallized in Sullivan's memory. Yes, the old man looked more like one of those fragile Jewish prisoners who had stared out at him from behind the barbed-wire fence at Treblinka. In those days the whole world had been wrestled from the siege of evil. But evil had left its mark. God, so many pitiful, wasted souls. They had looked like woeful, big-eyed skeletons. Sullivan—not yet twenty years old at the time—remembered thinking, How in God's name can they stand up? How can they walk?

But in one way, perhaps, those liberated prisoners were better off: the old priest in the bed couldn't move at all. There would be no escape, nor could he be rescued from the forces that bound him.

Resting on his side, curled tightly in a fetal position, the withered priest's arms crossed at the wrists. The fingers of both hands had tightened into firm little knots that pressed against his collarbone. Beneath his fists, the skin of his chest looked raw and red; it glistened with salve.

For a moment Sullivan was lost in thought. As if hypnotized, he watched bubbles of clear liquid dropping one by one from the IV bag—nourishment and moisture.

Motion caught his eye. The nun, Sister Elise, tugged the gray sheet over the old man's shoulders. Sullivan spotted the vivid red bedsore before it was concealed. Such things are unavoidable, he thought, but it made him sad.

He looked at the old man's eyes; one open, the other closed. Hoping for a sign—any small indication of awareness—Sullivan bent down to look directly into that single open eye. It seemed to be covered with a milky film. As Sullivan's head moved closer, the pupil didn't widen. The eyelid didn't flutter. Sullivan knew he could touch that eye, put his finger directly on the iris, and the old man wouldn't know.

He drew back, wrestling with a moment of atavistic revulsion. Though he had read the chart, read it over and over, he just hadn't understood. He had completely failed to prepare himself for the old priest's condition.

Seeing the reality of it now, he realized that empathy was beyond him. The old man—Father Mosely—couldn't be hurt, couldn't be helped. He felt nothing, thought nothing, had no aspirations, experienced no emotions. An irritating phrase from Sullivan's childhood intruded: nobody's home upstairs.

The skin of the old priest's face was almost translucent. It looked like candle wax. Father Sullivan realized that pale skin could be sliced, indeed major surgery could be done without anesthesia, and the old man would never know.

Sullivan shuddered, taking a deep breath through his nose in an effort not to cry. As he inhaled, the odor of urine, diseased flesh, and of some pungent antiseptic solution, struck him as a nauseating breeze.

"He was my teacher," Sullivan said. Then, needlessly, "It was a Catholic school."

The little nun looked up at him and nodded.

"That was in the early forties. He seemed an old man even then."

Sullivan stroked the patient's wispy hair. It felt strange, like a spiderweb.

"As bitter as I was in those days, I never objected to calling him Father." He paused, thinking back, remembering. "Father Mosely was the closest thing I ever had to a real father. Sounds maudlin, doesn't it?"

The little nun smiled, but there was confusion in her eyes. It occurred to Sullivan that she wasn't understanding him. This time he spoke to her in French. "How long has he been here?"

"How long? Ten years. Almost ten years with us."

"And all the time, just like this?"

"Just as you see him, Father. Not alive, not dead."

"A coma?"

"Yes, always the coma. He is a very old man, yet he does not die."

Sullivan touched one of the priest's hands, thinking he would take it in his own, hold it for a while. The gnarled fingers would not open, the elbow joints would not flex. Stiff as a corpse, Sullivan thought.

"Do you know what caused it, Sister?"

She would not meet his eyes. "Perhaps it is better if you talk with Father LeClair about this."

"This is not simple curiosity, Sister."

"Yes, I know. But didn't Father LeClair's letter explain all these things?"

"Sister—"

"I know, I know. It is not for me to question. My apology, Father."

"Well then . . . ?"

"The lay doctors say it is the result of a . . . a stroke."

"Go on."

"But Father LeClair, he says . . . he says . . . Please, Father, I cannot!"

Sullivan took a long slow breath, trying to control his impatience. "Of course. It is I who should apologize. I'm being rude and insensitive. Please forgive me, Sister Elise."

She dropped her eyes, folded her hands in front of her, as if praying.

Father Sullivan continued: "Perhaps you will be good enough to go and see if Father LeClair will speak to me now. I'll stay here. I'd like to spend a few moments with Father Mosely."

The little nun scurried from the room. Father Sullivan was alone with the old priest.

* * *

Boston, Massachusetts

It all happened so fast.

And every time it was just the same. He'd nod, close his eyes just for a minute, and he'd be there.

Soaring.

Free of the earth. Part of the sky.

The engine sound, the roar, ascending the scale until it became high-pitched and insect-shrill.

Far below, the compression of the bombs—blasting bamboo into splinters and men into mud—was the rhythmic pulse of his own heart.

And he soared.

Clouds crowded the sides of his plane. He was a scissors cutting through cotton, a knife plunging through snow.

And as he slipped along the ethereal corridor, he saw the faces flashing by, faces fabricated from the filmy material of clouds. White faces, ghost faces.

Smiling.

And he knew them, knew them all. These were the ones he had rescued. These were the souls his bombs had liberated from the sweltering hell of the jungle. Now they rose to take their places in the mansions of the Lord. American faces. Asian faces. All ascending because of him.

He was their savior.

The engines whined in his ears as he sped along the white tunnel, soaring toward the brilliant yellow opening at the end.

The beautiful golden light.

And if he could make it all the way, if he could just complete the journey one more time, he'd look upon the face of God—

The phone rang.

He opened his eyes.

The dream had lasted the duration of a blink.

He answered on the second ring.

"McCurdy," he said.

* * *

Montreal, Quebec

"Yes, Father Sullivan, exorcism. Just like in the Middle Ages; just like in the movies." Father Gaston LeClair leaned back in his rocker, resting his folded hands on top of his ample, black-covered belly. He seemed to enjoy communicating in English, like a proud schoolboy reciting his catechism.

Sullivan, now that he had LeClair's attention, didn't know what to say. While his mind raced, his eyes explored Father LeClair's office. Books—medical and theological—crowded sturdy oak shelves. Some rested properly, side by side, spines outward, titles displayed. Others lay on their sides, piled haphazardly, leaning like Pisa's tower. Some filled cardboard boxes on the floor, others were heaped directly on the carpet. File folders and medical charts littered the desktop. They were stacked helter-skelter as if LeClair were trying to build a wall of paper between himself and the world at large.

A crudely elegant cast-iron cross hung on the brick chimney above the fireplace.

Father Sullivan stood up and walked around the desk to look out the window behind the seated priest. Three stories below a walled courtyard was full of benches and flowers and statues, but it was empty of people.

Still, Sullivan could think of nothing to say, his mind had locked on those four alien syllables, so he spoke them: "Exorcism?"

Father LeClair swiveled in his seat, looked up at the younger priest. "Father Sullivan, Bill, I know what you're thinking. I went through the same thing myself. You can't accept it, right? It sounds primitive, superstitious."

Sullivan didn't answer, didn't look up from the courtyard.

"Bill, how can we spend our whole life serving God, then refuse to admit there's a devil even when he jumps up and spits in our face?" He tamped the bowl of his pipe with an ash-blackened fingertip.

Still, Sullivan didn't speak.

LeClair got up and stood beside him at the window.

"I think Sister Elise misunderstood me. I said the stroke may have resulted from the strain of the exorcism. I didn't say the devil caused the stroke. Do you see?"

Sullivan said nothing.

"Bill, the reality of exorcism is not important. If somebody thinks he is possessed, we have a choice: we can fight the demon with the Bible and holy water, or fight the sickness with the therapy and our arsenal of drugs. It doesn't matter to the victim—"

"But it does; it matters to Father Mosely."

"Of course. Exactly. Perhaps Hamilton Mosely *believed* it was a demon. But remember, Father, he was under a lot of stress. He was old and sick. *That* was his problem—"

"Then how could the bishop let him proceed?"

LeClair shrugged, fell silent for a moment. He took a gold lighter from his pocket, flicked it, and put the flame to his pipe. Then he shook his head. "I don't know. As I understand it, Father Mosely was a spirited and independent man. Perhaps the bishop was never consulted. It was a long time ago, and I'm afraid no one has ever given me all the details; they're not essential for the service I must provide here. I do know that Father Mosely was the only one—maybe in all of your New England states—who'd had experience with the Roman ritual of exorcism. He'd performed . . . I think three, and successfully, before the one that . . ."

Sullivan looked him in the eyes. "That crippled him? Destroyed his mind. Turned him into a—"

"Please, Bill, I was not involved then. I just do what I can for him now."

The little office had quickly filled with pipe smoke. Sullivan waited, controlling an urge to cough so he could speak. "Is there any chance that he'll . . . he'll . . ."

"That he'll come out of it? Probably not. It would truly take a miracle, Father. My position here has never allowed me much opportunity for optimism. I care for sick old men who never married, never had children. Most of them have outlived whatever family they may have had. Now they have nothing, no one. They have only the Church, because they have given themselves to the Church. Until their death, I'm afraid this place is for the hopeless."

"How many are here, Father?"

"We have eighteen. Only two are comatose. Two more have Parkinson's, very advanced. And there are five Alzheimer patients, gentle old men with the eyes of children. The rest . . . the rest are . . ."

"Irreversible dementia?"

LeClair lowered his eyes. "Yes, Father Sullivan."

Sullivan walked back to the leather couch and sat down heavily. Father LeClair returned to his desk.

"Father LeClair . . . ?"

"Yes, Bill?"

"Please. Can you tell me what happened?"

* * *

Boston, Massachusetts

"Sooner or later, everyone gets to see the computer," said Ian "Skipp" McCurdy.

Jeff Chandler followed him along a narrow brick-walled corridor toward a green metal door. Above, pale neon tubes cast cold bluish light that emphasized McCurdy's freckled bald spot and the horseshoe of limp, rusty-colored hair surrounding it.

Jeff tore his eyes away, feeling rude and petty. He should make it a point to judge his boss on criteria more substantial than his slightly clownlike appearance.

"Call this your *rite de passage*, Jeff. I guess you've been with us long enough now so you can see the entire operation. Especially if you're going to be . . . promoted." McCurdy laughed his irritating staccato laugh as he pulled open the green fire door. He held it as Jeff walked through.

The room was large, twenty by thirty feet at the very least. Though brightly lighted and comfortably cool, it felt institutional, alien. Perhaps that was because the room had not been designed to accommodate people. Instead, it was merely functional, containing but two objects: the computer, which was easy to recognize, and the mysterious twelve-by-twelve-foot glass structure beside it, which was a puzzle.

The computer looked about the size of an upright piano. On its front panel, colored lights flashed in seemingly random patterns. A row of five-inch video screens across the console's angled top filled with letters, numbers, and vividly colored graphics. Images appeared and vanished faster than Jeff's eyes could follow.

"What you see before you," McCurdy said grandly, "is the heart of the Academy, our central processor, InfoWork Industries' BLZ-28/22."

Jeff nodded. "It's not as big as I thought it would be."

McCurdy smiled; his cheeks turned into little red balls that supported his eyeglasses. "Amazing, isn't it? A state-of-the-art computer—world class, really—yet not much bigger than a washing machine." He looked directly at Jeff, as if waiting for an "Ooooo" or an "Aaaaaah."

"Amazing," was all Jeff could say.

"But when you stop to think about it," McCurdy continued in his tones of affected informality, "for five bucks you can pick up a pocket calculator at the K mart that'll do a whole lot more than the original Univac did back in the fifties. And that monster filled *rooms!*"

Jeff nodded, trying to look impressed. "Computers have sure come a long way."

McCurdy beamed, proud as a parent. "But this one is special, one of a kind. It's on the cutting edge of computer technology, and frankly, I think it's going to stay there awhile. It'll do tricks you or I could never even imagine. Tell you something, Jeff, even the Japs aren't making anything like this." He winked conspiratorially.

McCurdy looked on proudly as Jeff studied the dancing lights.

"No doubt about it: Bubb puts on an impressive light show," McCurdy beamed, "but to me, quite honestly, the computer's the boring part of this operation."

Jeff looked at him quizzically. "Bubb?"

McCurdy laughed. "That's what we call it, at least those of us on a first-name basis with the thing. Officially, it's InfoWork's BLZ-28/22. We nicknamed it Bubb. Clever if not quite appropriate, don't you think?"

"Ah . . . yeah, I guess. . . ." Transfixed, Jeff watched fluid, undulating designs on a liquid crystal display screen. He had to wrench his eyes away from the choreography of hypnotic patterns, shifting his interest to the room-sized structure beside the CPU. It looked a bit like one of those aluminum and glass filling stations he'd often seen tucked away in the corners of so many shopping plazas. Nestled within it was a smaller glass cube about the size of a walk-in closet. Within that, positioned on a stainless-steel laboratory table, he saw what appeared to be a fifty-five-gallon aquarium filled with crimson liquid. Bundled wire and clear plastic hoses were embedded in the aquarium's cover. Mystified, Jeff waited for his tour guide's explanation.

"Ah-ha!" said McCurdy, noticing Jeff's bewilderment, "this is a nifty little item. Watch." His palm flattened against a dark amethyst panel on the Plexiglas partition. A door hissed open. "See that? Recognizes my palm print," he said proudly, and winked.

Jeff looked away, put off by the repeated winking.

The electronically opened door admitted them to the glass corridor formed between the outer and inner aquarium walls. It hissed shut. Jeff noticed how much colder it was in the passageway.

Examining the transparent wall that separated the men from the innermost and smallest aquarium, Jeff asked, "How do you get in there?"

"You don't." McCurdy clicked his tongue as if Jeff had said something naughty. "That's a sterile environment. Technicians have to suit up and go through decontamination in this passageway before they can go inside." Holding his finger as if it were a pistol, McCurdy mimed shooting at a series of nozzles recessed almost invisibly in the ceiling.

Jeff understood the nozzles were gas jets.

"See," McCurdy explained, "this corridor is also a security device. It's fully capable of decontaminating intruders far larger and more threatening than bacteria."

Jeff shivered, but not from the cold; it was McCurdy's matter-of-fact reference to killing. He wondered—and not for the first time since he'd joined the Academy—just what he had gotten himself into. "The security measures I can understand," he said. "I can even appreciate the dust-free environment; I know airborne particles can wreak havoc on electronic components. But you said sterile? A sterile environment?"

"That's right."

"Why's that? Why sterile?"

McCurdy chuckled, tossing his head to the side. Obviously he thought Jeff was joking. When he saw his error, he sobered. "What do you mean?"

"Well, dust-free and sterile aren't the same thing."

"Oh. Right. Okay." McCurdy pursed his lips, looking momentarily puzzled. "To tell you the truth, it's a little out of my line, but as best I understand it, this computer uses an experimental kind of bioelectronic circuitry. It's some kind of . . . well, quite simply, it's synthesized organic material. That's what the tank in there is holding."

Jeff studied the aquarium.

"You can't see them, but inside that tank there is a series of glass plates, upright, side by side, almost like the plates in a car battery."

Jeff nodded.

"Each plate is coated with the artificial tissue just one cell deep. The system contains a layer of input units, and a layer of output units. Between them, the intermediate 'hidden' units are capable of assessing data and directing the various electrical responses. In effect, the only thing this experimental unit does is channel data. All the information it recognizes, it passes along to the CPU, if useful. Or it eliminates the information if irrelevant. If it doesn't recognize a piece of data, it spits it out and lets a human being evaluate it. The more data it ingests, the more it learns to recognize, and ultimately the 'smarter' it becomes."

"Which is essentially the way a human brain works."

"Right, Jeff. That's just exactly right. The psych folks tell me it's called 'associative learning,' and it's identical to the way a human being learns. In fact, they say the synthetic material used here is very much like the composition of our own brains."

Jeff shook his head slowly. "Laboratory-produced brains. Wow! So what you're telling me, really, is that this thing's alive?"

McCurdy clicked his tongue, looking thoughtful. "Well, no. I mean, that would be stretching it some—"

"It's all fascinating, Dr. McCurdy, but I don't get it. I mean, what's the point of synthetic tissue? Why not simply use conventional hardware and software? Why this experimental stuff, this—what would you call it?—wetware?"

McCurdy smiled benignly and shrugged. "Hey! Nobody tells me nothin'. Just because I'm project designer and executive director doesn't mean I can explain everything that's going on in my shop. Fact is, Jeff, we're just test driving the thing, not manufacturing it. We try it out, InfoWork lets us use the whole computer free of charge. Hey, in the government biz, that's called fiscal responsibility."

Jeff nodded.

"But I'll take a stab at answering, just so nobody gets his feelings hurt." McCurdy winked.

Jeff watched McCurdy frown and become more serious. "Okay, we know that even the most sophisticated computers, including Bubb here, cannot replicate the speed at which the human brain is capable of accessing information. Heck, we're accessing information all the time and we don't even know it! And when we access information, we learn, am I right?"

Jeff nodded cautiously.

"Okay. And once we've learned something, we are then capable of using the new information intellectually and intuitively, right? But the computer has no intellect, it has no intuition. And certainly—at least from my point of view as a Christian—it has no soul. So, by extension, we can accurately say the computer is a *brain*, but we can't say it's a mind. Simply put: it can't make sense of the world and it can't generate complex thoughts.

"The relatively new field of Computational Neuroscience tries to analyze and explain how the human brain uses electrical and chemical signals to represent and process information. Mainstream computer scientists are approaching the problem by trying to design software that will *mimic* the way the brain works. It's an unmanageably big project. In fact, many scientists think it's impossible."

"Yes, I've read something about that," Jeff mumbled.

"The approach here is radically different. This 'wetware'—as you call it—doesn't try to *imitate* the human brain. Instead, it's being developed to *replicate* the brain, to work exactly the way the brain works. It's cellular engineering, and it's working with a limited degree of success right here. This unit is the proof of the proverbial pudding."

Jeff reflected for a moment. "I don't mean to be obtuse, Dr. McCurdy, but you still haven't answered my question."

"How's that?"

"Why?"

McCurdy rolled his eyes and clicked his tongue. "I guess I did sort of tap-dance around that, didn't I. That's 'cause I don't really know. Tell you the truth, I suspect it's all working toward programmable human beings. But, hey"—he winked—"don't tell anyone I said so, okay? Maybe in the not-too-distant future some descendant of this machine will be able to transfer information directly into a human brain. Imagine going to sleep in English, and waking up in Russian, or French, or German!"

Jeff shook his head, more overwhelmed than ever. "So you keep the synthetic tissue in a sterile environment because you're afraid your staff could actually . . . infect the machine?"

"That's right. This computer has no immune system. And I don't know what kind of job performance we can expect from Bubb if it catches a cold or something. There's nothing about sick days in its contract."

This time both men laughed, Jeff a bit uneasily.

McCurdy turned away as if to say, Let's get on with the tour. But Jeff lingered a moment, entranced by the rusty-looking fluid flowing into and out of the aquarium. At that moment he knew he was completely out of his league; he had no hope of understanding anything that he was seeing. "I'm curious," he said, "how much do you suppose it cost to develop something like this?"

"The 'wetware'? Beats me. Like I said, IWI is developing it for the Defense Department, so various subcontractors—and we're among them—get to try it out for free. We haven't had to worry about cost."

Still smiling like a first-time home owner, McCurdy tugged Jeff's sleeve, coaxing him to follow. Magically, another sliding door opened and they left the glass enclosure.

"'Wetware,'" McCurdy chuckled, shaking his head with amusement, "that's pretty good . . . ."

* * *

Jeff gawked as McCurdy led him through another basement corridor. "I had no idea there was so much space down here," Jeff said. "It's like another complete building below ground."

"Ah, yes. Well, appearances are deliberately deceiving. From outside, the Academy looks exactly like all its neighbors. Just another unremarkable three-story brownstone. But!"—he raised his index finger dramatically,—"this one used to be owned by one of the scientists involved with the Manhattan Project, an MIT man. I guess the work he did scared the poor fella so bad he had this palatial bomb shelter constructed in complete secrecy during the nuclear terror of the early fifties. All the work was done at government expense, too, which I can understand. But I'll tell you the one thing I can't figure out . . ."

"What's that?"

"How did they get all the dirt out of here without the neighbors realizing something was going on?"

Jeff smiled. "Good question."

"So," McCurdy chuckled, his cheeks glowing like ripe apples, "the place saw weapons development in the early fifties, and in a sense, that's what it's seeing now. A completed cycle. And a perfect home for Bubb, don't you think?"

Jeff raised his eyebrows noncommittally. McCurdy led him through another green metal door that opened on a strangely barren room with cinder-block walls. The men crossed the brown carpeted floor to one of a half-dozen modular carrels lining the western wall.

"This is what happens to the data Bubb doesn't recognize," McCurdy explained. "He kicks it out and real human beings work with it here."

Jeff's eyes came to rest on a woman he had never seen before. Her brown hair was primly balled in a tight bun, her eyes, behind thick, dark-tinted glasses studied one of the terminals. Beside her keyboard she had a pile of color photocopies depicting pages of what Jeff took to be an ancient manuscript. He saw some kind of medieval script accompanied by pictures of flowers and plants.

"And speaking of real human beings," McCurdy said, "this is Yonna Keel. *Doctor* Yonna Keel. She's on loan from the CIA. Speaks ancient Greek and Latin like a native and is probably the most accomplished cryptanalyst in the country."

"Hello, Yonna," Jeff said, but she paid no attention. The screen before her was filled with tiny words that Jeff could not read.

"She's trying to decipher the mysterious Voynich Manuscript. The cipher is so clever it's eluded translation for—we guess—six or seven hundred years. Most likely it was written in the thirteenth century, but no one knows for sure. We also don't know who wrote it, or why. We don't even know what language it's in. With its drawings of plants, one might mistake it for an ordinary medieval herbal. That is, until you realize all the plants depicted here don't exist anywhere in nature!

"One thing we do know is that for a while it was in the possession of Dr. John Dee, the infamous Elizabethan magician. And as recently as 1912 it was kept in a Jesuit monastery in Frascati, Italy. So I guess we can't say for sure if it belongs in Heaven or in Hell. . . ."

Jeff shook his head. "Good luck, Yonna," he mumbled.

McCurdy lowered his voice. "We have researchers like you and Yonna on payroll all over the world. The full-timers are directly under contract to the Academy. Part-timers get their salaries laundered through educational grants and university work-study programs. All are assigned to libraries, museums, even monasteries and private collections. They use keyboards and scanners to collect vast quantities of raw data. Of course, no one doing fieldwork knows what the data gathering's all about. The cover is they're assembling reference information for an experimental hypertext program for Bubb—a huge interactive encyclopedia. We see to it they keep inputting a fair amount of worthless information, red herrings designed to keep folks from getting too close to what's really going on. They send it along, Bubb kicks it out, and we forget it."

The four unused monitors danced with color and moving designs. To Jeff, the screens looked like windows opening on to an unfamiliar dimension or an alien world. Shapes in space whirled and shifted in ultra rainbow colors. Points of light—amber, red, and gold—pulsed brightly and vanished.

"This is the stuff that's really exciting to me," said McCurdy, "the stuff that's right here in this room—the keyboard, the screen." He rested his hand on the top of a monitor like a doting father with his arm around a favorite son. "This is the spot where human meets computer, where man and machine come together in a wildly unprecedented way. It's here, you might say, that they mate and marry."

"So what's the punchline?" Jeff asked. "Do I have to keep guessing, or are you going to tell me what all this is about?"

McCurdy clicked his tongue and patted Jeff on the shoulder. "Time's up for today, my friend. But I won't keep you in suspense forever. Think about it. See what you make of all this. Then we'll continue with some clarifications first thing next week."

5

The Widening Gyre

Boston, Massachusetts

Karen decided to wait outside the restaurant for exactly fifteen minutes. If Jeff Chandler hadn't appeared by then, she would leave. Period. End of discussion.

She had been foolish to accept this dinner invitation. Well, maybe not foolish exactly, but certainly careless. After all, she didn't even know the man. Why, he could be anybody, even some kind of . . . well, she'd definitely been too quick to trust him.

But then again, he seemed nice . . . .

And what was wrong with a little adventure?

Another glance at her watch.

It probably didn't look good for her to be hanging around, *lurking,* outside this Commercial Street restaurant. She should go inside, maybe have a glass of wine. She could use the waiting time to calm down.

The two hours spent with Dr. Gudhausen had been terribly draining. Showing him the tape had been difficult, not because of its unsettling content, but because she was ashamed of the way she had lost control of the therapy session.

Afterward, she'd had to race back to her hotel to shower and put on fresh clothes. God, she'd been nearly frantic, tearing around like a flustered schoolgirl preparing for her first date!

At least *she* had arrived here on time.

Yes, by gosh, a glass of chilled wine would be just the thing. But somehow—this is really stupid, she thought—she found it difficult to go into the restaurant unescorted. Humph, some liberated woman.

She looked at her watch. Seven thirty-five. Ten more minutes to wait.

Traffic zipped back and forth in front of her. Horns blared; an auto alarm wailed. Somewhere in the distance she heard the shrill screech of a siren. The collection of noise was awful. She hated it. Too bad there wasn't some gadget to mute ugly sound the way her sunglasses softened the evening light.

Oh, nothing is going right! Maybe she should forget this "date," go back to the hotel, check out, and drive directly back to Vermont. At least there it would be quiet, and she could relax.

No, she thought, recognizing her all too familiar approach-avoid pattern, *you gotta do it.* She simply could not permit herself to be scared of everything and everyone all the time. It was stupid. She was a grown woman for goodness' sake, a professional.

Karen bit her lower lip, as she always did when contemplating decisive action. With great finality she turned, grabbed the brass handle, and pulled open the heavy glass door to Maxie's Fish House.

Right away the world was quieter. The conditioned air felt cool and inviting. Soft orchestral music played; it was almost subliminal so she couldn't hear it well enough to identify the piece. To her right, the bar was complete with brass foot rail, suggesting an old-time waterfront saloon. Above the bar, dim Tiffany lamps hovered colorfully. Most of the stools were unoccupied, but the dining room was busy.

Must be a good place, she thought, noting all the customers.

Karen sat down on an end stool. Two empty seats separated her from a fat black man eating oysters on the half shell. She looked away; there was something vaguely obscene about eating raw oysters. She placed her purse securely on her lap.

"May I help you, miss?"

"Oh, yes, thanks." She took off her sunglasses and put them on the bar. "I'd like a glass of white wine, please."

The bartender smiled as if to say, Good choice, and reached below the bar for a bottle and glass. He was a nice-looking guy. Dark hair, perfectly trimmed mustache, serious features. He wore a pink and white striped shirt, its sleeves rolled up just enough to expose a tiny, tasteful tattoo. Karen tried to see exactly what it was, but she couldn't. And she didn't want to stare.

When he poured her a generous serving in a large goblet, she noticed he had a small gold ring in his left earlobe. It looked good. Elegant. A little exotic. Like a pirate.

The wineglass felt pleasantly cold in her hand. Her first sip went down so smoothly that she felt some distant tension ease. Already she was starting to relax.

Then she remembered—

Five minutes more, she thought, checking her watch again.

Karen suspected that the bartender was looking at her, stealing quick questioning glances as he went about his business. No doubt he was thinking, What's wrong with this woman? Why doesn't she have a man with her?

Or worse yet, This woman must be an alcoholic, otherwise, why is she drinking alone?

I must drink this slowly, she cautioned herself.

Karen stopped before the self-deprecation soared out of control. It was stupid. Why did she always feel she was so conspicuous? In reality, she faded into the background like some potted palm, so inconsequential that people didn't check to see if it was real or plastic.

Conspicuous or invisible? Which is it? You can't have it both ways, kiddo.

No. The pretty women were the ones who got stared at, not her. Never—

Jeff was now twenty minutes late. She'd waited five minutes too many!

Karen bit her bottom lip and stood up. She placed her purse solidly on the bar and dug around in it for her billfold. She took out a five and left it by her half-empty wineglass.

She felt as if every diner's eyes were on her. She's been stood-up by her boyfriend, they thought. Karen felt herself blushing. Without looking around she walked straight to the glass door and stiff-armed it open.

Jeff was pulling up in a taxi.

"Hey!" he called, pushing the cab door open, nearly tumbling out of the back seat. "Hey, Karen, wait!"

She heard him but didn't acknowledge.

From the corner of her eye she could see him groping at his pocket for money. He produced a money clip, fanned the bills, selected one, and nearly threw it at the driver.

Karen crossed to the other side of the street.

"Karen! Hey, Karen!"

The cabbie shouted after Jeff, "Hey, buddy, your change. Hey, man, dis is a twenny!"

Karen stopped. *Darn.* She had left her Ray•Ban sunglasses on the bar. Could she just forget about them? Just keep going, eyes focused straight ahead, ignoring Jeff?

Darn. *DARN.*

Those sunglasses had cost her over sixty dollars. An indistinct voice that sounded very much like her mother's echoed from somewhere in her memory, "That's just throwing money away, Karen."

She turned.

She was enough of a Freudian to believe there are no accidents. Maybe she hadn't really forgotten her sunglasses, maybe she—

Jeff was zigzagging through the traffic to get to her. Horns drowned his cry, "Karen! Come on, will ya. Wait up!"

She stopped. Now, she wanted the sunglasses more than ever; she didn't want him to see her eyes.

He stood in front of her, sweating and harried. "Look, I'm sorry, okay? Something came up."

"You could have called."

"How? You didn't tell me where you were staying. I tried to call that guy Godunov's office, but I couldn't find him in the book. So I tried directory assistance and they didn't have a listing. I even . . ." He looked over his shoulder in the direction he'd come from. "I even brought you a flower, but I left it in the damn cab."

"It's not Godunov," she said.

"What?" He looked greatly offended. "What do you mean not good enough? You think I'm lying?"

She couldn't hold back the smile; she didn't try. "The doctor. His name's not Godunov, it's Gudhausen."

They laughed as they walked back to the restaurant, her thoughts of Herbert Gold and Lucy Washburn, and all the other stresses of the day, vanishing like dew on a sunny Vermont morning.

* * *

Montreal, Quebec.

"Exorcism," said Father William Sullivan. He wasn't speaking to anyone. He was simply articulating the uncomfortable word—"Ex-or-ciz-um"—trying to get it outside his head where he could turn it around, examine it, attempt to understand it, somehow.

Striding briskly, he tightened the collar of his blue jacket against drafts of cold air coming from the St. Lawrence River far below.

Beside Sullivan, Father LeClair puffed his pipe. "The bottom line, Bill, is if Father Mosely attempted an exorcism without the bishop's consent, he was out of line. He never should have acted alone; he never should have acted in secrecy. There should be a doctor present. Always. And there should be another priest to assist. Everyone involved should be in a state of grace . . . ."

Sullivan didn't want to hear it. He was ready to argue, to defend the old priest, but what was the point?

Heading south on Peel Street, Sullivan switched his attention from the brownstones on the left to a high-rise on the right. Its semicircular windows made the building look like a giant cheese grater.

"Remember," Father LeClair said, "whatever happened to Father Mosely, happened without benefit of witnesses. So I'm afraid—"

"But what do you *think* happened, Gaston?"

"You want an opinion—how do you say it?—off the recording?"

"Yes, if you would."

"You know, Bill, I am a curious hybrid of physician and priest, the product of two belief systems which are often irreconcilable."

Sullivan looked at him. "What do you mean?"

Father LeClair shrugged. "Well, he could have fought a demon and lost, but, frankly, part of me never really believed that. For me it is easier to believe that Father Mosely suffered a stroke, only that. I know his health was not good; I've seen his medical records. He had an ulcer. His blood pressure was high. He reported chronic sleeplessness. He was fatigued, exhausted, really."

"You think the exorcism is just a story?"

"Perhaps. There were no witnesses. Think about it. Someone would have heard if parishioners were being tormented, tortured, or actually possessed by demonic spirits. Someone, even today, would surely remember. If there really were such people, Father kept their secret; he keeps it still."

"Yes." Sullivan walked a few paces. "Ten years," he said. "Ten years in a coma; ten long years lost in some mindless limbo."

LeClair puffed his pipe before responding. "It's an intriguing conundrum, isn't it? A philosophical and theological puzzle. The person is as if dead, but still alive. So where is the soul?"

Sullivan's mind returned to that clouded, empty eye, the waxen, vein-streaked skin, the pale, cracked lips scabbed with crusty spittle. "Yes, where . . . ?"

* * *

Boston, Massachusetts

"You're a shrink! My God, I can't believe it!" Jeff Chandler leaned back in his chair. Grinning broadly, he lifted his wineglass in a salute. "Here's to you, Dr. Sigmund Bradley!"

Karen felt herself blushing; God, she hated that. Her gaze fell to her half-empty plate of scallops. "Well, to be completely on the up-and-up, I'm a clinical psychologist, not a medical doctor."

"Hey, a shrink's a shrink. And I'm a physicist, not a physician. Neither of us is an M.D. so that's something else we have in common."

She raised her head and gave him a quick smile.

"But that doesn't make me any less curious," Jeff said. "Can you talk to me about this heavy-duty powwow that lured you all the way from scenic Vermont to this vile pesthole known as Boston?"

"What do you mean! Boston's a beautiful city!"

"Yeah? Not if you gotta live here. Try getting stuck in a broken-down trolley sometime in ninety-degree weather, one of the myriad joys of urban existence. Or try playing hide-and-seek with one of the gangs. Or . . . Hey, I didn't hear anything about 'beautiful city' when that taxicab almost flattened you this morning."

Karen laughed.

"So tell me, Dr. Bradley, what is so important that you would risk life and limb on the mean streets of our state's capitol? Are you planning a career change? Interviewing for a job, perhaps? Thinking of forsaking your pastoral paradise and relocating to Beautiful Bean Town?"

Karen dabbed her garlic and lemon sauce with a piece of crusty bread, popped it into her mouth, and chewed thoughtfully. "I'm here for a case consultation. I came to confer with a psychiatrist named Stanley Gudhausen. Dr. Gudhausen is a world-class authority on Multiple Personality Disorder—"

"Like *The Three Faces of Eve*? That kind of thing?"

"Yes. Just exactly. MPD is still considered somewhat rare, but I think I've diagnosed it in a patient of mine back home."

Karen forced herself to stop before she told him any more. Of course, she was eager to discuss the incredible coincidence—if coincidence it was—of two completely unconnected patients, two hundred miles apart, who both manifested the same alternate personality. The "Splitfoot" alters were completely identical right down to the name, the facial characteristics, even the patterns of speech. It wasn't that discussing the cases with Jeff—in only the most general terms—was a violation of either patient's rights. It was simply too soon. She'd wait until after her second meeting with Dr. Gudhausen tomorrow; then she could talk about it all he wanted.

"So, that's me," she said, rerouting the conversation. "Now, how about telling me something about *your* work?"

Before Jeff could begin, the waiter came around to ask if he could bring another bottle of Chablis. Jeff held up his hand, asking the waiter to wait. Then to Karen, "My turn to get third-degree, huh? Do you want the complete or the abridged version?"

"Oh, complete, by all means."

To the waiter: "Then yes please, we'll need at least one more bottle."

The waiter responded with a brief emphatic nod, and vanished.

"Well, let's see. I'm employed by the Massachusetts Technological Academy—we call it the 'Academy' for short, that way we don't confuse it with the Metropolitan Transit Authority. . . ."

"Like 'Charlie on the MTA'?"

"You got it." He chuckled. "The Academy is a privately run think tank that prospers only because of the American taxpayer's supreme sense of generosity, and the government's willingness to keep the public as generous as possible."

"Do I detect a well-disguised note of skepticism?"

"Oh God, is it that obvious? No, it just irks me the way our leaders continue to squander tax dollars on any crackpot enterprise that can even remotely be termed 'related' to the almighty D.'" He leaned forward and whispered conspiratorially, "The D stands for De-fense."

"You don't sound like a man who loves his job."

"There you go, playing shrink again. Whatever gave you the idea I don't like my job?" He held up both hands, palms toward Karen, and assumed a wide-eyed expression of innocence. "Am I really that transparent?"

"An open book. What do you do there?"

"Well, most people consider it 'Top Secret.' Do I have your word you won't violate the doctor-patient confidence?"

"You have my word. I swear it on my DSM-III-R."

Jeff's expression suddenly became serious. As he sipped his wine, a faraway look darkened his face. He spoke quietly. "Among other things, we're into UFO research."

Karen suppressed a laugh. Her hand shot to her lips, trying to keep the wine in her mouth.

"What's so funny?" Jeff pretended to take offense. "I didn't laugh at your multiple personality stuff."

"It was so . . . well . . . it was so completely unexpected. You're not serious, are you?"

"Of course I'm not serious, but I'm telling the truth."

"About the UFOs?"

"Yup."

"You don't believe in them, do you? I mean people from outer space and all that?"

"No, I don't believe in them; I don't disbelieve in them, either. I'm a skeptic in the true sense of the word. But, dear doctor, I'll tell you this: Most of my less speculative colleagues don't believe in them at all. Period. End of discussion. In fact, they don't believe in them because they're paid not to. Part of our job is to think the whole idea is lunacy, which, I take it, puts us in the same ball park as you, right?"

"I guess. I don't know. I never gave it much thought. Then again, there are still people in my profession who don't believe in MPD. I guess we're both destined to be misunderstood. And that's another thing we have in common." She finished the wine in her glass. "But seriously, Jeff, how can you work at something you don't believe in?"

"Oh, I've got my price. I can be bought."

"Seriously now, come on."

"Seriously? Okay. I believe people are seeing something in the sky. I believe folks have been seeing airborne phenomena for a long time. If these shapes and lights and flying bugaboos aren't from outer space, then where else can they come from? Ever think about that?"

Karen shrugged as Jeff continued. "And what could be causing them? What do they mean? That's what I'm working on—I'm trying to make a complete list of possible solutions to this mystery. And, as mysteries go, this one's a crackerjack. UFOs have been around, and fairly well documented, for hundreds, actually thousands, of years. Take the biblical descriptions of fiery chariots, for example, and wheels within wheels. Or more recently, in 1883, a Mexican astronomer named José Bonilla photographed 143 circular objects moving across the sun. And starting about 1897 people all over America started seeing huge flying 'airships'."

The waiter returned with the new bottle of wine. He went through his presentation ritual and Jeff made a big deal of sniffing the cork, looking dismayed, then holding it between his lips like a wooden cigar. When he reached for the lighted candle, Karen looked away, embarrassed but amused. The waiter about-faced and made a hasty exit.

"Alone at last," Jeff said, tossing the cork onto the tabletop. He leaned forward. "Tell me something, Karen. Have you ever treated one of these people who claim to have been abducted by a UFO?"

"No, I really haven't." She thought a moment while pouring each of them another glass of wine. "But I've read something about it in the journals. I guess it's not all that uncommon these days. Oh, and I also read that book—it was quite a long time ago—about that couple from New Hampshire who were supposedly taken aboard a UFO where they underwent some kind of medical examination."

"Sure, Betty and Barney Hill; that's a famous case. The psychiatrist who worked with them practices right here in Boston. But, Karen, is it safe—or should I say, accurate—to conclude that as of now, right this minute, you have no professional interest in the topic?"

"Yes, that's true. I think I can honestly admit to being personally curious, however."

"Right. Good. I'm curious, too. Our files are full of 'contactee' cases where people believe they've been abducted, actually lifted off the earth. In some instances, whisked away to some distant planet. I don't know if these alleged abductions are literally, physically, true, or if it is some brand-new variety of mental aberration. Something not listed in your bible—what did you call it?—the DSM-III-R?"

"Right, the *Diagnostic & Statistical Manual*."

"So what's your diagnosis, Dr. Bradley?"

Karen had no idea what to say. "Well, I . . . I don't know. I haven't read all that much about it. Of course, I recall what Dr. Jung said about projections of the unconscious collective psyche, but—"

"But that's nothing more than a polite, scientific sounding way of saying they're imaginary. Don't forget now, Jung later retracted that view. Not long before he died he said he'd come to accept that UFOs are real, three-dimensional objects."

Karen started to feel a bit flustered. "Well, you're the expert, Jeff. Doesn't your 'think tank' have an opinion?"

"Strange you should ask. Yes, as a matter of fact, we do. Our—I need a drum roll here—our *official* level-one opinion is that all UFO activity, all the way from sightings to abductions, is pure bunk, hoaxes and hallucinations. That goes for close encounters of the first, second, and third kind. All of it. Everything. The whole shootin' match. My open-minded colleagues and I are being paid to reinforce that attitude on the American public every chance we get. How's that for objectivity? We have our conclusion right from the start, all we have to do is assemble the data to prove it. We are traders in swamp gas, Dr. Bradley. We're vendors of hot-air balloons, weather satellites, and sunspots. I'm one of a proud army of professional debunkers, dauntless soldiers in the U.S. government's war on truth, reason, and honesty."

"Oh, I'm beginning to see now." Karen leaned forward, as if she were conspiring with him. "You've researched it enough that you're starting to believe there's something to these UFO stories, right?" She narrowed her eyes. "You're starting to believe in them, aren't you?"

"There you go, playing shrink again. Well, Doctor, you got me. You're absolutely right. I do believe."

"The skeptic becomes a believer. And right before my eyes! Wow!"

"It's the wine. It loosens my tongue."

Now it was Karen's turn to lean back in her chair and raise her wineglass. "Then we'd better order another bottle, 'cause I'm curious as hell. I want you to tell me all about this."

"You're getting me drunk and plying me for top-secret information."

"Guilty as charged. Now, Dr. Jeffrey Chandler, let's come directly to the point. I've never talked to anybody professionally involved in the UFO business. Suppose you try to convince me. Suppose you tell me what you, personally, consider the strongest, most convincing case of a UFO."

For a few moments Jeff thought in silence while Karen stared at him, smiling patiently. All his frivolity disappeared, his joking stopped. When he finally spoke, he was completely serious. "It is a comparatively recent sighting. And one that was heavily witnessed and thoroughly investigated. What would you say about a sighting witnessed by an estimated seventy thousand people?"

"Seventy *thousand!*" Karen raised her eyebrows. "I'd say it was pretty convincing."

"Sure, so would I. Among the seventy thousand witnesses there were scientists, newsmen, film people. There were politicians. Doctors. Religious leaders. In fact, a broad sampling of the population, from all over the world. And I'm talking about credible witnesses, mind you. People whose testimony would be readily believed in a court of law. People whose word, under oath, could send a criminal to jail, even to the electric chair."

Karen held her eyes on his. He was talking directly to her, with no hint of humor in his voice. "If thousands of people really witnessed this UFO," she said, "then it would be big news. Is the government hushing it up or something? How come I've never heard anything about it?"

"I bet you have. It took place at about noon on October thirteenth of 1917 in a little town in Portugal, a town called Fatima."

Karen tensed. Her cheeks became hot. She felt as if she were being set up, tricked. "You're talking about the miracle of Fatima! The appearance of the Virgin Mary to those three little kids! That's not a UFO sighting—"

"No? Think about it. Sure, now it's viewed as a miracle. And we're in the habit of thinking of it as a religious experience. But that's mostly because the visions were first seen and interpreted by three Portuguese children whose strong Catholic upbringing was their only frame of reference. Today, when we read about the strange goings on at Fatima, the events continue to be colored by a Catholic perspective. But consider what really took place there. The children saw a lady who was described as having an angular face, long fingers, and a vaguely oriental cast to her features: these are the classic features of many so-called UFO occupants. Evidently our mystery woman's appearance was sufficiently otherworldly so the little Catholic kids thought they were seeing the Virgin.

"Most of the seventy thousand witnesses who assembled in that field called Cova da Iria in Fatima saw a large pearly disk come spinning down through the clouds. They thought the sun was falling. It was raining that day, but the disk was radiating so much heat that people's clothing dried instantly. It was that same radiation—infrared, I suppose—that cured ailing people with diseases like arthritis, and—"

"So what appeared? What did they see?"

"That depends. The people who were at a great distance saw only a ball of light. The people who were closest to the light had the richest images and experiences. If they were of one religious persuasion, they'd see Joseph, or an angel, or whatever. If they were of another persuasion, they'd see Jesus, or Mary, or—"

"Didn't anyone take pictures?"

"Sure. Lots of movie and still photographers were on the scene, but by and large cameras only recorded a ball of light. Later, many but not all of the photographs and movies were collected by the Catholic Church during an investigation some thirteen years after the fact. Man, I'd love to see that stuff, wouldn't you? I guess it's all stashed away in some vault deep within the bowels of the Vatican. I know they've never released it. They're more into secrecy than any government."

Karen listened attentively, her sense of fascination growing rapidly. "Wasn't there something about a prediction?" she asked. "I seem to recall—"

"That's right. This mysterious lady—whoever she was—told the children many things. She foretold the end of the war, and—in its own way a little more scary—she predicted that two of the children would die soon. And they did. Weird, huh? But supposedly there was a written prediction. I bet that's the one you're thinking of. It was sealed in an envelope and locked up in some safe in the Vatican."

"What did it say?"

Jeff shrugged. "I really don't know. In 1960, Pope John XXIII opened the prophesy, but then, for some reason, he chose not to make it public."

"Gee," said Karen, "censoring the word of God. Why would he do that? What do you suppose it said?"

"I have no idea. To explain the pope's behavior, I suspect the prediction relates to one of three general areas: first, it might have been a prediction about the end of the world, with zero hope of redemption. That kind of news would do very little to promote the domestic tranquillity."

"And second . . .?"

"The envelope's contents may somehow have suggested that the miracle at Fatima was a hoax, or a mistake, or something other than what it appeared to be. Discovering their miracle was some cosmic April Fools' joke would be bad news for the Catholic Church. Especially after they—in their infinite wisdom—had gone through all the trouble and expense of investigating the event and granting it miracle status. You know how those Catholics hate to admit it when they're wrong about something . . ."

"And third?"

"Third?" Jeff took the last sip of his wine, and tried to pour more from the empty bottle. "Third is a tough one to figure. There just might have been something written in that envelope that would negate, or redefine, every religious concept that we as a race have embraced for the last two thousand or more years. In fact, there might have been something that would change our whole concept of reality."

6

The Secret Birthday Wish

St. Albans, Vermont

It was Edmund Washburn's birthday, but he was too tired to celebrate. All day, as his fatigue grew, he became more and more convinced something was about to go wrong.

Now, driving home from work, he wondered what "something" would be.

Hope Lucy's okay, he thought. She was his biggest concern. Worrying about his daughter was one thing, but with this multiple personality business, it was like worrying about half a dozen daughters. Anything could happen. Anytime.

Ah, he was just tired. By morning the whole world would look better. Good thing he and Winnie had had the foresight to put off the party until tomorrow. They'd be able to have more fun on Saturday, when he was well rested. Maybe they could take the kids to a matinee or something.

It was about eight-thirty—just as the brilliant red sun began to sink behind the Adirondack Mountains beyond Lake Champlain's western shore—that Ed pulled his pickup truck into the driveway of his home.

He noticed that his wife's Buick was in the dooryard. Good, that meant she was here. So why hadn't she answered when he phoned to tell her he'd be working late?

The next thing he noticed was that the wide interior shade was drawn behind the big picture window he'd installed last spring.

Funny.

At this time of day, Winnie always liked to sit in her recliner, watching the sunset or listening to the songbirds that hopped from fence to lilac bush.

Ed slammed the door to his pickup. The hinges resisted a little so he made a mental note to put a couple drops of WD-40 to them pretty quick.

Halfway up the front walk he stopped and looked around the yard. Where were the kids?

Usually, neither of them was difficult to spot. Most days Randy would be grinning from the porch, holding the screen door wide open as an invitation to Dad and to hordes of flies and mosquitoes the boy just couldn't seem to become aware of. But the screen door was closed. And so was the heavy door behind it.

Odd.

Ed still had his key ring in his hand. The collection of keys jingled like Christmas bells as he separated his house key from the rest.

As he turned the key in the lock, he figured the three of them had gone over to Winnie's mom's place. Of course. She'd probably picked them up in the Ford.

But why?

As he pushed the door open into the dark interior of the house, the first thing he noticed was the absence of cooking smells. During their fifteen years of marriage, Winnie always had supper waiting for him when he got home from work. Even on days like today when he worked overtime.

On those rare occasions when she was away at supper time, she'd unfailingly leave something hot in the toaster oven for him.

Damn it, she should be here. He was grateful for the extra work and by God she should be, too. These weren't easy times, and his overtime pay would be a help to the family.

Lots of new buildings were being put up along the lakeshore. Vermonters weren't buying them; Vermonters couldn't afford them. It was new residents—born-again Vermonters, Ed called them—and out-of-staters wanting second homes who were footing the construction bills. Luckily for Ed, every new house and condo complex wanted cable TV. So today's workload was nothing new; installing the lines often kept Ed Washburn from getting home on time.

So where is she?

He had to reach around the door frame and flick on the living-room lights because all the interior shades had been pulled and the house was dark.

Strange.

Why wasn't Winnie right there to reward his extra work? When you got right down to it, she should have made something a bit special; after all, not only was it a Friday night, it was his birthday!

He'd worked overtime every day this week, and he'd get another half day tomorrow. Time and a half meant he'd be earning $13.50 an hour before deductions. You'd think she'd be proud of that. Least she could do was have a hot meal ready the minute he walked in the door. She should realize he'd be hungry and tired after such a long day.

Jeez, she hadn't even left a christly light on for him!

Damn woman, he thought, doesn't give a fart how hard I work; probably thinks I'm made of money the way she spends it out fast as I bring it in.

No. That wasn't fair. Winnie wasn't like that. In addition to tired and hungry, Ed realized he was grumpy, too.

Now he was more convinced something might be wrong. Maybe she'd left him a note somewhere.

As Ed walked through the living room he saw the school portraits of his two kids smiling at him from the top of the television set. Randy, looking like a toothless pixie; Lucy, starting to look a bit . . . well . . . womanly, in spite of the silver line of her braces.

Entering the kitchen, he flicked on the light. The blue-painted plywood cabinets reminded him how Winnie had been stashing money to replace them with oak. She'd put away a pretty fair nest egg before Lucy's "trouble" began. Then the money had depleted so fast Ed didn't even see it go.

The therapy sessions had started at just one a week, and that wasn't too bad; the doctor's fee was covered by Ed's insurance. Then the number of sessions increased to two a week, then three. And pretty soon the insurance allowance was used up. Now the therapy was all coming out of his own pocket.

Still, he had to be fair. Winnie had offered to take a part-time job as a clerk at the Ben Franklin Store; he had to give her credit for that. But her taking a job wasn't right. No wife of mine's goin' out to work, he'd told her. He'd have no part of it. Providing for the family was a man's job, simple as that.

But with three therapy sessions a week—Ed pulled a Bud out of the refrigerator—why that was $180 a week that went straight out of his paycheck and into the pocket of that female doctor—what's her name?—Karen Bradley.

Ed extracted two pieces of salami from the white waxed-paper packet, rolled them into the shape of a cigar, and bit off about an inch.

That lady doctor was okay, though, he had to admit it. She was doing all she could to get rid of Lucy's "trouble." She had even offered to give them every third session for free. But Ed would have no part of that, either. "I pay, same's I expect to get paid," he had told her.

If he had to work, then by God he'd work. Lots of families had troubles far worse than his. But $180 every week required an awful lot of overtime. And when the overtime stopped, he'd have to take a second job. Good thing they'd bought the house back when they did; mortgage payments were only $257 a month. But as the area around them got more developed, taxes kept right on going up and up . . . .

Ed opened the back door and looked out at the yard. No one there, either.

"Randy! Lucy!"

The tire swing he'd put up for the kids was unoccupied. It moved ever so slowly in the breeze, like a pocket watch dangling on a long chain.

The four Adirondack chairs he'd made last summer—one for each of them—were similarly vacant. Too bad he'd never built that picnic table he'd promised the kids. It was to have been Randy's first lesson in carpentry. Instead, he'd had to sell his table saw before he got around to making anything else. Next, he feared, he'd have to start selling off his guns.

Ed put the empty beer bottle into the space between the counter and refrigerator where they kept shopping bags and empties. Chewing the last of the salami, he walked to the cellar door, opened it, and looked down. "Hey, Winnie, you down there?" But of course she wasn't; the cellar light wasn't on.

"Winnie! Kids! Where the hell is everybody?"

Sure enough, they must have gone off with Winnie's mother. Okay, so where was the note? Least they coulda done was leave a note.

No sir, this wasn't like Winnie at all. Somehow, Ed knew things weren't going to be that simple.

"Winnie!"

God! What if one of the kids was hurt? What if an ambulance had taken everyone to the hospital in Burlington?

"Aw, shit . . ." Ed smacked his forehead with his palm. He chuckled happily. They're hidin' on me. A'course. Pretty quick they're gonna jump out from someplace yellin' "Happy Birthday!"

The front door slammed shut.

Ed jumped. Almost cried out. His heart pounded.

The living-room light flicked off.

"Winn, zat you?"

The kitchen light went out automatically the moment he stepped across the threshold and into the living room. What's going on with the friggin' lights around here? Can't be a circuit breaker, both lights would've gone out at once.

"Edmund." It was Winnie's voice, coming from the direction of their bedroom. "Edmund." She sounded funny.

"You're lucky, Edmund. You're so very, very fortunate."

Lucky? What was she talking about? Why did her voice sound so dry and scratchy? Was she sick or something?

He moved toward the hall that led to the bedroom just as Winnie stepped into view. In the darkness her appearance was strange. It was as if she were somehow darker than the shadows in which she stood.

Ed stepped toward her, squinting. She appeared to be dressed in some sort of transparent, filmy outfit. She was naked beneath it. He smiled, taking another step forward. So this was his birthday present! She looked good, too. Her waist was still thin, her thighs were tight, and her tits could still turn a lot of heads.

Smiling, Ed stopped when he realized he wasn't seeing things exactly right. She *wasn't* dressed in some provocative negligee. Instead, she seemed to be wrapped in an opaque veil of black swirling smoke. It was a form-fitting cocoon of mist that flowed over her body like the glaze of water in a shower.

That's what it looked like, anyway, and that was impossible.

He stopped, unbelieving, tried to blink away the dream image.

Her voice grew stranger now: windy-sounding, hollow, and distant. Was she trying to sound sexy or something? "Your great good fortune is to be envied, Edmund my love. . . ."

Beneath the cloak of flowing shifting vapor, Ed could see her heavy breasts swaying as she shifted her weight from one foot to the other. The vertical scar from her C-section seemed to glow, pulsing with an unearthly ruby light. Her beautiful red thigh-length hair was tightly braided. Draped over her shoulder, it hung like a crimson cable that dropped almost to her pubic thatch.

"W-what's going on here, Winnie? What's wrong with you? How come you're runnin' around naked like that? Where's the kids?"

She continued as if he hadn't spoken. "All your worries are as memories far, far behind you. Your future is bright, a clearly lighted path—"

"What are you talking about, Winnie? What's happened to you?" He wondered if Lucy's craziness could be contagious; could Winnie have caught a dose of it like some sort of mental influenza?

When he tried to take another step, he couldn't. His feet wouldn't move.

"Think of it, Edmund, love. Think of that one eventuality men fear above all else. The intriguing perplexity that humbles the magnificent, that levels the insignificant—"

"Damn it, Winnie, why are you talking crazy like that?" He tried to move again; couldn't. His voice slid up a register. "Help me. Something's wrong. Jesus Christ. I . . . I can't move!"

"Then listen, damn you."

"To what? What are you talking about for Christ's sake?"

"I'm talking about the sublime inevitability; I'm talking about headin' west, the end of the line . . . ."

"Winnie—"

"I'm talking about the grimmest of reapers, the old man down the road—"

"What old man?" He could feel a useless tide of adrenaline sloshing dead-ended within his paralyzed limbs. What was happening to him? Was this a heart attack? Was he having a stroke?

"The thing, Edmund . . . I'm talking about the very thing that makes the mightiest of you grovel with the peasantry in terror. The eternal footman. Azrael. Man's ultimate uncertainty. For some, Edmund, but not for you. You are the exception. For you, my Edmund, the grand uncertainty is no uncertainty at all."

She stepped closer to him. "Did you ever wonder, dear one, just what it's like to die?" She ran her fingertips ever so softly along his cheek. Her thumb came to rest upon his lips.

"Wh—" Now his lips wouldn't move. It was as if they'd been shot full of Novocain. He wanted to ask her for help—God, Winnie, I can't move, help me, please, call an ambulance—but now, dear God, he couldn't speak at all.

"When we pass on, dear Edmund, do the billions of cells in the body die all at once, a perfectly coordinated whole? Or does it happen slowly, cell by cell, piece by piece, a section at a time?" In a graceful curtsy she lowered herself before him, stroked the petrified muscle of his right calf. Numbness took it. It wouldn't support his weight. He collapsed onto his knee in an awkward genuflection. She touched his right thigh and he toppled.

"It's my birthday gift for you, honored husband." She smiled sweetly down at him. "Imagine the terror it must hold for the infirm, the diseased, the elderly. Imagine the solitary crone, her family far away and gone, living in the ancient house alone. Think, Edmund. Think how she makes her way to bed each night, night upon night, and always alone. Think how she wonders if she will survive till morning. Think how the terror will take her, night after night like a sadistic demon lover: Will this be the night? Will she see her children just one more time? Will she see another birthday of her own?"

Ed's eyes hurt. They burned something wicked, but he couldn't blink to lubricate them. His wife took a step closer, straddled his head, looking down. Slowly she lifted her copper braid.

What are you going to do, he wanted to ask her, but his tongue was a dead thing lying dry and fat in his mouth.

"For you, Edmund my love, there is no more questioning, no more guessing. Fancy it? Freedom from dread, freedom from trepidation. For you, Edmund, uncertainty becomes certainty. There will be no more birthdays—"

She lowered her head, puckering her lips as if preparing for a kiss. The limp braid dangled above his face. Impossibly, its bristled end scraped across his forehead spreading pain like sandpaper on an open wound. Yet he could not cry out.

She straightened. Hands on hips she sauntered around his prone form, continuing her one-sided litany. "No more birthdays, no more Christmases . . ." Her black smoky cloak slid around on her naked body like the tide slipping across the sand. Ed thought he saw tiny sparks here and there within the black intricacy of the smoke. Little pops and flashes, like a miniature lightning storm.

Then she knelt beside him, pulled her hair forward, and draped the braid across his chest. When she pulled it back toward herself, slowly, incredible white-hot pain seared through him. It was like getting whacked with 220 volts. Yet he couldn't pull away, he couldn't scream.

"It's my gift to you, dearest Edmund. Tonight you may enjoy an absolute certainty: tonight is the night you will die."

His fear mounted, raced toward hysteria. But there was no way he could release it, no emotional escape valve. He couldn't pull away, couldn't utter a cry, he could only lie there as she pranced around him, grinning, laughing, flicking him repeatedly with her braided whip. Every time it touched him, pain surged with the ferocity of lightning.

"And again you're fortunate; you'll not endure a lonely death. No, nothing quite that horrible. Your loving family will be with you at the end. We'll surround you, comfort you . . . ."

Little Randy stepped out of the hall. Although he was fully dressed in a jersey and overalls, he too was shrouded in that shifting smoky veil. He held a fifteen-inch wood chisel from Ed's toolbox, and he grinned crazily.

It's a nightmare, coaxed Ed's racing mind. But I can't wake up! Why. Can't. I. Wake. Up?

Randy walked over to his father, squatted flat-footed beside him, and tore open Ed's shirtfront. The little boy swayed as he positioned the chisel's blade against Ed's nipple. Randy held it there, metal against flesh, as Ed's mind reeled.

Oh my dear God, why can't I pass out?

Winnie circled behind him, quickly moving out of sight. The reflex to follow her with his eyes was there, but it was out of commission.

Just then Lucy stepped out of the shadowy hallway. No veil of smoke obscured her delicate features.

Help me, Lucy. Help me, he thought. He wanted to cry out to her. He would plead, if that's what it took. She could help him; she was normal, unaffected.

Then she looked at him, terror in her eyes. Had she seen the smoky fabric screening her mother and Randy?

A pressure built inside Edmund. Terror and frustration grew to lunatic proportions. He thought he would explode. Yet the undiminished voice of the protective father still screamed loudly somewhere in his combusting brain: Run, Lucy! Run before they get you, too!

Even in the darkened room Ed could clearly see how his daughter's face began to contort. Grotesquely rippling, flattening, stretching, and pulling into the frightful mask he had seen far too many times before: it was Splitfoot.

Randy moved aside as Lucy approached, but he never took the sharp chisel away from Ed's chest. The hideously smiling girl stepped up to her paralyzed father, dropped to her knees between his dead legs. She tugged his belt away from his stomach and unbuckled it.

Then, leering at him, the tip of her pink tongue tucked into the corner of her lips, she undid his zipper. "Come on, Daddy," she said in Splitfoot's voice, "haven't you been thinking about this? Haven't you been wanting it?"

She parted the fly of his boxer shorts, reached inside.

Somewhere in the midst of Ed's terror and humiliation, there was still a shrinking oasis of rational thought. Before it too surrendered to hysteria, Ed discovered that he was erect.

"I wouldn't want my daddy to die without making his most secret birthday wish come true."

She bent forward, holding his member in both cold hands. She kissed it with icy lips, then took it into her mouth.

In a moment she stopped, looked up at him, an offended pout on her lips. "Oh, but you're not moving, Daddy. Don't you like it?"

Ed felt the sweat streaming down his face, trickling over his ribs beneath his arms. He felt the icy edge of Randy's chisel pressed tightly against his chest. Its broad metal tooth ready, but it wasn't biting yet.

He thought of Lucy's wire braces as she leered up at him.

"You know what might be fun, Daddy? Wouldn't it be fun to see if you can keep from moving all on your own? Let's try it, can we? See if you can hold perfectly still, okay?"

"NO!" he roared. The word exploded from his mouth and he knew he was in control again.

The actions that followed came more from pent-up panic than rational thought. He rolled to the side, away from Randy and the chisel's shiny blade, pushing Lucy back with his legs.

And he sprang to his feet.

Winnie was right behind him. She snapped the hairy whip around his throat and pulled it tight. God she was strong! She was lifting him off his feet.

This time he could scream. The blade of the carpenter's chisel found the skin of his arm. Its bite felt like a fiery razor. It seemed to cut and burn at the same time.

Somehow he was able to shift his weight to the left. That pulled Winnie slightly off balance, just enough so they both staggered. Ed smashed her hand with his own and she let go of her braid. Enraged, Winnie screamed like a demon. She kicked at him savagely, but missed his genitals.

Now he had his balance. He raced toward the front door.

It wouldn't open.

Desperately he turned the key on the deadbolt, first left, then right, all the time shaking the heavy door. By the time he realized it was useless, they were all over him.

He felt the blade of the chisel slice into his shoulder, heard it shred the back of his shirt. Whirling, Ed caught the glazed expressions on his attackers. Mindlessly, he bolted toward the hall, screaming as he went.

Winnie's hair caught him slightly, stinging like an electric fence. He didn't slow down.

It was a short dash along the hallway and into the spare bedroom. There! No more than five paces in front of him: his gun rack on the wall between the two windows.

Something relaxed when he touched the blue metal of the shotgun barrel. It was a familiar sensation. It was sanity and order.

As he lifted down his twelve-gauge, he groped in the drawer for shells. "Please God, let them be here."

Winnie appeared in the doorway, teeth bare, growling like an animal.

Ed pushed the fourth shell into the magazine.

Advancing, she held the end of her braid as if it were a pistol.

Ed lifted the shotgun.

Winnie took a step forward just as Randy tore around the door frame and into the room. He didn't stop. He didn't look around. He just lunged at his father, swiping at him with the bloody chisel. The boy's body was a wild and mindless beast. He growled and snarled.

Ed stepped to the side. Randy's swift attack with the blade missed the target. The boy lost his balance, almost tumbled.

"Yes! Yes!" Winnie screamed.

Ed pulled the trigger.

The fiery roar was deafening in the small room. Scores of invisible pellets smacked the child against the carpeted floor. Warm blood splattered Ed's face. His son lay still, one chubby hand twitched and flexed.

"Yes, Edmund, yes. Calm down now." Winnie inched toward him.

Somehow, in that minuscule reserve of sanity, Ed realized it was his panic that was protecting him. The thing that had been his wife could not control him when he couldn't control himself.

But his rational thinking had gone on far too long; it had a deadly calming effect. She continued to speak soothingly as he felt the joints of his elbows begin to freeze up like rusty hinges. "Yes, Edmund, we need the deaths. Yessssss."

The shotgun was suddenly immensely heavy.

Winnie smiled almost prettily; she knew she was getting to him again. "Yes, that's right, you know what we need . . . ."

Ed concentrated, willed his fingers to move.

"I won't calm down," he screamed.

And he fired.

7

Pig On A Spit

Andover, Massachusetts
Saturday, June 18

Herbert Gold woke up at six o'clock, just as he did every morning. He showered, shaved, and vigorously brushed his close crop of wiry copper hair. All the time he grinned at himself in the bathroom mirror. Then he dressed and walked downstairs to the kitchen. His wife, Dora, moved silently from refrigerator to counter. She wore a floor-length, pink terry-cloth robe with long full sleeves. When she had first worn the robe, more than a year ago, Herbert had said she looked like a pink ghost. This morning he said nothing at all.

Dora put on water for instant coffee, put bread into the toaster oven, and set out the NutriGrain Wheat & Raisins beside a half gallon of one percent milk.

Herbert sat down and grunted a reluctant good morning.

"We got no juice," she told him. "Wish just once you'd think to stop and pick up juice."

"I can do without it," Herbert said.

"Well I can't," she told him. "You know how I like my juice in the morning."

Her breakfast responsibility completed, Dora left him alone in the kitchen and went back upstairs. Herbert knew she would crawl back into bed and stay there, watching television until he had left for work. On weekdays, her habit was to stay in bed at least until the end of the *Donahue Show*. But this was a Saturday. What would she do up there on a Saturday? Watch cartoons?

After a while she'd shower for about thirty minutes, steaming up the bathroom. And then? God knows what.

One thing for sure—even if she went grocery shopping, she wouldn't buy any juice. That had become his job now, even if Dora had to do without it for a month.

The moment his wife was out of sight, Herbert dumped his cereal and coffee into the garbage disposal, rinsed the dirty dishes, grabbed his lunch pail, and left the house.

His station wagon was at the curb.

Herbert crossed the lawn and got in, just like every morning. Then he drove to the stop sign at the end of the street.

This morning, however, instead of making his usual right turn and heading north to work, Herbert turned left.

Going south.

Toward Boston.

* * *

Boston, Massachusetts

After finishing an expensive room-service breakfast, Karen began to pack her suitcase for the drive back to Vermont.

It was almost a quarter to eleven, and Dr. Gudhausen still hadn't phoned. Yesterday he had agreed to do a little research, maybe call a colleague or two, then get back to her with whatever insight he could offer about treating Lucy Washburn. Their plan had been to meet, maybe have lunch, before Karen left for home.

So why hadn't he called? Had she failed to impress on him that she had to check out of her hotel room by eleven?

Or had he been humoring her from the start, politely feigning professional interest in the strange coincidence she had discovered?

Of course not! That was her insecurity talking; Dr. Gudhausen had not been faking interest. He had been concerned, even, it seemed, a little nervous. The whole bizarre situation clearly had started his mental wheels turning, she was sure of it. "If I were a superstitious man," Dr. Gudhausen had said, "I'd be pretty spooked right now. I've seen a lot of these MPD situations, but never anything quite like this. It's . . . well, frankly, Karen, it's uncanny. The only conclusion I can jump to right now is that Lucy Washburn and Herbert Gold have somehow stored separate sets of identical memories, assimilated independently, but apparently from the same source. Highly unlikely, I admit. It would have to be something they've both experienced, but experienced distinctly separate from one another: a movie, perhaps, or something on television? Possibly a book? Maybe even a magazine article? Who can say?" He shrugged his heavy shoulders. "Lame, I admit, but beyond that, I'm stumped."

Karen glanced at her watch. Ten to eleven. Okay, she'd wait exactly ten more minutes, then go to the lobby, check out, and call Dr.

Gudhausen from a pay phone. Still, it irritated her: his time was no more valuable than her own. After she'd traveled all this way, could he really expect her to hang around a hotel room waiting for his call?

Karen had to bare down with all her weight to close her suitcase. Jeez, she laughed to herself, I come to Boston for two days and I bring clothes enough for a week! It was a good thing, though, because she'd had a pretty dress to wear at dinner last night with Jeff.

She picked up the bulging suitcase and put it by the door. Then she leaned her attaché case against it and looked around the room for things forgotten.

Yes, by gosh, it *had* been a pleasant evening, in spite of her initial reservations. Jeff was bright and entertaining— rather silly actually, she thought, then quickly added—in an endearing sort of way. In retrospect, she was pleased with herself for not running away before he had arrived at the restaurant. If she had, true to her entrenched patterns of behavior, she'd have spent the entire evening cursing herself for her cowardice. Oh, she had blown similar situations before. Over and over she kept learning the same lesson: sometimes it's good to be a little adventurous; sometimes a bit of courage pays off.

The bottom line, of course, was that she'd had a great evening. She wanted to see Jeff again. She just hoped he felt the same way.

Did he?

Well, she'd find out soon enough. A good indication would be whether he would follow through on that trip to Burlington they had talked about.

The phone rang.

Karen jumped a little, having all but given up on Dr. Gudhausen. She stepped quickly around the unmade bed and picked up the receiver. "Hello?"

"Dr. Bradley?

"Yes?"

"Oh, good; glad I caught you. Stan Gudhausen here. Look, I'm sorry about cutting this so close to the wire, but I've been trying to track down an old friend of mine. Haven't accomplished much of anything except running up my Sprint bill. Anyway, the guy's a priest. A Jesuit psychologist. Crackerjack clinician. Listen, Doctor, if I may, I'd like to invite myself up to Vermont for a day or two. I think I'd like to examine that little Washburn girl in person, if that would be all right with you?"

"Oh yes, yes of course. It would be a great privilege—"

"Privilege nothing. I think, Doctor, that we may be on to something rather disturbing here. Look, I wonder if I can talk you into delaying your return trip to Burlington for an hour or so. I'd like to get some things together and ride up with you, that is if you don't mind a hitchhiker. We'll have plenty of time to talk in the car. Then I can catch a flight back."

"Yes, certainly, of course."

"I'll need an hour and a half, max. That'll give me time to make some arrangements and get a few things cleared up before I leave."

"Okay, sure."

"Can you pick me up at my office?"

"Just tell me when."

"Shall we make it one o'clock?"

"One o'clock it is. Thanks for calling. Oh, Dr. Gudhausen—"

But he had already hung up.

                              * * *

Montreal, Quebec

The brasserie on Maisonneuve was quiet and dark at midday. As they entered, the two priests attracted surprised glances and pleasant greetings. "Hello, Father," the bartender said directly to Sullivan.

"How do they know to speak to me in English?"

LeClair smiled mysteriously. "We can just tell."

They sat down at a table and gave their orders to a buxom young waitress in a white peasant blouse.

Father Sullivan had polished off three Molson ales before he finished his thick smoked meat sandwich. LeClair drank sparkling cider and picked at his *poutine*, a platter of french fries swimming in brown gravy and melted cheese. Little swirls of steam rose from the potatoes.

"Food was always my undoing," Sullivan said after rinsing his mouth with ale. "I was always a little fat kid. At the orphanage, St. Luke's—gosh, I must have been fourteen, fifteen years old at the time—they wouldn't exempt me from physical education in spite of my weight and my asthma. And, man, I hated to go to that gymnasium, not because of Father Mosely—he was the coach—but because of the other kids. They made fun of me." Sullivan chuckled sadly as he remembered. "When Father wasn't looking they'd pull down my shorts, or snap me on the ass with a wet towel. Then they'd remind me to turn the other cheek. After a while I refused to shower at all. Father would overlook this little breech of protocol and let me go directly back to class, drenched with sweat. Then they'd make fun of my smell. 'Do you smell bacon frying?' they'd say."

LeClair half smiled. "Children are such . . . savages, but I've always thought the little Catholic children were the worst of all. Little demons. Horrible little sadists."

"You can imagine what my self-image was like. I remember one time when physical education was the last class of the day. We all had to do ten chin-ups before we were permitted to leave. The meanest kids, of course, were also the strongest—it must be some kind of natural law—they'd do their chin-ups and get out. But there were enough kids left over to give me plenty of guff. ·

"After a monumental effort—a small miracle, really—I had just two chin-ups to go. Just two. I'll never forget it. After the eighth, my arms felt like they were going to stretch and rip apart; my shoulders hurt like hell. I pulled and pulled, grunting all the time. Kids were cheering and laughing. Someone oinked every time I grunted. Sweat just pumped out of me in buckets. Finally, I hung there like a fat apple on a limb, almost ready to drop. 'I can't do it, Father,' I said. I think I was crying but no one could tell because I was sweating more. 'Please, Father, I can't.' I was begging, actually begging; I remember every humiliating syllable. All I wanted to do was give up and get out and hide forever. I was terrified that I couldn't hold on much longer and I knew if I lost my grip and fell I'd be even more of a laughingstock. So I was trying to get Father Mosely to excuse me. I wanted him to let me off the hook, comfort me. I wanted him to say, 'It's all right, Billy.' But he wouldn't; he'd have no part of it.

"He said, 'You *can* do it. Concentrate, William.'

"And of course, I did. I hated him just then. But only for a while. Funny, isn't it, how a little thing like that can change the whole direction of your life? He'd taught me something, you see. The moral of the story is nothing I can articulate, but I definitely learned something important. After that, I took care of myself, lost weight and stayed fit. In fact, I think it was then that I first thought about becoming a priest."

The waitress brought another ale and another cider. Sullivan smiled at her. "I think you're trying to get me drunk." She grinned back at him and winked mischievously.

A high-pitched beep, its source unknown, puzzled the men for a moment. "It is my pager," Father LeClair said in surprise. "Please excuse me, Bill. I'll just be a minute."

As LeClair got up to phone the hospital, Father Sullivan took a folded piece of paper from the pocket of his jacket. It was a photocopy of a church document; the subject: Father Hamilton Mosely. Again Sullivan looked at the form, nearly certain he wasn't reading it correctly. Could it be a misprint? A typographical error? Yes, he thought, it has to be a mistake. Father Mosely had seemed like an old man even then, back in high school, in 1941. On the folded paper, the old priest's birthday was given as January 5, 1886. That would make him more than one hundred years old! Was it possible? Could the withered fetus in the hospital bed be the same Father Hamilton Mosely listed on the paper? Was there some possibility that the shriveled old man was not the person Sullivan remembered?

No. Impossible. There could be no mistake.

"Bill." Father LeClair hurried toward the table. He looked worried. "Something's wrong at the hospital," he said. "We have to go back."

8

The Foolish Fates

Boston, Massachusetts

Stanley Gudhausen phoned Gloria to tell her she could take Monday off. There was no reason for her to keep the office open while he was up north in Vermont.

Now he looked around with great satisfaction at the orderly way she had left everything before leaving work yesterday. If there is a God, Dr. Gudhausen chuckled, I should thank Him for creating obsessive-compulsives. The trouble with them—with Gloria away—was that he couldn't *find* anything! Where would she have filed Dr. Ralph Aldrich's paper on the dangers of treating multiple personality? It wasn't under "A-L" for Aldrich. Or "APA" for the annual American Psychiatric Association meetings.

Damn it, he should have asked her while he had her on the phone.

Gudhausen sighed and looked at his watch. In less than an hour Karen Bradley would pick him up and they'd be off to Vermont. He couldn't afford to waste any more time poking around in the filing cabinets.

He returned to his office and sat at his desk, eagerly fishing around the bottom drawer for one of the Cuban cigars he'd smuggled back from Toronto.

With Gloria away, he could smoke in peace, without listening to her sputter about the smell and his heart condition and the bad example he was setting for his patients.

Gudhausen laughed out loud in the empty office. She's a great gal, he thought, and I'm lucky to have her. But when she puts something away, God damn it, no one can find it but her! Must be some feminist plot to make herself indispensable.

Reclining, feet on the desktop, he puffed and thought, trying to recall the controversial assertions Dr. Aldrich had made about multiples.

The various personalities a patient displayed—called alters—were often remarkably dissimilar. Different, highly contrasting IQs were routine among alters, so were different aptitudes and talents. But Aldrich had gone further than that. He had argued that there were sometimes physiological changes, too. Some alters had eye problems, some did not, suggesting the shape of the eye had, in reality, changed. Muscle and skin tone varied dramatically. Wounds and blemishes could appear and vanish. Aldrich had demonstrated that changes in personality are always accompanied by changes in brain activity. He had used PET scans to show separate cortical activity in the brain of each personality.

The extent of physical change possible, of course, remained to be determined. Aldrich had suggested that in certain advanced instances, crimes committed by mutated alters might make identification impossible.

But the most controversial assertion of all was when Aldrich stated that certain of the alter personalities can be quite psychic. He emphatically encouraged his assembled colleagues to study multiples in order to learn how science can help develop psychic capabilities in healthy subjects.

That notion had gone over about as well as a fifty-pound sack of horse shit, Gudhausen recalled.

Still, his imagination locked on that one charged word: *psychic.*

At that time Gudhausen himself had been skeptical, but he hadn't rejected the possibility out of hand. Now he wondered, could a shared consciousness exist, psychically, between two multiples who were two hundred miles apart? Suppose little Lucy Washburn of St. Albans, Vermont, and Herbert Gold of Andover, Massachusetts, were in some kind of "psychic link"? Might that not explain the arrival of the mysterious Mr. Splitfoot?

"Hell," he said, "I'll just phone Aldrich. I could easily spend the rest of the day looking for that goddamn file." He began to rotate his Rolodex, looking for the California number, when he heard a gentle tap at the study's door.

He looked at his watch; too soon for Karen Bradley. Must be Gloria coming in to tidy up or do a little weekend organizing. "Come in," he said, thinking, What luck! Now she can find the file and save a long distance call. He wouldn't mention the call, of course; she always teased him about his unnecessary and inconsistent frugality.

Again the tapping.

"It's unlocked, Gloria."

The door opened a crack and the smiling face of Herbert Gold peeked in.

Gudhausen stood up. "Herb! I must be psychic; I was just thinking about you."

Gold kept smiling.

"Well, come in, come in and sit down. This is a wonderful surprise!" Dr. Gudhausen extended his right hand.

Grinning like a goofy redheaded farmboy, Herbert Gold shook hands and shuffled his feet. "Hope you don't mind me walkin' right in. Guess Gloria must have stepped out or something."

"Of course I don't mind. But Gloria doesn't work Saturdays. I know she'll be sorry she missed you. Hey, it's great to see you, Herb."

Gudhausen sensed something wasn't right. Something was just a little off, a little . . .

"But how'd you get in? Wasn't the main door locked?"

"Oh no, nothing's locked, but if this is a bad time—"

"No, I don't mean that. It's just that it's such a surprise. Sit down, Herb. Tell me how things are going. How's the family?"

Herbert sat in the chair next to Gudhausen's desk. The strange grin never leaving his freckled face.

Gudhausen extruded a mushroom-shaped blast of cigar smoke, then he thought: "Does the smoke bother you? Should I put this out?"

"No, hell, I like smoke."

"Can I offer you one?"

"Tryin' to quit. But you'll smoke enough for both of us." He took an exaggerated deep breath and laughed nervously.

"So tell me, Herb, what brings you here? I was beginning to believe I might never see you again."

Still smiling, the big man squirmed in his seat. "Well, I . . . know you've been awful good to me and my family. . . ."

Dr. Gudhausen could see that Gold was struggling with something. The man shook his head, his lips pressed tightly together. Still smiling, he began to perspire.

"Is there someone else who wants to talk to me?"

"Ah, no. Not really. The others, they all left me to do it."

"Do what, Herbert? You are Herbert now, aren't you?"

"Yes, I'm Herbert. We're all Herbert. That's what you showed us, Doctor. We're all Herbert."

It was as if Gold could not keep from smiling. His lips and cheeks seemed to stretch and lose color. Sweat and plump teardrops rolled down his face.

"Herb . . .?"

Gold stood up, visibly agitated. He paced around the office. "You know me better'n anybody else, Doctor G. I mean you're the one who found out what kind of sickness I got. You understand I ain't a bad man. . . ."

"That's right, Herb. I know you're a good man, no matter which of the voices is speaking out of your mouth."

"And you know I've never done nothin' bad, nothin' really truly bad."

"Yes, I know that."

"So I gotta tell you, Doctor, somethin' real bad's happenin'. Somethin' real, real bad. And the thing I don't understand is that it's me who's doin' it. I feel it happenin'. I see it. I watch through my own fuckin' eyes as I . . . as I . . . ."

"It's okay, Herb. We've got time. You relax now. Just sit back down in the chair and try to relax."

The big man dropped heavily into his seat beside the doctor's desk. He held his hand above the desktop. "See that," he said, "steady as a statue. But inside I ain't steady; I'm all tore up. I don't know what's happenin' to me."

"Go on. . . ."

Herbert let his hand fall to the desktop. Pale and freckled, it lay before Dr. Gudhausen like a squid on a dinner plate.

After a moment the big man shook his head, violently, like a dog throwing off rainwater. "I got this song or poem or somethin' rollin' around in my head. Don't know where I picked it up, don't know where it come from. And, Christ! I can't shut it off!"

Gold lifted his head to face Gudhausen. His cheeks were slick with tears. Instantly, the frightened look vanished and the unsettling grin returned.

"Can you tell me the poem, Herb?"

Herb shook his head. "No, I don't think I can do that."

"Can anyone tell me the poem?"

Betsy Bottom's voice spoke through Gold's mouth, high-pitched, simpering, petulant. "It's not a poem, silly, it's a riddle."

"Say it."

"Noooooo." Gudhausen recognized Sasha's low, sensual tones coming through the rugged mechanic's grinning mouth.

The doctor tried an old tack. "Then tell me something else instead."

Now Thornton: "The raging rocks, with shivering shocks, shall break the locks of prison gates; and Phibbus' car shall shine from far, and make and mar the foolish Fates."

After all his years of experience and study, this was a phenomenon that continued to baffle Gudhausen: just how was it possible for a burly middle-aged automobile mechanic with an eighth-grade education to quote satirical doggerel from Shakespeare?

"Is that the riddle?" Gudhausen asked.

Betsy Bottom shook her head coyly and pouted, "No, silly."

"I'd like to hear the riddle. I'm pretty good at riddles."

"Okay, now I'll tell it to you." Prissily, Betsy Bottom began to recite:

> "No one has ever seen me,
> For I'm always what I'm not.
> And no one's ever heard me,
> For a mouth I haven't got.
> My home has been forever,
> And forever I'm at home.
> And you can never know me,
> For forever I'm alone."

Herb's head rolled forward until his chin touched his chest. He was asleep.

"Herb," Dr. Gudhausen said gently. "Herb, wake up."

Herbert Gold's head jerked up. His eyes were clear now, the smile gone from his mouth.

"Are you all right, Herb?"

"Oh yeah, I mean, no. I mean, I'm sorry. I'm awful sorry."

"Sorry? For what?"

"For comin' here. For what I have to do."

"What do you mean?"

"I mean you know what kind of man I am. I'm not a bad man. You know that, don't you, Doctor?"

"I know that, Herb." Gudhausen could see the agony in the man's face. Gold was wrestling with some powerful compulsion. Perhaps he should suggest hypnosis, try to get the patient to relax. If Herb could relax, then maybe he could articulate exactly what was troubling him.

"No!" Herb snapped. "No trances, no hypnotics."

Gudhausen hadn't spoken, yet Gold knew—

"Can you tell what I'm thinking, Herb?"

"Yes. And what you're not thinking." Gold's tone was rapid-fire, staccato. Gudhausen had never met this alter before.

"Who are you?"

"Someone else."

"Let me talk to Herbert."

"Herbert can't talk."

"Herb, I want to talk to you. Come out."

"He can't talk. Nobody can talk. Not even you."

Gudhausen attempted a response, but it didn't work. He could not—*Good God, what's happening to me?* He couldn't speak. He couldn't move. His body's only reaction was to squeeze perspiration from every pore. *Oh my God!* His eyes filled with tears but he could not blink them away.

"I have come here to tell you something," the changing Herb-thing said in its clipped, militarylike diction.

Gudhausen thought of Dr. Bradley. Where *was* she? Would she be here soon?

"You are not paying attention, Doctor."

Gudhausen felt a bolt of electrical energy arc between his temples. And he couldn't see.

"You must learn to concentrate, Doctor. Ignore distractions. Here, let me help you."

Gudhausen tried to control his racing thoughts. There must be something he could do. There must—

He heard Gold's finger tapping the desktop—"Now pay attention, Doctor"—somehow he knew it was Gold's index finger. Very slowly: tap . . . tap . . . tap . . .

"Concentrate on that sound, Doctor. Hear it. It sounds very like a metronome, does it not?"

Yes, the slow rhythmic beats were exactly like a metronome.

"And if I speed it up a bit, it sounds very like a heartbeat. (Tap-tap; tap-tap; tap-tap . . .) Is that not so, Doctor?"

Yes, Gudhausen thought, a heartbeat.

"In fact, it sounds very much like *your* heartbeat. Don't you think so, Doctor?"

Gudhausen fought it. He didn't want to listen. All his nerves shot panic messages to his motionless limbs. Pressure built. He was a boiler without a valve. His nervous system was about to explode. He was shorting out. He was frying. He could almost smell himself burning. He needed to imagine . . . something. Anything. He imagined he could not hear the persistent tap of Gold's finger, now perfectly synchronized with his own pounding heart.

(tap-tap; tap-tap)

"And if I should tap a little faster, Doctor, do you think you can keep up?"

(taptap-taptap-taptap)

Gudhausen felt his heart rhythm accelerate, keeping time to that horrible finger.

"It's like taking a brisk walk; don't you agree, Doctor? Invigorating. Give the old ticker a workout. . . ."

Gudhausen could feel hot blood speeding through him. His heart kept pounding out that maniac rhythm. Why couldn't he move? Where was Karen Bradley? Could she help him?

"Suppose we step up the beat just a little. What do you think? Does this sound like a rainstorm to you, Dr. Gudhausen?"

(taptaptaptaptaptaptaptaptaptaptaptaptaptap)

His heart sped. It bashed maniacally against his chest. Pumping blood. Pumping sweat. Pounding, pounding.

(TAPTAPTAPTAPTAPTAPTAPTAPTAPTAPTAPTAP)

Sweat in his eyes. Stinging.

Muscles cramping, contracting. Pulling his useless arms to his chest.

TAP

Pain burning. Pain smashing. Muscles tearing.

TAPTAPTAP

Heart erupting.

He screamed. Falling. Convulsing on the floor.

Before the world fell away, he heard Herbert Gold whisper, "Dr. Gudhausen, I came here to tell you that you shouldn't have messed with it. I came here to tell you you're a dead man."

The telephone rang.

"You have reached the offices of Stanley Gudhausen, M.D. There is no one in the office who can help you just now. . . ."

* * *

"Oh my God!" said Karen Bradley, standing up suddenly and bumping the table hard enough to shake both cups of coffee.

Jeff Chandler looked up at her. "What's this? Your imitation of an earthquake?"

"No. I mean it's after one o'clock! I'm supposed to pick up Dr. Gudhausen!"

"Hey, slow down, Karen." Jeff smiled at her. "He's not going to leave without you."

"I know, I know, but I'd better call him. I mean . . ." She left the sentence hanging as she fished around in her purse, looking for change.

Jeff said, "Here you go." He displayed an empty hand, then closed it into a fist. When he opened his fingers, Karen saw that a shiny quarter had appeared in the middle of his palm.

She did an exaggerated double take. "Physicist, UFO debunker, and now I discover you're a magician, too!"

"Ah yes, I'm known for my multiple yet uniformly unappealing personalities."

"That's your diagnosis, eh? Let me worry about the treatment later, when you come up to Burlington." She smiled and winked at him, feeling delightfully brazen.

"It's a date. But don't run off without your consulting fee." He held out the quarter, then dropped it into her outstretched hand.

"Thanks, Houdini. I apologize for the vanishing act I'm about to do."

Jeff looked humorously crestfallen as she left the table and walked toward the pay phone near the entrance of the coffee shop.

He *is* cute, she thought, and his surprise appearance at the hotel had gone a long way toward convincing Karen that he truly liked her. But, darn it, he'd made her completely forget about Dr. Gudhausen!

Again rummaging in her purse, she pulled out her Day-Timer in which she had carefully entered Gudhausen's phone number. Her fingers shook just slightly as she punched in the seven numbers.

* * *

The thing that was Herbert Gold closed its eyes for a moment, then stepped over the body of Stanley Gudhausen to pick up the telephone. The answering machine cut off. In a neutral, nondescript tone the thing said, "Yes?"

"Hi, Dr. Gudhausen? It's Karen Bradley."

Gold looked down at the fallen psychiatrist. He knew the man's voice very well—he'd heard it often enough—but the face? Well, that might take some practice. He studied the doctor's features, distorted now in death. The skin resembled blue ice. Blood caked the lower lip, dribbled from the ears. The cheeks, just moments ago round and florid, were sunken, waxylooking. Gold twisted his face, trying to imitate that of the corpse.

"Yes, Karen, what is it?"

"Well, I know I'm supposed to be there now, but I'm running a little late and I'm sorry. I just have to say good-bye to a friend and I'll be on my way. I hope you don't mind waiting."

"A friend you say?"

"Why, uh . . . yes . . .?"

Shit! He'd said the wrong thing, made her suspicious. "Well," he thought fast, "normally I'd suggest that you bring him along. But, Karen, I'm afraid it is I who must apologize. Something . . . ah . . . something unexpected has happened, and I have no choice but to . . . ah . . . stay here."

She paused briefly. "You mean you won't be coming to Vermont with me?"

"I'm afraid not, my dear. I simply can't do it now. It's impossible. I wanted to call you, but—"

"I know, I'd already checked out."

"Yes. Right. You'd already checked out. But don't worry, Karen. You'll be seeing me again soon. Yes, I'll be coming to Vermont very, very soon."

Before she could speak again, the grinning thing that was neither Herbert Gold nor Stanley Gudhausen had hung up the telephone, breaking the connection.

9

The Crouching Man

Montreal, Quebec

Father Sullivan hurried to keep pace with Father LeClair as they raced across the courtyard toward the front steps of the seventeenth-century mansion that was Hospital Pardieu. Sullivan's heart pounded, not from exertion but from the other priest's contagious air of alarm.

The bright afternoon sun had disappeared behind a swelling bank of gray clouds. A drizzle of rain had begun. It collected on Sullivan's eyeglasses, making it difficult to see. His light jacket was useless against the blast of arctic air that met them as they dashed up the hospital's stone steps.

LeClair pushed open the heavy door and entered.

The moment Sullivan stepped across the threshold, he felt an undeniable change in the atmosphere. Even in the vast marble-floored entryway, the air seemed close, stuffy, somehow brooding and tangibly alien. Sullivan controlled an irrational impulse to turn around and leave.

A pervasive odor of urine and excrement mingled in his nostrils, offending him, making it difficult to identify the true source of his unease. A frail old man dressed in a soiled white hospital gown, and clutching a wooden crucifix, stumbled along amid the shadows of the far wall. When he saw the two priests he gave a short shrill cry and sank to the floor, his johnny billowing around him like a parachute.

Sister Elise, the little French-speaking nun Sullivan had met when he arrived, scurried from an activities room to meet them. "Oh, Fathers, I am so thankful you have returned. They are upset, all of them are upset. I do not know why; I do not know what is wrong."

"Show me," LeClair said.

"See there." She waved her arm toward the back wall and led them across the room to the crouching figure.

By now the elderly priest with the crucifix had pressed his right side against the dark wainscoting. He'd pulled his knees up nearly to his chin as he cowered there, hands on his forehead, face buried in his arms.

They slowed down, approached him cautiously. The slight man turned his face to the wall. His breath came in rapid wheezing pants.

"Father Hubert," LeClair whispered in French, "what is the matter? Tell me why you are so frightened?"

The old man screeched like a terrified squirrel and closed his eyes tightly. A horrible stench rose around him.

"They will not go into the bathrooms, Father. They say they are too dark. But look!" She pointed. "They are messing in the halls, in their rooms." Sister Elise spoke frantically. "And upstairs, Father Lemire will not come out of his room. The pass key will not work; somehow he has broken the lock. Oh, Father, there are only the four of us here. We do not know what is wrong. We do not know what to do. We cannot help them."

The little nun, her face a confusion of empathy and terror, began to cry quietly. Father LeClair put his arms around her. "There, there, my sister. You have done what you can. But please, just now I need your help."

"Yes, of course, Father. Forgive me." She sniffed and braced her shoulders. "Come, let me show you upstairs. Sister Agnes is up there; she is alone with Father Rabidoux."

The two priests had to race to keep up with the little nun. At the top of the stairs Sullivan heard sobbing coming from the room behind a partially opened door.

"Father Rabidoux is an Alzheimer's patient," LeClair whispered as he led Sullivan into the room. The interior reeked of urine. A yellow puddle spread from beneath the old priest who sat on the floor below the window. His small brown eyes glittered senselessly with tears. One hand clutched a Bible to his chest.

Sister Agnes knelt beside him, holding his hand. Lines suggesting deep sorrow dignified the sister's face. Her eyes, never leaving the old man's, were warm and compassionate. She spoke to him gently, as if to a child. "Here is Father LeClair"—she nodded to the two priests, smiling thankfully—"can you tell him what is wrong, Father Rabidoux?"

The old man spoke rapidly, almost too rapidly to understand. He piled words upon words as his apparent terror heightened. "Soul of Christ, sanctify me. Body of Christ, save me. Blood of Christ, exalt me. WaterfromthesideofChrist, wash me . . . washmewashme . . ."

When his aged, tear-glazed eyes met those of Father LeClair, the old man somehow managed to push himself to a standing position. Legs unsteady, he lost his balance, lurched backward against the window. Glass shattered. The old priest tottered, ready to fall.

He screamed.

"Grab him!" LeClair shouted.

Sister Agnes maintained her grip on his hand and tugged him forward. Fangs of broken glass tore at his delicate skin.

But she had him. He was safe. "Thank you, Lord Jesus," she whispered and made the sign of the cross.

When Father Sullivan moved to stand beside Sister Elise, the old man's sudden cry stopped him in his tracks.

"Sister Elise," LeClair snapped at the little nun beside him, "quickly now, bring me some sedative."

Three more old men, two dressed in cassocks, the other naked, found their way into the room, perhaps attracted by the shouting. All three stood by the door, shaking with an uncontrollable palsy. One spat on the floor. A lengthening cable of drool flowed from the naked priest's toothless mouth. It shimmied, groping downward, until it attached itself to his pale flaccid stomach.

Sullivan had to look away. Father LeClair stood up to face the newcomers. "Fathers, please go back to your rooms. I beg of you."

Docile, they turned and stumbled back into the corridor, leaving behind the oppressive reek of sweat and bodily waste.

"Good God," Father Sullivan said to no one. He felt his pulse quicken as he slipped into the hall. His racing thoughts were of Father Mosely, lying helpless and alone, unprotected in his coma.

An unfamiliar man in a cassock was stretched facedown in the dark hallway. He crawled along the floor like a broken grasshopper, using his elbows and forearms to drag his useless legs. In his hand the old man clutched a photograph of some smiling children.

Sullivan froze momentarily in an overwhelming sadness. Where is that peace that comes with old age? He shook his head, trying to throw off the bitter thought. Then, in motion again, he sprinted along the corridor.

He threw open the door to Father Mosely's room.

Inside, all was exactly as he remembered. The ancient, hollow-faced priest was in the same position, his shrunken body pulled into its perpetual S shape. Father Mosely stared senselessly from the single clouded eye. The thumb of his skeletal hand had found its way to his mouth and had crawled in. He sucked it silently, his lips flexing ever so slightly.

Thank God he's safe, Sullivan thought.

Sullivan sighed heavily and took a seat on the rock-hard ladder-backed chair next to the old priest's bed. Screams and terrified cries resounded in the hall outside. Father Sullivan's vision blurred as moisture filled his eyes. He prayed, concentrating deeply, trying to direct his mind away from a dreadful and selfish certainty: one day I too will become as these dear creatures are now.

Unaccountably, he felt as if the same sinister force that had destroyed these men of God was slowly working its fearful magic on him, trying to break him, make him its prisoner. In his memory he was a boy again, hanging like a fat apple on a limb. His taunting classmates screamed and whistled. But Father Mosely could not come to his rescue.

* * *

Sometime later, Father Sullivan heard a strange tapping outside the old priest's hospital room. The tapping changed to a scratch, then to a tapping again.

Sullivan concentrated on the sound, almost recognizing it, but still unable to identify it for sure.

Curious, he was about to get up and look in the hall when the door to Father Mosely's room opened slowly. Sullivan kept quiet as the tip of a thin white stick whipped back and forth against the floor tiles, scratching between the open door and its frame. Sullivan held his breath, watching in silence.

A dark form entered the room. Father Lemire. Sullivan recognized him by his white cane.

Father Sullivan watched in silence as the blind priest made his way across the room. The old man was mumbling, his singsong cadence sounded like quiet prayer. All the while he searched for objects and barriers with his scratching cane. A rosary dangled from his left hand.

Puzzled, Sullivan remained quiet and observed.

As the blind priest's cane connected with the metal frame of the bed, he stopped. His left hand patted the linen sheet, apparently searching for Father Mosely's body.

He discovered Mosely's inflexible arm, wrapped the rosary around the knotted hand, mumbling as he worked.

Although nearly fluent in French, Sullivan was not up to translating these mumbles and half-pronounced syllables. Still, he was able to recognize a word now and then. "No time . . . Coming . . . Lazarus. Dead. Not dead."

Careful not to startle the blind priest, Sullivan prepared to speak softly. Before he found the right words, he saw Father Lemire raise his cane and bring it down swiftly against Father Mosely's temple.

"Stop!" Immediately, Sullivan was on his feet. He grabbed the blind priest from behind, one arm around his chest, the other raised, holding the cane, preventing Lemire from delivering a second blow.

"Let me *go*," the old priest cried. "Do not stop me. You do not know the trouble you cause."

Sullivan tried to be gentle as he forced the cane-wielding hand downward. The old man fought like a captive animal. "They come. They are near! Can you not feel? Look what they do. Look!"

The cane clattered to the floor. From behind, still restraining Father Lemire with a bear hug, Sullivan backed away from the bed.

"No! You do not understand. It gets stronger. Can you not feel it? Can you not see? It is here! It comes for the old ones! It wants our deaths. Our souls. Oh, *mon Dieu!* It is here *now!*"

"There, there, Father Lemire. Calm yourself, please. It's all right. Everything is all right. I will not harm you." Sullivan felt the old man's chest heaving rapidly up and down like an overworked bellows; he felt the heart pounding within the bony chest. Still Father Lemire fought.

"Not *you*, not *you*." The old priest was in tears, nearly hysterical. His frail body twitched and thrashed. "It is the others. The bad ones. They are getting stronger. Can you not feel? Can you not see? They are as Lazarus. They grow strong. We must end it. Here. Now."

The blind priest's back arched in a mighty heave. Then the strength seemed to leave him. He softened, collapsed limply in Sullivan's arms.

Gently, Father Sullivan lowered the old man to the floor. He checked the scrawny neck for a pulse. Finding none, he lowered his ear to the old man's chest.

No heartbeat.

Sullivan shouted, "I need help in here! Quickly!" He tore Father Lemire's white shirt away. Then he began to pound the old man's chest.

* * *

By the time Sister Beatrice came into the room, Father Sullivan was finishing his prayer for the dead.

10

Crawling Things

St. Albans, Vermont

Lucy Washburn wasn't in the spotlight. Instead, she was tucked away in the darkness, way far up inside their head. She couldn't move. She couldn't speak. All she could do was watch through the two eyes, twin portholes that all of them shared.

The Mean One was in the spotlight. He'd been there for—Jeez, it seemed like days! Didn't he ever sleep? Didn't he get tired?

How come he wouldn't let anyone else take a turn?

Lucy wanted to come out for a while, feel the sunshine, pick the flowers. Too bad she had given up control—though she couldn't remember doing it. Now the Mean One wouldn't even talk about giving it back.

Still, she could see everything. Even the things she didn't want to see. And if the Mean One got hurt, Lucy would feel the pain; he wouldn't.

Lucy was the only one among them who could feel pain, everyone's pain.

And what was he doing with their body? Where was he going? Where was he taking her?

She saw their hand reach out and pick up a newspaper from the rack in front of the drugstore. And then they were running away. Running fast. So they wouldn't have to pay for the newspaper.

Then they were in the park, hiding behind a big green trash barrel. She could see the bandstand, and the historical society, and the big churches with their tall steeples.

The Mean One didn't let her look around for long.

They dashed from barrel to bandstand.

Their hands pulled away that secret loose board that worked like a door, admitting them to the crawl space under the bandstand. On hands and knees they crept underneath. Lucy didn't like it there. It smelled musty, and the earth always felt damp against her hands and her bare knees.

Lucy was sure there were worms and spiders crawling all around her. Maybe even snakes. She hated those icky crawly things. But the Mean One didn't hate insects and snakes. Maybe, Lucy thought, insects and snakes were the only things the Mean One liked.

Sun shown brightly through the wooden lattice around the bottom of the bandstand, making crisscross patterns over the newspaper as the Mean One spread it out on the damp musty earth.

"Look, Lucy," the Mean One whispered.

Lucy looked hard, and she too could see the print:

ST. ALBANS MAN KILLS FAMILY, SELF

ST. ALBANS—In an unexplained shooting incident last night, Edmund Washburn, 36, a cable company employee, apparently shot and killed his wife Winona, 36, and their 6-year-old son, Randy. Then he turned the weapon on himself, officials theorize.

Police Chief Michael Couture was the first on the scene responding to a neighbor's telephone call after hearing gunshots. Couture said there is no known motive for the slayings. "In fact," the visibly shaken policeman stated, "I just can't believe Ed did something like this. Why, him and me went to school together. I've known him all my life."

One family member, 12-year-old Lucine Washburn, was not accounted for at the crime scene. Couture suspects she was not present at the time of the shootings. "At least I hope not," the distraught official told this reporter. "Maybe she escaped and ran away. Or worse yet, maybe she came home and discovered the bloodbath. Either way, if she ran off, it might not be so easy to find her."

Neighbors were questioned long into the night. Area police and firemen have been contacted to search for the girl. . . .

(Cont. Pg. 4: Slayings)

Lucy couldn't read any more. If she had had the eyes, she would have wept. If she'd had the mouth, she would have screamed.

But the Mean One had the body now, and he was laughing.

11

Strange Awakenings

Hobston, Vermont
Sunday, June 19

Alton Barnes woke up screaming.

Sweating like a fat man in a steambath, he swatted away the clinging covers, as if they were restraining him. Hyperventilating, wheezing, chest heaving, he sat bolt upright in bed and looked around. His bedroom was dark and that disappointed him; it meant there was still a long uneasy time until morning. Hand trembling, he groped for the bedside switch, found it, flicked it on. A comforting incandescence filled the room. Alton tried to control his breathing as his gaze darted from corner to corner, inspecting the shadows, examining the furniture, trying to detect any motion that might suggest he was not alone in the old house.

For a moment the dream was clear in his memory:

Footprints.

Bloody footprints in the snow.

Alton following them. Crusty snow crunching underfoot. Up a hillside to the domed top of the bluff.

Oddly, the footprints end. They simply . . . stop.

Alton feels the wind, the strange strong wind that rushes upward from the ground itself. Now, he too is leaving the ground. Flying. Can't stop. Can't resist.

Far below, he sees where his own foot marks—like those beside them—stop. Far, far below.

He looks up, way above him in the sky. There, like a dazzling monstrous sun, he sees a face. A giant bearded face, big as a mountain, its mouth saying NO. NOT YOU. NO.

And he's falling away. Speeding toward the ground. He screams as he falls, screams at the anticipated impact, screams as the blood-rain splatters on his face and hands. And he's tasting the blood. He knows whose blood it is, and the huge face, looking down . . . with something in its mouth. Something kicking and screaming and flailing in its mouth. . . .

The picture is fuzzy. . . .

It's fading now. . . .

And he screams until he wakes himself up, sweaty and hoarse, from his nightly ritual.

As he screamed—just like last night and the night before—the dream was already fading from his memory.

Within a few minutes Alton had no idea what had frightened him. The ghastly images had fled like an intruder, leaving him alone, terrified without reason. The only reminders were his racing pulse and a dreadful shortness of breath.

The alarm clock beside his bed told him it was 2:49 A.M. The middle of the night.

Even as he tried to relax, his ears strained against the silence of the house. Of course there were noises, many noises, but none that were unfamiliar to him: a sprung shutter way in the back of the house slapped against the clapboarding with each passing breeze; the water pump cycled off and on because of that leak in the bathtub; mice skittered within the plaster walls.

Any of those noises could be easily eliminated, forever, if only Alton would put in the effort. A nail, a washer, a trap. But why bother?

He lay back on his pillow and thought about his dead wife, Angie, and of the children they never got around to having. She had left him alone—and the pain had been tremendous—but he had never been lonely, not real gut-squeezing, empty-hearted, bullet-to-the-head lonely, until his friend Stuart Dubois had—

Had what?

With the thought of Stuart, Alton's tension returned. He knew he'd better get up, start doing something, anything, so he wouldn't have to think. This was almost a conditioned reaction: every time Stu came to mind, Alton experienced panic. Why? Stu had been his good friend—his best friend, actually—after Angie had died. Alton didn't want to stop thinking of him altogether.

He got out of bed and pulled on his slipper socks. Then, naked, he padded downstairs to the bathroom. An agonizing pressure strained his bladder, reminding him of the two six-packs he'd polished off last night before he dared to attempt sleep.

After relieving himself, Alton stood in front of the sink and slapped cold well water against his face. He lifted his gaze, expecting to see how horrible he looked, forgetting that he had painted over the bathroom mirror because he simply couldn't stand the sight of himself, of what he had become. . . .

Or was becoming. . . .

"This has got to stop," he said aloud. "I just can't go on this way. I can't do this no more."

Alton had never been one to tell folks his troubles. Even after Angie had died he had never spoken to Stuart and Daisy about how badly he felt. But with them he didn't have to; the old couple just seemed to know, without words. They seemed to know that Al's kind of trouble needed lots more than words to set right.

God how he missed Stuart, in some ways more than he missed his wife. Sure, he knew how that sounded: odd. Maybe faggy. But Alton knew what he meant, and that too was something he'd never be able to explain to another human being. To Alton it was simple: somehow Stu had helped keep him from missing Angie too much.

Now, right this minute, there was nothing in God's green earth that could get in the way of his missing Stu.

The shower water dribbled onto his head and shoulders. The water pressure was shot to hell and the pump needed replacing, but these were fleeting concerns, inconveniences quickly forgotten when the reminders were gone.

Maybe he should pull himself up by his bootstraps and go on a marathon cleaning and fixing binge. If he spruced things up a bit he could probably sell the house and acreage for a tidy sum. These days property values were sky high. City folks would gladly pay a thousand dollars an acre for the 128 acres of land Al's daddy had paid less than a hundred dollars for! Christ, Al might as well take advantage of it like so many of his friends and neighbors had done.

He could keep a little bit for himself—two, three acres, maybe— and build a one-man cabin with a garden way up on Perkins Bluff. From there he could look down and watch the hungry metropolis of Burlington as it moved eastward, gobbling up woods and farmland and grand old homes, shitting out highways and condos and tacky convenience stores. It's an ugly thing, he thought. But it's progress.

Still naked, Al walked across the living room. The coffee table was piled with mail that he'd never bothered to sort, all held in place by unwashed supper dishes and empty, foul-smelling glasses with milk-scummy interiors. A big black fly buzzed around the rotting leftovers. Dozens more like it buzzed at the eastern window, repeatedly smashing their little black bodies against the unyielding barrier of glass. And they were screaming; he could actually hear them scream.

Al opened the front door and stepped out onto the porch. The eastern horizon was a wavy red ribbon that joined a range of silhouetted mountains to the black sky. The dawn is a beautiful thing, he thought, and the night air is fresh and chill.

He turned and faced the squalor of his living room, the cluttered furniture, the rotting food, the buzzing army of flies.

"Shit," he said. "Oh, fuckin' shit."

Then he started to cry.

* * *

Alburg, Vermont

"Hey, I'm talkin' to you!"

Lucy stirred, her senses returning one at a time. She felt heavy jolting bumps.

"So what ya doin', clammin' up on me?"

Then she heard the low throaty growl of an engine, the hum of tires on pavement.

She was in somebody's car. No, not a car, a van. She could smell grease and stale cigarette smoke, and a musty, sickening odor, like a pile of damp blankets. She wrinkled her nose. Cautiously, she opened her eyes.

"Cat got yer tongue?"

Squinting, she studied the man behind the wheel and realized he was a stranger.

She looked around. It was dark outside, but the van's bright headlights showed they were traveling on the interstate. North or south? She couldn't tell.

Where we going? she wanted to ask, but she could not. Somebody else was in control, and she didn't know who it was. Normally, she could tell who was in the spotlight, but this time she had no sense of it.

Lucy blinked at the stranger, willed real hard to speak, Who are you? she wanted to ask, but her tongue was held in check by someone else's will.

At least she could see, so she examined the driver more closely. He didn't look like a nice man. He wore a dungaree jacket with both sleeves cut off. A tattoo on his right forearm said, "Born Crazy." Lucy saw it clearly as the man lifted the beer can to his mouth.

He turned his head, looked directly at her. His left eye was missing. Where it should have been, a little hollow was covered with wrinkled, pasty-looking skin. She wanted to look away, but her head wouldn't move.

The man spoke. "So you don't want to talk no more, zat it?" His fat wet tongue poked through the space where two bottom teeth should have been. Whoever had been in the spotlight must have had a conversation going.

Lucy forced her mouth to work. "N-no," she said. Good. Now she could speak.

"So how come you're so quiet all of a sudden?" She could smell his breath way across the front seat.

"I . . . I don't know. I'm tired. I musta dropped off to sleep."

"To sleep!" He blew air through his lips and they vibrated nastily. "You tellin' me you dropped off in the middle of a sentence?"

"I do that sometimes—"

"Ya do, do ya? That's pretty fucked up."

"I . . . I—"

"Okay, miss prissy pants, we was talkin' about how we're gonna get you acrost the border into Canada."

"Canada! I don't wanna go to Canada!"

Quick as lightning his right hand jumped from the beer can between his legs. It slapped loudly against her cheek. And she felt it! It hurt, and she started to cry.

"Now yer turnin' into a little cock-tease on me. Hey, that's nothin' to fuck around with, kid. I make jokes about lots of things, but money and pussy I take real serious."

Lucy pressed herself tightly against the passenger door. She looked down, trying to see the handle, thinking maybe she could open the door and jump out.

"I want to get out." She wasn't trying to whisper, but that's the way it came out. Her voice cracked, "Will you let me out, please?"

"Will I let you out, please?" He spoke in high-pitched tones, mocking her, just like some bratty kid at school. But that was all wrong. He was a grown man, maybe older than her father; he wasn't supposed to mock her.

He opened his one eye real wide. "Okay," he said with a sigh. "Guess I might's well let you out. If you're goin' all mental on me, I sure ain't gonna risk takin' you acrost the border." He was trying to be matter-of-fact. "Yup, if you say so, I'll just pull right on over first chance I get and I'll let you hop right on out." He took a pull from the beer can, then went on in his airy singsong voice. "Can't really figure it though. I mean right up to now you struck me as a pretty together little chick. I figgered you was grown up, older than your years. Head on straight as an arrow. But if you want to be a little crybaby, I'll just pull right on over and say bye-bye."

The sign said: *LAST EXIT BEFORE U.S.-CANADIAN BORDER.* The man spun the steering wheel, and they were going off the exit ramp. The van's headlights lit stubby aluminum posts and guardrails.

All of a sudden Lucy knew where they were. Daddy had brought her and Randy here fishing not too awful long ago. It was the dark swampy flatlands north of Highgate Springs, near the eastern shore of Lake Champlain.

"Anyplace special Your Highness wants to get out? Does right here suit you?"

There was nothing but darkness outside the van. No traffic, no lights in from distant houses. Lucy looked out and felt afraid. "Yes," she said, trying to hold her voice steady, "yes. Right here. Let me out here."

But he didn't slow down.

"Don't ya think it's awful dark out there? I mean, who knows what's out there. Could be bears. Bears are real mean this time of year. Could be wolf, or coyote. They get ravenous-hungry this time a night."

Lucy said nothing. She stared at the window, thinking about red-eyed animals with sharp bloody teeth.

The man turned off the paved highway onto a narrow dirt road with grass growing down the middle.

He flicked off the headlights, but continued to drive in the darkness. Lucy saw fireflies blinking amid tall silhouetted stalks of swamp grass.

The man said, "This looks like a good place to let you out, doncha think?"

The van stopped right in the middle of the road.

She grabbed the door handle and pulled it. It moved too freely, like it wasn't connected to anything.

"Oh, forgot to tell you, Sweetie Bumps, that door don't work."

She looked at him briefly, then down at her knees. She knew her hair had fallen on both sides of her head like a curtain. She could see him, he couldn't see her.

"Course, I gotta be honest with ya, I hate to see you go. And that's flat truth. You're one awful pretty little thing. Anybody ever tell you that? You're prettier than some of them grown-up girls I know. Prettier'n most."

Lucy's hand tightened on the door handle. She wondered if she could pull it off, use it as a weapon.

Then she felt something shift inside her head, like bone grinding against bone. She winced.

"You really think I'm pretty?" It was her voice, but she hadn't said anything.

"Why would I lie to you?" He gave her a cautious smile. "'Fore you go, you wanna hand me another of them beers from in back?"

"Okay. If I can have one too. I need something . . . wet." She felt the tip of her tongue as it moistened her upper lip.

"Well a'course you can, Sunnyshine. You can have anything you want."

Lucy's body turned in the seat, reaching far behind her toward the aluminum milk crate where the beer was stashed. She had to put her knee on the seat and stretch way over to get hold of the can.

His hand grasped the back of her thigh, squeezing it, pushing his coarse fingers up toward her bottom. Lucy wanted to scream, to claw at him, to smash the Budweiser can right in his face.

Instead, she giggled.

"That's better now, yesssss," he said. Lucy knew he was trying to sound friendly, but he sounded disgusting.

She tried as hard as she could to get back control of her limbs. She had to run, had to get out of that awful, smelly van. She willed her legs to propel her into the back of the van. From there she could jump to safety through the back doors.

NO, said a voice from inside her head, DON'T. YOU CAN'T HANDLE THIS, STUPID. LET ME TAKE CARE OF IT.

Always before, when Lucy found herself in even a mildly threatening situation, someone else would take the spotlight and Lucy would nap until the episode was over. She had never been permitted to observe the really frightening stuff. Something bad was going to happen now. She didn't want to stay awake. She didn't want to watch it.

The man had his arms around her. He smelled like sweat and grease and dirty clothes. His big left hand pulled at the back of her blouse, tugging it from the waist of her skirt.

"You're such a nice little girl, such a pretty little girl." His impatient whisper came in stinky little puffs. Rapid breathing hissed in his nose. She felt slimy lips on her face, felt his sandpapery hand pulling down her bra, fingering her nipple.

"Ohhh," he wheezed, his voice went all soft and high, "are you my pretty little girl? My pretty, pretty little girl . . .?"

His frantic mouth found hers. Lucy's mind recoiled in soundless disgust as her own tongue slid into the space between his teeth. He kissed her—too hard!—his hot spit dribbled down her chin. Then he took her hand, forced it against the damp hardness between his legs.

"Ooooh," he moaned. "Ooooh, God. Oh, my sweet, sweet God."

With the mention of that name something else shifted inside Lucy's head. Her terror vanished. She was no longer an unwilling passenger inside his van and within her own body. No, now she was at ease. It was as if she could direct this scary situation, control its outcome.

A fury possessed her limbs. She found herself kneeling on the seat, pressing her chest against him, coiling both arms around his neck. He moaned, hummed, rubbed his pelvis up and down against her leg.

She pushed her mouth tightly against the sandpaper stubble on his face. Her lips worked like copulating worms, inching along his cheek until they found the cavity of his mouth. For a moment their tongues batted heads like warring serpents.

Lucy's mouth opened wider. Now her lips completely surrounded his. They continued to stretch, continued to widen. Her upper lip touched the bottom of his nose. Impossibly, her mouth opened more. Pain jabbed at her as her braces strained, snapped like cables against the soft flesh of her palate.

She felt the delicate connecting tissue that joined her upper lip to her gum line begin to stretch. Opening wider, that tissue began to tear as her upper lip slithered over his nose. Her mouth was open so wide it engulfed his nose and mouth. Her lower lip elongated, vacuum-sealing itself to his chin.

Then she began to suck.

His low passionate moaning turned into panicky gasps. "Ummp," he grunted. "Uuummmph! Ummp." The sounds vibrated inside her mouth, tickling her tongue.

He fought to push her head away, but she clung to him like a parasite. And still she sucked, increasing the vacuum that locked their heads together.

He thrashed under her. Slammed his fists against the arch of her spine. He bucked, kicked, jammed his hands against her forehead in an effort to push her away.

She inhaled again. Surely he was suffocating; surely she could feel his strength fading just a bit.

Intensifying the suction, she recognized the wet, rude pressure of colliding flesh as his lungs collapsed. Finally, in that joyous moment of victory, his strength vanished with his life.

The tremendous suction relaxed. Lucy realized that her lips had stretched so much that they had covered not only his nose and mouth, but most of his face.

When her lips released their iron grip, she spat his one remaining eyeball from her mouth. It struck his livid hickey-red face, then rolled out of sight. Slippery reddish-gray matter plugged both eye sockets and nostrils.

"Thank you," the voice in her mind whispered. "We grow stronger now."

Lucy took a deep invigorating breath. Before she could rest, another, stronger compulsion seized her.

Pushed her.

Prodded her northward, as if she were the needle of a compass.

She knew she had to finish the journey she had begun.

She had no right to rest; there was something more important—vastly more important—she had to do.

Now everything would be okay. Lucy could permit herself to sleep, while her body continued northward on its own.

12

Blue Monday

Burlington, Vermont
Monday, June 20

It was an omen: if Monday got off to a bad start, the whole week was likely to be terrible. For Karen Bradley, "Blue Mondays" very much deserved their reputation.

The Monday following her trip to Boston, she arrived at the Lakeview Health Center at ten to nine. Two messages were waiting for her. The first was from Gloria Cook, informing Karen of Dr. Gudhausen's fatal heart attack. The news hit her like a blow to the stomach. Holding the two pink "While You Were Out . . ." slips in her hand, she sat down before reading the second message.

Number two was from the St. Albans Police Department, asking her to call Officer Chaput regarding the Washburn family.

The Washburn family?

Karen stood up again and walked out of her office. "What's this all about?" she asked her receptionist. "What do the police want?"

"Oh dear God, you haven't heard." Laura Welsh's right hand rose to her lips; her eyes widened. "It was in Saturday's paper." She took a breath before going on. "Karen, Lucy's father flipped out. He . . . he shot his wife and the boy—"

"Little Randy? Oh my gosh! And Lucy? What about Lucy?"

"They didn't find her. The police think she ran away. They're afraid she's in hiding or something. Officer what's-his-name thought maybe you'd have some insight that would help them locate her."

"Me?" Karen didn't know what to say. All her energy had drained away. She felt as if she'd been blasted with some metaphysical double-barrel shotgun: the man who was going to help treat Lucy was dead, and now the poor kid's world had just jumped out of orbit.

Odd that both messages should arrive on the same day. Overkill, even for a Blue Monday.

Standing as if frozen, hand on her throat, Karen felt light-headed, oddly defeated. She had no idea what action to take. Finally, "Both of them? Ed Washburn killed both of them? Winnie and Randy?"

Laura closed her eyes and nodded.

"I can't . . . I just can't believe it. Ed Washburn? No, no way. There was nothing wrong with Ed Washburn, I'd stake my reputation on it. Did . . . did they arrest him?"

Laura shook her head. "Karen, he turned the gun on himself."

"Dead?"

Laura answered with a single nod. Karen dropped heavily into the chair beside Laura's desk. "Oh dear God, that poor little girl."

"I know. I'm so sorry, Karen. Can I get you something? Coffee? A glass of water?"

Karen touched Laura's hand. "No, but thanks. You're sweet." She closed her eyes and shook her head. "I'd better get myself together and call that policeman." She stood up, absently straightening the front of her skirt. Then, "She was doing so well in so many ways. She was trying so hard. My God, I hate to think about the defenses she'll have to create to deal with this one. Wow."

"I left Lucy's file on your desk, Karen."

"Yes. Okay. Thanks, Laura."

Walking into her office was like walking in her sleep. She drifted around her desk and sat down, totally unaware of what she was doing. This one had really trashed her; she knew she'd be useless the rest of the day.

God, she thought, does it ever get any easier? Were more experienced therapists like Dr. Gudhausen able to deal any better with this kind of thing?

She remembered her first suicide. It had happened over two years ago, when she was just beginning her internship. Mike Tucker was the young man's name. His face remained clear in Karen's memory; she'd never be able to forget him. Mike's wife had left him in the fall of that year, right after they had spent the entire summer building a home in the country.

The first room they'd completed was to have been the baby's room. Belinda Tucker was nearly two months pregnant. One day—God, that had been a Monday, too—Mike had come home early from his job on the Lake Champlain Ferry. He found Belinda packing her car. Quite matter-of-factly she told him that she'd had an abortion and that she was leaving. Period. No questions. No explanations. End of discussion.

There had been no scene, no histrionics. Belinda just drove away, leaving Mike with an empty house and a shattered expression on his face. That expression had become a permanent part of his appearance. It rarely changed during each of his three sessions with Karen.

Sure, he had tried to project a positive attitude. He even forced a smile at appropriate times, but his eyes never lost their haunted, hollow look.

In less than a minute, Mike Tucker's world had changed forever. The day Karen and Mike were to have met for the fourth time, Mike's father called to say Mike wouldn't be coming; he had hanged himself.

For Karen the poignant part of the story was Mr. Tucker's stalwart Yankee sense of responsibility: he had thought to phone to cancel his son's appointment on what must have been the most difficult day of his life.

The thing that drove this episode permanently into Karen's memory was the realization that she hadn't seen it coming. Not a hint, not a clue. She'd been sure Mike's superego was stronger than it was. But she was supposed to be an expert in human behavior; she was licensed by the state as a psychotherapist, and yet she hadn't spotted a thing. She had failed. Permanently, irreparably.

Even today, every time the incident came to mind she felt ashamed. It was still humiliating to recall that her case notes, prepared after their final session, had said it was little more than an adjustment reaction and that Mike was doing fine; the prognosis was excellent. God, she had even been proud of the work she was doing with him.

* * *

After lunch, Karen tried the St. Albans number again. As before, the phone seemed to spit its busy signal into her ear. That's just great, she thought, the line's still busy at the police station. What are we supposed to do if we need a cop? Mail an appointment card? Send a smoke signal?

Laura tapped lightly at the door and walked in. "Are you okay, Karen? Your one-thirty appointment's here."

"Yes, sure. I'm fine."

"You don't sound fine. You want me to cancel? Take the afternoon off? I can come up with something to tell him."

"No. That's nice of you, but no thanks. Who is it anyway? Do we have a file on him?"

"It's an initial. Dr. Sparker at the clinic in Hobston called it in this morning."

"Sparker? Really? That's a surprise. Did he give you any background?"

"Apparent sleep disorder. Symptoms of depression. Some paranoid ideation. You know how Sparker is; he's still not too sure about all this new-fangled 'psychology business.'"

"Well, at least he made the referral."

Karen saw the look of concern on the receptionist's face. "I'm okay, Laura. Honest. You can send him in now. Oh! Wait! What's his name, anyway?"

"The patient is a Mr. Barnes, Mr. Alton Barnes, from Hobston."

* * *

Highgate, Vermont

Lucy crawled out the back door of the van. She'd been hiding inside, waiting for the sun to come up. Her stay had not been pleasant; it was too hot inside. Her nesting area reeked of wet dog and the sharp smell of her own pee. She threw aside the mildew-rotten sleeping bag that had belonged to the dead guy, and stood up straight, facing north.

As long as she faced north, everything was okay, there was no pain grinding and splintering inside her head.

Somehow, with much stalling, bucking, and racing the engine, Lucy had been able to drive the van to this little turnoff beside the northbound lane of Route 7. Here she had released the emergency brake and let the van tumble down a twelve-foot incline and into the juniper bushes and scrub pine where it couldn't be seen from the road.

That remote part of her mind—the diminishing part she still identified as Lucy—felt disgust at the way she must look in the morning light. Blood caked the area around her mouth; she could flake it off with a fingernail. Her lips hung limply; they felt slack and fleshy like the puckered mouth of a sucker. They hurt wicked where they'd stretched and torn away from the gum line. And the roof of her mouth was sore, probably cut to ribbons when her braces snapped. Her hands were bloody, too, but that blood was hidden beneath layers of other dirt: grease from the van, dust from the road, and rich black loam from the earth. Most of her fingernails were torn away and her hands were ripped and raw from hand-digging the guy's grave. Her hair was a tangled foul-smelling bird's nest; her skin, except for blood and filth, was colorless.

A northbound car passed the turnoff. Lucy watched it from her hiding place behind an ancient oak. She shook her head: no.

A big truck roared by, leaving behind a swirling ghost of roaddust and exhaust. That wasn't the right one either.

It was nearly impossible for her to resist the urge—no, the *need*—to begin walking north. Could she make it all the way on foot? She didn't know. She didn't even know if she was tired because she no longer had a sense of her own body. Hunger meant nothing to her. Thirst and fatigue were somehow alien. Strangely, she was still able to feel hot and cold, she could sense pain and certain physical discomforts, but she had no idea if she was dead-tired or newly energized. She just felt as if she were being . . . pulled.

Also, she felt as if certain specialized parts of her brain weren't working right. Those, she reasoned, must be under the control of one of her internal travelers. One such function had recently announced itself: her bladder had let go and she didn't know it, not until she felt warm liquid running down her left leg. The Lucy-part of her was ashamed, now. Embarrassed.

Then a strong unnamed sensation excited her. She felt herself breathing in hard excited gasps. She looked south and the twin glowing headlights were like the eyes of a close friend. She stepped into the road, willing the car to stop.

The vehicle slowed down, pulled over, came to rest beside her. The man inside leaned over and unlocked the passenger door.

Lucy pulled the door open. She saw red hair, a crew cut. The man was smiling at her.

Neither spoke as Lucy got in, but somehow she knew the man's name was Herbert Gold, and just like her, he was heading up to Canada.

* * *

Burlington, Vermont.

"Mr. Barnes, right this way, please . . ."

Alton felt his face redden as the receptionist led him into Dr. Bradley's office. Looking around, he expected to discover some eccentric-looking wild man with Coke bottle glasses, wearing a white coat.

Instead, he saw a pretty young woman.

That can't be the doctor, he said to himself, she's just a kid. What can a kid tell me about all this crap I'm going through?

She smiled warmly and stood up, extending her right hand. "Mr. Barnes, I'm Karen Bradley."

He wiped his sweaty palm on his green work pants before shaking hands. At least folks around here were polite enough to call him *Mister* Barnes. Doc Sparker's nurse started calling him "Alton" the first time they'd met. He didn't like that; it wasn't right, it wasn't good manners.

"Please sit down, sir, make yourself comfortable."

Alton felt oddly oversize, awkward as a bear in the presence of this young lady. She was so different from him: youthful, poised, graceful, and highly educated with all her fancy diplomas papering the wall. Rich too, he guessed, like all doctors. Why, she was even good-looking with her long red hair and bright blue eyes. He took a careful step toward the stiff-looking chair in front of the doctor's desk.

Dr. Bradley stepped out from behind her desk, motioning toward a pair of easy chairs next to a wide window that overlooked Lake Champlain. "I think we'd be more comfortable over here."

Alton noticed a vase of cut flowers on the coffee table that separated the two chairs. Roses, he could smell them. Nice, he thought.

Each took a seat. Alton looked out at the lake; Dr. Bradley looked at Alton.

Immediately he felt beads of perspiration leaving cold trails as they rolled down his sides. Stinging droplets of salty sweat from his forehead seeped into his eyes, irritating them, filling them with tears. She's going to think I'm crying, he thought, brushing the moisture away with the backs of his hands.

"We can open the window, if you like. . . ."

"No. I'm okay. But thanks."

Alton crossed his legs, trying to look comfortable and at ease. The doctor was watching his foot; it was vibrating up and down like a tap dancer's.

"You're a little nervous to be here, aren't you, Mr. Barnes?"

"No, I—" he caught himself before he lied. "Yeah, but it ain't you, miss. I was nervous before I come in."

She smiled sweetly. "And how long have you been feeling this . . . nervousness?"

"How long? I can tell you exactly when it started: last fall, first day of huntin' season. But it's got a lot worse since then."

"Would you say you have always been a nervous person, Mr. Barnes?"

He thought about it, thought of his childhood on the farm, thought of school and of the time he dropped out from the tenth grade. He thought of the army, the war, the torture, the death of his parents, the years in a custodial position at the high school. "No, not always, I guess. I mean, no more'n the next fella."

"But the nervousness has gotten worse lately; is that right? Ever since hunting season you've been getting more nervous?"

"Yeah. It's gettin' so bad I can't sleep at night. Never had that problem before. Used to sleep like a baby. Now I get to feelin' scared, like somebody's watchin' me. I imagine awful things. An' pictures, ugly awful pictures roll around in my head so fast I can't shut 'em off.

Then, during the next day I'm tired. No energy. Not worth a good
goddamn."

He looked away, down at the carpet. "Excuse me, miss."

"It's all right, Mr. Barnes. Swearing is perfectly all right. Please go
on."

He still didn't look her in the eye. "And I'm cranky, too; get mad
about nothin'. And whenever I do get a little sleep, I have these
dreams, these awful wicked nightmare dreams. I have to fight 'em hard
in order to wake up."

"The dreams, do they have anything to do with hunting season?"

Alton was surprised. "Yup. Yup, that's right."

"So maybe we should start at the beginning, don't you think? Why
don't you tell me about hunting season. Tell me everything you
remember. After that we can talk about what's happening in these
dreams of yours."

Alton cleared his throat and settled back in his chair. He took a
deep breath and realized he was starting to calm down. Maybe this
doctor was just a pretty young gal, but she sure was easy to talk to.
Leaning slightly forward in her chair, she seemed truly interested in
every word that he said. By God, he was almost ready to level with her,
but before he could go on, he had to check something. "You ain't
gonna tell nobody about this. That's what Doc Sparker told me. Is that
right?"

"Absolutely. Whatever we talk about in this room is private. It's
just between you and me, and it's strictly confidential. I won't even
give my notes to the secretary to type if you don't want me to."

Alton held her gaze for a minute, searching those deep blue eyes
for a suggestion of treachery and finding none. He nodded once,
emphatically. "Okay then, that's good." Alton locked his fingers
together and rested them on his stomach. He closed his eyes for a
moment. When he opened them again, he started talking.

* * *

"Tell you the truth, miss, what I remember 'bout huntin' season's
pretty much what I seen in the papers. It was in all of 'em, you know:
Free Press, Herald, all of 'em.

"I'm talkin' about the disappearance of my friend Stuart Dubois.
Stu and me, we always went out first day together. First day huntin',
first day fishin', didn't matter one bit, we was out there.

"Stu, he's a little bit older'n me. Not much, fifteen, twenty years,
mebbe. An' we been friends a good long time. I think of him like an
older brother, mabbe even, you know, kinda like a father in some
ways. That sound kinda funny, does it? I guess it prob'ly does.

"We was in that stretch of woods up behind Stu's place. An' jes' like always we split up: Stu goes one way, I goes another.

"Pretty quick, after we put some distance between us, I hears Stu yellin' an' cryin' out to high heaven. Sounds like he hurt himself or somethin'. God, but that was a frightful sound. Stu's wailin' away like he's sufferin' wicked and's half scairt out of his wits.

"I go runnin' in that direction when the shoutin' stops. I keeps goin' though. Pretty quick I find Stu's rifle in the snow. That give me a funny feelin', 'cause . . . well, I can't imagine Stu puttin' down a weapon like that, not in the snow. That ain't the way Stu treats a firearm.

"And I see his tracks headin' up this little slope, so I follows him. Then, 'bout eight, ten feet up—goddamnedest thing I ever seen—them tracks jest stop. Jest plain stop, like some big ol' eagle'd swooped down outta the sky and carried Stu off.

"Now, next thing I done—

"You *sure* all this is off the record? I mean, I ain't gonna lie; I ain't gonna hold nothin' back. That's the promise I made myself when I decided to come here. I figure they ain't no point in holdin' nothin' back. See, the way things been goin' lately, I'll do most anything to put a stop to it. But what I got to say, well, it's gonna sound crazy as hell from here on in, and I know it.

"Okay. Good. I 'preciate it. B'cause, ya see, I never told the police or game warden about them tracks. I brought 'em up to the site and everythin', jest the way I'm supposed to, but by the time we got there, well, the snow had melted off, so there wasn't nothin' to show but wet ground and Stu's rifle.

"And I didn't tell the police what happened next, neither. See, I'm standin' there with Stu's weapon in one hand, mine in the other, and I'm callin' out for him. I'm lookin' around like crazy, an' callin' out for Stuart. An' then . . . then . . .

"Excuse me, ma'am, but this is the tough part. See, I'm lookin' around, but there's no place Stu coulda gone. I mean, cripes, it's a wide-open clearin'! Trees all around, sure, but none close enough to jump to. Didn't have to look up to know nothin's up there. Nothin' but spindly little branches way up overhead.

Had to force myself to look up. That's 'cause there's no place else to look. And when I did, it was jest as if the sun was right up above my head. There's this bright white light jest floatin' up there, hangin' in the air up above the treetops. It's weird, too, 'cause you'd expect a light bright as that would be makin' big black shadows on the ground. But it wasn't makin' shadows, and it wasn't makin' noise. But it was there, I swear to God, it was there and I seen it.

"Now here's somethin' else pretty damn strange: that's *all* I can remember. The light, then nothin'. Ain't that funny? My memory jest stops right there. Don't remember leavin' the woods, don't remember callin' the police or the Fish and Game boys. Everything I seen and done between spottin' that light and when Ted Mavis showed up at my house with his deputy and the game warden is a total and complete blank. It jest ain't there."

* * *

When Alton stopped talking, he looked the young doctor right in the eye as if he were defying her to say his story was not true. She didn't pull her eyes away, and her facial features gave no indication that she questioned any of it.

"Look . . . I know how it sounds, miss, but what do you think? You think I might be crazy?"

She leaned forward and put her soft hand on top of his. "No, Mr. Barnes. You're not crazy; we don't even have to think about that or talk about it. Crazy is simply not in the picture." She leaned back in her chair, her eyes never leaving his. "Next we're going to start finding out what actually happened that day in the woods. We'll also talk about all the things that have happened between then and now. We're going to find out what it is you can't remember, and we're going to discover *why* you can't remember it. Does that sound okay to you?"

"Yes, ma'am, it does. That's what I come here for."

"Good. So how about we get started right now. Can you tell me how your life has changed since that day in the woods?"

"Changed?"

"Yes. You've already explained that you feel more nervous than before, and that you feel you get angry too easily. But what else has changed? For example, do you smoke more than you used to—"

"Don't smoke. Never did."

"—or have you been drinking more alcohol than you used to? Have you sought out other people, or have you avoided them? That kind of thing."

"Well, one thing sure, I'd like to be doin' more for Daisy—that's Stu's wife—but I keep avoidin' her. I guess it's because I got nothin' to say that can comfort her, ya know?"

"Do you think Mrs. Dubois blames you for what happened to her husband?"

"Blames me? Oh no, ma'am; it ain't that. Daisy ain't like that. It's me. I'll plan to go over there, take her grocery shoppin' or somethin', then I'll bury my nose in a book and forget all about everythin'."

"A book . . .?"

Alton paused to think about that. "Yeah," he said slowly. "You know, I been readin' an awful lot lately. I can't say if I'm doin' it to forget my troubles or to try to understand 'em."

"That's a very good question, Mr. Barnes. What kinds of things have you been reading?"

Alton ran his hand across his mouth, stalling a little so he could decide whether he should tell her. What the hell, he thought, if she laughs at me now, I'll just get up, walk right out of here, and never come back. He cleared his throat. "Well, ma'am, it's the kinda readin' I never had much use for before. But now . . . well, it started with them little newspapers, the kind, you know, like at the supermarket checkout. Then I started usin' the library, then I started buying hardcovers at fifteen, twenty bucks a whack."

"What kind of books, Mr. Barnes?"

"They're strange books, ma'am. I been readin' all about ghosts, and flying saucers, and magic. Crazy stuff, you know?"

13

Foul Spirits

Montreal, Quebec

In the guest room at Hospital Pardieu, Father Sullivan threw a handful of tourist brochures on top of his packed suitcase. He dreaded the two-and-a-half-hour drive back to the United States, though he didn't know exactly why. Perhaps it was because he had to leave everything unchanged.

Permanent Vegetative State. God, it sounded grim. But, finally, Sullivan had come to accept it. He could do nothing for Father Mosely.

This morning, to lighten his spirits, he and Father LeClair had strolled along Boulevard St. Laurent, once the east-west dividing line of the city's English and French populations. In time the barrier obscured, as a vast cultural melting pot took shape: Italian, Portuguese, Jewish, Polish, and Greek, coming together like many distinct personalities within the same body.

The city is so *alive*, Sullivan thought.

Walking along "the Main"—as Gaston called St. Laurent—cooking aromas from that cross-cultural stew spiced the air with savory, unfamiliar fragrances—smoked meats, sausage, spiced breads and pastries. Unable to resist, Sullivan had stuffed his belly full of knishes, golombkis, souvlakis, and other exotic concoctions the names of which he couldn't remember.

"Food will be the death of me," he told his companion.

At noon he had done penance for his gluttony by visiting St. Joseph's Oratory. Here, until his death in 1936, Brother Andre had invoked his patron saint, the husband of Mary, to heal the sick.

Miracles happened here.

Sullivan had watched the afflicted as they moved about him, seeking intercession, seeking relief. He had knelt, chastised himself for his indulgence, and said a prayer for Father Mosely.

* * *

He took the handle and lifted the bag to the floor. His holiday was over. Tomorrow morning he was scheduled to meet with Bishop LaPoint in Burlington.

A tapping sounded from behind him.

"Father!" It was Sister Maria calling from the doorway.

"Come in, Sister."

She opened the door about a foot and peeked around it. "Excuse me, Father Sullivan," she said in the slow, cautious English of an occasional speaker, "but I cannot find Father LeClair just now. Can you to come at once? Something . . . something is happening with Father Mosely."

* * *

Boston, Massachusetts

McCurdy's office was in the house proper. Elegantly paneled in rich black cherry, the magnificent woodwork contrasted harshly with the bureaucratic plainness of the room's furnishings. Two green four-drawer filing cabinets looked like army surplus rejects. The one closer to McCurdy's metal desk had a dog-eared NO SMOKING sign attached to its side. Browned transparent tape flaked from the sign's border. Some pencil-pusher's hopeless crusade, Jeff thought, noting an oversize ashtray brimming with cigarette butts. It balanced precariously on the edge of the desktop.

McCurdy too noticed the accident-about-to-happen and pushed the ashtray to a safer spot. "Smoke?" he asked Jeff.

Jeff shook his head and sat down in a blue plastic and aluminum armchair.

"I shouldn't either," McCurdy said, "it's no good for me and it's sinful as all getout, but . . ."

Not paying attention, Jeff continued to look around. This was his second time in McCurdy's office, and he wanted to take everything in. He noticed another incongruity: there was a crucifix on the wall. Close by, on one of the exquisitely crafted bookshelves, he saw the black spine of a Bible, stacked beside it *The Oxford Concise Concordance* and the *Annotated Apocrypha*. And there were other books, but strangely, most seemed part of a devotional collection.

"As you can see, up here in the visible part of the operation, we like to keep our overhead pretty low." McCurdy broke the filter off his Marlboro and popped the cigarette into his mouth. "This way we can show the world a thrifty face. As you might guess, our ledgers reflect remarkable fiscal restraint: conservative admin costs, low working expenses, modest salaries. We're a model government operation, highly cost effective and properly respectful of the taxpayer's hard-earned dollars. Of course what goes on behind that secret door to the basement is another thing entirely."

Jeff nodded, not knowing what to say.

"I suspect right now you're thinking: Jeez, I was hired to investigate UFOs. Now I discover the Academy's into all sorts of strange and interesting stuff—right?"

"You read my mind." Jeff offered a weak smile.

"Then it's time I put my proverbial cards on the metaphorical table. Symbolically, Jeff, the day-to-day operation of the Academy represents a microcosm that reflects the workings of the U.S. government itself: some of what we do is overt, the rest is covert."

"Not a flattering analogy."

McCurdy cleared his throat. "Maybe not, but accurate. We're realists here, Jeff. We have to be. Over the years, especially since the late 1940s, there's been a tremendous amount of covert government activity centering around *many* situations, not the least of which is the UFO question. Outwardly, UFOs are our raison d'être. The Academy's ongoing UFO research demonstrates to a wary public that, yes, the government *is* looking into the matter. And yes, we are looking out for the welfare and safety of our citizens."

McCurdy lit a match and touched it to the shaggy end of his cigarette. Smoke gushed as he spoke. "And it's true. The simple fact is, hundreds of thousands of ordinary people—cops, waitresses, mechanics, even Sunday school teachers—are seeing strange things in the sky. I'm talking about people from all over the globe, even people like former President Carter, as you may recall. In spite of all that, our government has perpetuated a position of irrational denial.

"That's where the Academy stepped in. Thanks to that blasted Freedom of Information Act, dozens of civilian UFO investigators are suing the air force and the CIA to release UFO-related documents. Enough information got out so Defense had to demonstrate an apparent interest in the UFO question. Ignoring the obvious just didn't work anymore.

"Okay, so the Academy is kind of reactionary. Ours is a Band-Aid solution to a worldwide quandary. But hey, we're thorough and honest in our investigations. And, yes, we're slippery and very clever in our public relations program."

Jeff linked his fingers. "You know, Dr. McCurdy, I'm pretty much on the side of the public. I'm curious about UFOs; I believe I have a right to know what they're all about. And it's not just civilian UFO investigators; a lot of people feel the government has been . . . well . . . less than forthright. In fact, I think a lot of people feel their elected representatives are out-and-out lying to them."

"And they're right." McCurdy slapped his desk, belching smoke like a dragon. "To this day the official U.S. government stand—in spite of former President Carter's promise of complete disclosure—is that UFOs are nothing but airborne baloney: kites, weather balloons, ball lightning, anything but extraterrestrial visitors who travel to impossible places using unknown technology.

"Historically, the government has made a series of halfhearted public gestures: Project Sign, Project Grudge, Gleem, Pounce, and the rest; the laundry detergents, I call them."

"That's what they sound like," Jeff chuckled. "What about Project Blue Book?"

"Right." McCurdy puffed his cigarette. "Blue Book's certainly the best known."

"But the results were inconclusive, as I recall."

"Yup. So was the Warren Commission's report on the Kennedy assassination."

"Huh? You lost me."

"Jeff, we're talking smoke screens. It's time you understood that. Every official smoke screen operation—up to and including the Academy—has, as a matter of policy, debunked *all* sightings, even those by credible witnesses. The United States has conducted a campaign of ridicule so effective that most witnesses choose not to speak out about UFOs at all. Meanwhile, behind the scenes, we're spending hundreds of thousands of dollars, millions actually, trying to learn everything we can about these flying saucers. At the same time we're swearing they don't even exist!"

Smoke hanging in the closed office was making Jeff queasy. His nausea grew worse as he watched the other man pick flecks of tobacco from his pink tongue.

McCurdy went on, "Official curiosity is tied into national defense. First, regardless of where the saucers come from, we want to know if they pose any kind of threat to government operations and the civilian population. And second, if they are in fact alien technology, how can we benefit from that technology? Especially in the realm of warfare and weaponry."

McCurdy put the still burning cigarette butt into the ashtray, broke the filter off another, then lit it, inhaling deeply. In a moment a thick bluish cloud extruded from his pursed lips.

"Do you believe in God, Dr. Chandler?"

Jeff gave a start, grinning awkwardly; the question took him completely by surprise. "I . . . I . . ."

"It's a hard question for some; I know that. Please, take your time." McCurdy held Jeff's gaze with a chilling concentration.

"You want the truth?"

McCurdy nodded.

"Well, the truth is, I don't know. I mean . . ." He cleared his throat.
"That's an awfully strange question, Dr. McCurdy."

"Call me Skipp, remember? We've been colleagues awhile and I hope we're going to be friends. But this time"—he smiled—"friendship won't get you off the hook. I'd like you to answer my question, Jeff."

"But what does it have to do with—"

"Look, the law says I can't base my hiring decisions on an applicant's religious preferences, nor can I discriminate against him on the job for the same reason, right? But you've already got the job, Jeff, and your answer won't effect your advancement or alter the way we work together here at the Academy. So come on now, it's perfectly safe, answer me. Even a hard-ass atheist shouldn't be afraid to state what he believes. Hell, boy, this is the United States of America, for heaven's sake."

Jeff cleared his throat again. "Well, I guess, I mean . . . I really don't know. I suppose the issue of God isn't really part of my belief system one way or another. Why do you ask, Skipp?"

McCurdy arched his back in the chair so he could fish around for something in his pants pocket. In a moment he flipped a bright silver disk to Jeff. Jeff caught it—a twenty-five-cent piece.

"See what it says right under Washington's chin?" McCurdy asked.

"'In God we trust.'"

"Right. So, Jeffrey, it doesn't really matter what you believe, the motto of this country is identical to the motto of the Academy. Remember your logic: we Americans *have* to believe in God in order to place our trust in Him, don't you agree?"

"Well, yes, I—"

"And by extension"—McCurdy combed his fingers through his sparse red-brown hair—"if one believes in God, it follows that one must believe in the devil, too. Am I right?"

"Well, yeah, I guess. I mean, you can't believe in one without believing in the other, I suppose."

"Exactly. And while you are in the employ of this project, at least during working hours, you, and I, and everyone here will proceed as if we believe in both of them: God, and the devil."

"I—"

"Let me finish, please. Things will come clear in half a second." He took a long drag on the cigarette, and leaned back in his chair, as if he enjoyed prolonging the suspense.

Jeff crossed his arms over his chest. He could feel the stone-on-stone pressure of his clenching teeth.

McCurdy continued quietly. "How about magic, Dr. Chandler? Do you believe in magic?"

"M-magic?"

"Yes. In your application papers you indicated an interest in magic."
Jeff smiled. "I was talking about tricks, sleight of hand, stage magic, amateur stuff. It's a hobby of mine."

"What about *real* magic?"

"Real magic . . .?"

"You know, the means of producing natural effects or reactions that are not the result of natural causes—magic."

Jeff fidgeted in his chair. The plastic seat squeaked rudely beneath him.

"I'm somewhat tolerant of the concept of extra sensory perception, if that's what you mean?"

"It's not what I mean, but let's talk about it anyway. It's relevant, after all. Since the late sixties, when the United States discovered the Russians were experimenting with 'mind weapons,' the Pentagon, and virtually all the U.S. intelligence agencies, began taking a closer look at psi phenomena. As you may recall, we even experimented with telepathic communication as part of our space program."

Jeff nodded.

"The biggest spender, of course, was the CIA. However, in the mid-seventies they had to scale down their visible involvement with psychic research while they were under intense scrutiny on Capitol Hill. After that, much of the ongoing research was farmed out to innocuous-looking facilities like the Academy, and paid for from various black budgets. Recently a U.S. Army study disclosed that 'the Soviet Union has achieved significant progress toward developing mind-control weapons.' What do you think of that, Jeffrey?"

"Isn't that just a lot of hype?" Jeff's crossed arms squeezed him tighter. "Scare tactics?"

"Is it?" McCurdy stared at him with wide-eyed defiance. "Most of us realize the awesome potential of psi-warfare: mind-jamming, remote viewing, psychic persuasion, telekinetic assault. Frightening, isn't it? That's why you and everybody else want to deny it. But it's real. We're stuck with it."

Jeff worked to keep the disbelief from his expression. Was this some sort of test McCurdy was putting him through?

"In fact, Jeff, the Ruskies were so busy we had to increase our own effort to keep up with them. Since the early seventies millions, probably billions, of tax dollars have been directed, one way or another, into psychic research."

McCurdy took a breath, as if trying to slow his speech. "So, Jeffrey, now tell me: what, in your mind, is the difference between extrasensory perception and magic?"

Jeff fidgeted. He was uncomfortably hot. He caught himself tugging at his necktie, loosening his collar. Rolling his eyes, he explored the room. Was this discussion being recorded? Was there a video camera somewhere? Finally, his gaze met McCurdy's. "Well, ESP might very well exist. I mean . . . well . . . I suppose it's possible. But even if it does work, it must be governed by certain natural laws. It's just that—as far as I know—we haven't identified the laws in question yet."

"Okay, good. It's like saying gravity existed long before that apple landed on Isaac Newton's head in the eighteenth century?"

"Right."

"And magic? What about magic?"

Jeff crossed his legs. He wrestled with a smug smile as he decided to be provocative. "I can emphatically state, with conviction if not authority, that magic *does not* exist. It's fantasy, pure and simple superstition."

McCurdy's tongue went *tch-tch-tch*. He raised his eyebrows and blew a plume of cigarette smoke into the air. "What would you say, Dr. Chandler, if I told you that you're wrong?"

* * *

Montreal, Quebec

Slowly, a little at a time—here, a twitch of nerve; there, a flutter of muscle—the expression on the old priest's face was changing.

Sullivan watched in disbelief. In slow motion the cloudy eye widened. The closed eyelid raised. The dry chalk-white lips slid across yellow teeth and suddenly, like an image developing in a photographer's tray, Father Mosely's wrinkled face showed an expression of agony.

He's waking up! Sullivan thought, his mind fighting to deny the miracle that was taking place before his eyes. He dropped to his knees beside the bed. Mumbling a silent prayer, he searched the pocket of his coat for his rosary.

There was noise behind him. He recognized the sound of Father LeClair's footsteps coming into the room. As Sullivan finished a Hail Mary he felt a hand resting on his shoulder.

"It is nothing, William."

Sullivan looked up at Father LeClair. He whispered, "Nothing? Look at his face, Father. He's moving. Both eyes are open. I think he's waking up."

LeClair shook his head. "It is nothing, William. Sister shouldn't have concerned you with this."

"Nothing? How can it be nothing?" Sullivan stood up. He felt himself becoming angry. "Look at him, for Christ's sake!"

"It happens sometimes, William. It is reflex, nothing more. These occasional overt responses torture the families of coma victims. They see a facial change, they see some eye movement, a muscle tremor, sometimes even a familiar smile. But it is nothing. It is reflex. In their comas these people can grin, they can grimace, sometimes they even make sounds. But, William, these things happen without consciousness. There is no association with real emotions or real experience. There is no thought of self, no awareness of surroundings, no—"

"But—"

"Please believe me, William. What you see is motor reflex, or it is the product of some glandular patterns ingrained into our species for thousands of years. It sounds cruel, William, I know it sounds cruel and I'm sorry. But you must accept it: the man you knew as Father Mosely is gone. His brain has irreversibly and permanently shut down."

Father Sullivan looked away, giving all his attention to what had become a heartbreaking expression of undiluted terror now frozen on Father Mosely's face.

And there was something else. There was no point in bringing it to Father LeClair's attention, of course, but Father Sullivan was sure of what he saw.

Teardrops, like tiny jewels, rested in the corners of the old priest's eyes.

14

Ghosts

Burlington, Vermont
Tuesday, June 21

Karen couldn't seem to relax.

After dinner she'd tried sitting at the kitchen table attempting to write this week's letter to her mother. After three false starts she gave up, crushed the stationery into a ragged sphere, and tossed it, basketball style, into the trash. She got up, loaded the dishwasher, then absently opened the refrigerator and stared unseeing at its contents. "Why am I *doing* this?" she said, because she wasn't hungry at all. After pushing the door closed, she walked into the living room and put a new CD into the player, Ennio Morricone's soundtrack from *The Mission*. Before the first track could pick up steam, she'd flicked on the TV, then flicked it off again.

She just couldn't unwind, couldn't shake the persistent feeling that something was wrong. It wasn't the death of Dr. Gudhausen, though that weighed heavily on her mind. And it wasn't the tragedy of the Washburn family. It was something else, something closer. Something immediate.

She thought about Jeff Chandler, her new friend in Boston. He was a pleasant distraction. Frequently his smiling face had interposed itself between her eyes and whatever she might be working on. Jeff had promised to call her and he hadn't. Was it too soon to hear from him? Was she being impatient? Should she wait a few days more?

Or maybe she should call him?

"Darn it all," she said aloud, "I'm acting like some love-struck schoolgirl." But what could she expect? She was as inexperienced as a schoolgirl. During high school she had rarely dated. All through college, between her studies and her home obligations, she had always been too busy. And now, in her roll as a young professional, she easily kept the world at bay. What dating she'd done was quick and antiseptic. Like her therapy sessions, her relationships were limited to a meeting or two and then—

Okay. She had to admit it. She lacked courage. But once something got started, well, who could say where the resulting whirlwind could carry you?

But Jeff seemed so very nice, so funny, so timidly sincere—

Stop it!

Impatient with herself, Karen moved to her front window and looked out, searching the lakeshore panorama for something else to think about.

Trouble was, whenever she pulled her thoughts away from Jeff, her new patient Alton Barnes came to mind.

Alton Barnes.

Was he the reason for her nervousness? Was she overlooking something important? Had she missed some vital detail he'd disclosed to her.

Karen liked him a lot, saw him as a definite "type," one of those no-nonsense, intensely proud, kind-to-a-fault Vermonters, the sort who'd rarely seek the aid of a physician, much less a psychotherapist. Karen smiled sadly as she looked out at the lake. Their session yesterday had reminded her to write to Mother. Because Mr. Barnes, she suddenly realized, was just like her father.

The fact that Mr. Barnes had accepted a referral to therapy assured Karen that whatever he'd seen in the woods had frightened him terribly.

What could scare that kind of man?

What could be frightening enough to make him step forward to ask for help?

Initially, Karen had suspected a hallucination, but she'd quickly rejected the idea. No, Mr. Barnes *had* seen something. Something too horrible to recall. And that kind of fear looked out of place on Alton Barnes.

Karen had never seen any kind of fear in her father. Never. Not once. Even during those last days, when the cancer had rooted itself in every part of his body, he hadn't shown fear. At least none that a ten-year-old girl could recognize.

The last time she had seen him, his powerful six-foot frame had been replaced by some hollow-eyed changeling that seemed to be fashioned from sticks of wood and wrinkled parchment paper. It was a grotesque imitation of the father she loved.

On the last day, the doctor allowed her only five minutes with Dad. Odd how little space he required in the narrow hospital bed. She looked down at him, hating the thing beneath the sheets, not knowing what to say to it. Not knowing what to do.

Its lips were moving. She watched, fascinated, not understanding that it was trying to speak. When visiting time ended, she forced herself to lean over, readied her lips for a good-bye kiss. As her ear moved closer to his mouth, she realized he was talking. "Family'll all be together again, someday," he whispered, "so don't you worry." He paused then, as if trying to summon enough strength to continue. "Till then, you take care of your mama for me, okay, honey?" He'd been able to move his head just enough to kiss her on the cheek. His dry lips had felt like autumn leaves against her skin.

And she *had* taken care of her mother.

They'd lived together in the family place, with Karen commuting sixty miles every day to attend classes at the University of Vermont. Then she continued the drive, Bristol to Burlington, throughout her first year on the staff of the health center. The routine had become second nature: hot coffee and a muffin in the car, reviewing case notes on the cassette player, bringing home pizza or subs for a nine o'clock supper.

Only foul weather—when the snow-slick roads were too dangerous for driving—would keep her in Burlington overnight.

It was on just such a night that her mother had the stroke. Phone lines down, roads impassable, Karen didn't find her until eight o'clock the next night.

A lengthy hospitalization followed. Then long grueling sessions of physical and occupational therapy. Mom eventually regained some mobility on her right side, but she couldn't speak, and the doctors said she was not well enough to go on living at the family place.

With that, something had come to an end.

Karen thought of all the people she had counseled, good, well-meaning couples who came to her guilt-ridden and profoundly sad because they had to consider putting an ailing parent in a home. Having faced the same decision, Karen would never underestimate their discomfort.

Maybe the outcome was easier for Karen than it was for many people. Mom had made the choice herself. She would go to Florida for her "retirement." Now she lived in the same rest home as her sister Gladys. Karen understood Mom's decision: her mother simply was not willing to remain a burden to Karen.

They had sold the farm and divided almost two hundred and fifty thousand dollars. It met Mom's expenses and allowed a sizable down payment on Karen's lakefront condominium.

Karen blinked at the sunset and wiped the moisture from her eyes.

Gotta do something, she thought. *Gotta get busy at something.*

Mother was so generous, so prideful, always so careful not to trouble or inconvenience. Why then was it so hard for Karen to write her just one lousy letter a week?

What kind of person am I, anyway?

Repulsed by her dying father, neglectful of her ailing mother . . .

What makes me think I can help anyone?

How will I mess up Alton Barnes?

What have I done to scare Jeff Chandler away?

Bingo!—there was the problem.

Self-doubt had inspired uncertainty and inaction.

Gotta get busy. Gotta do something.

In the distance the sun, a bright fiery ball, hovered in the dark sky beyond Lake Champlain, above the silhouetted spine of the Adirondacks. Deep red rays lined the clouds and rippled brilliantly on the surface of the water. It was a beautiful sunset. Her wide eyes drank in the scene like a soothing tonic.

Finally, she knew what she had to do. She would make the phone call she'd been putting off since she got back from Boston. Why not? There was nothing that said she shouldn't. Why was it any more his responsibility than hers?

After a short hunt for her purse, Karen removed her Day-Timer and looked up the number. She punched the keys, silently rehearsed what she was going to say.

Someone picked up the phone during the third ring. "Hello?" A woman's voice answered, catching Karen off guard.

"Is . . . is this Jeff Chandler's residence?" She felt as if she were stammering.

"Yes," said the voice. "Just a minute please."

"No, wait!" But it was too late. Karen heard Jeff coming to the phone. "Yes? Hello . . ."

"Ah . . . Jeff . . . hi. This is—"

"I know who it is," he said. "Listen, I'm glad you called, but I can't talk to you now."

"But—" Karen feared that surprise, maybe hurt, was evident in that single word.

"No buts. Not now. Sorry."

Before she could speak again, he'd hung up.

15

Hand

Boston, Massachusetts

Dr. Ian McCurdy studied the hand on the table in front of him. He poked it gingerly, feeling the warm flesh yield and wrinkle beneath his fingertip. He ran the nail of his right index finger between two pink knuckles, leaving a thin white line that faded quickly and disappeared.

More adventurous now, he pinched the web of skin between its thumb and forefinger, tugged it, dug into it with opposing nails.

The hand was an alien thing, a five-legged creature that seemed locked in some anesthetic dream. It was an amputee-octopus on a dissecting tray. A starfish on a dinner plate.

McCurdy closed his eyes, breathing deeply to steady his nerves. What he was about to do was important. He knew that, yet he hesitated. And his hesitation, he confessed, was selfishness. And selfishness was sin.

Offering a silent prayer, he bent the hand's three longest fingers under the palm. Then he folded the thumb against them and taped the fist closed with eight feet of surgical gauze.

Now the knob of a hand was a girdled fist with just the little finger extended. Its nail was ragged with tooth marks. Its cuticle was an imperfect crescent of opaque skin with a hangnail drooping from its left end.

McCurdy placed the hand on the tabletop next to a marble slab. The little finger, lying on the elevated marble, was an ugly white grub sleeping on dark stone. He positioned the wrist tightly against the table.

Everything was in position.

Everything was ready.

I offer this as a symbol, he thought. I offer this as a sign and as a symbol, he prayed. I offer this to show my devotion, to show my commitment and my determination, to show that I am ready for the greater sacrifices that are to come.

The ten-inch Sabatier blade was solid in his hand. The steel was still cold though he had removed it from the refrigerator fifteen minutes ago. He had sharpened it that morning, cleaned it with alcohol, and stored it on white linen. Now its ebony handle felt like ice within his sweating palm.

McCurdy studied the hand. The fingers and wrist were a forest of tiny hairs. Thick blue veins bulged like glutted snakes. He poked the expanse of skin with the point of his knife. It dented. A pinprick of red appeared when he took the blade away.

Swabbing the hand with alcohol, McCurdy readied his mind for the sacrifice. Carefully, he positioned the thickest part of the blade across the little skin and bone bridge that separated the first and second joints.

"Oh my dear Lord," he whispered, "I offer this to show that I am strong."

Then he pushed!

Leaning heavily, he added his body weight to the cut.

It happened so fast! Blade hit stone, skidded along the polished surface now slick with blood.

He had time to think that the severed digit looked like a french fry before the impact of pain brought tears to his eyes.

He screamed.

McCurdy lifted his damaged hand from the stone slab, plunged it into the nearby bowl of ice water.

"It is done," he whispered through clenched teeth. "It is done. It is done. It is done."

Tears splattered against the bloody stone cutting board.

McCurdy smiled. He was very happy.

16

A Coming of Serpents

Montreal, Quebec
Thursday, June 23

The redheaded man crouched beside the dirty little girl with the drooping lips. Neither spoke. Motionless as stone gargoyles, they waited amid the depth of shadows outside the cold masonry wall.

Soundlessly, the man put his duffel bag aside and stood up. The little girl followed his lead. With one hand on each side of her waist, he lifted her to his shoulders so she could peer over the wall and look at the hospital. For a moment he sensed her confusion. It doesn't look like a hospital, she thought, it just looks like some big old three-story house.

Without exchanging words, he knew she could see lights in some of the second-story windows. Somehow, he also knew the window they were looking for was not on this side of the building. So much the better; the building's back side would be invisible from the road. They would not be troubled by passing cars or pedestrians. What they had to do would be hidden completely.

He let her down, feeling the skin of her knees tear as it scraped against the rough masonry. She made no sound.

In near-perfect unison the man and girl dropped and flattened themselves against the ground. With the man in the lead, pushing his duffel bag before him, they crawled like lizards through the damp dark passage formed between the lowest cedar branches and the base of the wall.

In time the man came to realize that the eight-foot wall completely surrounded the hospital building. He also knew that the wall would be interrupted here and there by wrought-iron gates. Some gates would be narrow enough for pedestrians, some wide enough for vehicles. But it was nighttime now; all the gates might be closed, maybe locked.

Still, the wall was more a convention of seventeenth-century architecture than a genuine defense fortification. The man was confident that even if all the gates were locked, they could get in with little difficulty.

He tried to clear his mind, hoping to receive some message or signal. He needed some indication about which of the many windows looked out from the room they were searching for.

The man rounded a ninety-degree corner, still slithering along under the protection of heavy vegetation. Without having crawled much farther—surely no more than ten feet—he came to an opening. With his left cheek pressed tightly to the earth, he looked up. Above him there was a spiked iron gate. A quick push with his fingertips proved it was unlocked. The gate swung heavily; its rusty hinges groaned. The man, like an obese serpent, crept through the opening and into a garden. The little girl slithered along behind him.

Scanning the dark face of the building, the man was somehow certain that none of the four lighted windows was the one they were seeking. His eyes kept pulling toward a darkened window at the far end of the second floor. When he fixed his gaze on that window everything else vanished from his attention.

The window was less than three feet wide. It was five feet tall, maybe more. Its irregular shape was not a problem. Nor was its distance from the ground—almost twenty feet.

Behind the window there appeared to be a faint green incandescence, like the glowing face of some electronic instrument. Also, he saw a point of white light inside. It seemed to be reflecting off glass; maybe it was a bottle or some shiny metal surface.

But somehow he knew, there was no question: he was looking at the right room!

It wasn't necessary to inform the girl; if he knew something, she would know it as well. Her unblinking eyes had locked on that same distant spot of light.

Hidden by the fathomless shadow of a magnificent oak tree, the pair dashed to the side of the building and flattened themselves against its cold stone surface.

Backs to the wall, they moved silently, invisibly, toward a narrow wooden door.

In a moment the man's hand was on the latch. He tried it. Found it locked.

With the girl standing watch, the man opened his duffel bag and removed a small hydraulic jack and two twelve-inch lengths of iron pipe. He screwed the pipes together, making a two-foot bar. This he attached to a fitting he had welded to the head of the jack. He positioned his creation horizontally, running from one side of the door frame to the other, just in front of the lock. Then, with a crank he had fashioned in his workshop, he began to turn the jack. The jack lengthened until it held itself in place. It extended some more. As pressure increased, both sides of the door frame strained and creaked. Soon the ancient wood began to split. Slivers popped out like tiny switchblades. Within moments the vertical door frames started to bow, screeching as the wood bent outward.

When the man tried the door again it opened easily, now too narrow for its widened frame.

Slowly, carefully, the man collapsed the jack and removed his apparatus from the doorway. He disassembled it and returned it to the bag.

Then he and the little girl entered the building.

They stood in the center of a long unlighted corridor that ran left and right the entire length of the building. The closed door directly in front of them probably led to the main hall.

Following a powerful instinct, the man ignored this nearby door and went left. He knew they'd quickly find a stairway that would take them upstairs and almost to the room they were looking for.

Rapidly he led the the girl along the shadow-crowded corridor. They were in luck! Everything was exactly as he'd imagined.

They climbed the steps as quickly and quietly as they could. At the top they stopped and peered through a doorless opening that would admit them to a dimly lighted hallway.

As the man transferred the duffel bag from one hand to the other, the pipes it contained clanked together. He stepped back quickly, his heart pounding.

In French, a woman's voice said, "What's that? Who's there?"

The man held his breath as a white-garbed figure carrying a flashlight and a stethoscope scurried toward them.

He grabbed the little girl and threw her out into the corridor. She stumbled, her bare feet skidded, and she hit the floor. There she began to cry softly. The white-clad figure hurried to assist her.

"What's this?" said the nun. "Who are you, child? What are you doing here?"

From the shadows, the redheaded man watched the nun kneel to comfort the fallen child. "What has happened here, little one? Oh my heavens, you're filthy dirty! Come, child, let me clean you up."

The girl lifted her head until she faced the nun.

Seeing the child's ruined face, her blackened eyes, her grotesquely distended lips, the nun recoiled in surprise. At that moment the man seized her. His left arm coiled around her neck, jerking her upright. His right hand slapped across her mouth. He spun her around and pushed her headfirst against the rock wall. Her knees gave out. As she slumped, he snatched his duffel bag and slammed it against the back of her head.

Then the man and the little girl ran down the corridor toward Father Mosely's room.

* * *

Hobston, Vermont

The persistent electronic beep wrenched Father Sullivan from a troubled sleep. This was his first night at St. Joseph's rectory and he'd never been able to sleep well in unfamiliar surroundings.

When the electronic trill sounded again, Father Sullivan realized it was the telephone. "What's the matter with good old-fashioned bells?" he mumbled. "At least a man can tell what he's listening to." Before summoning the energy to open his eyes, he groped for the bedside lamp. His floundering hand knocked over the half-full glass of water on the bedside table. He knew the tumbled glass had emptied its contents into his slippers.

"Damn," he muttered, and begrudgingly let his eyes open—just a slit—to discover it was already light in the bedroom.

The phone rang.

Sullivan poked at the various objects on the table looking for his watch. He found it on his wrist. Ten after six in the morning!

He flopped back on his pillow, thinking how great it would be if he could just sleep another couple of hours.

The phone rang.

This time he managed to grab the receiver without lifting his head from the pillow. "Yes? Hello? Good morning?"

The voice spoke in French. It sounded a long way off. "Hello, Father Sullivan?"

"Yes."

"This is Sister Marie from Hospital Pardieu in Montreal. . . ."

"Yes, Sister. Good morning."

"I am calling for Father LeClair. Can you wait please?"

"Yes, Sister, of course." They wake me up and put me on hold! Where is the justice?

Sullivan heard the familiar French-accented tones. "Father Sullivan? Bill? It is Gaston LeClair. I am sorry to have awakened you at this hour, Bill. But . . . well, we have had the strangest thing happen. Of course I am aware of your interest in Father Mosely, so I have called you at once."

"Something's happened to Father Mosely?"

"Bill, he is gone—"

"Dead?"

"No. He is *gone*. Vanished. Someone broke in here last night and took him—how do you say?—kidnapped him."

"Kidnapped him? That's crazy."

"Yes. Crazy. The police are here now."

"Didn't anyone see what happened? Didn't you hear anything? I mean to kidnap an old man in a coma . . . ?"

"Sister Elise was hurt—"

"Oh good God. How bad?"

"She is unconscious. The doctor is with her." Father LeClair's voice cracked, "They were brutal, Father, and she is not a young woman. They . . . they smashed . . . with her head . . . against the stone wall. Made her unconscious. Her nose is broken. Teeth, too. She will be scarred, Father, disfigured. . . ."

"Dear God."

"Bill, the police want to talk to you. They want to know if you have any idea who could have done such a thing. And why? What reason can there be to kidnap an old man in a coma?"

"I don't know, Father. I have no idea. But I promise you this: I intend to find out."

* * *

Boston, Massachusetts

At exactly twenty-three hundred hours the automatic timer locked Dr. McCurdy in his office.

The precise metallic *click* of the mechanism jolted him from his reverie and reminded him that he was the only person in the Academy building.

Metal window blinds clattered shut, his FM radio switched off, the electric circuits to his office—all save one—disconnected. A single electronic tone told him the telephone line was inoperative. No incoming calls, none going out.

Although he couldn't hear it, he knew that low-frequency electromagnetic waves were eliminating any possibility of electronic surveillance.

His pulse throbbed in the bandaged stub on his left hand. Nervously he picked at the white surgical tape.

"Okay, boss," he said to himself. "You're on."

He pressed a good half of his cigarette against the marble ashtray and brushed an accumulation of ashes from the front of his cardigan.

Standing up, McCurdy stretched, yawned, then walked away from his desk, moving to the computer terminal that was appearing from behind a rising panel on the far side of the room.

Eleven o'clock had also activated a communications program McCurdy was required to use once a week for exactly one hour. He knew that messages originating at either end of the hook-up would be temporarily saved, scrutinized electronically, then deleted a character at a time as they were transmitted in nonsequential patterns, millicharacter after millicharacter. The entire process, hidden among scores of inconsequential data, would be dispatched immediately if urgent, or randomly and intermittently if routine. Routine transmissions—the simple manipulation of data—took place over the seven-hour period between midnight and seven o'clock in the morning, exactly one electronically measured hour before the office officially opened. McCurdy's coded message would arrive hundreds of miles away. And somewhere within the Pentagon, each tiny character would become an electronic needle hidden within billions upon billions of electronic haystacks.

It was safe, a foolproof system that couldn't be detected, much less decoded.

Message or no message, security required Dr. McCurdy to remain locked in his office until midnight, when a precise electronic timer would unlock his office door, restore telephone lines and electrical circuits.

McCurdy sometimes wondered who, exactly, he was communicating with? Was there really a human being on the other end of the line, sitting in some dark air-conditioned office before an identical keyboard? Or was he communicating with the machine itself, holding cryptic conversations with some experimental data bank equipped with a state-of-the-art artificial intelligence program?

If the truth were known, might McCurdy discover these late-night hour-long sessions were actually a test or some kind of verification procedure? Were his reactions, thought processes, reasoning ability, and general awareness being probed and examined by some phantom federal employee at the other end of Bubb's long extension cord? He didn't know. And in truth it didn't matter. The bottom line was that he was doing his job. It wasn't his responsibility to question, to agree, or to disagree; it was his responsibility to do. Exactly as ordered. Period. The annual renewal of the grant money made it all worthwhile.

Still, McCurdy was certain of one thing: there were many secret checks and balances built into the system, enough to verify beyond doubt that the user in Boston, Massachusetts, was, in fact, Dr. Ian McCurdy.

Since security did not allow him to know the various check mechanisms, his single great fear was to inadvertently trigger one. If the machine believed him to be an impostor, the office would not unlock, and there would be no way to abort Bubb's CONTAIN command.

McCurdy stared at his reflection in the empty screen. While he waited, he hypothesized about the various "check and verify" systems operating at the Academy. He enjoyed guessing, although he didn't know much about what he called "gadget technology," the electronic instruments of surveillance. One device, he guessed, might have to do with how much he weighed. Every Monday, without exception, the nurse took his blood pressure and recorded his weight. This weekly routine was part of ESRP—Esrep—their bogus Executive Stress Reduction Program. Maybe his desk chair, or the chair at the computer terminal, weighed him and compared.

Or maybe it had something to do with his car. His instructions were most emphatic: he was always to park the Academy's car in the spot reserved exclusively for him.

But no, these seemed clunky and imprecise.

Then again, perhaps one of the keys on his computer terminal could recognize his fingerprint. But which key? And which finger? Whoa! Realization struck with a jolt of adrenaline—he no longer had a print on the little finger of his left hand! What if—

His attention locked on the CRT as it began to glow neon purple, a color out of some flashy science fiction film. Or, as his trainer had remarked three years ago in a rare display of humor, "It's just like the color of a bug-zapper." Right now McCurdy didn't like to contemplate the irony in that statement.

Although these weekly contacts were boringly repetitive, not to mention routinely uneventful, there was always a moment of suspense as the computer's logo—BLZ-28/22—appeared at the center of the screen.

McCurdy could never anticipate exactly what information might be required of him, or what instructions he might receive. But tonight, more than usual, he had an idea of what was coming.

A white smoky image began to take shape on the monitor. It undulated and solidified, assuming the characteristics of a human hand. A left hand, with a truncated little finger.

McCurdy couldn't believe it. How? How did they know?

But he knew the routine. He placed his left palm on the video screen, directly over its mirror image. When he took his hand away, its hazy outline remained imposed upon its video twin. In the center of the electronic palms, a message had appeared:

MCCURDY VERIFIED

The two words blinked twice. They vanished and were replaced with:

                    INFORMATION
                    REQUEST
                    TO FOLLOW

He waited, oddly tense, nearly certain of the next display.

                    INDICATE STATUS
                    EMPLOYEE
                    NUMBER U-7734
                    + + +
                    NAME: CHANDLER, JEFFREY.

The instruction faded; controlled choices appeared.

                    YOUR ASSESSMENT OF
                    PROMOTION POTENTIAL
                    1 : SATISFACTORY
                    2: UNSATISFACTORY
                    PLEASE RESPOND:

McCurdy marveled at how simple it seemed. For Jeff Chandler, without his even knowing it, the entire world had suddenly been reduced to two one-word states of being on a tiny computer screen. The simple words were almost Zen in their austerity. Either could connote complicated life situations, motives, reasons, rationales, explanations, layers of subtlety, personal drives, loves, ambitions, interpersonal affections. Here, any imaginable complexity of situation had been reduced through electronic objectivity to a simple binary, a simple choice: one or two, A or B, true or false, right or wrong, bad or good, light or dark, on or off, life or—

Briefly, McCurdy wondered what would happen if he lied. Should he try it? Should he hit number two? THE EMPLOYEE IS UNSATISFACTORY, UNSATISFACTORY, UNSATISFACTORY . . .

For a moment he speculated that if the machine knew enough to ask the question, it probably knew the answer as well. In fact, this entire exercise could be phony, a setup, nothing more than one of security's seemingly motiveless checks and balances.

But what if the proper response really couldn't be communicated by a simple one-word answer? Suppose he wanted to reply more completely than either choice would permit?—*I found I actually like Jeff Chandler. He impresses me as an oafish, six-foot kid, a lovable, charming clown who'll never appreciate the full responsibilities of his position here. Jeff impresses me as a small-timer, not even one hundred percent security cleared—*

He didn't dare test his hypothesis. Fearful to wait any longer, he reached forward—remembering to hold down the asterisk anytime he entered data—and pressed "1" on the keyboard.

YOUR SATISFACTION IS NOTED,

DOCTOR MCCURDY.

The thirty-six letters tumbled away into the screen's purple infinity. Where they vanished, more appeared.

YOU HESITATED.

WHY?

PLEASE RESPOND:

McCurdy tensed. Never before had his behavior—not even his response time—been questioned by the machine.

*because i understand the consequence of my answer

AND KNOWING,

DO YOU STILL HESITATE?

PLEASE RESPOND:

*no

GOOD.

PLEASE VERIFY.

McCurdy typed:

* new employee, number u-7734
* chandler, jeffrey:
* evaluation rated satisfactory.

THANK YOU, DOCTOR MCCURDY.

PLEASE PREPARE FOR DISCUSSION TO FOLLOW.

McCurdy prepared, knowing he would have to read rapidly as words flashed in hypnotic pulsations on the purple screen.

DOCTOR MCCURDY, THE WORK YOU DO
HAS GREAT VALUE. IT HOLDS THE
PROMISE OF AFFECTING PEACE AND
HARMONY IN A TROUBLED WORLD. YOU
UNDERSTAND THAT YOU WERE GIVEN
THIS R&D PROJECT BECAUSE
  —YOU ARE A SKILLED ADMINISTRATOR
  —YOUR MILITARY RECORD IS WITHOUT
  BLEMISH
  —YOUR RELIGIOUS BELIEFS
  DEMONSTRATE THAT YOU ARE
  SINCERE IN YOUR DESIRE
  FOR A PEACEFUL WORLD
  —YOUR UNDERSTANDING OF THE
  NATURE OF EVIL IS THE ONLY
  UNDERSTANDING THAT CAN LEAD
  TO ITS EXTINCTION.

PLEASE RESPOND:

Respond? What was he supposed to say? For an instant he thought he had to choose among multiple responses.

DOCTOR MCCURDY, PLEASE
ACKNOWLEDGE THAT YOU UNDERSTAND.
        PLEASE RESPOND:
        PLEASE RESPOND:
    * i understand
THANK YOU. I HAVE BEEN INSTRUCTED
TO INFORM YOU THAT THE NATURE OF
YOUR ASSIGNMENT WILL SOON BE
MODIFIED. IT IS TIME FOR US TO MEET.
I WILL CONTACT YOU BEFORE THIS
TIME NEXT WEEK.
        PLEASE RESPOND:
    * yes, understood
    * question: where am i to meet you?
DOCTOR MCCURDY, I WILL CONTACT YOU.
THAT IS ALL. TRANSMISSION TERMINATED.

The screen went dead. A tone told him the electrical and communication circuits were operative again. He heard the whir and clatter of the metal shutters uncovering the windows.

McCurdy didn't rise from his desk, though a metallic *click* told him the door was unlocked and he was free to go. Instead, he sat staring at a paneled wall where the keyboard and CRT had been. Doubt flickered somewhere in the back of his mind. His mangled hand began to itch.

Had he been dialoging with a machine or with a human being?

McCurdy's heart jumped against his chest as he prayed silently, moving his lips without speaking, Oh my dear Lord Jesus, let this be the beginning. . . .

17

Invaders

Hobston, Vermont
Friday, June 24

Bingham Creek Road ended at a turnaround in Daisy Dubois's dooryard.

The home she had shared with Stuart was a weather-beaten, sway-backed farmhouse beside a tumbled barn. Nowadays, Daisy was sometimes a trifle embarrassed by the state of the property, but more often she found in its disrepair a special kind of pride: she was convinced she would outlast both structures, house and barn. Though the porch roof was collapsing, and myriad broken windowpanes were mended with squares of linoleum, Daisy did all she could to keep the place running. Certainly she did as much as Stuart had when he was here. And besides, the place was important, it was the last real bit of civilization between Hobston town and the vast Green Mountain forests.

Phone and electrical lines didn't stretch quite far enough to supply her with either service. But she and Stuart had gotten by without them for sixty-plus years. There was surely no reason for such luxury at this time in her life.

Although theirs had been a childless marriage, they had been a heaven-matched pair. They'd got on well and always without complaint. They had devoted themselves to each other, their garden, their livestock, and their God. Even when Stuart took sick back in '71, while Daisy'd had to run the farm alone, they'd held Christian services every Sunday in Stuart's sickroom. She'd light the pretty-smelling candles and he'd sit up in bed—pillows steadying him, holding him upright—and read passages from the Bible, often in a voice too weak for Daisy to hear. At those times she'd kneel at his bedside and pray, fearing she'd never again hear his powerful tenor voice singing the hymns they both loved, beautiful Christian songs that brought tears to the eyes of their tiny congregation.

The Good Lord had pulled him through that time. But now the loss of Stuart's music made her sad. *Dear Lord,* she thought again, *what's happened to him?*

Every other Wednesday, back in the old days, Father Mosely had made the trip up the hill for an evening visit. "I enjoy the hike," he always said. Some folks might have thought it odd that the priest should take such a long walk to see a couple of Baptists. But Stuart hadn't seen it as strange: "The Good Lord never said a Protestant and a Catholic can't be friends."

Now smiling at the recollection, Daisy stared into the starless sky beyond her parlor window. She rocked in her creaky wooden chair, the faded carpet below worn threadbare in two spots, one beneath each shoe. "So many mem'ries," she whispered to no one. "Oh, me, so awful many mem'ries."

Even after Stuart . . . left . . . that new Baptist preacher never looked in on Daisy. Once he had dispatched the town's interdenominational church social worker to see if Daisy was all right and to find out what assistance the congregation could provide. Silly. Both were questions old Father Mosely would have known better than to ask.

Of course she was all right, thank you very much. And there was nothing she needed that she couldn't make for herself, or buy outright when Al Barnes, or somebody, drove her into town. Come to think of it, those trips to town were getting more than a little bit off schedule. She hoped Alton was all right. Truth be known, in his own way, he had probably loved Stuart just as much as she did.

Daisy had just started reminiscing about that church social worker—a nice young girl who seemed awfully nervous, spoke too quickly, and acted as though she didn't want to touch anything in the house—when she heard the distant sound of an automobile engine.

"Hummm," she said, "can't be Alton at this hour."

Standing, looking out the window, she failed to spot the source of the noise. Moonlight cast a pale silvery brilliance over the hilltop. For a moment Daisy was captivated by moon shadows and the playful flirtation of a million blinking fireflies against the rich blackness of the forest.

She took the kerosene lamp from the kitchen table and stepped out onto the porch where she waited to meet whoever might be coming up the driveway. One of her cats, the fat one, Bertha, pushed open the screen door and sat between Daisy's feet.

"Looks like us old gals is getting some callers," Daisy said to the cat. "Wonder who's comin' up the hill at this time a night? Nobody with no good news to bring, an' that's for certain."

Moths surrounded the burning lamp as Daisy set it on the porch table. Their shadows looked like bats flickering across the clapboarding and the peeling newel posts.

Daisy thought about the shotgun she kept just inside the doorway. "Awful thing the way a person has to be afraid all the time nowadays," she said. "Wasn't never that way in the old days. Used to be you'd know who was trouble and who wasn't. Not no more."

Bertha rubbed her sleek side against Daisy's ankle and uttered a tight raspy cry.

The automobile engine grew louder as it approached. Now Daisy could hear its tires grinding against the gravel drive. Pretty quick she began to make out its bright headlights dancing among the lush shadows and towering trunks of thick evergreens.

"Awful late to come calling," Daisy said, her eyes narrow, peering into the night. "Why, I believe it must be nearly eleven o'clock. Maybe little after."

Then the car did something strange. As it reached the last stretch of driveway—that exposed area between the woods and the open dooryard—it turned its headlights off. Yet it continued to move toward the house like a fat black beast, crouching, growling, inching forward in the shadows.

"This don't look right to me," said Daisy. She looked around for Bertha, but Bertha was gone. "Don't look right to you neither, does it, Mama Cat?"

Daisy stepped back and opened the screen door just enough to get her hand inside. Without taking her eyes from the car—now she could see it was a station wagon—she reached around the door frame, moist fingers wriggling, until she touched the cold metal barrel of Stuart's twelve-gauge shotgun.

The station wagon ground to a stop about ten feet from Daisy's front steps. The engine continued to run, and for a moment no one got out. Daisy noted several things at once: her mob of curious cats didn't swarm silently into the driveway as they normally would when investigating a new arrival; even fat old Bertha, the nosiest of all, stayed out of sight. The scores of fireflies held their light, returning the landscape to utter darkness.

Daisy noticed something else, too: the air was full of noise. Dogs and coyotes far in the distance howled into the black sky; chickens in the coop beside the barn raised holy heck, squawking and flapping as if a fox had come a-calling.

Daisy pulled the shotgun onto the porch. Holding it by the barrel, she let it stand beside her, its butt on the porch floor. She knew the people in the station wagon would see it, but they'd see, too, that it wasn't shouldered and ready.

When the passenger-side door opened, Daisy was surprised to see a child get out. It was a girl, a grimy little girl, with filthy hair and a dirt-smeared face. She looked like some poor street urchin, dressed in a tattered jumper. The girl slammed the car door, but it had been open long enough for the interior light to reveal a man behind the wheel.

The little girl stood beside the car, looking up at Daisy. "Pweef, miffif," she began, but she was awful hard to understand. Daisy squinted at her, a signal that she should try again.

"Please, missus," she said, more slowly and carefully this time. "Can you please help us?"

Now, with difficulty, Daisy could make out what the child was saying. "We got lost on the way to the hospital. My grandfather's in the back, and he's awful sick."

The child's voice was sure odd. Why did she pronounce her words so strangely? Daisy stared at the little waif, studied her, not at all sure of what she was going to do. "There ain't too much I can do for you, honey. I 'spect I can give you directions—"

"Can we phone, ma'am? Can we phone for an ambulance?"

"No, honey, I'm sorry. I got no phone, I got no way to call for the doctor."

She froze, immobilized by terror's icy touch. It was as if a blast of arctic air had suddenly filled her, freezing up her insides. Silently, heart beating faster, she cursed herself. Stupid! she thought, stupid old woman! What had made her say a stupid thing like that? Why had she given away that information? When her slippery fingers tightened on the barrel of the shotgun she knew how badly she was sweating.

Ah well, what's done is done. Maybe there was still some way she could maintain control of the situation. It was *her* house after all. And she *did* have a shotgun. She lifted the weapon and held it across her chest. "Whyn't you come up here little closer to the light, so I can get a look at you."

The girl took a tiny step forward. "How come you wanna have a gun, lady?"

"'Cause I don't know ya, that's how come. Now who's that fella behind the wheel?"

"My pa." The little girl inched a bit closer to the porch steps. Now Daisy could see the peculiar deformation of the child's mouth. Her lips hung low, slack like the limp bodies of dead snakes.

Poor thing, Daisy thought, but she knew better than to drop her guard. "Why don't you tell your pa to come on out where I can lay my eyes on him, too."

With that the driver's door opened and the interior light revealed the face of a redheaded man with very short hair.

He was smiling.

PART THREE

Revelations...

"... this workaday actuality of ours—with its
bricks, its streets, its woods, its hills,
its waters—may have queer and,
possibly, terrifying holes in it."

—Walter de la Mare

Excerpt from
The Reality Conspiracy:
An Anecdotal Reconstruction of the Events at Hobston, Vermont

On Saturday, June 25, Jerry Finny was ten minutes late for Bible School.

He had dallied and dreamed and dragged his feet all the way from home. His only stop had been at Gorman's Drugstore where he'd unloaded part of this week's five-dollar allowance. Gorman's was the only place in town that still carried packs of Marvel Universe cards. They also had a super selection of comic books.

As he walked, Jerry hugged his purchases to his chest. Jeez, he thought, this business of going to Bible School on Saturday is for the birds. It's ruining the whole morning!

He glanced at his watch. Almost ten. Gotta hurry!

Next year he wouldn't have to rush. Next year, when he'd be twelve years old, his parents wouldn't make his allowance dependent on Bible School attendance. At least that's what his dad said, and Dad didn't lie. Usually.

Jerry took a minute to hide the cards and his *Punisher* comic amid the pages of *Bible Stories and Christian Tales;* they'd give him something to think about during class.

Pausing in front of the old brick Baptist church, Jerry looked up at the steeple and watched puffy white clouds drift across the blue morning sky. In Jerry's mind that pointed spire was not a church steeple at all; it was a rocket ship aimed at Europa, one of the moons of the planet Jupiter.

He checked his watch again. No sweat. So what if Captain Finny was a few minutes late for boarding. The passengers would already be in their seats. The mission could get under way the moment he took his place at the control panel. He hoped.

Jerry walked up the huge stone steps to the church doors, confident that he walked in silence. Slowly, carefully, he opened one side of the heavy double doors and looked inside. The scent of burning candles was the odor of rocket fuel, and the vacant interior of the church told him his fellow travelers were already assembled in the seating rooms below.

If Miss Beth Damon, otherwise known as Deathdemon, wasn't teaching today, he might just get away with this late arrival. If the Deathdemon was aboard, he'd get away with nothing.

Deathdemon, that three-legged monster, had been around forever. Even when Jerry's mom and dad were kids in Baptist Bible School, Miss Damon had been there, waving her cane, insisting on punctuality. And she'd always said the same thing: "You young ones better learn to keep your appointments with the Lord. Learn it now, and you'll be better prepared for that one appointment nobody misses."

The Lord, of course, had manufactured the Deathdemon way back in the days He was kicking Satan and the boys out of Heaven. That important bit of history meant two things: first, that she was about a million years old; and second, that the Lord could still control her behavior.

With that in mind, Captain Jerry Finny offered a little prayer to the Lord, asking for a safe delivery. Now, if he could make it to the captain's chair before the Deathdemon saw him, he could spend the next forty minutes touring the universe undisturbed. If she saw him, however, there'd be hell to pay.

Most of the crew and passengers had entered through the church's side door, which led downstairs to a lengthy corridor, lined on either side with classrooms. Jerry had long ago discovered that if he went directly into the church, then downstairs through a narrow door near the altar, he would end up at the back of his classroom. Today, if he was in luck, he could dash to one of the desks in the back row while the Deathdemon was looking away, or sharpening her claws on the blackboard.

At the bottom of the narrow stairway, Jerry peeked into the classroom and his heart sank like a stone in a frog pond. There she was, her blue hair fluffed out like rancid cotton candy, her pasty, puffy face knotted in wrinkles like a piece of chewed gum, her skeleton hand clutching that ever-present walking stick. She was using her stick to point out something on the blackboard.

To Jerry, the Deathdemon's voice always sounded like the last words of a strangled chicken. "Now, children," she squawked, "what we're really talking about is *faith*. Faith helps us to believe things, even if we can't *prove* them. No matter what scientists—or even your parents or your teachers—may say, there is no *proof* of the theory of evolution, not at all. There may be *evidence*, I don't say there isn't. But—and this is for certain, boys and girls—there is absolutely no proof, none whatsoever."

Smugly, the Deathdemon turned to the blackboard and underlined the word FAITH several times. The moment her eyes left the fifteen pupils, Jerry dashed to an end seat and slouched nonchalantly, as if he had been there long enough to get bored.

He watched her turn back toward the class, studying her eyes to see if she'd spotted him. Her expression revealed nothing.

"Now, boys and girls, faith is one of the most important of God's gifts to man. You don't have to study science to have faith. You don't have to be rich or famous to have faith. In fact, boys and girls"—here she contorted her face full of wrinkles into something resembling a smile—"if you have faith, real Christian faith, there is very little else you need."

Her gaze jumped from face to face as she clobbered everybody with her creepy false-toothed smile. "I've worked with Christian youngsters for almost fifty years. No one knows better than I how much children need faith. Not *facts,* boys and girls, *faith.* Yet scientists, yes, and even educators, continue to bombard your little heads with half-truths and radical opinions. All that chips away at your belief systems like ocean water eroding rock cliffs."

Wow, thought Jerry, she's really wigging out today. He kept his Bible reader closed and his Marvel Universe cards in his pocket. Right now the Deathdemon was far more entertaining than either.

She went on: "Now, I believe you children are living in one of the worst times of all, a time of tribulation. We are living in a 'scientific' age, an age where unholy science tries to replace God's truth with its own half-truths, and its guesses, and its 'scientific demonstrations.'

"Each year hundreds—no, *thousands*—of young people just like you drift away from God's love. They sin, they blaspheme, some even say there can't be a God, there can't be a Heaven. They say they *can't* believe in these sacred things because there is no *proof!*

"That's where faith comes in handy, boys and girls. These poor dear wanderers have lost their faith. But they miss it; we can tell because they try to replace it with science, or rock and roll music, or, worst of all, drugs.

"Children, science teaches you to look for proof, it teaches you to *need* scientific truth, do you understand? Science teaches you that if something can't be proved, then it's not true. Now I'm not saying science is no good. Maybe it helps you keep your bodies healthy, perhaps learning about it even exercises your minds. But, children, science does nothing to strengthen the spirit. You may be healthy of mind and body, but if you're sick in spirit, Heaven will be lost to you."

Jerry scrunched down even farther in his seat as the Deathdemon's gaze darted from face to face, fast and random, like the metal bearing in a pinball machine. He kept his own eyes looking down, focused on his folded hands in his lap.

"Now, children," said the Deathdemon, gearing up again, "I want to talk to you about the value of prayer. I can promise you—without proof—that God understands perfectly well that Miss Beth Damon is a most loyal servant. He understands that my entire Christian life has been devoted to strengthening the spirits of His young people. I prayed, boys and girls, I prayed and I asked God, 'What do I do, Lord? They're drifting away from me . . . all those lovely little lambs, Lord. I watch them drifting, more and more of them, year after year. They've learned to want proof, dear Lord, proof of the things they need faith to understand.'"

The Deathdemon took five short tottering steps away from the blackboard. She moved around the teacher's desk and stood directly in front of Diane Bixby, who always sat, back straight, hands folded, right up in the front row.

Then the Deathdemon tucked her walking stick under her arm and stood unassisted. She picked up the Bible from Diane's desk, licked her fingers, and began flipping pages.

She whispered now, apparently confident she had everyone's attention, "And God spoke to me in my heart, boys and girls. He said to me, 'Miss Damon, the lambs need a sign.'

"And, just like anytime when I need an answer, I riffled through the pages of my Holy Book, and when it felt just right, I dropped my index finger onto the page"—she acted this out as she spoke—"and do you know what that finger pointed to, boys and girls?"

No one answered.

"No? Well, I shouldn't wonder. Listen now; I'll read it to you."

She read:

"Then Moses answered, 'But behold, they will not believe me or listen to my voice, for they will say, "The Lord did not appear to you."' The Lord said to Moses, 'What is that in your hand?' Moses said, 'A rod.' And God said, 'Cast it on the ground.' So Moses cast it on the ground, and—"

In deep concentration she looked from face to face, and whispered hoarsely, "'Moses cast his rod onto the ground, and it became . . . *a serpent!*'"

Jerry heard someone giggle as Miss Damon lifted her walking stick high above her head. The lights in the classroom seemed to dim, just a bit, hardly enough to notice, but Jerry was sure the room had suddenly become just a shade darker.

The Deathdemon held the walking stick above her head, one hand on each end. With her eyes squeezed shut, she began to speak faster than Jerry had ever heard before. "And I know you young people don't believe me so the Lord has said he'll give you a sign so you will believe what Miss Damon tells you and so you'll go home and tell your parents and you'll tell your teachers and you'll tell your friends and other little boys and girls who would stray away from the Holy Spirit of the Lord. . . ."

Jerry gripped the edge of his desk with both hands until his knuckles whitened. He gritted his teeth and looked up, openmouthed, as Miss Damon continued.

"You'll tell them all that you have seen and all you have learned." She bowed her head, dropping her chin to her chest, and she said, "God told me, 'Miss Beth Damon, you cast your rod away,'" and with that she flung her walking stick, pushing it away from her with both hands. It sailed over the heads of the motionless children.

Jerry heard his classmates gasp. He saw the stick stop in midair, directly over the head of Dickie Laymon and parallel with the floor. It hung there for a moment, suspended from nothing, until it began to rotate. Slowly at first, then the speed of rotation increased, gathering force, like the blade of a helicopter revving up.

Kids made noise. Frightened sounds. One of the girls, Linda Allen, began to cry. Miss Damon remained at the front of the room, eyes pinched shut, arms over her head, palms toward the class. "Quiet, children, quiet in the presence of the Lord."

Jerry couldn't pull his eyes from that magical stick; it righted itself now, turning like the wheel of fortune at the firemen's carnival.

The Deathdemon pointed. "Look, children! There is your proof! There is your proof of the Lord!"

Joey Arnold shrieked and ran for the door. The stick sailed like a javelin leaving an athlete's hand. It connected with the back of Joey's head—Thwap!—knocking the boy against the wall beside the coat rack. Joey lay on the floor, scrunched into an S shape, hands and arms trying to protect his bloody head from further assault.

Now the stick righted itself and stood in front of the exit, weaving ever so slightly back and forth. No visible hand held it, but it stood there just the same.

"Lord knows your sins, boys and girls. You can't hide anything from the Lord!" Miss Damon was screeching now. Linda Allen and her friend Rose sat on the floor, hugging each other and wailing. Dickie Laymon hid under his desk. Johnny Coon, Coon the goon, had his arms folded on his desktop and his face buried in the folds.

Jerry watched the cane. Now it was jumping up and down. It looked like a pogo stick with an invisible rider as it bounced down the aisle. Occasionally it paused, snapping to the right or left to whack some kid in the head.

Most of the kids were crying. Some pressed their palms tightly against their eyes and shook their heads left and right. A girl, Debbie Swale, was chanting "Nonononono."

Jerry watched the stick make its way up the center aisle, tapping loudly on the floor tiles like Long John Silver's crutch. It stopped, still standing under its own mysterious power, right beside Diane Bixby, directly in front of Miss Damon.

Diane leaned to the left, trying to get as far away as possible, yet not daring to leave her seat.

Miss Damon's fingers were linked together, pressing tightly against her solar plexus. With eyes closed, her lips moved rapidly in silent prayer.

The walking stick stopped swaying, snapped to rigid attention.

Jerry couldn't tear his eyes away. He held his breath while all the other kids got quiet at the same time.

The stick leapt into the air and started spinning like a majorette's baton. Three times in rapid succession, faster than she could move away, it struck Diane in the face.

"Sinner!" screeched Miss Damon as Diane, her nose and mouth red with blood, slumped to the floor. Jerry couldn't tell; he thought she might be dead.

The stick did cartwheels from desktop to desktop, tapping rhythmically, dancing, pausing unpredictably to rap someone in the temple.

Kids cried, screamed for their parents.

Without leaving his seat, Jerry pushed his entire desk backward a few inches at a time. Its metal legs scratched loudly on the tile floor. He could feel the vibration, but knew no one could hear it above the cries of his terrified classmates.

Now the stick had stopped whirling. It hovered parallel with the floor, a ropeless trapeze, gliding over the heads of the cowering children. It seemed to dare them to move.

Jerry pushed his desk back another inch.

Miss Damon dropped to her knees in the aisle, clenched hands against her mouth, her eyes tightly closed. "Thank you, dear Lord, for all your gifts, and for rewarding me with this magnificent display of your majesty. Thank you for the children, Lord. And thank you for your love—"

The rubber sole of Jerry's sneaker squeaked on the floor as he retreated another inch. Now he could almost make it to the rear stairway. Almost . . .

The horizontal walking stick floated toward Miss Damon. "Thank you for your love—"

Ever so gently, almost like a caress, the stick placed itself under her chin.

And leapt upward, lifting the old woman into the air, dropping her on her back atop the teacher's desk.

Jerry wasn't sure what happened next. When Miss Damon went down, he jumped up. Two rapid steps brought him to the bottom of the stairs. He risked a quick look back, just to be sure the stick wasn't following him.

What he saw was to be a puzzle etched forever on his memory.

Either the stick was lying beside Miss Damon on the desktop, resting against her leg, and partially hidden within the folds of her clothing, or—and Jerry didn't hazard a second look to make sure—it had actually transformed itself into a snake and was crawling underneath Miss Damon's skirt.

The confusing picture was vivid in his mind as he raced up the back steps and into the church.

18

Earl King

Burlington, Vermont
Monday, June 27

"Karen, your ten o'clock is here," said Laura Welsh as she peeked through the slightly opened door to Dr. Bradley's office.

Karen looked up from her newspaper. "My ten o'clock?" She glanced at her calendar. "I don't have anybody written in for ten o'clock."

Laura stepped through the door and closed it. "Oh-oh, my fault; I forgot to put it in your book, sorry. It's a Mr. Earl King. He called first thing this morning; said you'd asked him to come in."

"*I'd* asked him? I don't remember any Earl King."

"Oh boy!" Laura rolled her eyes. "What shall I do?"

"I'll see him, of course. The hour's open, and now I'm curious."

Laura flashed a grateful smile. "Thanks, you're a pal. I'll get him." She turned away and spoke to the man in the waiting room, "Please come in, Mr. King."

Karen watched the door, eager to find out about her mysterious appointment. When the man walked in, she stiffened with surprise, then anger.

Jeff Chandler closed the door and took three swift steps to the chair beside Karen's desk. "May I sit down," he said.

She nodded once and he sat. Not knowing what to say, her eyes automatically scanned him head to foot. Jeff looked much changed from the man she had met in Boston. There was no sign of the tailored three-piece suit, the styled hair, the careful professional grooming. Today he wore jeans, running shoes, and an oversize T-shirt advertising Ben and Jerry's Ice Cream. His dark hair was wild; springy curls uncoiled in every direction. He had shaved his beard, then let it grow back for a day or two, giving his face a rough, almost unsavory look.

Jeff's body language told her he was uncomfortable. It took a few moments of fidgeting before he could start talking.

"Karen," he began, "I know how you must feel. I was unforgivably rude to you on the phone the other day, and I know it. I knew it while it was happening, but I had no choice. I sincerely apologize, and if I may, I'd like to explain. Will you listen to me?"

"That's my job," she said, feeling the icy edge in her voice. Leaning back in her chair, she crossed her arms over her chest. "I'm a professional listener."

His eyes left hers as he lowered his head. "Okay, I had that coming. But can we have a cease-fire for a few minutes, at least until you hear me out?"

Karen allowed the muscles in her face to relax. "Okay."

"Thanks." He took a breath, momentarily appearing confused and hopelessly lost. Karen studied every subtle look and gesture. Something's terribly wrong, she thought.

"Wow," Jeff said. "Where to start?" His ultra-blue eyes explored the office until they again met Karen's. "Let me begin by explaining why I'm here. Remember, I told you about my work at the Massachusetts Technological Academy?"

"Sure. You debunk UFO sightings."

"Right. I do that and lots of other things as well. But UFOs make the most entertaining dinner-table conversation. They're also the most public of our many activities. In reality, the Academy is involved in all sorts of . . . well, arcane research. Most of it's highly classified. UFOs are just the visible tip of the proverbial iceberg."

Jeff stood up, paced over to the window, and looked out on the lake. "Late last week I got word that I'm being considered for some kind of promotion. Ian McCurdy, the executive director, called me in and spoke quite candidly about some of the other things the Academy is involved in. It's stuff I didn't know about, scary stuff. Scarier than I would have imagined."

"So you're not upset about the promotion, but you don't think you can be a party to these . . . other things?" Karen heard herself being the psychologist when she knew Jeff needed a friend.

"I *know* I can't. But I'm upset about the promotion, too. I'm afraid it, like everything else at the Academy, is not just exactly what it seems."

"How do you mean?"

Still facing the window, Jeff spoke, never looking at Karen. "I have a friend there, an administrative assistant. She tipped me off, told me to be careful. I think she did it because she's somewhat sympathetic to my stand on . . . certain of the Academy's policies. . . ."

Karen leaned forward, elbows on her desk, listening with greater concentration.

"While I was talking with Dr. McCurdy, I had the feeling he was sizing me up, testing me, trying to get me to tip my hand about something. He was probing into areas that have nothing to do with my skills as a researcher, administrator, or scientist. The whole interview just didn't seem to be . . . on the level."

"So what exactly did this administrative assistant tell you?"

"That she'd noticed a pattern. That promotional interviews often resulted in firings."

"Firings? Why do you think they'd fire you?"

He turned from the window to face her. "I don't fit in. I'm too much of a maverick. And I've made the mistake of articulating certain . . . ethical concerns—objections, really—about what the Academy is hiding from the general public."

Karen nodded, careful to appear interested but not too sympathetic.

"But I'm getting ahead of myself," Jeff paused, as if collecting his thoughts. "Dismissals at the Academy are rare. That's because employee compatibility is measured in advance by intense preemployment screenings followed by absurdly in-depth reference checking for security clearances. But when somebody gets the boot, believe me, it's serious business. As I understand it, firings are always sudden and normally they're a complete surprise. When they occur, the sacked employee gets a couple months severance pay and is hustled out the door."

"So why all the game playing? Why this promote or dismiss business?"

"Just a trick to get me to drop my guard. They want to find out what I really know. What I believe. How likely I am to be a thorn in their side."

"Are you hiding something?"

"No. Well, yes, in a way. No big deal. I don't have a record or anything like that. When I was in college I was into computers. I programmed a virus and set it loose in the ROTC data bank. Wiped out a lot of records, replacing them with the names of all my favorite albums. Stupid, I know. I could have been expelled. Could have been convicted. But I got off with a slap on the wrist and a good talking to. They weren't storing anything vital and had backup my virus couldn't touch."

"Does the Academy know about that?"

"Probably. But I didn't tell them. There was no conviction; it's not part of my record. Maybe McCurdy just wanted to see if I'd fess up."

"If they're not confident of you, why don't they just give you some kind of warning or put you on notice or something?"

Jeff shrugged. "Same thing as sacking computer programmers, I suppose. What if you fire one who's really into retribution? If he continues on the job, he can sabotage your operation, do stuff that'll cost you thousands of dollars to correct. He can delete irreplaceable data or disable programs, he can mess up files, input bogus information, cause all kinds of general damage that can be irreparable."

"Right, I see."

"In my case, not only do I have access to computers, but also I have access to lots of classified information unrelated to UFOs. And they know I don't go along with their secrecy. Right now they're probably thinking, What if this guy goes to the press . . . ?"

Karen stared at him for a long time. "I still don't get it, Jeff. Why avoid the inevitable? Why didn't you just report for work today? Why come here of all places?"

Jeff dropped into one of the easy chairs by the window. From her desk Karen watched him slouch, long legs stretched out in front of him, nearly horizontal. He combed his fingers through his hair.

"I didn't go in because I'm afraid."

Karen waited for him to continue. When he didn't, she prompted, "Afraid?"

"Yup. Here's something else my friend told me. About two years ago, right after I started work, a guy named Vince LoBianco was fired. He was a research assistant and not involved in the UFO project. Then last year a woman named Merrilee Hubbard resigned, a protest resignation." Jeff straightened in the chair, crossed his legs. His foot tapped nervously. "Today, both of them are dead. They died within two months of leaving the Academy. LoBianco had a heart attack. Hubbard wrapped her car around a tree."

He raised his head looking Karen in the eyes. "You're thinking, coincidence? Maybe. If not, you can see why the woman who tipped me off has taken a tremendous risk. Thank God she gave me a little time to get the hell out of Boston, to disappear. By warning me, she put a lot more than her job on the line."

"I see that, if what you say is true. But what I don't understand, Jeff, is why you came here? Why are you telling all this to me?"

Jeff tapped his fingertips together. "Karen, I didn't have time to think about it. I didn't have time to plan. On one level, I realize I may have put you in danger by coming here, but on another level, I hope to God you can help me."

Karen felt herself softening. Recognizing the outward symptoms of Jeff's tension and fear, she thought a moment before speaking. "Okay, maybe I *can* help you. Tell me how."

When Jeff blinked, relief was evident on his face. "I think there may be a couple of ways. First, you're safe; no one at the Academy even knows you exist. So they have no way of knowing you and I are acquainted. Think about it: we met by chance; there's no record that we went to dinner together; I didn't even put it in my calendar, and the restaurant doesn't take reservations. And another thing, I paid in cash—no credit card, no written transaction. I've thought about this, Karen, and I'm pretty sure there's no record that I know you or anyone at all in Vermont."

"Record? What kind of record?"

"Their so-called personnel records, in depth, highly intrusive files kept by the Academy."

"They actually keep a record of your *friends?*"

"Wow, do they keep records! They maintain extensive files that include preemployment security investigations conducted by—get this—the FBI. And the bureau continues its involvement with ongoing random checks and updates. Man, there's more people looking at us than at the Dallas cheerleaders. I know how this sounds, Karen, it sounds paranoid as hell, but it's *true.* If they ever want to find me, they can produce a list of everyone I've ever known since I was, Christ, fifteen years old."

Karen shook her head. "This . . . .this is all so . . . weird!"

"Yup. See, Karen, it was just dumb luck that you and I ran into each other, even dumber luck that we didn't leave any kind of a trail. Shortly after we had dinner, I got word what might be coming down. I didn't know how else to behave on the phone when you called. I wanted very much to talk to you; I know I was terribly rude, but I just didn't dare have a conversation. I was afraid my line was bugged, or something. This way, maybe they know I got a call, but at least I didn't let you give your name."

Karen sat quietly, studying the end of a Bic pen. Finally, "That's reason number one: I'm an ally the Academy doesn't know about. What's the other reason?"

Jeff smiled a long, sad smile. "You're a psychologist."

Karen raised her eyebrows. "What do you mean? What's that got to do with it?"

"Well, when you give me the go-ahead, I'm going to tell you the whole story. . . ."

"Yes . . .?"

"If I told it to anyone else—the police, the press, even some of my closest friends—they'd think I was nuts, totally paranoid, delusional. You, on the other hand, have the professional expertise to hear me out and diagnose that, okay, I may be a little stressed out, but I'm perfectly sane."

"And . . .?"

"And if you believe me, maybe you'll help me. Maybe we can decide what to do?"

Karen stood up and walked from behind her desk. She took a seat in the armchair across from Jeff, searching his eyes for any suggestion of deceit. "Okay, Jeff, I'm with you so far, at least I think I am. For now, anyway. But for my own piece of mind, just tell me one more thing."

"Okay. Sure."

She looked away, momentarily losing her resolve. No, she thought, I won't back down. "When I phoned you at your apartment, a woman answered . . .?"

The guilty, caught-in-the-act expression she expected didn't occur.

"That's exactly the reason I'm so scared, Karen. And it's the reason I'm running away. That 'woman' is my sixteen-year-old daughter, Casey."

"Your daughter?"

"Yeah. I'm scared for myself. Scared as hell. But I'm more scared for her. Right now she's out in the car, waiting. I haven't told her much about this, but she's a bright kid, she knows something's up. At the moment she just thinks I'm in here seeing a friend. And . . . Look, Karen, if I could leave Casey with you, just a day or two, until—"

The look on her face must have stopped Jeff midsentence. Karen hadn't been prepared for anything like this: first a fugitive friend, now the possibility of a teenager in the house.

"Oh, Jeff, I don't know. . . ."

"It's a lot to ask, I know, but—"

"Let me think about it, okay? I'll have to think about all this. But now I've got appointments. Tell you what: Can you meet me back here at the end of the day?"

Jeff nodded. He looked more than a little disappointed.

"I've just got to process this," Karen said, forcing herself to smile. "I'll let you know at five. In the meantime, I don't want you or Casey to worry. As I told you at the restaurant, any discussion with me is strictly confidential."

* * *

Hobston, Vermont

The shotgun roared.

The flying disk exploded into a cloud of white dust.

Alton Barnes placed another stack of clay pigeons into the mechanical launcher. Holding his weapon ready, he hit the switch with his foot. The white and black disk shot into the air like a bird taking off.

Alton fired. The disk burst and vanished. He launched another. *Blam!* Vaporized in a driving hail of pellets.

He was already working on his second crate of pigeons; he knew he'd run out of ammunition before the disks were gone.

By now the single barrel of his twelve-gauge pump was too hot to touch. Discharging round after round heated it up like the grill on a barbecue.

He tripped the mechanism.

Another disk sailed.

Alton fired. The gun clicked uselessly.

He pumped. Pulled the trigger.

Nothing.

No more shells. Four boxes empty. Alton checked the pockets of his pants, his jacket.

Out of ammo.

About two dozen clay pigeons remained. He seized the shotgun by the barrel, heard the sizzle of his palms on the blistering metal.

Screaming, but not letting go, Alton used the gun stock to pound the remaining disks into powder.

* * *

Burlington, Vermont.

At five o'clock, immediately following her last appointment, Karen stepped from the front door of the Lakeview Health Center. She looked around the parking lot for Jeff and Casey. After much deliberation, she was prepared to give them her decision.

Almost at once, she saw Jeff leaning from the driver's window of his Dodge Colt, waving. She saw the uncertainty in his smile.

Jeff opened the car door and got out. Karen hurried toward him.

She had no intention of equivocating. "I'd like you both to stay with me," she said with finality. "I have a guest room and a couch. I also have an awful lot more I want to hear about all this. We'll take time to sort things out and decide what to do."

Jeff seemed genuinely surprised. "Thank you," he said softly. "This is very . . . brave . . . of you."

"Yeah? I'm learning that sometimes I have to be. Besides, when you cut me off on the phone I didn't get a chance to ask my question."

"What question?"

"Never mind; there'll be plenty of time for that, later."

Without thinking, she touched his arm and kissed him briefly on the cheek. Instantly, she was aware of what she had done; oddly, she felt great about it. With that simple kiss, delivered spontaneously and with a cautious trust, a barrier between them evaporated.

They walked around the front of the car to the passenger's door. Inside, Jeff's daughter, rolled down the window and smiled at Karen. Then she extended an arm. "Hi, Dr. Bradley, I'm Casey."

Karen took her hand, smiling back. "Hello, Casey, it's nice to meet you. And please, my name's Karen."

"Oh, good. I feel like we already know each other. I mean Dad's been talking about you nonstop all the way from Boston."

Karen looked at Jeff and caught him rolling his eyes and cringing in exaggerated embarrassment.

Somewhere in the back of her mind she felt an uncomfortable tickle: why had Jeff waited until today—this morning—to tell her he had a daughter? And why had— *No! Stop it!* Karen was determined to ignore these moments of recurring suspicion. Instead, she spoke up, "Then it's only fair that you and I talk about him the minute we get a chance. Maybe we can send him out to get us a pizza for dinner."

"Yeah! That's Dad's specialty: going out for pizza."

"Hey, thanks a lot!" Jeff mugged, now mock-offended. "At least I'll know enough to buy gourmet pizza for highbrows like you two."

Casey's smile was wide and bright, her skin unblemished and silky smooth. What a beautiful girl, Karen thought, looking the teenager full in the face. Casey's lush brown hair was as curly and abundant as her father's. Her dimpled cheeks shone with a rosy blush. Her white teeth were perfect gemstones.

For a moment Karen was lost in Casey's most arresting feature—her eyes. She caught herself staring, envying them. Like bright pools of mountain water, they reflected the blue Vermont sky. In their enigmatic depths the innocence of youth mingled provocatively with the mystery of womanhood. At sixteen, Casey Chandler seemed everything Karen had never been: socially adept, poised, intelligent, and very beautiful. At that moment, Karen caught a glimpse of the girl's mother, Jeff's wife.

"How about if you two follow me home," she blurted, yanking herself from the reverie. "It's a little less than three miles from here."

"Sure," said Jeff, "but take it easy, okay. I'm not used to this big-city driving."

* * *

Checking again to be sure the Colt was behind her, Karen drove south along North Avenue, parallel with Lake Champlain. Farther south, traffic had bottle-necked beside Battery Park, where bumper-to-bumper commuters ignored panoramic lake views and a profile of the Adirondack Mountains beyond.

Waiting at the red light, Karen looked at the park. Afternoon loungers were scattered like worshipers at the foot of a giant carved wooden Indian. White walkways sliced acres of lush green grass. Pretty young mothers pushed strollers or held hands with bowlegged toddlers. In a rusty flash, an Irish Setter jumped and bit a Frisbee out of the sky.

A horn blared. Karen looked at her rearview mirror and saw Jeff grinning and pointing at the green light.

Slowly, the two-vehicle convoy continued down Battery Street. They passed clothing stores, delis, florists, boat shops, and souvenir vendors. Bright-colored signs beckoned throngs of balloon-carrying kids. Young women in baggy shorts walked beside short-sleeved, khaki-clad men. Anyone not carrying an ice-cream cone or frozen yogurt was sure to have a camera or binoculars. Karen hoped the festive atmosphere of Vermont's Queen City would appeal to Jeff and his daughter.

Soon, a stretch of new blacktop signaled the road to Karen's house.

Checking once more for the Chandlers, she led them down Colonial Lane, which skirted scenic Burlington Bay. An extra-wide, recently constructed covered bridge brought them over the Vermont Railway tracks to the landscaped grounds of Colonial Condominiums.

Each unit was assigned one division of a long garage built to resemble a carriage house. An additional parking space, numbered 37 to match Karen's home, was closer to the condo's walkway. Karen directed Jeff to the space, then she parked in the garage.

She grabbed her briefcase and crossed the roadway to help Jeff and Casey with their luggage. Casey remained in the car when Jeff got out. He pulled his seat forward so he could remove a conical package of green waxed paper.

"Here, Karen," he said, "these are for you." His blue eyes twinkled.

"Jeff, thank you!" She folded back the paper, revealing a bouquet of roses. "Oh, they're beautiful!"

"I wanted to surprise you, but there's no way I could've smuggled them inside."

"But they *are* a surprise! No one's ever—"

It was true: no man had ever given Karen flowers. Again she kissed him on the cheek, this time deliberately. "That's awfully sweet of you, of both of you. Thanks so very much."

He pulled a canvas suitcase from the back seat and put it on the asphalt. Beside it he placed his briefcase, and a smaller traveling bag.

Karen watched as he unlocked the Colt hatchback. It sprung open like a mouth. Jeff removed a blanket that covered something bulky. Soon he was wrestling with an odd plastic and aluminum contraption with wheels. As he lifted it from the car, Karen guessed it was some kind of collapsible bicycle.

When Jeff pulled the arms apart the object took on a more recognizable shape. It was a wheelchair.

He rolled it to the passenger's side. While Casey pushed the car door open, Jeff positioned the chair and locked the brakes against its rubber wheels.

With her father steadying the door, Casey turned to the right and slid toward the edge of the seat. When she got both legs out the door, her feet dropped limply to the ground. Then, with one hand atop the door, the other gripping the back of her seat, she quickly, somehow gracefully, transferred from car to wheelchair.

With Karen holding her roses, briefcase, and the overnight bag, and with Jeff carrying his attaché and suitcase, they walked on either side of Casey as she wheeled herself toward Karen's door.

* * *

Dr. Lloyd Sparker paused outside Beth Damon's hospital room. He didn't want to go inside. He didn't want to talk to her. For a moment he closed his eyes, bracing himself for a difficult conversation. This could be tougher than last night's consultation with Jake Townshend and his wife. "I hate to have to tell you this, Jake, but that cancer you got, it's gonna kill you."

Sparker opened his eyes and peeked around the door. If she was awake, he would have to talk to her about leaving the hospital. Medicare wouldn't pay for many more days of in-house treatment. So, what was he going to do with Miss Beth Damon? She wasn't strong enough, or—he had to admit it—lucid enough to be released to her own care.

Dr. Sparker looked at the chart again. The space beside "Next of kin?" was a blank. The poor old woman had remained unmarried all her life. No husband. No children. No family left at all. Now there was no one to take care of her but the state. If he discharged her, chances were she'd be taken into some kind of custody until the Bible School incident could be fully investigated. A rest home, a mental health facility, or a jail. All options seemed equally bleak.

On tiptoes, in the half-light of the hospital room, he approached the bed.

"Miss Damon?" he whispered.

Her eyes were partly open, only the whites showed between wrinkled parchment lids. A plum-dappled hand stirred atop the white sheet like a spider waking. Her tongue poked at the dry corner of her toothless mouth.

He took her hand. "Can you hear me, dear?"

Her lips seemed to pucker. "Lloyd?" He could barely hear her.

"That's right, Miss Damon. I'm right here with you."

Her eyelids flicked up and down like curtains blowing in a window. She couldn't keep them open.

"Lloyd, you tell 'em for me. Lloyd . . .?"

"Tell them what, love?"

"You tell 'em that I never hurt those young ones. You tell 'em I'd never do a thing like that."

"Don't you worry, I'll tell 'em. But I think they know that." It was a lie. Last Friday Miss Damon had been loved by the entire community. Now, Sparker knew, some of the townspeople were asking for revenge. What had happened to all the love, the tolerance, the Christian forgiveness? It was a question Sparker had asked himself many times, about many things.

Her hand was cold in his. She lay quietly for a moment, then: "I can't go back there, not now I can't."

"Back where, Miss Damon?"

"To the church. You know . . . back home to Hobston."

"'Course you can. You just gotta get some strength back first. That's all."

"All my life in the church. So many years. A whole lifetime of prayin' and teachin' His word."

"You've been a treasure, dear. Folks love you for what you've done."

"No. They think I hurt their children. I didn't. But all my life . . . all my life as a God-fearin' Christian woman . . . It simply wasn't enough, Lloyd."

"Enough for what, Miss Damon?"

"To gain the strength of spirit." She blinked. A single tear found a wrinkle below her right eye, followed it down, rolled into the wispy hair above her ear. "I just wasn't strong enough to protect those young ones, Lloyd. I just wasn't strong enough to keep the devil away from 'em."

Her hand tensed in his, then relaxed. "Miss Damon?"

Her eyes closed. Her chest sank . . .

"Miss Damon?"

. . . and she died.

19

Time to Kill

McCurdy walked along Newbury Street toward the Public Garden. His gaze jumped furtively from shadow to shadow as he fought the claustrophobic impression that he was trapped in a narrow canyon with high brownstone walls. Dark, disturbingly motionless automobiles lined the curbs like tumbled boulders. Street lamps and lighted windows gave the sidewalk a semblance of perpetual twilight. He was in a familiar place, but it was an alien world.

The night air, hot and still, was an uncomfortable contrast with the Academy's controlled climate. He'd walked less than a quarter mile; already sweat greased his forehead and clouded his eyeglasses. Taking off his sweater wasn't a consideration; if he did, he'd have to carry it. It was better to keep his hands empty and his mind alert.

The restful hum of air conditioners in upstairs windows gave way to a siren's wail. On the corner of Arlington Street, across from the Ritz Carlton, somebody's auto alarm screeched. Yet, it attracted no one's attention. The alarm could as well have been a rape victim's scream, or the cry of an old man being beaten.

Someday all this will change.

Day or night, it didn't matter, the city of Boston was always the same. The streets were rotten with crime, more every day, spreading godless filth like a putrefying contagion. McCurdy saw it clearly, without benefit of newspapers or television. Evil was growing; rearing its hideous head unchallenged, its deep obsidian eyes, cool, its Latin accent whispering threats.

On Boylston Street, near a hedge, an elderly man, unsteady as a toddler, stepped out of the shadows. He was pissing in the bushes, McCurdy thought.

The old man, his arms full of plastic shopping bags, staggered and swayed.

If he asks for money, McCurdy thought, I'll give it to him. But he didn't. He stumbled past, eyes cast down. When McCurdy turned to take another look, the old man was gone.

A cab went by; one of its headlights was broken. A limo followed, its windows tinted dark, its interior invisible, its occupant anonymous. Perhaps some wealthy lawyer cruising for girls. Or a fat North End don with some *melanzana* bitch sucking his lap, sharpening vampire teeth on his zipper.

McCurdy clicked his tongue.

He glanced at his watch: oh two hundred hours. And suddenly the street was empty.

For a long frozen moment the world was quiet and deserted, just as it should be at this time of night. There was a warm wind, scented vaguely with seawater. He sauntered across Tremont—*no hurry*—carefully staying within the designated crosswalk.

On the sidewalk in front of some Chinese fast-food place a cop scraped the sole of his boot against the curb. McCurdy could almost hear him cursing unleashed mutts.

Ever since he'd been a child in South Boston, McCurdy had fancied that the city held two populations. And that's the way it used to be, really. Daytimers and Nighttimers, he called them. Entirely different races that never met because they never occupied the city at the same time. It was as if there were two different worlds, different universes maybe, completely dissimilar but forever identical in the one place they intersected—the city of Boston.

The Daytimers were the people McCurdy knew, and the people he remembered from his Southie childhood. Some were men in dark suits—politicians and bureaucrats—who walked to the trolley. Others carried black barn-shaped lunch boxes (dinner pails, his dad had called them). The latter might stop for a newspaper, the former to buy a flower for his lapel.

Daytimers said *good morning!* to the merchants who emerged at daybreak from their tiny shops like squinting groundhogs from their burrows.

Daytimers drove the ice-cream trucks, or juggled bowling pins on the Common. They went to church, cheered at Fenway, walked their kids to school, and coached Little League in the summertime.

It had been their city and it had been grand.

Then little by little the Nighttimers intruded like a rising and polluted tide. The days seemed to grow shorter, the shadows farther reaching. And the warning signs arrived before the Nighttimers came: wind-lashed litter danced in schoolyards; rushing air blasted stench from subways; dark-skinned men with barely human faces dispensed liquor from the trunks of battered Cadillacs, or bought and sold adolescent girls using white plastic packages for currency.

"Gimmi dollah, man."

McCurdy started, stepping around the black man in the woolen navy coat. The crazy ones always dressed for winter on the hottest nights. *They don't feel things the same way we do. Not them. Not the Nighttimers, not the soulless ones.*

Jake Wirth's was closed at this hour, its doors and windows locked away, safe behind metal webbing. McCurdy walked past this final symbol of civilization, securely caged until the dawn.

And he entered the last circle of hell—the Combat Zone.

It was midday under garish neon suns. The whores were here, and the sailors, and the college kids looking for trouble. Huge windows that once displayed furs or finery now screeched with crude hand-stenciled signs: "Everything Half Off," "Checks Cashed," "Live Dancing Girls." There were dildoes and stroke books, magazines in cellophane, martial arts weapons. And videotapes, their packaging ersatz-tasteful with black censor-circles separating pursed lips from pimpled bottoms. Leather mysteries hung like hides on a rack, sun-faded bedroom ware hid the firm torsos of headless mannequins. Topless, McCurdy thought. A windowful, an eyeful.

"Hey, man, want some lovin'?" Was it a man's voice or a woman's? McCurdy scurried across the street to avoid finding out.

A giant spotted cat winked its neon eye from the far side of the street. *The Polka Dot Pussy.* A big black man with tattooed arms crossed upon his chest stood beside the door. He partially obstructed a glass panel where nude photos of timpani-titted temptresses beckoned indiscriminately. "Must be 18," a peeling sign reminded.

As McCurdy hurried by, loud music belched from the bowels of the cat.

More windows ahead. Rap booths. Adult movies. Live sex shows.

"Step right in, m'man," grinned the silver-toothed hustler outside The Golden Ring. The window sign offered "Fantastic Fighting Foxes." Beside it, a poster-size photo of a blonde in striped micro-shorts, her breasts bigger than her boxing gloves, smiled enticingly. Above it, a hand-lettered sign said, "This girl can't wrestle, but cum in and see her box."

A sailor staggered out of the next doorway, almost colliding with McCurdy. The lurching man steadied himself against the side of a parked van and threw up against the windshield.

The driver, a skinny spic in bell-bottoms, got out, grabbed the sailor by the epaulets, and threw him to the sidewalk. One swift kick, and the sailor puked again.

Nighttimers, McCurdy thought. The soulless ones.

Two black women stood on a street corner talking in loud staccato voices and waving at the infrequent passing cars. "Com'on, Daddy. Two fo'da price a one," McCurdy heard one of them say. His eyes rested a moment on her purple, high-heeled boots.

When he turned away a man was in his path.

McCurdy stopped short.

The haggard specimen made no move to get out of the way. Slack-jawed, lips crusted with sputum, he stared at McCurdy with vapid, nearly dead eyes. The long greasy hair on the right side of his head was swept back. The left side grew wild and sparse, as if someone had pulled it out by the fistful. A scabby scalp glistened like Vaseline underneath.

In the hot moist air the man's stench of urine and filth was almost powerful enough to push McCurdy back. He turned aside, forced to detour around the standing garbage. Garbageman, McCurdy thought.

Before McCurdy could walk away, the man spoke. "Spare a half, Doctor?"

"No . . . I . . ." McCurdy arced around him, about to hasten away. Then he stopped.

He called me Doctor. How did he know?

McCurdy turned. Squinting, he searched the dirt-streaked face for some recognizable feature. The man was smiling oddly. Missing front teeth seemed to hold the squirming tongue at bay. The bulbous nose was a crimson weavework of burst capillaries.

Chuckling, the man reached down to the curbside for half a cigarette. He broke off the filter, tossed it away, and popped the remainder into his mouth.

McCurdy's stomach lurched wetly when the man began to chew the tobacco.

"You come with me now, Doctor." The man's voice was gruff, garbled. "Tonight's your night. It's time for us to meet. Come on. I want to lead you away from here."

McCurdy didn't move as the man turned away. Streaks of some slippery-looking brown substance smeared the back of the man's shapeless, ill-fitting trousers. A pint flask, brown paper twisted around its neck, protruded from a hip pocket.

The man didn't look back. "Come on now, Doctor. Your time's a-wastin'."

McCurdy couldn't believe his eyes. His ears were lying to him, too. How could he follow? Was this some kind of undercover operation? Could this be the man with whom he'd corresponded via the computer? Was this his contact?

"Wait."

The man stopped, turned. Now he wasn't smiling.

Somewhere, a car door slammed and McCurdy jumped. The man glared at him. "You're not cooperating, Dr. McCurdy. We can't talk here. You were informed we would meet. Now you must come with me."

"But I . . . You—"

"Enough. Come now. We have work to do."

"But first . . . Wait. Don't you have some kind of—"

"Identification?" The smile was back. It was thin, tight, deadly as a razor. "No. None at all. I'm homeless. Nameless. Without hope. But in a moment you'll have little doubt who I am. Come. Walk with me. I'll explain."

McCurdy took a guarded step. The next one came easier, and in a moment he was beside the man as they made their way north on Washington Street. "Where we going?

"My house. Come on. Just follow me."

"Why?" McCurdy slowed his pace ever so slightly.

"I want to tell you things," the man said. "Things about yourself." He spat on the sidewalk. "It is important for you to see how well I know you. Quite possibly as well as you know yourself. I've studied you a long time."

They were walking swiftly enough so that the man's acrid odor was not so nauseating.

Turning left, there was an unlighted, trash-littered alleyway between the old Flynn Theater and St. Catherine's Roman Catholic Church. The garbageman stepped into the lush shadows, but McCurdy held back. Without turning, without looking over his shoulder, the man said, "Come now. Almost there."

"Where are you taking me?" The shadows in the alley loomed thick and deep. The smells were foul.

"Church. We're going to church. Don't be afraid."

McCurdy watched as his companion hunkered down and lifted a rectangular metal mesh from the cellar window of St. Catherine's. Uneasily, McCurdy hovered over him, bending down just a little. He could see the three-paned cellar window was nailed shut. The man took the head of one of the loose-fitting nails in his fingertips, and pulled it out of the wooden frame. The nail moved easily, like a bolt in a lock. He pulled out a second nail and the window swung up. Carefully, he placed the nails on the windowsill.

"You're probably not used to going to church my way," the man said with a soft, noncommittal chuckle. Then he slithered through the two-foot opening.

A crippling, immobilizing fear seized McCurdy. It would be so easy to turn and run. He could be back at the Academy in twenty minutes, or he could hail a cab and be home in half an hour. But this—unlikely

as it seemed—was his contact. This was the man he'd been waiting to
meet. Duty overrode fear as McCurdy sat on the ground and slid his
feet through the open window.

* * *

The great, brass-piped organ was directly below the steeple. On
either side of the three-tiered keyboard, light oak panels of wainscoting
connected the organ to the wall, making it appear that the instrument
were solidly and forever built into the structure of the church.

The man slid a panel of wainscoting aside, revealing a passageway
that led behind the organ. Work space for repairmen, McCurdy
thought.

"Gimme a match," the man said.

McCurdy fished around in the pocket of his cardigan for his
lighter. The garbageman took it, lighted it. Using it as a torch, he led
McCurdy through the sliding wooden door and into the tight
passageway.

The area behind the organ was the size of a closet. At a glance,
McCurdy guessed the total floor space was no more than three feet by
eight feet. Coffin-sized. The hideaway reeked of tobacco smoke and the
sour scent of mildewed fabric.

It was obvious that the man lived here in this claustrophobic nest.
A pile of ratty blankets formed the vague shape of a bed on the floor.
Stuffed plastic bags passed for pillows. Near the head of the bed, on
top of an overturned milk crate, two stubby candles occupied red glass
holders. No doubt stolen from the altar. An open box of Blue Diamond
matches lay equidistant between the candles.

Here and there, litter—McDonald's bags, plastic foam boxes, and
empty plastic cups—suggested meals were taken here, meals no doubt
salvaged from the trash cans of the Combat Zone.

The man lit the candles and returned McCurdy's lighter. Then he
motioned for McCurdy to sit on the floor.

"We'll be safe here," the man said, the jagged nail of his right index
finger picking at an infected-looking pimple on the lobe of his right ear.
"They don't open the church till nine in the morning, so we got time.
And it's quiet here. We got the whole place to ourselves."

McCurdy sat on the wooden floor, avoiding contact with the filthy
blankets. He studied the man's face in the pulses of candlelight. If the
garbageman was wearing a disguise, it was an awfully good one.
Stringy hair dangled limp and filthy around a face wild with whiskers,
slashed with grime. Eyes, lifeless and discolored, teeth and gums, a
brown, pulpy mass. And the smell, the odor of human waste and
decay, surely it was something impossible to fake.

The man spoke in a hoarse whisper. "You were in the war, a fighter pilot in Vietnam. There, you had a religious experience. Am I right?"

McCurdy nodded, very much on his guard.

"What you saw there is not important to our discussion or to the work we must do. But let me say simply that it is your religious conviction that makes you ideally suited for your role at the Academy. The work you do there must be tempered by a strong Christian spirit. It is dangerous work, as you well know; it requires a sound mind and a sturdy Christian soul. What you are doing with your electronic equipment would not have been possible at any other time in history. That it can be done now marks a whole new step in human development. Would you agree with me?"

Again McCurdy nodded. His stomach had contracted into a tight, lumpy knot. He was sweating and his mouth tasted strongly of copper. For a moment he thought he was going to faint.

The man settled back against the wall, stretching his legs out in front of him. McCurdy could see the holes in the soles of his mismatched shoes.

"Your theories about the degeneration of mankind are not far from wrong. What's happening to the human race is a problem of numbers, really. There are more people now than ever before. I mean the number of people alive right now, as we speak, by far outnumbers all those who have ever been born, and who died throughout the entire history of this planet. And soul, Dr. McCurdy, soul is a commodity of which there is a precious limited supply. In short, for way too long there just hasn't been enough of it to go around."

McCurdy's head reeled. How could this man know about soul? McCurdy had never shared this theory with anyone.

"Do you believe that, Dr. McCurdy?"

McCurdy cleared his throat. "Ah . . . believe what?"

"That soul is quantifiable. That it is in limited supply. That there is nowhere near enough of it to go around. That it is a precious resource that has been shamefully squandered."

"I've . . . ah, well, I've considered it."

"And if it is true, would you agree that it is therefore possible for certain people to be born with too little of it to be called human? Would you say it is possible that some individuals are born with none at all? That they can mature, mate and marry, then give birth to generations of soulless progeny?"

McCurdy had secretly considered all these things, but he had never spoken of them, not to his father, not to Rev. McNaughton, not to the other members of the congregation. And hearing them spoken aloud made McCurdy realize how eccentric they sounded.

"Is this a difficult question for you, Dr. McCurdy?"

Still, he didn't answer. Nonetheless, it had always been clear to him: if soul is the quality that can make human beings divine, then the absence of soul is the only thing that could explain the rabid growth of evil in the world. Terrorists, serial killers, preteen murderers, opportunistic politicians. The soulless ones. The Nighttimers.

Without soul there can be no incentive to accomplish good works, no possibility of redemption, no chance for earning divinity.

"Dr. McCurdy . . . ?"

The walls of the little cubicle seemed to close in on him. The candle appeared to lose its light. Suddenly the humid heat was unbearable. McCurdy tapped his fingertips against his knee. His eyes darted from side to side. He swallowed rapidly, feeling his gorge rising. How could this man know his unspoken thoughts? How?

A series of memories presented themselves in a revealing sequence: in McCurdy's mind the Combat Zone was a vision of Hell on earth, something he was compelled to study, night after night on his aimless walks among the Nighttimers. Yet this man had said, "I want to lead you away from here."

Then he had taken him to what he described as "My house." Only it was a church.

And now the stranger was articulating some of McCurdy's deepest, most carefully protected suspicions.

Without changing visibly, the soiled and homely face suddenly took on a different light. And suddenly McCurdy was in his plane above bamboo shacks and rice fields. Below, the brown earth exploded into churning smoky mushrooms. Machine guns spat and charges erupted. Jet engines roared like dragons as again McCurdy rolled out of a dense cloud and soared toward the blue-black heavens.

And again he saw the light, the brilliant white flaming pillar that divided the horizon like a slice cut out of the sky. *A vision. I'm having a vision!* It was then—way back in 1969—that he had seen the face of God.

And now he knew the stranger across from him. "What would you like me to do?" he whispered.

* * *

Burlington, Vermont

Karen stared in terror at the television screen.

The black and white videotaped image had all the newsreel immediacy of a Fredrick Weisman documentary.

She had watched the image of the masked, black-suited men as they tied the naked prisoner to a heavy wooden chair, watched the white-clad medic tape the sensor wires to the captive's skin, heard the electronically altered voice introduce the tethered Denny LaChance and read off his list of crimes.

And the recorded demonstration began.

When LaChance started to twitch, Karen felt ill. Bile sloshed against the back of her throat. She had to swallow rapidly to keep it down.

When he convulsed as if hit by a million volts of electricity, she looked away and reached for her gin and tonic. By the time LaChance bit off his tongue, Karen was in tears, her eyes hidden in her hands.

"Turn it *off*," she said, jumping to her feet. Before Jeff could find the remote, she had crossed the room. Just prior to hitting the TV's OFF button she noticed viscous liquid from LaChance's exploded eyeballs running down his cheeks, blending with the black blood surrounding his mouth.

Karen flicked the switch and the TV screen went dead.

"That's awful, Jeff. It's . . ." her voice was uneven, wracked by stifled sobs. "I've never seen anything so . . . so horrible."

Jeff walked closer, extending his arms to embrace her, but she pulled away.

"I don't care if he is a criminal," she said, "how could anyone do something like that to another human being?"

"I warned you it would be rough, Karen, but I had to let you see it. You *have* to understand what I'm so panicked about."

She used the paper napkin from under her gin and tonic glass to dry her eyes. The ring of moisture felt cool and good against her face. Then she sat down, trying to compose herself. She thought of Casey, sleeping in the spare room. How fortunate the girl was not aware of the ghastly research her father was involved in.

Hyperventilating, Karen wrestled with the urge to shout at Jeff, to tell him that he'd have to wake Casey and leave at once. How dare he involve her, not to mention his own daughter, in something like this? How dare he just bulldoze into her life and force her to watch something so grotesque, so inhuman?

Her anger, she knew, was born of a deep-rooted, bone-crushing fear. If only she didn't have to see, didn't have to *witness*, that such inhumanity existed. She felt sick. Sick in her heart, sick in her soul. She had never seen anyone suffer and die so violently. Swimming somewhere in her vague memory she recalled a news broadcast from the Vietnam war era. It involved a Vietnamese officer putting a pistol against the head of some skinny pajama-clad soldier and blowing him away, executing him with a single merciful bullet. The victim dropped out of sight and it was done. Ugly as it was, at least it had been quick. What she had watched tonight seemed to go on and on. It was torture.

"Where did you get that awful tape?"

"I told you, Karen, I took it from Skipp McCurdy's office. I stole it. I knew I would have to have some proof."

"W-what did they do to him? Was it electrocution or what?"

Jeff sat beside her on the couch. She fought the urge to get up and move away from him.

"I don't think it was electrocution."

"The wires . . .?"

"Just as they said, sensors. They recorded his vital signs and brain wave activity while they were killing him."

"Couldn't it have been a trick?"

"I don't—"

"Maybe they staged the whole thing, maybe the whole thing is bogus?"

"It would be great if that were true."

"You believe it, Jeff? You really believe they killed him with . . . with . . ."

"Magic."

Karen started to cry again, this time it came in great heaving sobs. "No, no it can't be. They poisoned him before he sat down, or . . . or . . . maybe they really did use those wires to electrocute him. How do you know they didn't? Huh, Jeff? How do you know for sure?"

Jeff rested his hand on her shoulder. This time she let it remain. He spoke quietly but insistently. "All I know is what McCurdy told me about what the Academy is up to.

"Look, Karen, I know how whacked out all this must sound. It smacks of witchcraft, and voodoo, and Indian magic, and all the other stuff our parents and teachers told us just *can't* be real. But the trouble is, it *is* real. I can't deny it; you have to stop denying it.

"The Academy has been using that damn computer to gather all sorts of magical data from all around the world: old, new, the well known and the seemingly insignificant. Everything. Crazy or not, that's McCurdy's million-dollar idea. And he was able to explain it convincingly enough to sell our government the kind of bill of goods that earned him a multimillion-dollar research grant.

"See, McCurdy believes in magic as much as he believes in God. And he believes that all the age-old magical beliefs might each hold a certain amount of magical *truth*. It makes a weird kind of sense: every culture in the history of mankind has had a tradition of magic. And within cultures there have always been subcultures, sects, and secret societies, all carrying some small part of a great body of hidden wisdom. How can something that is completely bogus have such staying power?"

"But, Jeff, how can you honestly—"

"Believe it? I'm not sure that I do. Not completely. But try this on: chemistry evolved out of alchemy, right? Astronomy is astrology all grown up. Maybe the arcane forces we refer to as *magical* conform readily to natural laws we just aren't aware of yet. Maybe McCurdy will be remembered as the terrible genius of the twentieth century who brought magic out of the closet and put it into the classroom. In any event he's succeeded in putting it on America's defense budget right along with psychic warfare and flying saucer research."

Karen heard herself sigh pathetically. She felt as if she wanted to hide and cry and forget everything that had happened today. She felt as if she wanted Jeff to take her in his arms and tell her it was all some great big joke, a campfire story designed to scare her half to death before she crawled into the snug security of her sleeping bag.

She glanced at the clock on the mantel. Thirty minutes after one o'clock in the morning. No wonder she was feeling so fragile—she was tired. Tired, but not sleepy. "Okay, Jeff," she said slowly, trying to control her voice, "one thing at a time. First, how do you know that tape is on the level?"

He got up, walked over to his open briefcase. He removed a file and brought it to Karen. "Here," he said, "this is a photocopy of the autopsy report. Look at it. Check out the cause of death."

Karen's eyes quickly found the entry in question, then raced over the typed pages for something that would argue with the medical doctor's conclusion.

After a while she closed the folder and handed it back to Jeff. "I'm sorry, Jeff," she said. Now her voice was stern and cold. "I just cannot believe this. It's impossible. It's a joke or a plot of some kind. This just cannot be true. No. No way."

She shook her head and, when Jeff took the file, crossed her arms defiantly.

"It *is* unbelievable. I admit that, Karen, but I have no choice but to believe it's true. Before the doctor performed the autopsy he found no cuts on the body, no intrusions whatsoever. Nothing at all. Nowhere. But when he opened the chest the heart was gone. Believe it, Karen, the man's heart vanished from his chest!"

* * *

Boston, Massachusetts

They walked up and down the aisles of the church. The tap of McCurdy's leather-soled shoes echoed ominously in the hollow of the vast marble-floored sanctuary. Lights from outside cast the silhouette of wire mesh against the muted colors of twelve stained-glass windows. Before the altar, rows of candles burned in red glass holders. Above, soft indirect lighting illuminated the great carved crucifix. On either side there were statues: to the left, the Virgin Mary; at right, St. Joseph holding the baby Jesus.

"A great change is coming," the stranger said to Ian McCurdy. "Until the millennium, God's presence will be felt upon the earth. It is time for a miracle, a vast and monumental change only hinted at in Revelations. It will be a time that will purge the soulless ones and bring God's children back to the altar of the Lord. There is much to be done, and I warn you, these will be the most difficult of times. But the help you can offer will be the greatest of all."

"I will do what I can, of course . . ."

"What we ask will not be easy. You have been given two visions, Dr. McCurdy. You have seen the filth of this world, and you have never been seduced by it. And you have seen the face of the Lord. You realize now that this is a drastic time that will require drastic measures . . .?"

"Yes."

"Have you ever killed anyone, Doctor?"

"Killed anyone? I . . . I was in the war. A fighter pilot—"

"A personal killing, Dr. McCurdy . . .?"

"The demonstration for the Pentagon, I did the programming; I pulled the switch, I—"

"But that was *with* the sanction of your government. What about on your own? Have you looked your victim in the eye? Offered him the chance to plead? Killed him face-to-face, taking his life in your hands?"

"No. Never like that. That's . . . well, wouldn't that be murder?"

"Murder? Hardly. Remember, the children of God do not die, Dr. McCurdy. They are reborn. Only the soulless ones die. And you cannot murder that which is not human. The soulless ones are not the children of the Lord."

"I'm not sure I could—"

The man rounded on McCurdy. "You *must* be sure. You must *know*." He took a breath, paused before resuming his pacing, shoulder to shoulder with McCurdy. Then softly, "If a Christian would willingly die for his God, wouldn't he kill for his God just as readily?"

"I don't . . . I'm not . . ."

The man stopped, turned slowly, looked McCurdy in the eyes. He put a dirt-smeared palm on McCurdy's shoulder. "You will be tested. You must prepare yourself for killing, Doctor. It is the Will and the Way."

McCurdy blinked back the panic that threatened to push tears into his eyes. He never thought it would be like this. His mind raced, struggling to understand. "Kill who?"

"The first, to see that you can. Then others when the time comes."

"But—"

"But why? Is that what you wish to know? To return God's kingdom to the earth. It's simple."

"I . . ."

"You don't believe me, do you? Yet you pride yourself on being a believer. You feel you are better than the rest, one of the elect, or so you think. You fancy you're one who feels personal outrage at the state of the world. But after all your rhetoric, after your research at the Academy, and after all your Sunday mornings filling up a pew, you really don't believe, do you, Dr. McCurdy?"

"I—"

"Tell me if you believe!"

"I—"

"Tell me!"

McCurdy whirled away from him and let himself fall onto the hard wooden pew. "I do believe." His voice was strained and cracking.

The stranger sat down beside him. Oddly, McCurdy was aware of the scent of rose petals, not the biting stench of this street person's breath as he whispered directly into McCurdy's face, "I know. I know you do."

Side by side, still as statues in the gloomy interior of the church, the men sat quietly for a while. Finally, when he felt composed, when he was confident he could speak evenly and well, McCurdy said, "Who must I kill?"

The man smiled with infinite patience in his sad soft eyes. "Me," he answered. "You must kill me."

Something seized up in McCurdy's chest as if an icy fist had clenched his heart. Sweat like bullets pushed through his skin.

"Now," the man whispered. "You must kill me now."

Some unfamiliar reflex, one McCurdy had never experienced before, propelled him from the pew. Panting, nearly breathless, he stood in the center aisle of the church glaring down at the changing face of the stranger.

It was as if a tiny spotlight illuminating the man's features were instantly extinguished. Tight skin stretching across his forehead relaxed into deep furrows. A webwork of wrinkles appeared around his eyes; the eyelids fell to half-mast; the eyeballs reddened. His smiling mouth drooped, became shapeless. Thick liver-purple lips quivered spastically. A glistening sliver of drool hid itself within the whiskered creases of the chin.

And the posture changed. It was as if the force that had controlled his limbs, allowing him to meander around the church at McCurdy's side, had suddenly abandoned him.

The man growled something incoherent and slumped in the pew.

McCurdy took another step backward, again responding to that novel reflex of revulsion. Could it be some atavistic reaction to the strange, the alien, the supernatural? Was this how our ancestors felt when they witnessed bolts of fire in the sky, or looked up, quaking in terror, as the black moon passed before the sun? Or might this be how men felt in the proximity of a spirit, a demon, or during some angelic visitation? Did Bernadette at Lourdes experience terror before the peace had come?

Now the odor of rank alcohol was ripe in the church, intensified by the stink of the man's fear. Crablike, the garbageman slid along the polished wooden bench, backing away from McCurdy. A trembling hand grappled in his back pocket for the paper-wrapped pint of liquor.

"Who dahell're you?" he slurred. "Wha dahell you doin' in nere?"

McCurdy shook his head, alarmed by the transformation.

"You da priest innis place? You da fahdah?"

The drunk's back pressed against the side of the pew; his knees pulled up—fetuslike—for protection. Even in his terror, he gulped from the bottle.

"It's okay," McCurdy said quietly, "it's okay, I won't hurt you."

The man's eyes widened, pupils darted back and forth. He could push himself no more tightly against the corner of the wooden pew.

McCurdy took a seat at the other end of the bench, a good six feet away from the cowering man. "Yes," he said, "yes, I'm the priest. Don't be afraid."

The package slipped from the man's trembling hand. McCurdy heard the muffled explosion when the bagged glass burst against the marble floor.

"I didn't take nothin', Fahdah. I jes' come in from owside. Tha's all. I jes' come in from owside."

McCurdy slid a little closer to him. "That's okay," he said, "everyone is welcome here."

The terror in the man's face didn't relax. As McCurdy slid another foot closer, the man shifted in his seat. Now his feet were on the floor.

He tried to get up, one hand on the back of his pew, the other on the pew in front of him. The man was obviously weak; he had trouble rising to his feet.

When McCurdy stood up the man recoiled. Legs unsteady, backing toward the aisle, he almost toppled. His foot connected with the fallen bottle, slid on the wet floor beneath the shattered glass. He stumbled. When his legs shot out from under him, he fell. The back of his head smacked hard against the floor.

"Ohh!" he cried. His hands jumped to his skull. "Oh God, ohhh."

Rocking back and forth on the marble floor, he hugged his head with his hands. "Oh my head. . . . Oh God, id durts."

McCurdy stood over him, looking down at the pitiful face contorted in agony. The man's eyes darted back and forth. He blinked once. Again. "Fahdah, good God help me, Fahdah. I can't see. Oh God, I can't see!"

"There, there," McCurdy said soothingly, kneeling by the writhing man. "You've hit your head, that's all. You're stunned. You'll be all right in a minute. Try to relax now."

"My eyes. Oh God, I'm blind."

"Take your hands away from your eyes, now. That's right." McCurdy let his fingertips rest against the man's temples. He could feel blood pulsing rapidly. "Relax now. You'll be okay in a minute. That's it, relax."

McCurdy passed his hand over the sightless eyes, watched their wild rotation in slightly different directions. "That's right, settle down. Stretch your legs out. That's it. Yes. Try to be comfortable. Okay now, take a deep breath . . ."

The man's breathing slowed. He dropped his arms to his sides. "Fahdah, I'm not gonna be blind, am I, Fahdah?"

"No. You'll be fine. Close your eyes, now. That's right, good. Just keep them closed a moment while I say a little prayer."

The man stopped thrashing and struggled to lay very still.

"Dear Father in Heaven, take pity on this unfortunate servant . . ."

Tears slid from beneath the closed eyelids. Now the vagrant was flat on his back, his arms slack at his sides. McCurdy knelt closer beside him, his right knee touching the man's arm.

"St. Joseph, let your healing light shine on this injured brother . . ."

Looking down at tension flowing from contorted features, McCurdy lightly massaged the man's temples with the fingers of both hands.

"Let your healing power flow to these damaged eyes . . ."

As lightly as the touch of a bee to a flower, McCurdy's thumbs rested on the delicate eyelids. He could feel the eyeballs moving below the thin layer of skin.

"And put an end to his suffering . . ."

Driven by the full weight of his body, McCurdy thrust his thumbs deeply into the eye sockets. He felt fragile bones give way like eggshells as the thumbs descended. An exquisite warmth flowed over his hands, a living softness caressed his fingers.

The man's heals beat a spastic tattoo on the marble floor.

When the thrashing stopped, McCurdy rose and walked confidently to the font of holy water at the back of the church. He rinsed his hands thoroughly and reached up under his sweater to dry them on his shirt.

He left the church the same way he had come in, stopping only to drop the nails back into their holes in the cellar window and to replace the metal grate that covered the glass.

* * *

Hobston, Vermont

The middle of the night.

Lucy wasn't asleep, but she was dreaming.

It was as if she'd been dreaming since Friday, when they'd arrived way out here in the boonies at the old woman's house.

Lucy wished the voices inside her head were part of the dream. For a while they had been almost silent, talking in whispers from far, far away. Then they got louder. Almost too loud. So loud she couldn't hear anything else.

This was a new thing—so many voices. Used to be just one, the Mean One, that would talk to her inside her head. But now there were a whole lot of them, all talking at once. Buzzing, screaming, and laughing. They never stopped!

Lucy remembered how they had urged her onward in roaring painful whispers, "Go on now, go ahead. She won't shoot a little girl like you." So Lucy went ahead. She had to. Just like when the Mean One spoke. The only time she could disobey was when somebody from outside gave her an order. She could disobey Mommy, or Daddy, or any of her teachers. She could even disobey Dr. Karen. But when a voice spoke inside her head, she had to do just exactly what it told her.

Lucy couldn't remember when she had quit trying to fight them. When they spoke to her on Friday night she had gone straight up onto the porch, grabbed the gun, and pulled it, barrel first, right out of the old lady's hands. Then the man—Mr. Red, she called him—who somehow seemed as much a part of Lucy as her own hands, had bounded up the steps and grabbed the old lady around the waist. She had kicked and cried—she seemed pretty strong for an old lady—but Mr. Red dragged her inside, and tied her to a wooden chair with coils of baling wire.

And there she sat, all through Saturday and all through Sunday, way on the other side of the room, her ankles and wrists dripping blood from the wire cuts, her head drooping down till her chin rested on her chest. Sleeping now. Snoring like a drowsing animal.

The voices stopped. Lucy's mind shut off. She saw only darkness. It was as if her eyes had rolled back all the way into her head where everything was blacker than a movie theater before the film comes on. Sometimes Lucy caught sight of things in the darkness inside her head, flitting forms or familiar faces that were gone before she could be sure who or what they were.

There! Her daddy was there! She could see him way off in a tiny circle of light, as if he were in a spotlight on some faraway stage. He was drinking something. Using a straw. A funny straw that was bigger and thicker than the straws Lucy had used at school. This one was *really* thick. Thick as a broomstick. And black. Shiny black. It shone as if it were made out of metal. Daddy's cheeks kind of caved in, forming little pockets because he was sucking so hard.

But something was wrong!

He was sucking *too* hard. *Way* too hard! So hard the liquid came up the straw and into his mouth much too fast!

His cheeks puffed out; his eyes snapped open. He jumped off the floor, flew backward as the top of his head exploded like a mushy red fountain, and—

What's going on? Lucy's mind raced around inside her head like a bumblebee in a jar. Even with her body rooted, beyond her control, her mind fought to escape. It battered against the inside of her skull, harder and faster, as if the captive bee had turned suicidal.

The voices in the blackness whispered excitedly, but Lucy couldn't quite make out what they were saying.

When she opened her eyes, the dream-pictures vanished. Her daddy was gone and the darkness of the old woman's kitchen came back into view.

"You're all alone," the voices told her.

Lucy saw the old woman was awake, too. Her wide, frightened eyes flicked back and forth like the eyes of the mechanical cat on the clock back home in Mommy's kitchen.

But the old woman wasn't supposed to be awake. Today, tomorrow, something was going to happen and the old lady wasn't supposed to see it.

As Lucy began to move, the old woman's eyes locked on her. They seemed to say, Help me, please, help me, little girl.

Lucy's body tensed, just as it did when she was angry.

She wasn't angry now, not even a little bit, but she couldn't stop herself from stomping across the room and standing right in front of the old woman.

Today, tomorrow, something is going to happen. . . .

The lady looked up at Lucy, scared as could be. Lucy wanted to tell her, Don't be scared, lady, it's okay. But even as the words formed in her mind, her hand reached out and tore away the top of the woman's raggy old dress. Lucy felt her body laughing at the woman's flat wrinkled old titties. And probably her toothless old mouth would be open in horror if Mr. Red hadn't stuffed her ugly cotton panties in there before wrapping her head with masking tape.

And—Lucy's body laughed some more—it was really funny the way he'd taken a Magic Marker and drawn a smiling mouth on the tape.

Today, tomorrow . . .

The old lady made a noise through her nose and jerked her head back and forth like she was saying no.

But the old lady couldn't be allowed to see what was going to happen.

Lucy's hand came up and she hit the old woman hard on the side of the head. The old woman's head snapped sideways. She heaved and groaned. She made sounds like coughing.

Lucy hit her again. This time she went back to sleep.

. . . something is going to happen. . . .

Lucy ran over to the screen door.

Sometime soon, today, tomorrow, someone new will arrive. . . .

* * *

Father Sullivan felt the chill dampness of the earth as it penetrated the knees of his pants. Shifting his weight, he picked up one of the Shasta daisies from the planter beside him. To his right, he saw a line of seven identical flowers, each supported within a symmetrical mound of gently patted earth. Sullivan saw an optimism in the cheery faces of the blossoms. If all went well, these perennials would pass the years with him. Together they'd welcome each new spring, each demonstration of God's miracle of rebirth.

Sullivan rose to his feet, his critical eyes surveying the yard. The buildings and grounds were a dreadful mess. The church and rectory had been closed for ten years. So he guessed he was facing a decade of yard work.

Already he'd begun to feel a certain affection for St. Joe's. In fact, he had begun to think of it as his home, bequeathed to him directly by Father Hamilton Mosely.

Sullivan had never lived in a home of his own. For him, growing up had been a six-decade game of hopscotch; he had leapt from orphanage to army, then to seminary. From graduate school, he'd jumped, finally, to a fixed location: a faculty position as psychologist in residence at St. Mark's College. There he'd had a private room at the campus rectory, a rectory shared with three other priests.

Sullivan marveled at the memory: when he'd joined the priesthood he'd fully expected to have a parish. All this time a shepherd, and never a flock.

He looked at his watch. Almost ten o'clock. Why, he'd been mowing and pruning and weeding and planting for three hours! He hoped his efforts would show the community that St. Joe's was coming back to life.

Sweat poured down his face. A while ago he had considered banding his forehead with a handkerchief, but he'd hesitated, fearing how that might appear to prospective parishioners. What if they mistook him for some gray-haired, sixty-five-year-old hippie, instead of their new spiritual leader?

Again, Sullivan chuckled, realizing that either description might be equally appropriate.

"Excuse me . . .?"

The voice came from over his shoulder.

Sullivan turned to see a youthful police officer standing behind him. He had to blink two or three times before he realized his uniformed visitor was a young lady. She wore mirrored sunglasses, her sandy blond hair was tucked up under her Stetson. "I'm looking for the priest," she said, "Father William Sullivan?"

Sullivan wiped his fingers on his pant leg before extending his shaking hand. "I'm Sullivan," he said, smiling, "sorry I'm out of uniform."

She didn't smile. "I'm Sergeant Shane," she said. Her handshake was firm and brief. "I'm from the Vermont State Police. We're cooperating with the RCMP in the investigation of the apparent kidnapping of a Father Hamilton Mosely who disappeared from a hospital in Montreal."

Sullivan nodded.

"I'd like to ask you a few questions, if I may."

She was exceedingly businesslike, but her professional manner did nothing to help Sullivan accustom himself to an attractive young woman in a state trooper's uniform.

"How may I help you, Sergeant?"

"You had been visiting Father Mosely just before the kidnapping incident?"

"That's right."

"Did he have any other visitors that you recall?"

Sullivan thought for a moment, remembering the old blind priest who'd struck out at Mosely with his cane. "No. No one from outside. Just the other patients. . . ."

"Right. And did any of these other patients say or do anything that seemed strange or suspicious to you?"

Should he tell? No one else had witnessed Father Lemire's attack on Father Mosely. What had the blind man said? Something about Lazarus . . .? "The other patients, they're all elderly priests. Some are not quite themselves. . . ."

She nodded stiffly.

"One thing I remember: they were upset about something. All of them. The fact is, they were *all* acting strangely—nervous, agitated—but no one could tell us why."

"You got any ideas, Father?"

Sullivan shook his head. He waited, expecting another question, but it didn't come. The young policewoman—possibly a lapsed Catholic judging from her deferential demeanor—shrugged helplessly. "Well, Father, thanks. Mostly I just wanted to introduce myself and let you know I'm on the case." She presented Father Sullivan with a business card. "Please call me if you think of anything, okay?"

"Of course."

"And if you should stumble onto anything in the house, or maybe in the church . . .?"

He nodded and held up her card.

"Okay then, thank you very much, sir." The young woman walked away. Sullivan watched her take about six steps down the walk, then she stopped, turned around. She removed her sunglasses and squinted at the priest. Now the youthful police officer looked like a puzzled little girl. "Father?"

"Yes, Miss Shane?"

"I just can't understand it. I mean, why would anybody kidnap an old man like that?"

Sullivan moved down the walk and stood in front of Sgt. Shane.

She looked at the ground for a moment, then back at Sullivan's eyes. "Could it be . . . do you think it could be some kind of blackmail setup, Father?"

Blackmailing the Catholic Church? A novel idea, but way too strange a notion. "I have no idea, Miss Shane, none at all. I wish I did."

He shook his head sadly. It was irrational, but he felt guilty that he had nothing to offer this young lady.

She put on her mirror sunglasses, covering her puzzled eyes. "Thanks, Father Sullivan." Sgt. Shane's posture stiffened; suddenly she was a cop again. "Don't forget to call me if you come up with anything."

"I won't, Sergeant. I promise." Again they shook hands. The young policewoman did a practiced about-face and strode back to her cruiser.

Father Sullivan watched until the green and yellow police car pulled away. Should he have mentioned the investigation he planned to conduct on his own? No, it would only make him look foolish. The discouraged young policewoman gave him an idea of what he—a nonprofessional—was likely to be up against.

Returning to the house, he chuckled to himself, wondering what the townspeople would think if they noticed their new priest's first visitor was a state cop.

* * *

Burlington, Vermont

Karen fidgeted at her desk in the health center. Leaning forward, elbows on the blotter, she massaged her temples, oblivious to the clutter of files, letters, and referrals before her. She was so tired. She hadn't slept much last night. Her conversations with Jeff had lasted far into the morning hours. When she had finally crawled into bed, alone, she was unable to sleep.

Now she was confused and nearly in tears.

Her mind churned with fantasies that had suddenly become impossible realities. The world had changed for her, changed frightfully, changed to a degree that, she feared, might never permit sleep again.

Karen glanced at her watch. Her session with Alton Barnes would begin in just fifteen minutes. She didn't want to face him. Maybe she couldn't. Surely, she was too foggy to proceed competently. But she had a responsibility. Mr. Barnes's problem had taken on an unexpected new depth. Karen had no choice but to go on with the therapy, to help him if she could.

Her mind seemed to get fuzzier as she considered all. horrendous implications of the many things Jeff had told her. The Academy, the UFO research, the outrageous use of a multimillion-dollar computer; it all seemed like something out of a paranoid's nightmare.

Paranoid?

Could she be wrong about Jeff?

She'd miscalled things before, that was for sure. Was Jeffrey Chandler nothing more than a classic paranoid, slowly coaxing her, through charisma and fatigue, into his magical delusions?

Oh, Lord, she just didn't know for sure. She couldn't tell. Again she was forced to consider how imprecise a science psychology really was. Today her own fatigue contributed to its imprecision.

If Jeff were telling the truth, then the fabric of what Karen thought of as reality had started to fray. If he were lying, or delusional, then she may have already backed herself into enough of a corner to result in professional suicide. Either way she was in trouble. By letting Jeff into her life she had dared to disturb her world. Now she was paying the price: she might be in great and possibly immediate danger.

She looked at her watch again. Five more minutes.

At the moment, her most important concern had to be for her patient. Her memory worked to isolate those parts of her marathon dialogue with Jeff that pertained directly to Mr. Barnes.

She tried to recall last night's conversation. Casey had just gone to bed and they were alone in the living room.

"So I'm dying to know, Karen, just why did you phone me at home? I'm sure it wasn't just to see how rude I can be."

She looked down at her glass, swirling the remaining gin and tonic, now mostly melted ice. "I couldn't help but remember what you told me about the miracle at Fatima, how you think it wasn't a religious apparition at all, but some kind of UFO experience . . .?"

"Right. I was serious about that, you know."

"I know. So am I." She wet her lips with the ice water. "Jeff, I can't tell you his name, of course, but I have a patient, a real nice older man, who experienced what I supposed might be a hallucinatory episode. But then I thought of that big ball of light you described. I think he saw something very much like that, and it made me think that maybe . . ."

"Maybe your man saw a UFO?"

"Is it possible, Jeff? I mean, your job is to debunk them, I know, but you told me—"

"I told you that I believe lots of people are seeing strange things in the sky. Seventy thousand witnesses at Fatima couldn't all be experiencing the same hallucination, right? And cameras don't hallucinate, yet photographers very definitely recorded a ball of light. Even now—almost every day—people are photographing all sorts of oddball aerial phenomena. At the Academy we've got literally thousands of UFO photographs, lots of fakes, I admit, but many—"

"Jeff, could someone have seen a UFO around here?"

"Why not? They're spotted just about everywhere. Not only do I believe it's possible, but I bet I can tell you where your man saw it."

"No—"

"In Hobston, Vermont. Right? That's close to here isn't it?"

Karen was speechless. She gawked at him, utterly silenced. When she spoke her tone was flat. "How did you know that, Jeff?"

Jeff smiled, apparently finding ill-timed amusement in his display of mind reading.

"Did I tell you it was Hobston, Jeff? Come on, how did you know?"

He got up from his chair and walked over to sit beside her on the sofa. She felt herself pulling away, experiencing something irrational, something like fear.

"Relax, Karen, it was just an educated guess. I've helped to collect an awful lot of statistical data about so-called paranormal phenomena: UFOs, disappearances, monster sightings, weird time warps, apparitions, both religious and diabolical, and so on. And yes, I'm talking about the kinds of stuff you read about in those lurid supermarket tabloids. But all the real data seem to suggest that there are certain places in this wonderful world of ours that, for reasons unknown, experience a disproportionately high percentage of paranormal phenomena. Fortean researchers call these areas 'Windows.' Occultists call them 'Gateways.'"

"Windows? Gateways? What do you mean?"

"Metaphorical descriptions of real phenomena. Both words suggest openings, places where the division separating the known from the unknown worlds has broken down, or, in some cases, has vanished altogether. The late Ivan Sanderson studied this 'Window' phenomenon—'vile vortices' he called them, somewhat melodramatically—and he identified at least six of them around the world. But as we gather more data we discover there are many, many more. Sanderson identified the biggies. Probably the best known is the so-called Bermuda Triangle. But there are others. For example, so many ships have disappeared in the Devil's Sea off the coast of Japan that even today fishermen are careful to avoid it."

"You believe in that stuff, Jeff?"

"I believe in the data I've seen. There's just so much of it . . ."

"And you're telling me that one of these 'Windows' is in Hobston?" Karen couldn't tell if she was experiencing honest skepticism, or if her mind was literally rebelling, denying, fighting against an uncomfortable truth. Perhaps her suspicion was some atavistic survival instinct that protected the mind rather than the body.

Jeff continued, heedless of her discomfort. "The fact is, you have at least two Windows here in Vermont, three if you want to count Lake Champlain and that monster people keep seeing there. One is in the southern part of the state, the area around Glastonbury Mountain, near Bennington. But the one in Hobston has always been more . . . active.

"Weird stories associated with both these places go back hundreds of years. In the Hobston area, there were Indian tales involving spirits and monsters. Then, when European settlers began to move in, they discovered what the Indians already knew—that there are some very strange places in this new land. Colonists reported weird lights, eerie screeching, inexplicable odors, giant lizards, and 'wondrous horny beasts.' More recently, in the late forties and early fifties, a total of seven people—some of them lifelong Hobston residents—vanished without a trace. And check this out: in 1987 the only color photo of a Vermont Bigfoot sighting was taken there."

"Bigfoot sightings?" Karen shook her head. "Oh, boy, I think I need another drink."

Jeff held up his hand. "No. Please wait a minute. I know how all this sounds. I know it's a lot to digest at once. But let's not discuss it seriously now, then tomorrow toss it all off as drunken blither."

She stood up. "I'm not drunk."

"No. I know. And neither am I. But you asked me, Karen, and I'm telling you, seriously, soberly: Hobston, Vermont, has had a bad reputation for a long time. Its well known as a haunted place; it's been perceived that way for hundreds of years. Even its name is almost a sure giveaway. It's an odd quirk of fate, I admit, but the word Hobston comes from 'hob,' which is an old English word meaning 'devil.'"

"Devil's Town, Vermont . . .?"

Jeff shrugged as if to say, See what I mean? Then he went to get each of them another drink.

* * *

"Karen, Mr. Barnes is here." Laura Welsh peered around the partly open door.

Jarred from her reverie, Karen looked up, bleary-eyed. Automatically, she began to straighten papers on her desk. "Is Jeff Chandler out there, too."

"Yes, he just arrived." Laura stared at her for a moment. "Karen . . .?"

"I'm okay, Laura. I'm just tired, that's all."

"Sure. But if you need anything . . ."

"I know. Thanks."

Laura turned away, almost closing the door. Then she stopped, turned back. "Oh, Karen, Gloria Cook, the woman from Dr. Gudhausen's office, phoned this morning from Boston. I guess she's been in there cleaning the place up, and that sort of thing."

"Yes?"

"She said you had asked her about the therapist Dr. Gudhausen had been trying to get in touch with . . .?"

Karen shook her head, confused.

"You know, that friend of Gudhausen's? The Catholic priest . . .?"

"Oh yeah, right. Dr. Gudhausen was going to ask him something about Lucy Washburn."

"That's it. Well, Ms. Cook located the name and phone number for you. She's pretty sure the man Dr. Gudhausen had in mind is on the faculty of St. Mark's College in Utica, New York. Want me to set up a phone consultation for you?"

"Oh yes, please." She thought for a minute. "What's his name, do you know?"

"Do I know? 'Course I know. His name's Sullivan, Father William J. Sullivan."

* * *

"Nope, no sir, I don't know if I can go along with nothin' like that." Alton Barnes shook his head. His gaze jumped from Jeff Chandler, to Karen, then back to Jeff. "I mean, talking to this lady, to Dr. Bradley here, is one thing, but I don't know about this hypnosis business. Doc Sparker never told me nothin' about no hypnosis." He crossed his arms and sat back, spine pressed tightly against the straight-backed chair.

Alton looked defiantly at Jeff. Jeff looked at Karen. She noted how the patient's eyes automatically gravitated to the man in the room. But, by gosh, *she* was the doctor, not Jeff, and it was up to her to win Alton's confidence and cooperation.

"Look, Mr. Barnes," she said, "no matter what you may have heard about hypnosis, as I use it here it's little more than a relaxation technique. It's no more painful than deep breathing, and nowhere near as dangerous as a cigarette after dinner. The theory is, the more you can relax, the more you'll be able to recall. You said it yourself: you can't remember anything after you saw that circle of light in the sky."

Alton uncrossed his arms and let his hands fall to his lap. He studied the back of his right hand like a penitent schoolboy in the principal's office. Karen too looked at his fingers. They were sun darkened, leathery, rugged-looking. She noted the gray crescents of dirt under his well-chewed nails.

On the phone, he had displayed only slight resistance to the idea of meeting Jeff and allowing him to sit in on the session. But when they introduced the topic of UFOs, Mr. Barnes had seemed to back off. Now the hypnotism. She was throwing too much at him too fast.

I'll let him alone for a minute, she decided. I'll give him time to think. Maybe he'll come around.

Alton systematically cracked the knuckles of his right hand, one finger at a time. When he finished he said, "I know how you're tryin' to do right by me, Dr. Bradley. I appreciate it and I don't mean to sound ungrateful, but . . . you know, this business about gettin' hypnotized, I mean . . ."

"I promise you, Mr. Barnes, hypnotism is nothing like it's portrayed in the movies and on TV. I guarantee you'll remember everything we talk about, and I won't ask you to do anything I wouldn't ask you to do right now. All I really want is to help you remember. When we find out what's bothering you, we'll be a lot further along toward helping you to feel better."

Alton raked the fingers of his right hand through his thick white hair. Then he looked at his hands again. Karen was afraid he'd start cracking the other set of knuckles. In a moment he looked up at Jeff. "And if we find out what I seen really is one a them flyin' saucers of yours, then what?"

Jeff looked to Karen for help. She decided to let him answer this one on his own, and she waited with Mr. Barnes to hear what he'd say.

When Jeff spoke it was directly to Mr. Barnes, never breaking eye contact. "Then we'll know you've had an experience that is shared by literally thousands of other people all over the world. And all three of us will know it's true. As it is now, none of us knows for sure what happened out in those woods."

Again Alton's gaze dropped to his hands.

"How about this, Mr. Barnes," Karen said, "I can record the session on videotape. Then afterward you can watch the whole thing so you can see just how it works."

He didn't look at her. It was obvious the man was monumentally uncomfortable. And it was her fault, too. Karen began to wish she'd never complicated the therapy by involving Jeff.

Alton Barnes sighed deeply. "Okay, miss," he said in a whisper.

Karen felt herself brighten. "Shall we give it a try then?"

"Yup. Now that I chewed on it a little, I recall that's why I come here at the start. So let's give her a whirl and see what comes of it."

"And will it be all right with you if Mr. Chandler observes?"

Alton looked up and smiled. "Sure. Why not? The more the merrier. But you don't need to bother about that tape machine of yours. I trust the both of ya."

"Thank you, sir," said Jeff. The men shook hands as if together they'd won a great battle.

* * *

Jeff left the room while Karen went about inducing the hypnotic state in Alton Barnes. She was surprised to see how adept a subject he turned out to be. In spite of his initial unease, he relaxed readily. Within a very few minutes he was in a deep hypnotic trance.

Fewer than twenty minutes after Jeff had left the room, she asked him to join them again. Now, Alton was reclining in one of the chairs by the window. His eyes were closed and he looked very comfortable. She handed Jeff a yellow legal pad and a pencil so he could make notes or, if need be, pass messages to Karen.

When she took a seat across from Alton, the session began.

"Now, Mr. Barnes," she said, "you will be very comfortable and very relaxed. You are perfectly safe in your soft cozy chair. It'll be easy to recall the events that occurred on November twelfth of last year. You'll be able to see everything clearly; you'll remember everything completely. And you'll be safe all the time. You're perfectly safe and comfortable here in my office. You'll be watching the events, just as if you were reclining at home, watching a television program. Do you feel relaxed, Mr. Barnes?"

"Yes. I'm quite comfortable. Thank you."

"Good. Okay then, now you're going back in time. Back to last year and the first day of hunting season. There is snow on the ground, and you have just entered a clearing in the woods. You're looking for your friend, Stuart Dubois. Now, Mr. Barnes, you see Stuart's footprints in the snow, is that right?"

"Yes. Right."

"Okay. Good. Then what happens . . .?"

* * *

"The footprints, I see 'em goin' up a little rise and then they just stop. They just . . . they just . . . end. And that scares me a little, 'cause I'm thinkin', they *can't* just stop like that. I'm standin' there with two weapons in my hands 'cause Stu musta dropped his. That ain't right, Stu droppin' his weapon. And it ain't right the way his tracks just stop like that, right out in the middle of nowhere."

"Go on, Mr. Barnes. What else are you thinking?"

"I'm thinkin' I wants to hightail it outta there. Somethin' ain't right and I want to get the hell away fast. But I can't. I can't because . . . because I know somethin's happened to Stuart, and I'm the only one around that can help him.

"But I'm . . . I'm awful scared. I don't know why, but I'm scared as hell. I keep lookin' at his tracks, just ending like that, and, and . . . Jeez, I can't find my voice. I try to find my voice so I can call out to him, you know. An' finally I call, 'Stu, hey, Stu.' But my voice ain't comin' out with no real force behind it. I try again:

"'HEY, STU!'

"But I know he ain't gonna answer me. And I look at them tracks, and there ain't nothin', I mean *nothin'* around he coulda jumped up on, and there ain't no place he could be hidin'. He's jest flat out gone, period.

"Trouble is, they ain't but one direction he coulda gone off in: straight up.

"So I figures I jest better look up. And . . . and . . . I don't wanta look up. Please. I don't wanta look up. . . . Oh. . . ."

"It's all right, Mr. Barnes. You're safe here. You're watching this on a TV screen. You're relaxed and comfortable. It's okay to look up now. You're perfectly safe. Nothing can hurt you. Go ahead. Go ahead and look up."

"Oh . . . I . . . I . . . Yes. Okay. There's . . . I see there's light up there. Oh God, oh God, there's light up there. It's real bright, but it don't make no shadows. And it looks, it looks . . . hot. White-hot. But I can't feel it. I can't feel no heat from it.

"Funny.

"Funny."

"What's funny, Mr. Barnes?"

"The light. I . . . I'm lookin' right into it and it don't hurt my eyes. It looks like . . . kinda like . . . a disk, or somethin'. Bright. Real bright. It looks . . . you know, round . . . like somethin' flyin'. Like one a them Frisbees, or a clay pigeon, maybe. But bigger. It's real big. I'm thinkin', Oh God, oh Lordy God, I don't like this. Oh God, let this not be happenin'. . . ."

"It's all right, Mr. Barnes. You're perfectly safe. Relax now. Take a breath. That's it. Let the breath push all of the tension out of you. . . ."

"Yeah. Sure. I'm lookin' up. It's . . . I see a big circle of light. . . . Right up over my head now. Must be forty, fifty feet straight up. And it's round. Perfectly round. Like a disk, like a big, glowin' disk.

"But . . . oh . . . it ain't a disk. It's—Oh God no, this can't be—no, it's not a disk at all, it's . . . it's . . . I think it's more like . . . Oh Christ, that's what it is all right. Oh God—"

"What is it, Mr. Barnes? What is it you see?"

"It's . . . it's a *hole.* That's what it is. It's a big hole in the sky! In the air. A hole. An . . . and it's moving! It's goin' up, and it's goin' west—

"And—oh God—and there's somethin' else. Somethin' awf . . . Oh, don't make me say it! I can't . . . Don't—"

"Mr. Barnes . . ."

"I . . . I . . . Yes. I see . . . I see Stuart! I see him dangling out of that hole, half in, half out. His legs is kickin', and he's twitchin' and floppin' around, puttin' up a fight.

"And he's screamin'. Oh. He's screamin' somethin' wicked. God, he's screamin' like a squirrel gettin' tore to pieces by a cat. I can't—

"Stuart! STUART!

"He hears me, I think. He hears me and he thinks I can help him. But . . . I . . . I . . . can't. I can't help him. 'Cause he's way off up above my head, and . . . I . . . I can see it now. I can see it."

"What do you see, Mr. Barnes?"

"I see what it is now. I see . . . For cryin' out loud, there's somethin' inside that hole! There's somethin' on the other side of it. I see heads leaning over, like I'm on the bottom of a well lookin' up, and there's two, three . . . people . . . animals . . . looking down the well at me. I see heads. I see arms. Good Merciful Christ, there's somethin' on the other side a that hole! And they got hold of him. They got hold of Stuart!

"STUART!

"They got him, they got him up there. They got him and they're pullin' him through!"

* * *

Boston, Massachusetts
11:00 hours

In his sealed office, McCurdy was sweating profusely when the monitor blinked on. He knew what was coming. It was his error, his mistake in judgment. He just prayed it wouldn't be his job to correct the situation.

Dear God, how could he have known?

INSTRUCTIONS
TO FOLLOW

Though it had already begun, he wasn't prepared for tonight's dialogue with the machine. He was tired. His mind was as fuzzy as his vision. In fact, he couldn't remember going to bed last night.

Trying to slow his racing mind, McCurdy stared at the purple screen with anticipation.

NUMBER U-7734
CHANDLER, JEFFREY
SECURITY
WILLFULLY
VIOLATED.
MAX. RISK.

There it was. Jeff had made his run.

On some level it didn't surprise him. But just the same, there was no way he could have *known*.

Thank God they had prepared for just such an emergency. Sure, Jeff had been smart. Smart enough to act fast. Smart enough not to use his own vehicle. Even smart enough not to use his credit card. But this was the big time, and Jeff's crime-show tactics simply hadn't cut it. What he'd failed to realize, of course, was that the tracking device was the credit card itself.

CHANDLER, J.
PRESENT LOCATION:
BURLINGTON, VERMONT

Burlington, Vermont?

Another nauseating flicker of disbelief intruded. My God, this time it's really happening! We've got a breach. A dangerous breach!

Jeff ran and he took something with him. Something highly classified. Something McCurdy himself had made the mistake of leaving unsecured.

McCurdy's fear mounted in white-hot surges as an instruction sequence appeared on the screen. He was gripping the arms of his chair when the first order appeared.

LOCATE

Of course. This one-word command was to be expected. And it was the easiest to obey. He had anticipated it.

The next would decide if Jeff was simply to be contained, taken into custody, or—

The screen flashed:

ABORT

McCurdy's heart jumped against his chest. His temperature soared.

He had never done an abort! Not in person, not by himself! He'd always been able to delegate something like that. Sure, he'd had ample experience with security's three-strike command series:

LOCATE—CONTAIN—ASSIGN

. . . and even the more dreaded, and twice used:

LOCATE—ABORT—ASSIGN

But—oh sweet Jesus!—this might be his first two-word directive.

He prayed silently, moving his lips without speaking, *Let me assign it. Please let me assign it.*

Of course, he had known all along that someday a critical situation might call for personal executive action. And the meeting this morning, the meeting in the church. That must have been to prepare him for something.

But maybe not for this.

Maybe that was one thing and this was another.

Maybe now wasn't to be the time.

Oh, he'd been lucky, so far. The Academy had suffered very few serious problems. No final resolution had ever been his personal responsibility. This time, however, the situation was different, unique.

Jeff had stolen a parcel. And—dear God—McCurdy knew exactly what that parcel contained.

He took a deep breath and realized his eyes were tearing. He concentrated on the blurry screen.

Oh my dear Lord Jesus, let it say ASSIGN!

He waited, holding his breath. If no additional words appeared on the CRT, this would be McCurdy's first abortion.

How could he? He couldn't. Not to Jeff. He just couldn't.

But it *had* been McCurdy's mistake. He *was*, after all, responsible. *Please, dear Lord, don't end the transmission here.*

Why, McCurdy actually *knew* Jeff Chandler. *Liked* him.

Jeff wasn't dangerous. Not in any personal way. He was just a good-natured clown with a skyscraper IQ. But he'd never been smart enough to appreciate the full significance of his position, and perhaps that was McCurdy's error, too—

No. Now wasn't the time to think about it. This was no time to get sloppy or sentimental. This was no time for McCurdy to debate with his conscience. He knew full well that the greater good would be served by the outcome of tonight's dialogue, however personally painful it might be. Lesser men had done far more for their country and for their God.

Again, McCurdy found himself mouthing a silent prayer. *Please*, he thought, *let there be one . . . more . . . word.*

And as if the machine had read his mind before answering his prayer, the display flashed the word for emphasis:

ABORT

ABORT

ABORT

ABORT

20

The Acolyte

Hobston, Vermont
Wednesday, June 29

Sullivan's sense of purpose had been reaffirmed by Sgt. Shane's visit. She had cut right to the quick of the thing: "Why would anybody kidnap an old man like that?"

Well, Sullivan wanted to find out; yard work and renovations could wait.

Now, sitting on the oak floor of what would become his study, he tried to decide where to start.

The rectory had been unoccupied since Father Mosely's "accident." Why had no new priest been assigned? That seemed odd. Why close down a church?

Last year the new bishop, Armand LaPoint, announced he was eager to revitalize St. Joe's. It should be easy to fill the church again considering the suburban overflow sloshing nonstop from Burlington, saturating every surrounding town in Chittenden County. "Just look," LaPoint had said during Sullivan's first telephone interview, "we've got well-attended churches in Winooski, Essex, Shelburne, and Williston. Why not Hobston?"

Why not indeed?

During their second interview, His Eminence explained the kind of priest he was looking for. An older man, one who can be viewed—quite literally—as a father figure by his young, educated, upwardly mobile flock. Yet, it must be a special man, one subtle enough to embrace traditional church values without frightening the parishioners away. "The new man must have a certain . . . charisma. Administrative skills alone won't get St. Joseph's up and running again."

Eager to escape his teaching position at St. Mark's College, Father Sullivan made it known, emphatically and without humility, that he would very much like the assignment.

"Psychologist to parish priest? That's a radical change of station," LaPoint told him. "But in an era when the number of available priests has dwindled unfortunately, perhaps we can make . . . unusual accommodations. . . ."

During a subsequent telephone conversation, Sullivan had learned Father Mosely was still alive. But LaPoint had no information about the old priest's condition, or the odd happenings surrounding the onset of his illness.

Exorcism?

It kept coming back to that.

Frustration mounting, Sullivan pushed away a cardboard box full of dusty old missals, financial statements, and mimeo-masters for Sunday services long past. The carton scraped across the gritty wooden floor as he wiped his fingers on his filthy khakis.

Where could notes about the alleged exorcism be filed? Were they stashed in a bookcase someplace, packed in a cardboard box, pushed to the back of some closet or drawer somewhere in the huge old parish house? Could useful information have been overlooked by whoever cleaned out the rectory?

What else could he check?

He'd tried to contact Mrs. Phalen, Father Mosely's housekeeper. She had passed away several years ago. And Bishop LaVallee, who had run the diocese in Mosely's time, had died also.

Then Sullivan tried to locate the physician who'd attended the old priest on the day of his "stroke." Only one doctor was listed for Hobston. A phone call to Sparker, Lloyd, M.D., was no help at all. "'Course I remember Father Mosely," Sparker had told Sullivan, "but I never treated him. Coulda been an emergency team from Medical Center; coulda been old Doc Blodgett. Blodge was a Cath'lic fella, as I recall. Dead now."

Dead end.

Might Father Mosely have mentioned the exorcism to any of the townspeople? Most likely not. Any casual discussion would have been a tremendous breach of protocol.

Who then would know about it?

Again he thought of the young policewoman: ". . .if you should stumble on to anything in the house . . ."

Okay, it was reasonable to assume the victim of the infestation, or possession, would have been a Hobston family. Probably a Catholic family. If so, their name should be listed in the church register for the year in which Mosely took sick.

That didn't narrow things down much, but at least it was a place to start.

Now, thought Sullivan, just where might those old church registers be?

* * *

Montreal, Quebec

When Ian "Skipp" McCurdy's plane touched down at Dorval Airport, the jolt of landing forced a sour belch against the inside of his tightly closed lips. He swallowed, then allowed the stream of foul-smelling breath to escape slowly. He felt hot and clammy; sweat stung his eyes. *Lord, I hope I'm not getting sick.* He reached up to adjust the stream of cool air so it blew directly on his face.

The hour and a half flight from Boston had seemed especially long. Time never passed easily without his cigarettes, and the chilled fruit salad he'd been served right after takeoff must have been rotten. It had turned to gas in his stomach. For the last forty-five minutes he'd been terrified he might have to use the toilet on the plane, always an unpleasant and often a messy process. Even now, as the nausea began to pass, McCurdy kept his flight sickness bag within easy reach.

Some fighter pilot, he thought, and clicked his tongue. Guess I just can't fly anymore. Not on these small commercial rigs. Out of practice or something. . . .

McCurdy's pulse throbbed in his bandaged finger. It hurt. And when it didn't hurt, it itched. Just something else to worry about.

The plane taxied in nauseating fits and starts to the terminal. When it stopped, and the attendant opened the door, McCurdy remained in his seat. He didn't want to rush or risk jostling anyone who might remember him later. No, he didn't want to make anyone angry. All he wanted was to avoid drawing attention to himself.

A little kid with bib overalls looked at him in surprise. "Mommy, that man burped," the child said, giggling.

On his feet now, inching toward the door, McCurdy nodded to the smiling flight attendant. Docilely, he followed the line of passengers down the ramp and to the customs desk. When he flashed his diplomatic passport, the smiling boyish official said, *"Bonjour,"* and waved him through. McCurdy walked around the metal detector. Well past, he breathed a sigh of relief, then wondered if anyone had noticed what he'd done. Looking around to check, he strained to appear nonchalant.

Why, he wondered, hadn't they flown him directly into Vermont, right to the Burlington airport? Why make him worry about customs and border crossings and fake IDs? Well, no matter. It wasn't for him to argue.

Because he'd never done anything like this before, it frightened him. Still, underneath, it wasn't so bad. Maybe it was even—just a little bit—exciting.

Mouthing a silent prayer, McCurdy braced himself to work his way through scattered groups of sweating travelers. He was on the lookout for signs that would direct him to the rental car area. Hertz would have a vehicle waiting for him. It would be prepaid by the SAC base in Plattsburg, New York, and would be for Col. William P. Northey—the name that appeared below McCurdy's photo on the passport.

There would be a weapon under the seat.

Now, he thought, the easy part is over.

He paused to check his watch—10:00 A.M. Then he computed rapidly: as of now, he was no more than two and a half hours from Jeffrey Chandler.

McCurdy gripped his briefcase more tightly, hugging it against his chest. His phony passport would get him across the U.S.-Canadian border, no questions asked. From there an hour's drive south would deliver him to Burlington, Vermont.

* * *

Waterville, Vermont

"You the one wants to see Clem Barry?" A white-suited orderly spoke as he trotted down the stairs.

"That's right." Father Sullivan noticed the tattoo on the man's left forearm: a dragon breathing fire, a woman squeezed in its talon. He also noticed the sweat-stained T-shirt below the neck of the man's white shirt.

"You're gonna freak him out, man. I mean, Clem never gets no visitors."

"I'll take my chances," Sullivan said coolly.

Sullivan followed the attendant up the stairs and through a rambling complex of green-walled hallways that connected building to building at the Vermont State Hospital.

The air was pungent with the sharp, sweet odor of some industrial-strength cleaning fluid. Occasionally, they'd pass another white-clad figure who'd nod solemnly without pausing. The attendant stopped when a pudgy young woman with a pock-pitted complexion stepped into the hall. She wore a gray uniform and held a stethoscope in her hand. Smiling at the attendant, she ignored Sullivan.

"You goin' swimmin' up the dam after work?" the attendant asked her.

"Sure. You?"

"Well, a'course."

"Great! See ya there?"

"You bet."

Sullivan felt an anger growing inside him. He wrestled with it as he might struggle to control a cough. He wanted to say something about the patients being better off in the streets, but he held his tongue. This young orderly, for all his apparent deficiencies, was not to blame.

Passing a vacant nurses' station, they walked toward a wooden screen door dead center at the end of the hall. A slack-lipped giant with drool glistening on his chin pushed his mop bucket, his mop, and himself out of their way.

Without breaking stride, the attendant said, "When you get the floor washed, Andy, you might try washing your face." He patted the patient on the shoulder, a gesture of condescending camaraderie.

Andy giggled nervously. Sullivan cringed. The attendant stopped at the door to the sun porch. "You wait right in here, Father. I'll go get Clem and bring him down."

"That'll be fine," Sullivan said with ice in his tone. He stepped onto the porch and sat down on the bench of a picnic table constructed from pressure treated-lumber. On the tabletop someone had carved, "The penis mightier than the sword." Sullivan smiled. I'll have to remember that one, he thought. Possibly the poet's envious understudy also tried his knife at wit: "Wanda drinks tolit wader."

When Sullivan looked up, the orderly had returned, holding another man by the arm. He pushed the man forward, "This's Clem Barry. Call me when you're done with him, Father."

Done with him? Sullivan bit his lip before finding a smile for Clement Barry.

The patient didn't smile back.

Barry was a slight man, fortyish, dressed in green, sharply creased work pants and a blue loose-fitting pocket tee. His head was shaved nearly bald, the skin of his face was white as a mushroom.

Gripped tightly in Barry's right hand, Sullivan saw a wrinkled white handkerchief. Vigorously, the patient used it to clean his left. Then, as soon as the orderly was gone, Clem used the handkerchief to scrub the spot where the man had handled him.

"Hello, Mr. Barry. I'm Father Sullivan, Bill Sullivan. I'd like to thank you very much for agreeing to see me."

The man pulled away. Sullivan knew he was afraid to be touched. Anticipating a handshake, Mr. Barry had backed off.

"Would you like to sit down?" Sullivan asked, indicating the bench opposite his own.

Barry looked at the seat, then at Sullivan. Slowly, he turned his head, looking around the sun porch. He saw a pile of newspapers on a table between two faded easy chairs, the arms of which extruded clumps of off-white stuffing.

Sullivan knew what the man was going to do before he did it. He watched Clem take a sheet of newspaper, shake it open as he might a linen napkin, and place it on the bench of the picnic table. Then, moving very slowly, he sat on the newspaper. Again he used the handkerchief to clean the fingers that had touched the paper.

Sullivan studied the man's face. If his drug-dulled eyes expressed anything at all, it was suspicion.

"I need your help, Mr. Barry."

Barry turned his head very slowly to the side, but his eyes remained fixed on Sullivan. When he opened his mouth, Sullivan saw his white-coated tongue. It looked dry as talcum powder. Sullivan heard a dull smacking noise as the tongue separated from the roof of Barry's mouth. The man was heavily medicated.

Barry's lips moved, but no words came. He cleared his throat, swallowed noisily, and tried again. "Whatcha want . . .?"

"I think you may know a very good friend of mine, another priest."

Barry's eyes moved slowly to the right and then to the left. "I dunno no priests. 'Cept maybe Father Bissonnette. He comes here for mass on Sunday afternoons."

"No. The man I have in mind is very old now. He used to be the priest in Hobston. Isn't that the town you come from?"

More suspicion darkened Barry's expression. "How d'you know that?"

Sullivan smiled. "Hobston is my parish, now. I found your name on some old announcement sheets. Then I asked around. If I'm not mistaken, you used to celebrate mass with him. You were an altar boy, weren't you?"

Barry looked down at his hands. His left was cleaning the right with the handkerchief. He whispered, "Father Mosely?"

"That's right. Father Mosely. When I was a boy, Father Mosely was . . . well, he was very much like . . . a real father to me."

Clement Barry lifted his head and looked directly at Sullivan. His eyes and cheeks glistened with tears. "Whatcha want me for?"

"I'm trying to find out what happened to him."

"Whatcha mean?"

"If I tell you, will you help me? I need your help, Mr. Barry. I need it very badly. . . ."

Again Barry's mouth made the sticky smacking sound. Sullivan tensed as the man's lips formed a circle that seemed to forecast a negative response. Instead, Clem Barry said, "Okay."

"Thank you," said Sullivan. "Now, you used to live in Hobston, am I right about that?"

"Yes."

"And you were one of Father Mosely's altar boys?"

Barry nodded.

"Mr. Barry, I have recently seen Father Mosely. He was being cared for in a Canadian hospital for old people. He was in a coma."

Barry's eyes were wide, his expression noncommittal. Sullivan wondered to what degree he was being understood. Determined, he pushed on, "His doctor told me he had been hurt when he . . . when he tried to perform an"— Sullivan cleared his throat. Why was it so difficult to say the word?— "an exorcism. Do you know anything about that, Mr. Barry? Do you remember anything at all?"

Now Barry was rolling the handkerchief between his palms. He molded it into a long, thin shape that resembled a white serpent. "I told him I would help him, but he wouldn't let me."

"So you *do* remember!" Sullivan tried to control his enthusiasm. "You're the only person I've talked to who admits remembering."

Barry nodded his head slowly. "Father Mosely, he kept it all pretty hush-hush. It's better folks don't talk about it."

"Why do you say that?" Sullivan cursed himself for the question. He didn't want to scare the man. He didn't want to push him too hard. Questions starting with "Why" were likely to sound accusatory, challenging, like an interrogation. But it was done, and Mr. Barry didn't seem any more agitated.

"Why? Because look what happened to me. If people talk about it, why then they'll sound crazy. And besides, I don't think many people in town knew about it. Father Mosely didn't tell 'em. I didn't tell 'em. It was a secret."

Sullivan folded his hands together and put them on the table in front of him. "Mr. Barry, please try to remember. What I need to know is this: Who required the exorcism? Which house did it take place in? Can you remember?"

Barry looked at him blankly. "Things flew around. I seen things rise right up off the floor. I *seen* it! Big things, heavy things, floatin' in the air. I heard banging. Powerful banging. Like thunder. Worse. It shook the walls, should've broke 'em; should've cracked the plaster."

"You saw all this?"

"Saw. Heard. I even felt stuff." His face twisted into a grimace of disgust. ". . . things touchin' me. Rubbin' on me. Scratchy, wet things . . . swimmin' in the air. They snuck under my clothes, made me itch and burn." Clement Barry worked the white handkerchief vigorously between his palms. "I couldn't see 'em, though. They . . . they were invisible things. Dirty. I could smell 'em. Awful. An' sometimes it was like they crawled inside me. Like I could—"

"So it was your house, Mr. Barry? Father Mosely performed the exorcism at your house?"

Clement Barry looked around. He looked at the floor, under the table, through the open door. He looked at the hospital grounds through the confining mesh that closed in the sun porch. Then he looked at Sullivan.

Leaning forward, he pushed his face toward the priest. "No," he whispered, "not my house. It was at his house. It was at the rectory. Father Mosely fought it there. Then he tricked it. Somehow he got it to follow him. He led it into the church. Wanted to trap it. Inside the church. Trap it so it couldn't get out. So it couldn't get into the town. So it couldn't hurt no other people. So it couldn't get inside of 'em, and . . . and . . ."

"Then what happened, Mr. Barry?"

Barry looked at him sadly, slowly shaking his head.

"You don't remember?"

"Remember? A'course I remember. He wouldn't let me go into the church with him. Father Mosely locked himself in there with the thing. They had to smash down the door to get him out after he had his . . . I don't remember what you call it?"

"A stroke. They tell me Father Mosely had a stroke."

"Yes. That sounds right. A stroke. I remember he wasn't very well. He was old. Awful old. Sick, too. He should have let me help."

"And the exorcism? Did it work?"

Clement Barry sat quietly for a long time, staring across the green fields toward the Winooski River. He wadded the handkerchief into a ball and squeezed it so hard his knuckles turned white.

"I think so," he finally said. "I think maybe it worked. Yup. The invisible stuff left me alone after that. Maybe Father Mosely got it to go away, I can't say. But I know one thing: they didn't open up the church again. They closed it down and they kep' it closed. Maybe, I don't know for sure, but maybe the thing is still trapped in there."

Sullivan tried not to betray the rippling sensation of dread that engulfed him right then. He simply nodded. "Mr. Barry, do you know what the thing was called? Did Father Mosely ever call it by any kind of name?"

"Name? I don't remember no name. Maybe it didn't have no name. I thought it was some kind of ghost, or something, you know? But Father Mosely, he said it wasn't no ghost. He said it was a demon. A demon in the church." Barry chuckled uncomfortably, "Weird, eh?"

"Do you know if Father Mosely told anyone what was going on? Did he talk to the bishop? Any of the parishioners?"

"Not's I know of. He was real tight-lipped about it. Didn't want to upset people. Didn't want to scare 'em away from the church."

"He must have trusted you very much to tell you about it."

"Maybe. But I knew about it on my own. I was the first one to see anything. It was the holy water. I saw the holy water in the basin had turned all red, like blood." Clem Barry shook his head.

"Mr. Barry, do you remember if Father Mosely kept any sort of records?"

Clement looked at Sullivan as if Sullivan were crazy. "Records? Whatcha mean, records?"

"You know, did he keep a diary, or journal? Did he write about any of this?"

"Yes. He wrote. He kept notes. He said he put 'em somewhere the demon couldn't find 'em."

"Where? Do you remember? Where are his notes?"

Clem Barry stared at him. His right cheek swelled as if he were pushing his tongue from the inside. His eyes darted from side to side. Then he froze as if listening to something Sullivan could not hear. The motion of his hands on the handkerchief had slowed, almost stopped.

Now he adjusted his grip on the rolled cloth as if it were the scrawny neck of a chicken. He squeezed it between both thumbs and forefingers as if strangling something. The heel of his right foot began to tap noisily on the wooden porch floor. His eyes darted from side to side.

"F-Father Mosely . . . he always said look in the Bible. If you have some kinda question about something, all you gotta do is jest look in the Bible."

* * *

Burlington, Vermont

When Karen got home from the office, Jeff volunteered to get dinner. She agreed readily, so he kissed her on the cheek and headed out to pick up a pizza.

"I don't know about you," Karen said, "but I could sure use a drink."

Casey nodded enthusiastically.

Karen left to get a couple of Cokes. As she walked, she noticed that someone had tidied the place up. The dishes from last night and this morning were washed and put away, the magazines were arranged neatly on the oak coffee table, the surface of the piano was dust free and shiny. And Karen could tell by the combed look of the carpet that someone had vacuumed.

Could Casey have done this?

She put a frosty glass on a marble-topped end table beside Casey. "I should thank someone for doing so much work around here."

Casey smiled. "Oh, that's okay. I'm glad to help out when I can. I always do it at home. . . ."

Karen sat down across from Casey. This was their third day together, and their first real opportunity to talk when Jeff wasn't there.

"So, Casey," Karen began, "what do you think of Vermont?"

Casey wheeled herself closer to Karen's chair. "I like it. I think Burlington's a nice city. And the drive up here was really pretty."

"Think you'd like to stay?"

Casey looked down at her lap. "I guess. If Dad can find a job and everything."

Quiet for a moment, Casey studied the fingernails of her right hand. Karen thought the girl was acting uncommonly shy. Clearly she wasn't interested in small talk.

"Karen . . .?"

Karen gave her full attention. "What, hon?"

"Karen . . . can I ask you something?"

"Sure."

"I'm . . . I'm worried about my dad."

"I know you are, Casey."

"There's more to all this than just changing jobs, isn't there?"

Karen shifted her position in the chair. Jeff had made a big deal about protecting Casey from the real reason he had made his impulsive trip to Vermont. But, in Karen's mind, the young woman had every right to know all the details, and all the possible dangers. From experience, professional and personal, Karen had learned that certain types of protection can be harmful. She didn't approve of Jeff's secrecy.

"You're right, of course, Casey. We've been silly to think you wouldn't notice our behavior and our late-night powwows. But this is tough for me because I really think it's up to your dad to fill you in."

"But—"

"When Jeff gets back, maybe right after supper, I think the three of us should have a family meeting, and—"

Karen stopped abruptly, self-conscious about her use of the word "family." On some level she *was* thinking of the three of them as a team. But a family? Why had the word tumbled out so easily . . .?

"Karen?"

"Oh, sorry, Casey, I was drifting."

"That's okay; I know you're tired. But will you tell me just one more thing?"

"If I can, sure."

"Is Dad in some kind of trouble?"

Karen felt the blood rise to her face. At the same time she was aware of a rock-solid lump in her stomach. What could she say to a question like that? *Yes, your father has fled Boston with national defense secrets and he can possibly be labeled a traitor? Yes, your father might well be a target for arrest and prosecution. Maybe even—*

"Casey, I just can't lie to you, honey. And to me an evasive answer is no better than a lie. But look, the fact is, this is between your father and you—"

"I know! But he won't *talk* to me." Both her fists came down on the padded arms of her wheelchair. "All he ever does is treat me like a kid. Ever since Mom died and I ended up in this chair. . . . It's like he's put me up on a pedestal or something. It's like I'm not a real person anymore. It's like—"

"I know, sweetie. He's scared for you just like you're scared for him. Let me tell you this for now: Jeff not only left his job at the Academy, he took something from there. A videotape. He did it because he really believes the Academy is"— She groped for the right word,—"misrepresenting itself to the public. And your dad thinks the Academy is into some . . . well"—the picture of the naked prisoner convulsing in the torturer's chair jumped unbidden into her mind,— "some highly unethical activities. He needed the tape as proof. What your father did, he did because he is a good and honest man, and he accepts that it is his personal responsibility to do everything he can to set something right. . . ."

As Karen's voice trailed off, her own words echoed in her ears, suddenly demanding all her attention. It was as if she'd revealed a great truth to herself. Yes, Jeff *was* a good and honest man. And that's exactly why she felt as she did about him. All at once she knew how very special he was.

"We'll talk about it when he gets home, I promise. Is that all right, Casey?"

Two forward thrusts on the wheels moved Casey to the side of Karen's chair. At exactly the same instant, each reached out for the other's hand.

* * *

At his room in the Radisson Hotel, Ian "Skipp" McCurdy turned away from the lake-view panorama and pulled the cord, closing the heavy drapes over the wide western window.

The room was in semidarkness. The air conditioner hummed. Wisps of cigarette smoke curled and drifted.

He sat down at the desk and opened what appeared to be a black leather briefcase.

Built into the top was a nine-by-fourteen inch liquid crystal display screen. Two thirds of the bottom was a keyboard. The other third was a powerful transmitter and receiver. McCurdy stretched an antenna that looked very much like a numberless metal tape measure. It extended about four feet from the side of the unit. Then he squared himself in his seat before the keyboard and hit the ON switch.

The outline of a hand with a truncated little finger appeared on the lavender screen. The moment he placed his left hand upon the image, he knew a confirmation signal was bouncing off a satellite miles above Burlington. Instantly, he was communicating with Bubb at the Academy in Boston.

When he took his hand away, its hazy outline remained. In the center of the electronic palm a message said:

MCCURDY VERIFIED

McCurdy typed:

 * installed at burlington, vt., ready

LOCATION VERIFIED.

THANK YOU, DOCTOR MCCURDY.

The words winked at him, then vanished. New words rapidly appeared, faster than he could read them:

YOU ARE IN THE PROXIMITY
OF YOUR OBJECTIVE.
THE SACRIFICE YOU ARE ABOUT TO MAKE
IS OF TREMENDOUS VALUE AND IMPORTANCE.
ARE YOU READY TO PROCEED,
DOCTOR MCCURDY?
1. YES
2. NO

McCurdy hit the "1" on his numeric keypad.

YOUR RESPONSE IS NOTED.
DOCTOR MCCURDY,
I MUST INFORM YOU THAT
BEGINNING NOW
WE WILL MAKE USE OF
A FASTER AND MORE DIRECT
FORM OF COMMUNICATION.

```
ARE YOU READY TO PROCEED,
DOCTOR MCCURDY?
1. YES
2. NO
```

McCurdy's finger hesitated, hovering above the "1" on the numeric keypad. A faster and more direct form of communication? What could that be? His imagination was fired, his curiosity piqued.

McCurdy clicked his tongue—"Tch, tch, tch."—hoping he wasn't due for another run in with some soulless street person like that disgusting garbageman he had killed.

Well, here goes nothing, he thought.

With a quick cavalier toss of the head, he pressed the key.

WHACK!

It was as if he had thrown a switch releasing a million volts of electricity into his body.

He bucked.

Legs jerked. Spine straightened. Instantly, rigid as a board, he snapped like a spring from the chair.

Paralyzing bolts of electrical pain coursed up and down his sides. The back of his head felt as if it might erupt like a volcano.

Blinking convulsively, he found himself on the floor, his tongue pressed against the pile of the carpet. Brilliant specks, tiny white stars, floated like dust in the darkened room.

He shook his head as if he had just surfaced from a dive. Then he laughed.

His body felt wonderful! Energized! Perfect!

His nerves were the strings of a celestial harp on which an angel played divine music. Beauty embraced him. Rushing blood sang in his veins.

And a voice spoke clearly in his mind. "I am with you now, Doctor McCurdy."

* * *

From across the room, Karen glared at Jeff. Neither spoke. In the uncomfortable silence she could hear Casey's sobs beyond the closed door of the guest room.

Jeff picked up the last piece of pizza from the box. Paused when it was halfway to his mouth, then threw it down with a look of disgust. He stood up. "It was a big mistake coming here; I can see that now! A big fucking mistake."

Karen crossed her arms. "No it wasn't, Jeff. It was the *right* thing to do under the circumstances. What's wrong is the way you keep trying to play God with us."

"Play *God!* I—"

"Yes. Right. You show up here, unannounced, and drop this whole thing in my lap. Okay. Fine. I can handle it. At least you told me what the risks are. But what about Casey? You dragged her along, right into the thick of things, and you didn't so much as tell her what she's getting into. That's not fair, Jeff. Think about it!"

"Not *fair!* I'm doing what's best for her, considering what we're up against. She shouldn't—"

"Shouldn't what, Jeff? You've kept her completely in the dark, yet you expect her to obey silently and not ask any questions. Come on, she's too smart for that. Casey's a very intelligent young woman. She has a right to know what's going on. And you . . . and you . . ."

Karen felt her voice cracking. She was afraid she was about to lose it and start crying. Somehow, she managed to hold on and charge ahead. "Jeff, you just don't have any right to control the flow of information like . . . like . . . like some censor, or dictator or something. That's where all this started, isn't it? With you objecting because the Academy refuses to be straightforward about what they're doing? You said people need to know . . . have a *right* to know, for their own protection, remember? Yet you're doing exactly the same thing with Casey. And now you're angry at me because I said all three of us should talk about it."

"You were siding with Casey against me."

"Siding? What are you talking about? I'm not on anyone's side. Are we choosing up sides here?"

"How I raise my daughter is up to me; it's not your business, Karen."

"It was my business the minute you walked into my life with all this high-tech horror of yours. Jeff, listen: all three of us are in this together. Right now, right this minute. And you're the one who put us here, remember? At least you told me about the potential dangers involved—I should think you owe as much to Casey. . . ."

"Naw. No way." Jeff turned his back. "This is too much for that kid to handle. She's—"

"It's too much for *any* of us to handle. But we're stuck with it. I know you want to protect her, Jeff. So do I. But this isn't the way to do it. She can better protect herself if she has some idea what we're up against."

Jeff whirled around. "Karen, you don't understand a thing. The more she knows, the more danger she'll be in. That's why spies don't even tell their families about the cases they're involved in. That's why—"

"Is that what you think you are, Jeff? A spy? Do you think we're all living in some James Bond movie? My job is reality, my friend, so let's keep real. Don't glamorize what you've done. Your decision to expose the Academy may be good and right—and I think it is, I think you're brave to have done it—but don't you dare start thinking of this as some kind of game. We're not pieces on a chessboard, Jeff. I'm your friend, and Casey's your daughter. That's the reality of it. And together, we have to decide what we're going to do about this. We've got to be clearheaded, and we've got to make a plan."

Jeff dropped into a chair and lowered his head into his hands. He rubbed his eyes vigorously, then stopped, keeping them closed for a few moments. He spoke slowly, "You're right, Karen, you're right. I'm not questioning whether I was wrong to come here. In some ways, it's probably the smartest thing I've ever done. But I'm sure having second thoughts about starting this whole mess to begin with."

Karen's impulse was to go to him, but for now she knew it was better to keep her distance. Let him think. Let him talk. Obviously, he was reconsidering, reevaluating. Karen waited patiently for Jeff to say something more.

After a while he buried his face behind his palms again. When he took his hands away and looked up, his eyes were red-rimmed and moist. "I guess . . ." He blew a long slow stream of air through pursed lips. "I guess I'm just scared, Karen. Okay, I admit it. And every time I think about it, or talk about it, I get more scared. I . . . I simply did not realize what I was getting into. What I was getting Casey into. Now I'm afraid that when I lay the whole thing out for her, both of us will see what a fool I was to set it in motion. There's no stopping it, you know; there's no turning back. It's going to keep getting worse and . . . God . . . I don't know that I'm up to it. Thank God the Academy doesn't know where I am. At least that gives us a little breathing room before—"

"But it doesn't give us any time to waste. If I were you—"

Jeff stood up. "Okay," he said, holding up his hand. "Maybe I'm a little slow, a little dense, but I finally got it." He walked over and kissed Karen on the forehead.

"Thanks," he whispered, and moved across the floor toward the guest room.

* * *

Hobston, Vermont

Light-headed and barely conscious, Daisy Dubois knew she had lost a lot of blood. Whenever she moved to get more comfortable, her shoes slipped on something thick and wet. The sensation sickened her.

For a long while she had been in terrific pain as the baling wire sliced into her wrists and ankles. With each movement, it sliced deeper. The only way to stop it was to sit quietly, like a statue.

At the moment, thank God, all the pain was gone. Probably that was because she was half asleep. Lately she couldn't tell for certain when she was asleep or when she was awake.

Some little while back, just as it was starting to get dark, she had seen her husband Stuart looking in the kitchen window at her. He looked young and fit, just as he had on the day of their wedding. He smiled at her as if to say, Hold on, Daisy, pretty quick I'll be coming for you.

She tried to smile to let him know she understood, but he was gone.

Yes, she remembered now, Stuart was . . . gone.

He wasn't hiding outside with a policeman, waiting for a chance to break into the house and rescue her. No, Stuart was gone. He'd been gone a long time.

And Daisy was alone.

She moved her eyes around. The redheaded man and the little girl stood motionless in the shadows. What a strange and frightening pair! In all her days, Daisy had never seen anyone like them.

Last night—or was it the night before? Daisy wasn't sure— after they'd tied her up, they filled her mouth with—oh my goodness, the thought was too humiliating—they had filled her mouth with *cloth* and secured it in place with masking tape. Then they'd laughed at her, pointing at whatever the man had written over her mouth.

Their laughter, loud ugly grunts, echoed in Daisy's memory, reminding her of how helpless she was.

Then the pair had become quiet, all at once, just like machinery shutting down. The man stood outside the closed bedroom, the girl took a place beside the screen door, looking out at the dooryard. Watching. Waiting. For what?

They'd been standing there ever since, saying nothing, hardly moving, not even shifting their weight.

All through the night they'd held their spots. Then all through the morning . . . Not talking. Not eating. Just standing there, hour after hour—the man grinning, the little girl rubbing the place between her legs.

What do they want?

What are they waiting for?

Were more visitors on the way?

Oh, heavens, what were they going to do with her?

Now, her mind clouding again, Daisy uttered a silent plea to the Good Lord. Her head nodded forward as her consciousness ebbed.

Motion caught her eye!

The redheaded man was moving! He didn't yawn or stretch, he didn't even shake his head to clear it. He just walked toward the porch, looked out, then moved toward the bedroom.

Before he pulled the door open, he turned and looked at Daisy. She saw something in that glance, something fragile, something like a real human emotion.

It looked for all the world like fear.

Fear as raw and as shattering as her own.

She thought he might speak, maybe even help her . . .

But no.

Instead, he turned away. And the little girl followed him into the dark interior of the bedroom. ·

* * *

Burlington, Vermont

It was almost midnight.

Karen still hadn't fallen asleep when she heard the tapping on her bedroom door.

Jeff opened it a crack and looked in. Light from the hall spilled in around his head. "Can I come in a minute?" he whispered.

"Sure." She sat up a bit, two pillows beneath her shoulders.

"I hope you weren't asleep," he said as he tiptoed across the carpeted floor. "Look, I just want to apologize. I really flew off the handle and I'm feeling embarrassed about it."

"I know. It's okay. You're under a lot of pressure. I understand that."

Jeff took a seat on her bed.

"Karen, I don't know what I'd do if you weren't here to . . . well, to . . . you know, to keep things in perspective for me. I behaved like a jerk and I'm really sorry."

She reached out and took his hand. It felt warm and good.

"I'm sorry, too," she told him. "It's just that I'm tired, I guess. Maybe I'm not being patient enough. Maybe I'm not handling things well. I guess I didn't get much sleep last night, you know? Too much talking, too much thinking. Way too much happening. We'll both be more clearheaded in the morning."

As she spoke he took her hand in both of his. She could see his face indistinctly in the subdued light. His features had softened, he seemed more relaxed. His wiry hair looked wild, silhouetted in the hall light.

"Casey and I had a good talk. I told her what I was up to, why I had come here. The whole thing."

"And how did she take it?"

"Just the way you thought she would: like an adult."

"She *is* an adult, Jeff. She's a very special young lady. You should be very proud."

He chuckled dryly, mirthlessly. "I am. I just wish I could be as proud of myself. You're *both* very special young ladies. Maybe some of it will rub off."

Karen smiled at him. She reached up and touched his face. "I'm proud of you," she whispered. "You're very brave."

Without speaking, he lowered his face and kissed her. Their second kiss lasted longer. Karen's lips flexed, sealing the bond between them. Their tongues met warily.

Karen slipped her hand from his grip. Without thinking, her arms were around his neck, pulling him closer. She felt the solid mass of his chest as it pressed against hers, flattening her breasts. She felt his hands in her hair.

His head was beside hers now. His mouth breathed warm air against her ear. "I have so much to thank you for," he whispered. "I don't know where I'd be without you. You're the only sanity in this whole crazy mess. I hope you know that."

She closed her eyes. Sometimes you have to be a little brave, she reminded herself. Sometimes you have to be a little adventurous.

Jeff kissed her again and stretched his body on the bed beside her. The box spring squeaked from the added weight. Only the thin sheet separated them.

It had been a long time since Karen had been kissed affectionately, passionately. Her body seemed to need it, feast on it as dry earth feasts on rain. She felt his hand running up and down her side, felt a pleasurable rush as her nipples hardened against the silky fabric of her nightgown. Her hips moved, pressing against his thigh.

But before she could release herself to the passion, dark thoughts intruded. Karen's mind fought her body, contrary forces experiencing the same event. This was the first time a man, any man, had been in the bedroom of her new home. But they weren't alone. In her mind's eye she saw her father, a wrinkled, hollow-eyed skeleton in a hospital bed.

Jeff's hand found the fullness of her breast, kneaded it gently. The silky nightgown felt delightful against her skin. A muted sigh escaped her throat.

Like a movie projected on the back of her eyelids, Karen saw her mother's tear-swollen eyes at Dad's funeral. Saw her limp, paralyzed form in the wheelchair.

She almost didn't hear Jeff whispering, "Sometimes I think we were thrown together by some benevolent power. I feel as if you were there for me when I needed you the most. Does that sound crazy?"

Again their lips locked together. Her hand was on his cheek and she could feel the warm blood there. In her mind she saw Mike Tucker spinning at the end of a rope after his wife drove away forever.

Karen slid her lips away from Jeff's. "Jeff, please, I can't do this."

"I . . . what's wrong?" He lifted his head, tried to look her in the face, but she wouldn't let him.

"Am I hurting you?"

"Oh no. Not that. It doesn't hurt. It feels . . . well, it feels good. But, oh, I can't, Jeff. I just can't. Not now. I'm just not . . . prepared, not ready."

He was sitting now. Still, he had one of her hands in his.

"Jeff, I've just never . . ."

"And I haven't either. Not since my wife died. I never thought I could be with a woman again. But, Karen, I can't tell you how much you mean to me. It's almost like magic."

She felt herself pulling away. Still she could not give up his hand; she liked the feel of his strong fingers around hers.

"We can't . . . we shouldn't let this get started. . . ."

"Why, Karen? Why not?" His voice was quietly insistent. "What's there to be afraid of? There's not someone else, is there?"

Karen squeezed his hand. "Oh no, it's not like that. It's just . . . Well, if we let it get started, then—"

Abruptly she pulled her hand free of his and turned away. Her bed tossed with the sudden movement. She covered her face, feeling tears push toward the surface. His warm hand rested on her shoulder.

"What is it, Karen? Can you tell me?"

"Oh, it's like you and your wife, Jeff. Don't you see?" She turned her head farther away, buried her face in her pillow. "These things . . . they always end . . . they always end in . . ."

"What? Tell me, Karen. Talk to me."

"They end in tragedy. Always. They always end in tragedy." Crying now, muscles tense, she tried to hold on, tried to keep the sobs away. "Go, Jeff. Please."

He didn't. He tightened his grip on her shoulder. "It's okay, Karen. It's okay, I understand."

He tugged at her shoulder, gently but insistently, trying to get her to face him. She allowed herself to be moved. Rolling onto her back, she looked up at him again. She smiled weakly, embarrassed by the tears, embarrassed by her timidity. "M-maybe it's that I'm just tired. Maybe it's that too much is happening . . . so many changes. . . ."

For a long while she just stared up at him. He didn't look away.

"Why don't you lie with me, Jeff. Just until I fall asleep. Would you do that?"

He nodded once, perhaps a bit sadly, and stretched out beside her, taking her in his arms.

21

Necessary Evil

Burlington, Vermont
Thursday, June 30

Bored with magazines and morning television, Casey Chandler decided to go outside for a while. Who would give her any trouble in broad daylight? Besides, Dad said nobody knew they were here, so what was he so worried about?

All she wanted to do was sit in the sun for an hour before Dad came back from Hobston. It would be nice to pass some time in the fresh air looking at the lake.

Casey wheeled to the door, unlocked it, and pulled it open. It was so wide she had no trouble getting her wheelchair over the threshold and onto the walk. With one hand steadying the rubber tire, she pulled the door closed. Then she began to move.

Following the sidewalk around the corner of the building, she hoped to get close enough to the lake to watch the sailboats. Or better yet, maybe there'd be kids on windsurfers zipping around in the morning wind.

Beneath her, the concrete sidewalk was smooth and flat. Maybe if I had a sail, she thought, I could let the breeze push me along. . . .

An abrupt incline ended the sidewalk. Way too steep, it must be some developer's poorly conceived acquiescence to handicapped accommodation. Still, it allowed Casey to descend to the blacktop if she gripped the push rims as if her life depended on it.

The smoothly paved road ran west, directly toward the lake. Its slope was gentle; Casey could easily make it back up when she needed to.

Soon she discovered another sidewalk leading to a long wooden deck covered with white plastic furniture. Colorful umbrellas shaded each cluster of table and chairs.

Casey was delighted with this observation platform atop steep red rock cliffs. Within seconds she was on that deck, looking out on the lake. The craggy shore of Lake Champlain was a hundred feet below.

Just as she'd hoped, there were sailboats weaving on gentle rolling waves. And yes, there were kids on their windsurfers—college guys in black and neon spandex—their features obscured by the distance, their bodies tanned and glistening.

To her right she could see the huge Champlain Ferry chugging its way toward Plattsburgh. Closer to shore, *The Spirit of Ethan Allen,* a humorously inept imitation of a nineteenth-century paddle wheeler, ferried tourists along the shoreline.

Casey felt good here. The sun warmed her face and a soothing breeze kept her from getting uncomfortably hot. She closed her eyes and listened to the birds, the wind, and the distant laughter of young people on the beach below.

* * *

From behind the wheel of his rented Plymouth, Dr. Ian "Skipp" McCurdy watched the young woman in the wheelchair as she left the condominium. He felt sorry for her as he watched the awkward leaning and pushing effort required to move the chair along the level sidewalk. How can she smile like that? he wondered. What does she have to smile about?

When she reached the steep ramp leading down to the roadway, McCurdy was sure she'd topple and hurt herself. Yet somehow she managed the maneuver easily and with a mysterious grace.

McCurdy had never met Jeff Chandler's daughter face to face, but he'd seen plenty of photographs of her. Many had been Academy file photos, but there was also the color five-by-seven school portrait Jeff kept on his desktop. Even without the wheelchair, Casey Chandler would be easy to recognize. Handicap or no, she was a beautiful girl. Absolutely beautiful. Briefly, the devil in McCurdy's mind forced him to wonder what it would be like to—

No! Good Lord. Stop it! I'm thinking like a psycho!

Shaken, he wiped the unclean image from his imagination by uttering a quiet prayer, asking for strength and forgiveness. *My dear God, what's happening to me?*

It's all right. I'm with you now, said a soft voice in McCurdy's mind.

He smiled and nodded, relieved. Then he took a couple of deep calming breaths. Yes, everything was fine.

When he was sure Casey had made it to the observation deck, he prepared by carefully considering the options. He had to plan, calculate, anticipate. He had to maintain a cold mind. Right, that was the phrase: a cold mind. At this point McCurdy could not afford excitement. As he knew full well, emotions deceive; they create mistakes.

McCurdy waited, offering another silent prayer to steady his nerves. *Please, Lord, make me strong of mind and heart, for what I do, my Lord, I do for you.*

We are strong, Doctor McCurdy, said the sweet, soft voice.

As McCurdy's lips continued to move soundlessly in prayer, his attention never wandered from the girl in the wheelchair.

How far was she now from the steep jagged face of the red rock cliff?

Was anything there that might cause her to fall?

Should he join her on the deck? Or should he go inside the apartment? Wait for her there?

Trust in me, the voice whispered.

When he was confident the girl's attention was occupied, McCurdy got out of the car. After closing the door as quietly as possible, he straightened his bow tie and tugged on the sleeves of his seersucker jacket.

Satisfied that he was presentable, he took a casual look around. Then, quickly, he crossed the parking lot to the front door of Karen Bradley's condominium.

His white-gloved hand went directly to the doorbell. He pushed it. Once. Twice. As he'd anticipated, no one answered.

No one is here, the voice said.

McCurdy looked around nonchalantly.

Not a soul watching.

He took the knob in his hand and tried the door. Unlocked; he'd been right about that, too.

Steady, now . . . steady, he thought. *Dear Lord God, let your tranquillity fill me. . . .*

Trust in me, the voice answered.

McCurdy pushed the door open about three inches. This allowed him enough room to put a hand inside and trip the lock.

Quickly he removed his hand, pulled the door closed, and tried to open it again.

No way. It was locked tight.

Then, removing his gloves, he walked back to the car and waited.

* * *

Hobston, Vermont.

"See there?" said Alton Barnes, pointing. "That's the Dubois place."

Jeff Chandler nodded, trying to keep up with the older man. They'd left the car at the end of Bingham Creek Road and walked the trace of a trail that skirted the vast field beside the house. Now they followed a stone wall, making their way toward the forest. From there they'd continue up the mountainside to the spot where Stuart Dubois had vanished.

Alton Barnes sliced through the green grass as the bow of a ship slices the tide. The older man moved with surprising alacrity; his head turned rapidly from side to side as he studied the trees, the brush, and the shadows. Jeff could tell Alton was tense. Even his voice sounded strained. "Stu's wife still keeps the place. Can't be easy way up here with no phone and no power. Tough old broad, Daisy Dubois."

Jeff glanced at the house. Quiet and dark, it seemed to shrink into the eastern distance. Looks vacant, he thought.

"Did you ever talk to her about what you saw up here?" Jeff asked.

"Heck no," said Alton, "never talked to nobody about it."

"Maybe we should stop in, ask her if she has ever, you know, seen anything strange."

"Reckon the only strange thing she's seen up here is you and me." The older man chuckled at his own joke. "But we can stop in and find out for sure. Probably wouldn't hurt to check in on her."

* * *

Daisy had been alone in the kitchen for a long time. Hours? Days? She just couldn't tell because she kept fading in and out, losing track of time.

Her shoulders ached because her arms were tied behind her back. The arms themselves—when she could feel them—tortured her with their prickles and throbs. They wouldn't let her forget the razor-bite of baling wire where it had scraped to the bone.

Her mouth was dry as sand. Every time she tried to summon some spit, she gagged on the ball of cloth. Lordy, how long had it been since she'd had any food or water? When one of those awful people comes out of the bedroom, I'll ask for a drink. They can't refuse a body a drink?

Daisy couldn't stop drifting in and out of sleep. Seemed like people kept coming to visit, old friends, relatives, even her husband Stuart. All were dreams, she knew, but they were good dreams and she welcomed them.

So what if she was going crazy? Maybe crazy was better than wired to a hard wooden chair in her own kitchen. But what if crazy were her only option? What if it were the only way to escape this mess?

Oh, what did they *want* with her, anyway? If they were going to kill her, why didn't they just *do* it and get it over with?

For the first time Daisy faced the other option: she might die in that chair. The memory of those friendly faces, and the sad, sweet smile of her husband, made her think death might not be so bad. Why not give up? Let go? Whenever she drifted off to sleep, her friends would be waiting.

Could be they're *not* dreams, Daisy reasoned. Could be they're honest-to-God real. And if that were true, Daisy had a pretty good idea what they were waiting for.

She started to pray then, giving the unsettling word emphasis in her mind. *If I should* die, *before I wake . . .*

There!

A noise. She thought she heard a noise!

Merciful God, maybe it's help! Maybe help's coming!

She listened hard. Yes! Voices! The far-off sound of men talking!

And to the west, through the window, she could see two men walking in the field! She gave her head a little shake, but they did not vanish. They were real.

If she could . . . if she could just make it to the porch . . . she could cry out for help!

She tried to move her fingers—thought she was moving them, too, but she couldn't tell for certain. The wire, she imagined, had filleted the flesh of her forearms like the sides of a bass.

She tugged on her right arm one more time. Yes! *Yes!* Wire and flesh resisted, but lubricated by blood, her hand came free!

Adrenaline surged. Suddenly wide awake, she brought her arm around, stared at the gore-slick pulp that had been her right hand.

She checked to make sure she could still see the men. She'd have to act quickly, before they were out of sight.

It was easier to free her left hand. Now, with both bloody stumps before her, she bucked in her chair. Rocked it. Pitched it forward. It clattered to the floor.

Her head struck hard, but she didn't pass out.

Wait! What if the man and the little girl had heard?

Eyes closed, Daisy held her breath, listening, praying. When she looked she saw the faded floral linoleum two inches below her nose.

Hands free, she was able to hook a paralyzed thumb under the wire that bound her neck. A jolt of pain flashed as her knuckle connected with a live nerve ending in the open neck wound. She didn't care. Gritting her teeth, she loosened the wire. A moment of tugging and she was able to pry it up and over her head.

She was free!

She worked to get the gag out of her mouth. When the soggy obstruction was clear, she spat several times, once again tasting her own spit.

She strained to elevate her head, hoping to see how far it was to the door.

Eight feet, no more. So very close. . . .

If she could crawl to the porch she could cry out for help—

But wait! What if she couldn't make herself heard? What if she was too weak to shout for the men as they moved farther and farther away?

She thought: When the redheaded man grabbed me, he threw the shotgun onto the porch swing. And she'd never seen him bring it in. Was it . . .? Could it still be out there?

If Daisy could get through the door and onto the porch . . . if she could get her hands on that shotgun . . . she'd be protected. . . . A signal shot would bring the men to her aid!

Facedown, she dragged herself a foot toward the door. Grit scraped her skin like sandpaper.

Another six inches. *Oh Lord, don't let them get too far away. . . .*

She pulled herself forward again, leaving tracks of smeared blood on the grainy linoleum.

Three and a half feet.

She heard herself breathing. Hard. Fast. Her chest pumped. When she exhaled, she blew dirt out of her path.

A noise!

She heard a noise behind her.

Oh, God! What was it?

She froze. Her fine-tuned ears listened for the latch on the bedroom door. Silent seconds passed. Daisy held her breath, knowing she was losing precious time.

Satisfied no one was coming, she reached forward, planted her forearms against the floor, and dragged herself a foot closer to the door.

Her heart beat even faster; her lungs worked like a bellows. Sweat ran down her face, trickled into her eyes, stinging, clouding her vision.

Another foot.

The door was within reach! She touched it to make sure. If she could get through it, if she could get outside, the shotgun would be less than four feet away.

Supported by her left forearm, Daisy arched her spine, reaching for the latch. Blood flowed down her arm in bright rivulets, tickling her, filling wrinkles, weaving and crisscrossing like a network of external arteries.

She hammered on the latch with the ball of her thumb.

Once. Again.

Cringing from the noise, Daisy listened for movement within the house.

Everything was quiet. She pushed the flayed ham of her hand against the metal latch. Metal scraped exposed nerve. Daisy bit her lower lip in an effort not to cry out.

The latch moved with a metallic *click.*

The door opened about an inch.

Just enough to see outside.

The two hikers were gone, but they could not have traveled far. No, she could still call them with a shotgun blast.

Daisy rolled onto her left side, hoping that would create enough room for the door to swing open.

Yes! Open now. Wide open. Yet she couldn't feel the sunlight on her body. She seemed to be lying in a shadow.

She bent her neck backward, forcing herself to look up.

A man stood in the doorway.

Thank God, she thought.

The first thing she saw was his bare feet, then bare legs. His bright white garment hung all the way to his knees. As her gaze traveled higher, her eyes clouded with sweat and tears. Straining, she could almost see his face.

"Help me," she wanted to say, but no words came.

His arm descended; she reached to take it. There was no pain as her ruined hand touched his.

The eclipsed sun glowed behind his head like a halo. He must be an angel, she thought. Yes, a white-robed angel come for me.

The man bent lower. She felt his strong hands probing underneath her shoulders and legs. He picked her up with ease, and now his face was close to hers.

He looked familiar. He looked so familiar. She blinked, and his smiling face came into focus.

And she knew!

Oh. Ooooh. So it *was* real. He really *was* out there.

She was so very happy to see her husband again. She wanted to kiss him, tell him that—

No! What was he doing? He was carrying her back inside the house! She had to warn him! Had to tell him about those people, in the bedroom.

"B-b'beh-troom . . ."

Now they were passing the kitchen table, passing it and . . .

Stepping toward the bedroom. He had misunderstood. He thinks I want him to take me into the bedroom.

"Nuuuh. Nuuh nununu." She couldn't tell him. She couldn't speak.

The bedroom door opened by itself, like magic. When he carried her over the threshold the strangest odor filled her nose. Sickish sweet like . . . like . . .

The room was empty! How could that be? The little girl, the redheaded man, even the old man in the bed—they were all gone. Vanished.

Oh, thank God!

When Daisy saw the open window with its lacy nylon curtains blowing outside in the draft, she understood.

Stuart put her on the bed, looked down at her, his youthful face full of love, his familiar eyes smiling with a mischievous delight. It was just like their wedding night.

He touched her forehead, brushed strands of hair out of her face.

He's an angel, Daisy thought, he's an angel now and the Good Lord sent him to fetch me.

But something wasn't right. There was something wrong with the gown that he wore. Stuart's radiant white cloak, it was nothing but a sheet. Daisy looked down. The top sheet was missing from her bed.

"W-wait . . ."

Her chest tightened, locking half a breath in her windpipe.

Still smiling, Stuart touched her face. His hands were warm. No, not warm, *hot.* They were burning.

Panic shot adrenaline throughout her exhausted body. Somehow, she got to her feet.

Reeling, Daisy took one, two stumbling steps toward the door, but he grabbed her hand, stopping her midroom. She stared in disbelief at her own reflection in the round vanity mirror. Could this haggard bloody old woman really be her?

Stuart's reflection was clear as he stepped behind her. The sheet fell away and she saw he was naked. His man-thing was hard and big, almost bursting, just like on their wedding night.

And when he spoke, sure enough it was her husband's voice. "I need you, now," he whispered.

He shoved her against the vanity, knocking over her Evening in Paris talcum, pressing her face against the vanity mirror.

Bending obscenely, she saw her own expression of agony as his man-thing like a bloated serpent wriggled against the backs of her thighs. She couldn't move, couldn't tear her eyes from their reflection.

The serpent bored into her, hot, scorching, like the barrel of a gun. A burning sensation moved from the pit of her, spread across her buttocks, along her arteries, over her solar plexus.

The serpent spat like a blowtorch, driving lava deep into her, yet she couldn't move, couldn't scream.

A tiny voice in her mind whispered, "This is death, Daisy. This is what it's like."

Her gaze locked on that horrid hot point at the middle of her forehead where the heat seemed to focus. The skin turned brown, like paper with a candle underneath. It darkened, turned black. As its circumference widened, blue flames danced in its center. Dense, sweet-smelling smoke poured from her skull, filled her nose, covered her eyes.

Somewhere, somewhere far beyond the smoke and the blue dancing flames, she heard laughter.

* * *

Burlington, Vermont

Using both hands, Casey pushed the door, then pulled it, then pushed it again.

Drat! she thought. I *know* I left this damn thing unlocked. I know I did!

She rapped on the door, then pressed the doorbell, thinking maybe Dad or Karen had come back. Nope; no such luck.

"Man, this is just *great*," she said. "Now what am I going to—"

"Hi!" a pleasant voice said from behind her.

Casey looked over her shoulder at the smiling man in the blue pin-striped jacket and light tan pants.

"Are you looking for Karen Bradley?" he said. His freckled face and bald head glistened with sweat. His red hair made an unruly halo.

Casey smiled back at him, embarrassed because she'd been caught talking to herself. "No, but I'm locked out of her apartment."

"Yes. So I see. Is the door stuck? Can I give you a hand?"

"No thanks. But I'll take a crowbar if you have one."

"Locked, eh? Karen's not inside?"

"No. She's at the office. I'm here by myself."

The man looked puzzled. He glanced down at a notebook in his hand, then he looked back at Casey. "You know, I bet I was supposed to meet her there, at the health center." He looked at his watch. "I've got a one o'clock appointment with her. Don't know what I was thinking, coming here. Guess I'd better hurry; I've only got fifteen minutes to get up there."

He turned as if to go, then stopped. "Sorry," he said, turning back, "a moment of confusion there. I'm Bill Graig. I'm a friend of Karen's and I'm a guidance counselor at the high school. We were going to talk about some referrals. Don't know why I came here instead of the office. Force of habit, I guess."

Casey raised her eyebrows. "You wouldn't happen to have a key, would you?"

The man seemed to blush. "Oh no, no. We're not *that* kind of friends. We just meet here sometimes after work; gets both of us out of the office." He cleared his throat, "Listen, you're locked out, and it just so happens I'm on my way over there. Karen and I'll probably meet for about an hour. No more. Could I give you a lift over? You could get her key and I could drop you off here on my way back to the school."

"All right!" Casey smiled. "I'm getting rescued. Hey, this is just like in the movies."

Both of them laughed. The man stepped behind the wheelchair and pushed Casey in the direction of the Plymouth.

* * *

Hobston, Vermont

Jeff saw nothing remarkable when they entered the woods. Of course he had no idea what he expected: flashy high-tech machinery? Helmeted spacemen? Big-eyed insects with ray guns?

He listened, but heard nothing unfamiliar in the wind. No saucer sounds, no half-human calls echoing from the granite cliffs? Nothing.

Instead, he was far more impressed with the woodland's beauty than with its strangeness. It was tranquil here, very lovely. He wished Casey could see it.

Ahead, from where the land rolled to the northeast, he could see a stark, bare-topped peak. "Mount Mansfield," Alton told him, "highest mountain in Vermont. Taller'n any building in the state. Kinda puts things in the right perspective, don't it?"

Jeff nodded, smiling. He enjoyed Alton's humor, but he could hear a nervous edge to every jest and chuckle.

Both men stared at the panorama. Pointing, Alton continued, "If ya look at it just right up on top, you can see the face of an Indian, forehead, nose, chin, and all. Like he's some giant, lyin' on his back, lookin' up, keepin' a watch on the sky."

Jeff studied it for a moment, then, sure enough, the rocky mountaintop really did look like the profile of a reclining Indian.

After they passed a row of evergreens, Alton stopped beside a hickory tree and cleared his throat. "This here's where I figger Stu stopped to rest after we split up. I 'member the imprint of his rifle butt in the snow. And the snow was all sorta tromped down, jest as though he'd stood here for a minute or two, shiftin' from foot to foot."

Alton seemed to hold back at the point where the slope steepened to become the base of Stattler Mountain. He took a few hesitant steps forward and stopped. "I ain't so sure I want to go up in there again." He wiped his hand nervously across his mouth, avoiding Jeff's eyes.

"We're getting close to where it happened?"

"A-yep, too close, for my money." Alton pointed with a trembling hand. "You jest walk right up there, straight ahead. Pretty quick you're gonna see a mossy rock with a big, kinda circular depression—what they call a bowl—right near it. That's the spot. You go on an' look. I'll wait right here."

Not wanting to pressure the man, Jeff went on alone. But—he had to admit—he felt a queasy spot in the pit of his stomach. Without Alton at his side, he didn't feel so brave.

Soon Alton called out behind him, "That's where I found his Winchester. Right there by your foot, lyin' in the snow."

Jeff looked down. He glimpsed the brown tail of a snake as it whipped out of sight under a rock. Then he looked over his shoulder. Alton was still leaning against a tree about one hundred yards below.

"You okay there, Jeffrey?" Alton called in an abnormally high-pitched voice. Its echo bounced around in the air.

"So far so good."

The sun beat on him warmly. Circular shadows collared the trees, hugging their trunks. Jeff guessed it must be around noon. Checking his watch to confirm, he found it was almost one o'clock.

Blood pounded in his ears from the exertion of the climb. His chest hammered. He looked around again, studying the landscape, feeling puzzled.

What had really happened here?

He experienced a melancholic chill identical to the one he'd felt years ago when he viewed the battlefield at Gettysburg. Or perhaps it was closer to the tremor he'd endured more recently when morbid curiosity led him to retrace the steps of the infamous Boston Strangler. It was as if some unsettling memory hovered permanently in the air. There was an almost tactile discomfort in the place's deceptive normalcy; the tranquillity was some kind of illusion.

Yet, all appeared commonplace, remarkable only in its loveliness. But try as he might, he just couldn't get beyond it—something *had* happened here.

What?

Had a man literally walked off the face of the earth?

Had a UFO swooped down and pulled Stuart Dubois into the heavens?

Had the old man stepped out of the third and directly into the fourth, fifth, or sixth dimension?

Or had the sky opened up, creating a porthole to another reality?

Every notion seemed so foreign, so unreal, so utterly incredible in this natural setting.

A breeze rattled dead leaves in the treetops. Jeff scanned the sky: clear, blue, perfect as exquisite crystal. It seemed to go on forever. The mountain slope ahead was bright in the sun. Dull rocks seemed to glow, greenery appeared iridescent. Shadow-choked trees formed walls on either side of the mountain trail.

What? What had happened here?

Something heavy hit a branch. Jeff tensed, looked up. A red squirrel vanished into a shadow. Somewhere beyond, a woodpecker tapped Morse code on a hollow limb.

Movement caught Jeff's eye! A flash of white darted among columns of dark tree trunks. Was it an animal?

There it was again! A good fifty yards away. An animal, yes. Moving on all fours. Whitish. Fleshy colored. The overall impression was of a starving pig with something—a snake?—in its mouth?

He took a step toward it, but it was gone.

"You all right up there, Jeffrey?"

He turned to see Alton approaching slowly.

"Y-yes. I'm fine. A bit perplexed, but fine."

The older man was close enough for Jeff to see his eyes darting around. Alton's face was slick with sweat. "You 'bout through? What say we head on down? I've had about enough of this mountain climbin'."

"Okay, fine by me." No point in prolonging this.

"You still want to stop in, talk to Daisy Dubois?"

"Sure, why not?"

* * *

Burlington, Vermont

Weird, Karen thought, gazing at the bay from her office window, really weird.

The arrival of Jeff Chandler and Casey had turned her life upside-down. Now her whole sense of reality seemed to be warping beneath the added weight of her surprise house guests. Suddenly, right out of the blue, she was forced to consider such way-out notions as unidentified flying objects, holes in the sky, murder by computer, and all sorts of new-age science fiction nonsense that could scare her silly if she thought about it enough.

What's happening, she thought.

Last night's scene at the condo had made sleep difficult. And, good as it felt, she had lain awake far too long in Jeffrey's arms.

Today she was paying the price: she felt drained, listless. And goodness, she had so much catching up to do! Where did all this work come from? Where should she start?

Karen stiffened her spine, forcing herself to concentrate on business. She looked at her appointment calendar. Ah, no one scheduled after lunch. She'd use the time to tackle some dictation. But for now, she'd work her way through the pile of notes and phone messages.

She picked up her short stack of pink "While You Were Out" slips. Right on top was a message from Officer Chaput of the St. Albans Police Department. Oh, Jeez, she still hadn't called him back! She read, "Called again. Wants you to phone and set up an appointment to discuss Lucy Washburn's disappearance." Laura had underlined the message in red ink.

The second message reminded her of another call she still hadn't made. It was from Dr. Gudhausen's secretary, giving her the name of the therapist Dr. Gudhausen had wanted to consult about Lucy's MPD.

A priest, Karen thought. Why a priest?

The words "St. Mark's College, Utica, NY" were clear and easy to read, but she had to squint to make out the name.

Father Wm. Sullivan—Psych. Dept.

Funny. That name sure looked familiar. Maybe she'd read one of his papers in a journal or something.

She picked up the telephone, determined to satisfy her curiosity about the priest before talking to Officer Chaput.

She began to press the buttons.

* * *

Hobston, Vermont

Even in the bright midday sun the house looked dark.

Jeff and Alton cut across lots, wading through a field of hip-length timothy dappled with buttercups. As they walked, Jeff studied the old place. The clapboarding had weathered dull brown, rust blemished the tin roof, and the porch sagged like the spine of a dying beast. Odd not to see power lines running to the structure. It was like a scene from another age.

Much of the barn roof had collapsed. Huge hand-hewn beams were visible through a hole, its edges scaled with rectangles of slate. Glassless windows looked in on darkness.

The whole dying farmyard seemed like a monument to a way of life that had all but passed.

"It doesn't look like anybody's home," Jeff said. "The place looks deserted."

"Naw," Alton assured him. "Daisy's there. She's probably got an eye on us right now, wonderin' who we are and what we're up to. Pretty quick, soon as she knows it's me, you'll see her out on the porch waving. You wait an' see what I tell you."

But she didn't appear as the men moved closer.

"That's funny," said Alton as he stopped and stared at the barn.

"What?" Jeff stopped, too.

"Lookit that, looks like there's a car in the barn."

"So?"

"Daisy and Stu never had no car."

The back end of what appeared to be a station wagon was vaguely visible beyond the open barn door.

"Maybe she has company," Jeff said.

They detoured a bit to investigate. When they moved close enough, Alton remarked, "Massachusetts plates, ain't that right?"

Jeff nodded, recognizing the familiar design. "Maybe we shouldn't intrude. She may not appreciate the kinds of questions I want to ask. Not in front of guests."

"Prob'ly won't appreciate 'em anytime."

Smiling, Jeff collected his thoughts, reviewed the things he wanted to ask the old woman. Had she seen or heard anything strange on that day back in—

"Alton?"

"Yessir."

"Tell me again when it happened. What was the date that you and Mr. Dubois were up here, do you remember?"

"Remember, hell, I'll never forget. It was huntin' season. First day of huntin' season, jest last year."

"But the date . . .?"

"It was on a Thursday. November twelfth. Why?"

"Just trying to get the facts straight."

Something about that date stuck in Jeff's mind. It seemed to click over and over as if it were a record skipping on a turntable. He just couldn't recall, but something about it—Thursday, November twelfth, last year—made him uncomfortable. Yes, that was it—uncomfortable. Somehow, he seemed to associate that date with discomfort, pain. His mind was spinning. His subconscious wrestled with a memory that he couldn't bring into focus.

"What's the matter, Jeffrey?"

Jeff realized he had stopped walking. He was staring at the ground as if he were in a trance. "There's something about that date . . . something I can *almost* remember . . . ."

Then it was there, like a vision illuminated behind his eyes. The date came into focus like a picture on a TV screen.

The tape! The videotape he had stolen from the Academy. The recording of the execution victim had been made on November twelfth of last year!

"Holy shit," Jeff said to no one. "Holy fucking shit!"

"Somethin' wrong, Jeffrey?"

"No . . . ah, nothing wrong, exactly." He was in motion again, striding toward the house. "Come on, Mr. Barnes. Let's go have a talk with Mrs. Dubois."

Jeff studied the house as he approached it. He could swear nobody was home. Even on this warm afternoon the windows and the side door were closed. No motion was obvious beyond the dark glass. It was as if nighttime filled the place.

Their pace slowed as they crossed the dooryard.

"I . . . ah . . . I got kind of a funny feelin' . . ." Alton said.

"Yeah," Jeff agreed, before he could rationalize the sensation away. "Yeah, me, too."

Alton touched Jeff's arm. "Somethin' ain't jest right."

They stopped their approach.

"Daisy!" Alton called. He cleared his throat and tried it again, *"Daisy!"*

They waited. Jeff thought he saw motion inside, but it was only the reflection of an airborne bird in an upstairs windowpane. The men looked at each other.

"Cats," Alton said.

"What?"

"Daisy's cats. I don't see her cats. They oughtta be climbin' all over us by now."

"Come on," Jeff said, leading the way to the porch step.

A car horn blared. Rapid staccato blasts caused both men to look at the road. A black Nissan was speeding toward them, leaving a cloud of dust thick as jet exhaust.

"That's Karen's car," Jeff said, turning in the driveway to meet her.

Before the Nissan had ground to a halt, Karen was opening the door.

"Jeff, oh God—"

He ran to her. "Karen, what is it? What's wrong?"

She was panting as if she had been running. Her eyes were wide with something very like fear. Jeff watched as she struggled to control herself.

"Jeff . . . it may not be anything, but—"

"But what, Karen? What's the matter?"

"Jeff, it's Casey—"

"What's wrong with her? Has something happened?"

"I . . . I don't know."

He grabbed her by the biceps. "What about Casey?"

Karen took a deep breath. "I . . . phoned her at lunchtime. Just wanted to say hi. I thought she might be lonely or something. She didn't answer the phone. I figured maybe she'd just gone outside.

But the more I thought about it, the more worried I got. She still didn't answer when I tried her again, so I drove home. She was gone, Jeff. The house was locked and she was gone. I looked all over for her."

"Well . . . well . . ." Jeff shook his head. "Maybe she just . . . just . . . Oh Christ, where could she *go?*"

Karen stared at him.

"We'd better get back there," he said. "I'll ride with you. Alton's got his own car."

After a hurried good-bye, Jeff and Karen were in the Nissan, racing down the hill.

* * *

Alton stood alone in the dooryard. He looked one last time at the house, then at his car where it waited down the road at a turnoff.

Before he could make a move he caught motion out of the corner of his eye. The side door to the house was opening.

A bent figure stood in the deep interior shadow.

"D-Daisy?"

"Alton Barnes, is that you?" It was Daisy Dubois's voice.

"Yes, ma'am, it is."

"Why, I *thought* that was you out there. Come in quickly, can you? I need your help with something."

* * *

Waterville, Vermont

His breathing eased. His thoughts slowed. The anger passed.

He could see it perfectly now: there'd been no real reason to get so angry. He had let Winston the orderly get under his skin. And he'd lost his temper again. For the first time in weeks.

Now he was flat on his back and shot full of Thorazine. And nothing, nothing in the whole world seemed important enough to get angry about.

All he had wanted to do was use the phone, to call that priest— Father Sullivan—over to Hobston, and to tell him the rest of the stuff about the bad thing in the church.

Clement Barry should have known this would happen. Every time he talked about the thing in the church, people thought he was crazy. And this time, wow, he had really lost it. God, he'd definitely blown it this time, but good.

"Why do you want to use the phone, Clem?" Winston had demanded. Winston's eyes were always half-closed and he always looked as if he were squinting down his nose at you.

"I . . . that priest, Father Sullivan, he asked me to call if I remembered anything else."

"Anything else about what, Clem?"

"About the church. You know, the church in Hobston. I used to be an altar boy there."

"Hobston's a long-distance call. You got any money, Clem?"

"No, I . . . I thought maybe I could use the phone in Dr. Ramsland's office."

"What's the matter with the pay phone?"

"I t-t-told you. I don't have no . . . any money."

"Maybe one of the nurses will let you use the phone at the nurses' station. You could ask, you know."

By then Clem was grinding the fist of his right hand into the palm of his left. "N-no . . . be-be-cause I need to speak in private. I need to speak to the priest. It's im-im-important."

"What could be so important that you can't tell me about it?"

"He . . . he's at that church. And something . . . you know . . . bad happened at that church."

When he realized Winston had tricked him into talking about it, the passion had come like a flame igniting at the base of his skull. His face heated as if sunburned. His fists clenched at his sides.

He pushed Winston out of the way and ran down the tiled hallway toward Dr. Ramsland's office.

When he slammed his shoulder against the wooden door it burst open, surprising Ramsland who was talking with a patient. The patient looked up in horror and started to scream.

Clem had tried to say that he needed to use the phone, but before he could explain, Ramsland was screeching for the orderly.

"The priest. I gotta talk to the priest," Clem shouted. He turned and bolted from the office, but failed to see Winston's foot.

Sprawling on the floor, Clem felt Winston sitting on his back. Then he felt the prick of the needle as it penetrated his shoulder.

* * *

Hobston, Vermont

The strange redheaded man snatched Alton through the open doorway, then threw him to the floor. With the impact, dishes rattled on the shelves of Daisy's old oak hutch. Some tumbled, shattered on the linoleum floor.

In spite of the familiar voice that had summoned him, Daisy was nowhere around. Waxy brown smudges beside him on the floor suggested something bad had happened here.

"Where's Daisy?" Alton said to the man, who towered over him, looking down with his red military crew cut and his toothy smart-ass grin.

Alton waited for an answer that didn't come. When he started to pick himself up, the man kicked him. Air fired from his lungs and he made a puking sound. Again he sprawled on the floor, overturning one of the kitchen chairs. He puffed and panted, the wind knocked out of him. But hell, he'd suffered worse beatings than this. Even that feisty little nip in Korea hadn't been able to make him talk. That tiny oriental—Christ, he couldn't have been over five feet two—had given Alton the worst beating of his life. That karate shit was nothing to mess with. After the war eight years of training insured that Alton would never suffer similar indignities again.

So maybe Alton was a little rusty, and a whole lot older now, but he could tell just by the way this guy moved, he didn't know anything about fighting. Bulk and muscle were all he had to show for himself.

The grinning man said, "Now, Alton, you jest settle down and behave. Like I was sayin', I got somethin' I need you to help me with."

It was a perfect imitation of Daisy's voice. Alton's flesh crawled as he listened; he found it difficult to believe his ears. "Who the hell are you?" he forced his voice to a commanding firmness, hoping to sound intimidating.

"I'm whoever you want me to be, Alton." This time it was Stuart Dubois's voice. For emphasis, the man spat from the side of his mouth, exactly as Stu used to spit his chewing tobacco. Thick saliva clung to Alton's shirtfront. He felt an immobilizing coldness in his gut. This was way too strange. It was unearthly in its strangeness. This guy was some kind of first-class fruitcake.

Sizing up his attacker, Alton steadied himself before he tried a second time to get to his feet.

"Alton, you jest don't never learn, do ya?" It was Stu's voice again. The grinning man's right foot rose like the bucket of a steam shovel. This time Alton was on his feet and ready. With a slight shift of position, he sidestepped the kick. Catching the ankle between his hand and thigh, Alton pivoted, raising his right leg. With all the force and muscle power of his full two hundred pounds, Alton brought his left foot down on the man's outstretched leg, just above the kneecap.

The kneecap slid when the attacker's foot hit the floor. The leg broke with a crack like splitting timber. Together the men tumbled onto the floor. The grinning man howled, his right leg bent backward like a stork's.

Alton rolled away and sprang to his feet.

"Now you son of a bitch, you're gonna tell me what's going on here. Too much weird shit's happenin', and I don't like none of it."

The roles had reversed; now Alton towered over the whimpering man, who, oddly, was still grinning. With the toe of his boot, Alton jabbed the wounded leg. The man shrieked in agony.

"Feel good, ya bastard? Now you tell me what ya done with Daisy before I bust that damn leg clean off."

The man was trying to sit perfectly still. Alton knew any motion would result in tremendous pain. He lifted his foot, let it hover over the demolished knee.

"No," the man pleaded, grinning. "Not no more." This time it was Alton's own voice issuing from the man on the floor. He was whining, just exactly the way Alton had whined on the floor of that nip prison. "No. Please. Not no more."

Alton bristled with an embarrassed dread. He fought the brutal urge to tromp the splintered leg, turned away, took a couple of steps toward the living room. "Daisy!" he called. "Daisy, you around here someplace?"

There was no sound but the wracked breathing of the wounded man.

"Daisy, you all right? Can you answer me?"

Silence.

Alton whirled on the man. "I ain't gonna ask you again, you son of a bitch. You tell me what you done to Daisy."

The man began to shake violently. Alton thought he might go into convulsions. He didn't care. "Where is she, ya bastard?"

Then a strange transformation began. Although his facial features were contorted in pain, the man's teeth were still set in that hideous grin. Suddenly the muscles below his skin twitched, moved, seemed somehow to shift. The skin, a moment ago taut as the head of a drum, slackened and wrinkled. The grin faded; lips covered teeth. It was not just that the man's expression was changing, his whole face was transforming. When he looked down at his misshapen leg an expression of helpless terror altered his features even more. In a moment, fearful puzzled eyes looked up at Alton Barnes.

Alton held his gaze, staring him down.

The man looked away, glanced around the kitchen as though his surroundings were completely unfamiliar. "My God," he said in tones unfamiliar to Alton, "oh my God, what's happened here? What have I done?"

Then he screamed. The hysterical sound quickly rose to a pain-filled demented wail.

A gunshot sounded.

The fallen man's head jerked back, split, sprayed bloody particles onto the wall behind it.

Alton whirled.

Another redheaded man, this one wearing tan pants and a pin-striped jacket, stood at the doorway. He was not smiling. The barrel of a small automatic poked from his fist. "You're full of surprises, Mr. Barnes."

Shaken by the killing, Alton looked from the gunman to the corpse and back again. "I'd sure like to know what's going on around here," his voice cracked.

The gunman clicked his tongue as if he were chastising a misbehaving schoolboy. "We have a great deal of work to do, Mr. Barnes, and unless I can persuade you to help us, I'm afraid you'll have to join the fallen Mr. Gold."

Seething silently, Alton waited. When it seemed the gunman wouldn't continue, Alton asked quietly, "Who are you?" He almost followed it with *and what do you want,* but all of a sudden he really didn't want to know.

"My name's McCurdy," the man answered pleasantly.

"Is Daisy all right?"

"Oh yes, very much so. She has given herself to the Lord."

"What do you mean? You mean she's dead?"

"She has . . . passed on. Just like our friend Mr. Gold. But that's *good.* No one really dies, Mr. Barnes."

"Where is she? What have you done with her?"

"Please, take a seat in one of those chairs." McCurdy gestured with the weapon.

Alton sat.

Just then he heard a commotion in the next room, as if a dog were coming across the floor. A filthy, pink-colored animal entered the room, moving awkwardly on all fours. It looked like some deformed ape that had shed its body hair. Only a greasy, matted mane remained, swept back on its bulbous head. Drooping, blackened lips hung limp like a boneless jaw. Alton needed a moment to realize the creature was human. A female. A little girl.

Again he shivered in the stark chill of unreality.

Without being spoken to, the girl lunged, dragged herself across the room. Rearing back on her knees, she pulled cords from the venetian blinds on two kitchen windows. Dust rose in clouds from the horizontal slats. Grunting and drooling as she worked, she used the cord to tie Alton to the chair. He watched her unskilled fingers move clumsily.

When she was done, she squatted beside the table, eyeing Alton keenly, as if she were a well-trained guard dog.

* * *

Burlington, Vermont

"We *can't* go to the police," Jeff raged, slapping his palm against the top of Karen's baby grand piano. She cringed as the strings rumbled and whined.

Taking a cautious step toward him, Karen held out her hand, attempting a comforting contact. Jeff pulled away. Ghastly pale, as if the blood had drained from his face, body rigid as a marionette's, he paced around the living room. His eyes blazed. Sweat glistened on his forehead like rainwater.

"Jeff, listen—"

"I was *wrong* to come here, I was *wrong* to bring Casey with me. I was *wrong* to drag you into this—"

"You didn't drag me—"

"God, Karen, now they know you're involved; they know where you live."

"Jeff—"

"I've put you in danger. Real danger. Y-you . . . God, Karen, you could be next!"

"Jeff, please, try to calm down. Whether you were wrong or right doesn't matter now. What matters is that Casey's gone and we've got to deal with it."

"I *know* she's gone, damn it. You don't have to tell me that. You don't have to talk to me like one of your goddamn patients! You love this sort of thing, don't you? Tell everybody how to fix their lives. Bury yourself in everybody else's problems so you don't have to deal with your own. You—"

He cut himself off, turned away. "I'm sorry," he said, almost in a whisper.

Karen bit her lip, wrestling with defenses that had sprung up like steel bars between them. *Of course* Jeff was devastated; he was scared, angry, and he didn't know what to do with it. So he lashed out. At her. Because . . . because Casey was gone.

Together they had searched the grounds of Colonial Condominiums. They'd checked the observation deck, the beach, they'd even knocked on doors and questioned Karen's neighbors. She was gone all right, and no one had even seen her leave. How could anyone not see a girl in a wheelchair?

Now Karen felt so useless. What help could she hope to offer? This was no counseling practice session, no role-playing exercise at a training seminar. How effectively could she expect to handle this real-life crisis? Above all, she hoped she wouldn't freeze up. She knew she might. If she did, she'd be no good to anybody.

Jeff stood looking out the window toward the parking lot. He was quiet now, but no less tense. Was this a good time to push for police involvement? Or would that make him fly utterly off the handle? He seemed so dangerously close to some kind of explosion.

Karen summoned all the authority she could muster. "Darn it, Jeff, you listen to me now. You came here and you asked for my help, remember? And I agreed. So for better or for worse, now you're stuck with me. And by gosh I'm going to help you, like it or not."

Jeff turned and stared at her; she had his attention.

"Think about it; you said it yourself: somehow the Academy located you, and now they've taken Casey. Okay, if they've got her it's probably to use her as some kind of a lever against you, right? So they'll keep her safe, won't they? I mean, they can't all be cold-blooded killers and psychopaths. They'll keep her safe so they can use her to bargain with you."

"But we've got to *find* her!"

"It's a job for the police, Jeff. I don't know what makes you think you can help her all by yourself. I don't mean to insult you, but you really didn't make a very successful fugitive, remember? What makes you think you'll do any better as a detective?"

Jeff turned from the window and glared at her, his eyes like lasers. "Jesus, Karen, wake up, will you. We're not talking about Officer Friendly here. The police could be in on this. Maybe they're the ones who took Casey."

"Jeff, you can't believe—"

"Believe? Hell, I'm in a position to *know*. You aren't. We're talking big government bucks here. Covert activities. Top-secret defense operations. Christ, I could be accused of treason!"

"Jeff—"

"If I call the police, they'll call the Academy; simple as that. Then they'll send a cruiser, pick me up, and deliver me in person."

She couldn't find a rebuttal. Could he possibly be right about all this? Could she have blundered, wide-eyed and innocent, into some vast and mysterious conspiracy? No. No way; it sounded too much like a Hitchcock movie.

At the same time she knew Jeff wasn't lying. And he wasn't delusional. In fact, if she had to, she could honestly testify under oath that he was perfectly sane and rational. But wow, the whole situation was crazy, inconceivable. Absurd.

She watched Jeff, undecided.

No. She *had* to believe him. Just because things were unbelievable didn't mean he was lying,

He caught her staring. "And don't look at me like that, God damn it. I'm not paranoid, no matter what you're thinking."

She walked over to him, took both his hands in hers, looked directly into his eyes. Then, softly, "I know you're not paranoid, Jeff. I never thought that. And even if I had suspected it once, I wouldn't believe it now, not after getting to know you, not after spending so much time together. Not after what's happened. I think I understand what you're feeling: you're angry as can be and you're worried sick about your daughter. And you have every reason to be. But there are people who know how to deal with situations like this. You and I don't. Let's face it."

He couldn't hold her gaze. Eyes cast down, he almost toppled forward. Moving in slow motion he wrapped his arms around her. Then he began to cry, burying his face in her long hair.

"Oh God, Karen, she must be so scared, so . . . terrified. . . ."

She held him tightly, and then her own tears came. When she felt the strength in his arms relax a little, she said, "Here, let me get us a couple of drinks."

"Yeah," said Jeff, sniffing, trying to smile. "Yeah, good idea. Thanks."

She continued to talk to him as she crossed to the kitchen for a bottle and glasses. "We're bound to hear from them," she said. "Maybe any minute. If the Academy's security is as tight as you say, then they've already done a complete psychological workup on you. They'll gamble you won't go to the police. Look, they know you're out on a limb, otherwise they wouldn't have risked a stunt like this." Karen pulled an ice cube tray from the freezer.

"And that forces me to admit the other possibility," she went on, "the possibility that you're completely right about this. About everything. That the police *are* in on it. At least to the degree that they'll believe some government official's story before they'll believe ours. But either way, what can we do? We can't go out looking for her. Where would we start, for heaven's sake? Like it or not, it looks like the next move *has* to be theirs."

She handed Jeff a glass containing two shots of Canadian Club, one ice cube, and a splash of water. She'd made one just like it for herself. They sat side by side on the sofa. Jeff tapped the upholstered arm soundlessly.

"God, Karen, I'm awfully frightened for her." Jeff's voice was quiet, hoarse from shouting. "No matter what I told her, Casey could never realize the extent of what's going on here. I never prepared her for something like this. And she's always so trusting. . . . Of everybody. . . ."

"I bet you prepared her much better than you think. It may be easier for me to see that than it is for you."

"Yeah. Sure. But she's in over her head. And so am I." He pounded the arm of the couch. "*Jesus*, I should never have done it. If I hadn't played hero like this, if I hadn't been the hotshot whistle-blower, wanting to expose the Academy, I'd . . . I'd . . ."

"We need heroes, Jeff."

"What?"

"I said we need heroes."

His eyes locked on Karen. After a moment his gaze drifted away and fixed on his empty glass. "Some hero." He took a deep breath, then continued talking in a quiet monotone. "Since her mother died, I've felt responsible. Overprotective. Sure, I admit it. Maybe you read about it in the newspapers. It was one of those random, senseless things that leaves everybody feeling like God has packed up, taken the afternoon off to go fishing. The *Globe* called it 'The Trolley Terror'; it got a fair amount of television time, too. Even made the tabloids.

"Casey and Jessica had gone into the city to see a show. I stayed home. I'd been away on assignment and I was tired and cranky. Hardly fit to be with at all. I should have gone with them. Least I could've done was drive them in. See, Jess hated to drive in the city; she was always scared she couldn't find a parking place or that the car might get broken into or ripped off. God, the stuff she worried about seemed so trivial. . . .

"Anyway, there's gangs in Boston. Maybe you've heard about them: kids, twelve, thirteen, fourteen, carrying switchblades and guns. Believe it or not, Karen, they identify themselves by the sneakers they wear. That's their uniform. What could be more appropriate for a kid, right?

"Three of these kids—I don't know how old they were, but they were just kids—they were chasing some rival gang member through the cars. Some guy, a retired fireman named Thomsen, told them to knock it off and he tripped one of them with his cane. The other two stopped what they were doing, turned around, and blew the old man away. Just like that. They took out a couple others in the process. Jessica was hit in the face, killed instantly, so they tell me. When Casey got up to help they shot her in the spine.

"What a conspiracy of circumstances, eh? I mean if I'd just been decent enough to drive them, you know? And now I wonder . . ."

"Oh, Jeff. . . ." Karen bit her lower lip and blinked away the threat of tears. She took his hand; it felt limp in hers. "I don't have any comforting platitudes for you. Certainly I can understand how you feel about Casey. But the rest of it, it's history now. It's over. None of it was your fault."

Jeff's ice cube had melted. He drank the water from his glass and reached for the bottle on the coffee table. Carefully, he poured himself another two fingers of whiskey.

Karen thought he seemed calmer now. Maybe this was the time to introduce the plan that had been taking shape in her mind.

"Jeff, I have an idea that doesn't involve the police at all."

He looked up, the glass frozen at the midpoint between the tabletop and his lips. His eyes, though slightly suspicious, coaxed her to go on.

"I spoke with a priest today just before I came home. A Father Sullivan. Turns out he's the new Catholic priest in Hobston. We had a pretty interesting talk and what he had to say, well, now that I think about it, it might have something to do with Casey and what's going on here."

Jeff narrowed his eyes, looking at her strangely, as if he had no idea what she was talking about.

"A priest?"

Undaunted, she pressed on. "Before moving to Hobston, he was a teaching psychologist at a college in New York state. I wanted to talk to him about a patient of mine, a little girl who . . . disappeared."

Disappeared: the word made Jeff snap to attention. He was listening now. She had his complete attention.

"Jeff, listen to this: It turns out Father Sullivan is also looking for a missing person, another priest, a Father Mosely." In her excitement she rushed the words, "And Alton Barnes, too. His friend Stuart Dubois vanished. And other things are going on. Weird things. Like an old woman Sunday school teacher who started beating kids for no reason—"

"In Hobston?"

"Right, yes, Hobston."

"Holy shit. . . ."

"Right. So, what do you think? Can all this be coincidence, Jeff? All this strange stuff? And each of us—you, me, Mr. Barnes, and Father Sullivan—each of us is dealing with a disappearance? What are the odds against that, huh? And there's lots of other weird stuff, too. How much of it centers around Hobston? You said it yourself, Jeff: weird things happen there. You were the one who told me about these 'Fortean Windows' of yours. I didn't know what to think of them then. And now? Well, now I still don't know. But to me it sounds like . . . like something's going on. What, I don't know, but something. I mean, how can I deny it? It's right in front of my face. It would be irrational to deny it."

Jeff nodded.

"And, Jeff, suppose Casey's disappearance has nothing whatsoever to do with the Academy. Suppose it's related to the other stuff that's going on around here. Or maybe . . . maybe they're both part and parcel of the same thing!"

Karen stopped talking, embarrassed from rattling on. Jeff's attention hadn't wandered. "Go on," he said.

"Well . . . well, what about this: Let's not call the police. Let's go back over to Hobston and talk to Father Sullivan. We can be there in less than half an hour. I'll call him. Okay?"

"Wait! No! We shouldn't use the phone. It might be—"

"Bugged? Yeah, right. Maybe we better stop at a pay phone."

"Hold it! Wait! Jesus, Karen, I can't leave here. What if they call while we're gone? What if they want to talk to me? What about Casey?"

"Don't worry, Ma Bell to the rescue. I've got Call Forwarding, remember? A necessary evil in my business. I'll punch in Father Sullivan's number. That way, if they phone here, we can pick it up at his place in Hobston."

"I don't know, Karen . . . A priest . . .?"

"I've talked to him, Jeff. He's not one of these sweetness-and-light types. He's down to earth. Bright. Dr. Gudhausen recommended him to me, don't forget. And I think we can trust him."

Jeff continued to stare at her, blinking.

"Come on, Jeff, snap out of it, will you! Jeez. . . ."

And suddenly he was grinning at her.

"Hey! What are you doing? What are you smiling about?"

"You. You never swear, do you?"

"W-what?"

"No matter what's going on, you never swear. You say things like 'darn,' and 'gosh,' and 'wow!'"

"What are you talking about?"

"You! You don't ever swear. You don't cuss, curse, use four-letter words, blaspheme."

"I don't . . . what do you mean? So what?"

"So nothing. It's just that I've never met anyone who doesn't swear before."

For a wonderful moment, they both laughed, embraced. Then more tears came.

* * *

Hobston, Vermont

"Cat still got your tongue, Mr. Barnes?" said Skipp McCurdy as he walked back into the kitchen, smiling pleasantly. "Well, no matter. You'll be talking soon enough."

Al heaved against the cords that bound him to the chair. He knew he had no chance of breaking free. Every time he moved, the naked child at his feet snapped to attention like a vigilant attack dog.

McCurdy pushed the child with the toe of his wingtip. "Settle down now, he's not going anywhere."

The child scurried back to the wall where she crouched, hugging her knees to her chest.

Chuckling, McCurdy took off his blue pin-striped jacket and loosened his bow tie. Then, as if someone had pushed a freeze frame button, he stopped. He straightened mechanically and cocked his head to one side, apparently listening to something Alton could not hear. In a moment he dashed outside, returning quickly with a black briefcase that he placed on the kitchen table.

When Alton saw the case, his stomach knotted tighter than the cord on his wrists. He had a pretty good idea what was in it and he knew what was coming next.

Again he flexed against his restraints.

McCurdy clicked his tongue. "Oh my no, Mr. Barnes. What do you think I have in here? Thumbscrews? Red-hot pokers? A cattle prod maybe? Such mistrust. . . ."

As McCurdy opened the briefcase, Alton saw the TV screen built into its lid. One of those portable computers, he concluded. But why?

McCurdy looked around for a place to plug it in. "Imagine that," he giggled, "no electricity. Thank the Good Lord for battery backup. What a fine age we're living in, Mr. Barnes! A fine, magical age. An age of miracles!"

Now he was pulling some kind of flat metal antenna from the side of the case. "I wouldn't want you to miss your afternoon game shows, Mr. Barnes." Again he laughed and the sound was ugly, like a beast growling.

"To start, I'm going to show you how we can use this magical little machine to bring your friends Jeffrey Chandler and pretty little Dr. Bradley to join our meeting. Would you like that? Would you enjoy a bit of company?"

Alton squinted at him, willing himself not to break eye contact. But he said nothing.

Then McCurdy froze again, listening to the silence. His tongue clicked and he said to no one, "Mmm-hmm. Mmm-hmm. Ooooh-kay!" He turned on Alton. "But first we have a little errand to do. I have a show here that I know you're going to enjoy. It's of an inspirational nature. Tell me, Mr. Barnes, have you ever seen a sinner burn in Hell?"

Alton glared at him.

"Still nothing to say, heh?"

Planting himself in a chair before his makeshift computer table, McCurdy switched on the machine. The impression of a hand appeared on the screen. When McCurdy placed his hand on the image,

Alton again noted his truncated little finger. He'd remember that—a good identifying detail.

MCCURDY VERIFIED

McCurdy's fingers deftly tapped the keys:

*clement barry. display visual.

The outline of a head took shape on the LCD monitor. The image waved and flexed as features clarified. Soon Alton saw a detailed photographic likeness of an unfamiliar face. A five-pointed star appeared around the image, started to spin. A light show of colors and shapes danced brilliantly on the screen.

Alton Barnes watched, almost hypnotized, though he had no idea what he was seeing.

* * *

Waterville, Vermont

Clem's strength was returning. It seeped into him like blood into sleeping limbs, restoring their senses, bringing them back to life. Little by little, the drug was wearing off. Clem Barry was waking up.

Yet even at his most lethargic he had been able to think. The tranquilizer hadn't stopped his mind from working. Instead it kept his thoughts, no matter how horrible, from bothering him too much. And so he loved this chemical freedom from the torture of his own mind. At the same time, he realized how helpless he was when under sedation, how totally and completely vulnerable.

But he had put the time to good use. He had thought the whole thing through, never recoiling from any of the ugly knowledge. Yes, Father Sullivan seemed like a good and strong man. If something was still hiding in the church, Sullivan should be warned straightaway. None of this cryptic business about looking in the Bible; in all probability Father Mosely's Bible wasn't even there anymore. So how could Sullivan look in it?

Clem had been in a position to help, and he had refused. That's not the way Father Mosely would have liked him to behave. In the beginning, so very long ago, Clem had freely offered to help. Father Mosely had refused. Then, when Clem tried to tell his story, people thought he was lying. And crazy.

How could they know every word of his story was true? What they called symptoms of mental illness were in reality rational behavior. Why couldn't they understand that he didn't like to touch things because he knew all things were infested? All matter was not exactly as we see it.

The easiest thing had been to acquiesce, accept his diagnosis and eventual confinement. In time he had learned to be grateful for his incarceration because he was safer here, locked away from the outside world, confined, protected. Here people kept an eye on him twenty-four hours a day. He'd never have that kind of security anywhere outside. Out there, he would have been on his own. Out there, he was at the mercy of—

For nearly ten years the bad thing had not bothered him. Not really. Except for little reminders. At dinner a fork would twitch in his hand. A bird might perch on the bars of his window and speak to him. Or it would rain inside his room and he'd get in trouble for spilling water.

But now, with Father Sullivan back in the church, suppose the bad thing started up again? Suppose, simply by keeping his silence, Clement Barry had given the new priest and the people of Hobston the Judas kiss?

Soon, as soon as he regained his strength, he knew what he had to do. When the drug wore off he would sneak away, leave the hospital. He would find Father Sullivan and tell him everything. He'd offer to help and he'd hope it wasn't too—

What was that?

With difficulty, Clem lifted his head off the cot and looked around his room. Water dripped in the sink in the corner. A breeze drifted through the open window, brushing his skin like a silk scarf. Air ruffled the clothes in his closet. The arms of his three long-sleeved shirts rose and fell as if they were waving to him.

Tiny specks of white plaster snowed from cracks in the walls and ceiling.

Why should that be?

Clem propped himself on his elbows as the locked door rattled in its frame.

Only the wind, he thought. *Only the wind. . . .*

But there was also that buzzing in his ears. He must have left his radio on. With a tremendous effort of will he moved his limp legs, heavy as the limbs of a statue. He flopped them over the side of his bed. His stocking feet plopped like dead things onto the cold tile floor.

Groaning, he shifted to an upright position. The effort made him feel like the heaviest man in the world. Somehow he stood.

Five unsteady steps brought him to the radio. Numb fingers found the knob—the radio had been off all along.

Yet, the buzzing grew louder.

He looked at the window. The black horizontal bars seemed to be bubbling. A closer look and he saw hornets, one after another, perching there. The sky beyond was an ebony cloud, as if a million wasps had assembled and were heading his way in an endless swarm.

Clem ran clumsily to the window, slammed it down, crushing tiny black bodies against the sash. They twitched and groped with hairlike legs.

More plaster rained from the ceiling.

The buzzing in his ears grew louder.

When he looked down at the floor he realized he was standing in midair a thousand feet above the distant rocky ground.

Clem gasped and flopped back onto his bed.

He knew what was happening. The thing was messing with him again. He had probably summoned it simply by thinking about it. He had learned, *don't think about it.* He knew thinking about it only made things worse.

"O-okay," he said in a tense whisper. "Okay, I won't say nothin'. I'll stay right here in my room and I won't say nothin' to the priest. Okay . . .? Okay . . .?"

Something wet, clammy, and invisible dragged across his face. He tried to brush it away, and his hands came away slick with blood.

It's not real, Clem thought, *it's just trying to scare me.*

Still, he frantically wiped the blood on his pants.

The buzzing in his head turned to a hissing, and the hissing became words, "Ssssstupid . . . sssstupid . . . stupid . . . Ssssssss."

Clem slapped his hands to his ears, but it did no good. He tried the floor again. Cautiously. It was an invisible barrier that easily supported his weight high above a shadowy pit seething with red dancing flames. They flicked at him, reached up like serpent tongues.

Without daring to look down, three sprinting steps brought him to the door. He tugged on it, pounded.

But the orderly had locked him in.

He opened his mouth to shout, "Hel—," but something like damp cotton filled it, gagging him. He tried to pull it out, but nothing was there.

Then he noticed the walls.

They were beginning to change. The beige paint was vanishing like mist evaporating from a windowpane. And all of a sudden the walls were gone.

One by one the pieces of furniture in his room fell into the lightless void. His bureau spun away and disappeared. His desk dropped out of sight, its chair flew off into space, and the bed hovered a second and soared off into infinity. Hairbrush, toothpaste, slippers, and a Coke bottle zipped around him like comets.

Clement clung to the solid knob of the invisible door. *It's not real,* he thought, *none of it's real!*

In his ten years as a mental patient he had learned much about the deceptions of the mind. And the bad thing did its work in the mind.

Clem saw sweat flying from his face as, frantically, he tried to look around. There was nothing else to see. It was as if he were suspended in space, enclosed in an endless, all-encompassing planetarium where tiny stars surrounded him in the heavens. They were white pinpricks, far away and out of reach.

"Stop it!" Clem screamed.

Something moved from behind him, coming into view. It was the wood-framed mirror that had hung over the washbasin. It floated surrealistically in the black infinity until it positioned itself directly in front of him. Clem wanted to swat it away, but he didn't dare let loose of the doorknob clutched in his aching, sweating fists. If he released the doorknob, he knew he would plunge to his death.

Gotta hold on, he thought. *This isn't real. None of it's real! I can't be in space. I couldn't breathe. I'd explode or something. . . .*

When he saw his face in the mirror, the pain came.

A sloshing sensation, like warm water in his stomach. Only this time it was in his head.

I shouldn't have thought "explode." Oh God, I shouldn't have thought "explode."

His terrified face glared at him from the mirror. He wanted to look away, but right now his face was the only real thing in the universe. The alternative—looking at the blackness and the stars—would bring madness. So he looked at himself, saw the skin of his face redden as if it were blasted by a scorching sun.

Saw the hair of his head and eyebrows singed and falling away like dust.

Saw his irises bleach white, turning his eyeballs into perforated eggshells.

And the pain in his head intensified.

Blood slipped from his nose, his mouth, his eyes. He looked like a painted savage in the mirror. His last articulated thought was that something inside his head has dislodged.

Then—*Oh my God*—he saw what might have been liquefied brain flowing from his nose and ears.

He screamed. But in space there could be no sound.

PART FOUR

Devil's Town

"Something entered people, something chopped, pressed,
punctured, had its way with them and
if you looked, bad child,
it entered you."

—Maxine Kumin
The Man of Many L's

Excerpt from
The Reality Conspiracy:
An Anecdotal Reconstruction of the Events at Hobston, Vermont

Dr. Lloyd Sparker lived just far enough out of town to enjoy a sense of escape when he went home after work. As a younger man, he used to drive the mile and a half between his office and his house. But now, and ever since his heart attack in '83, he truly believed that exercise was every bit as important as he told his patients it was. So on days when he didn't have to make hospital visits, he walked to and from work.

On Thursday, June thirtieth, his receptionist left at four-thirty. A little after five, Sparker locked the door to the office, checked the potted geraniums on the wide porch railing, and reflected on the events of the day as he started down the sidewalk toward home.

That morning had been oddly quiet at the office. Both appointments had canceled, so he had been free to ponder the *Burlington Free Press.* Surprising how much bad news thirty-five cents will buy, he mused, turning pages to get beyond the story about Beth Damon's death. He flattened the newspaper on his desktop and poured over the details of yesterday's Red Sox game.

Then, out of a deeply ingrained sense of professional obligation, he had flipped through the latest issue of *JAMA*, deferring gratification so he could get to the new *Yankee Magazine* that had arrived in the morning's mail. He was well into a short story by Howard Frank Mosher when the strangest emergency of his four-decade career began.

Over the years Sparker had often seen the disgusting product of solitary sexual experimentation. He had removed greased Alka-Seltzer bottles from vaginas, pulled knotted clotheslines from rectums, and once he'd even had to extract brittle brown pine needles from Dwight Gardner's penis.

In almost every case, people would sit there and innocently insist they had no idea at all how the foreign objects happened to be where they were. Sparker constantly marveled at the randy human animal's capacity for denial.

Today's first patient had been something else again.

Rich and Rena Michaels had brought their daughter Kimberly into the office. The howling nine-year-old girl, dressed in a light summer bathrobe, was wracked with severe abdominal cramps.

"I think something bit her when she was in the pool," Rena Michaels said in a voice thin with restrained panic.

Seeing the blood on Kimberly's leg, Sparker considered an alternative: the girl might be having her first period.

"Aah, aah, aah!" Kimberly gasped, twitching and bucking in her father's arms. Rich carried her into Sparker's examining room and tried to stand her on her feet. "Something's inside me!" she wailed, doubling over, arms locked around her stomach.

Her father lifted her onto the table and Sparker motioned for the agitated young parents to adjourn to the waiting room.

When they had left, he administered an injection of valium and, momentarily, was able to get the girl to lie still on the examining table. Speaking soothingly, he placed a hand on her lower abdomen. He could feel a slight but steady pulsation below the skin and muscle.

The girl moaned, trying to flex into a fetal position.

Sparker waited a moment for the drug to take full effect, then guided her feet into the elevated metal stirrups.

He pulled on his plastic gloves, all the time talking to her soothingly. "Did you put something in there, honey?"

But she cried, "No!" so plaintively he almost believed her.

"Did someone else put something up there?" He asked the abhorrent question in his most matter-of-fact and grandfatherly manner. On some quiet level he was appalled at the crazy antics some young people got into these days. However, in this case he wouldn't permit himself to consider the possibility of parental abuse. Rich and Rena Michaels were fine young people. Among the best in town.

"No, oh no!" She gasped and he could see the white skin above her silky pubic fuzz pulsate as if with a muscle spasm.

As he manually encouraged her to dilate, he spoke in low comforting tones, "There now. You're going to be okay, dear. We'll just have a look now and see what's hurting you."

Under his intense lamp he could see a triangle of some foreign black substance within the pink and bloody folds of skin.

With a deft turn of the forceps he was able to grab . . . something.

When he tugged, she screamed.

With the forceps locked on their target, he applied a liberal amount of K-Y to the vaginal opening. Then he pulled again.

Kimberly wailed.

If it were not for the spiky fins, the eight-inch trout would have slipped out as easily as it must have slipped in. Incredibly, it was still twitching.

Even now, six hours later, the memory turned his stomach.

He passed the last square of concrete sidewalk without noticing. When he felt the uneven gravel path under his wingtips, he knew he was a quarter mile from home.

There was a spike of cool air in the early June evening. The momentary fear of a storm passed when Sparker glanced up at the cloudless blue of the sky. Going to be a beautiful night, he thought.

He quickened his pace, eager to see his wife and the pitcher of martinis he hoped she would have waiting for him. He could sure use a drink.

He had instructed the bewildered and embarrassed parents to drive the little girl directly to the hospital in Burlington. No doubt there were some minor internal injuries. Nothing serious, he assured them. Still, he wondered how they would explain the problem to the admitting people.

That's sure one for the textbooks, Sparker mused as he heard a soft *plop* behind him.

He stopped, turned, looked around, but saw nothing.

Returning to stride, his house came into view. Again he noticed how the big maple tree in the front yard appeared to be dying. Too many leafless branches; too many limp leaves. Gonna have to take the chainsaw to it, he thought, before some storm drops it on the house. A pity, too. Beautiful old tree. Going to cut back on shade for the porch. . . .

Then he consoled himself thinking of all the firewood the tree would yield.

PLOP!

The sound came from right behind him.

He turned to look as something solid struck his shoulder.

"What the—?"

A twitching eight-inch trout tumbled from his shoulder to the ground where it joined its flip-flopping companion. Then another fell, striking the road with a fleshy *thwack!"*

"Holy Moses!" Sparker said as he bent to examine the fish. He watched its gills open and close along with its mouth.

Plop. Plop-plop.

More fish landed around him. They smacked the ground like clapping hands.

Standing up straight, he squinted into the clear sky.

Far, far overhead, more fish looked like distant dirigibles where they appeared—just appeared—out of nowhere. Then they fell, slowly, strangely slowly, seeming to gain speed as they descended.

Holy shit!

They struck the walk, the grass, the blacktop. They were all around, twitching and flopping.

"Jesus Christ in Heaven!" Sparker said, quickening his pace.

As he passed the big maple tree, he saw motion some three feet over his head. At first the alien animal looked like some odd variety of snake crawling out of a hole in the trunk. But no! A second look told him it was the head of another trout, a big one. Crazily, it was half-embedded in the solid wood of the tree, as if it had just . . . materialized there.

Sparker couldn't believe his eyes. The old man fairly ran across his yard, eager to show his wife what was happening.

22

Shepherds of the Light

Hobston, Vermont

The priest's house was dark and old.

Like the scales of a giant lizard, cedar shingles so brown they looked black covered the rectory, the church, and the walkway that connected them. A sign shaped like a coat of arms hung beside the church door. It said:

St. Joseph's
Roman Catholic Church
Established 1867

Someone had painted over the priest's name, and the paint, like everything else on this Hobston street corner, looked ancient.

Father Sullivan appeared at the entrance the moment Karen and Jeff pulled into the driveway. By the time they were out of the car, the priest had walked halfway across the lawn to meet them.

Karen noted his casual attire: blue jeans and a drab sweatshirt. His gray hair was thick, highlighted with yellow the color of tobacco stains. He looked fit, but older than she had expected. In his sixties, at least.

And there was something more. He looked familiar, as if she had met him before.

"I'm glad you came," he said, holding out his right hand. Karen took it, smiling shyly. All her life she'd been intimidated by clerics. To her they were the spiritual elite, privileged to know something she didn't. Something about life, and afterlife. Something about reality and happiness. But, she reminded herself, she'd come here, not because William Sullivan was a priest, but because he was a psychologist.

Jeff introduced himself.

"I'm terribly sorry to hear about your daughter, Jeff. I know the police can't help much in a situation like this. No matter what their instincts tell them, they have to wait a day or so to confirm a person's absence. Of course, I'm ready to help immediately if I can."

Jeff shook Sullivan's hand, then he followed the priest and Karen to the rectory.

With Sullivan holding the door, they walked single file into a tiny dark mudroom with coat hooks on either side. A second door brought them into a spacious living room where a mullioned picture window looked out at the darkening backyard.

Karen noted worn burgundy leather furniture around a fireplace. On both sides of the brick chimney bookshelves—mostly empty—rose floor to ceiling. Woodwork and exposed beams were stained a dark brown. The fading walls were off-white.

Directly above her head, melted stubs of candles lined a cast-iron chandelier.

A lovely old place, Karen thought; definitely a man's domain, a cozy hybrid of library and hunting lodge. No! She had it now—the place suggested an old world men's club. It lacked only the fragrance of cigars, brandy in snifters, and a scattering of white-haired men in tweed coats, pouring over newspapers.

She jumped when the grandfather clock chimed the half hour. Seven-thirty.

"Come in, please," Sullivan said. He walked toward an odd door frame, maybe eight feet wide, enclosing a series of dark, tightly stacked horizontal slats, almost like wainscoting.

Puzzled, Karen asked what it was,

Sullivan's face brightened. "It's a door!" He demonstrated by reaching to the floor and lifting it as if it were a window shade. The horizontal slats vanished into the ceiling. "This house was built for the church over a hundred years ago," he explained. "The man who built it made his fortune manufacturing rolltop desks. This may be the world's first and only rolltop study."

"That's terrific," Jeff said, but his features showed little enthusiasm.

Sullivan said, "Why don't we sit in here?"

They chose two old, comfortable chairs that smelled faintly of mildew. Sullivan took a place behind a big mahogany desk. After a volley of pleasantries the priest leaned forward and went directly to the point. "Jeff, after talking with Karen, it seems the three of us have a lot to discuss. If you don't mind, I'd like you to start. Please tell us everything about this . . . somewhat questionable employer of yours."

Karen liked the way the priest was so direct; it was probably the best thing for Jeff. She watched him moisten his lips with the tip of his tongue. He cleared his throat and started talking. "Well . . . a little more than three years ago, about six months before my wife died, I accepted a research position at the Massachusetts Technological Academy. In fact, they recruited me. I was with IBM at the time, but I was bored and eager for a change.

"I didn't know what to make of them at first; see, they wanted to hire me as a UFO investigator. The minute I realized they were serious, I went for it. I mean, hey, I've always had a real . . . curiosity . . . about flying saucers. I loved to speculate about, you know, visitors from other planets, the possibility of a totally alien technology, all that kind of thing."

The priest nodded.

"The money was good, the assignment was intriguing, and, well, it was almost magic: one moment I'm a drone at an IBM plant, then . . . Voilà! I'm a UFO investigator for a highly secret, government-funded research program.

"First off, I had to pass a security clearance. Then take an oath of secrecy. Lots of top-secret mumbo-jumbo. But hell, I didn't care about that, I just wanted to get the straight scoop on UFOs. Wouldn't you? Wouldn't anyone?"

Father Sullivan nodded noncommittally, never breaking eye contact as Jeff continued. "Their security made IBM look like kindergarten. They wouldn't even let me *talk* about my job. But that was okay, I didn't have to worry about my friends thinking I'm a crackpot.

"At first everything was fine by me: suddenly I've got access to all these government files on UFOs, dating all the way back to Project Blue Book. Earlier, too. You may be surprised to learn that our government has been tracking UFOs in a structured and organized manner since Calvin Coolidge was in the White House. That's the early 1920s."

Sullivan raised his eyebrows.

"And here's something else that appealed to me: the freedom. Mostly I'd be traveling or working out of my home. They gave me a computer terminal, a fax machine, an expense account, credit cards, clerical backup, pretty much anything I wanted. Every two weeks or so I'd go into the office and meet with the director, Dr. Ian McCurdy. Quite recently Skipp—that's McCurdy's nickname—gave me the grand tour of the Academy's covert installation while he explained about some of the other things—secret things—they're involved in. That was the turning point for me."

Karen watched Jeff fidget and hedge. She suspected he was trying to decide how best to introduce the topic of *magic*. He outlined the computer's data base of arcane knowledge, the artificial-organic processing unit, the worldwide staff of researchers and data entry people. When he was well into his description of the horrifying videotaped execution, he had still avoided the word.

She noticed how Father Sullivan paid close and uncritical attention. He would nod, prod with a gentle "Go on. . . ." and smile benignly at appropriate places. She liked the way the priest conducted things. Even his appearance seemed to encourage trust and confidence. Father Sullivan looked like a stereotypical Irish priest from a TV show. His silvery hair and heavy-browed eyes made him appear distinguished and wise. A strong jaw suggested a real no-nonsense quality about him, that if needed he could offer physical, as well as spiritual, protection.

But gosh, she wondered, why does he look so familiar?

"So as I understand it," Sullivan said, "your Dr. McCurdy pushed a button in Boston and somehow executed this unfortunate man in California?"

"That's right, Father. We brought the videotape. Karen has it in her purse. You can see for yourself."

"Frankly, Jeff, your description of this . . . atrocity . . . is vivid enough for me. I guess I'm lucky not to have a VCR or television set. But please be sure I believe you. So, how do you think this execution was actually accomplished?"

Jeff sat up very straight in his chair, his back rigid as a post. Crossing his arms over his chest, he set his jaw and spat out the word—"Magic."

Sullivan didn't crack a smile.

Jeff looked uncertainly at Karen, then back at Sullivan. "You . . . you believe that, Father?"

Sullivan massaged his chin with a big-knuckled hand. "Until we have a more precise word, yes."

Karen and Jeff traded glances.

"Don't forget, Jeff, you're talking with a priest, a person who has devoted his life to a world of invisible forces, mystical experience, and the survival of death. You're also talking with a man—and a woman—who've devoted their careers to the mysteries of the human mind, its frailty, and its apparently awesome power. Sure I believe you. And now I'm going to ask that you believe me."

Sullivan told them about his trip to Canada, the decade-old exorcism, and the kidnapping of Father Mosely. He paused only long enough to light a cigarette. "Within the last few days," he said, "I'm starting to believe that the world of the human mind, and the unseen world of mystical powers, may be more closely related than anyone—but perhaps the most advanced occultists—has ever believed. Apparently something incredible happened in this church. Ten years ago, some horrible confrontation turned Father Mosely into a human vegetable yet, impossibly, kept him from dying. Does that sound like magic, too, Jeff?"

Karen looked at Jeff. He shrugged almost invisibly and asked, "What really happened here?"

"Who knows? Far as I can tell, there's no official record. That's unusual. Notes are *always* taken in a church-sanctioned exorcism. Nowadays the proceedings are even recorded on tape. But there was a witness. He's now confined to a mental institution, diagnosed paranoid schizophrenic. Just yesterday I visited him, but he wouldn't—or possibly couldn't—tell me what happened.

"Yet there was something about that man that I can't put my finger on. He seemed to understand what I needed, seemed to know . . . something. Still, he was unwilling to speak. All he told me was, 'Father Mosely always said, if you have questions, look in the Bible.' Rather a cryptic answer. Too pat, you know? Too Bible-thumping. But when I thought about it . . . Well, the fact is, I *knew* Father Mosely. Like most Catholic priests, he *never* encouraged Bible reading. See the contradiction? So the more I thought about it, the more I realized that this poor man had given me useful information."

Sullivan pulled open the drawer of his desk and took out a black leather book with gold lettering on the cover, the Holy Bible.

"I found this just this morning. It's Father Mosely's Bible. He hid it in the bottom drawer of this desk, along with a vial of holy water. Whoever cleaned out the desk missed it because Father Mosely had fashioned a false back to the drawer, concealing its contents very thoroughly."

Sullivan opened the book as he continued. "See, he actually wrote right in the Bible. Used a heavy felt-tipped pen so he could write directly over the existing print."

Karen could see heavy script covering the two-columned text. As Sullivan riffled the pages, it appeared much of the book was filled with Father Mosely's notes.

"I gather Father Mosely believed something evil was loose in the rectory. Apparently he thought his journal would be safe if it were written in a Bible. Just to be sure, he placed the book under an additional protective barrier of holy water."

"A demon?" Jeff sounded skeptical.

Sullivan looked directly at Jeff. "That's what Father Mosely believed—"

"And do you believe that?"

Father Sullivan's chest rose and fell with a deep sigh. "As a Roman Catholic priest, I believe that spirit is real. In fact, I believe spirit is the basis, the actual foundation, for all reality. I also believe *evil* spirit is real and very much a part of our lives."

Sullivan said it as matter-of-factly as if he'd stated, "I believe whales live in the ocean, although I've never seen one."

Jeff's expression gave Karen no insight into what he might be thinking. But she could guess.

Noticing this silent exchange, Father Sullivan said, "Do you believe in God, Mr. Chandler?"

Jeff paled. "I . . . I . . ."

"Is something wrong?"

"No. Ah . . . it's just that McCurdy once asked me the same question."

"And what did you tell him?"

"Father, if I believed in God, I think I would be praying right now."

"Yes. Of course." Sullivan cleared his throat and leaned back in his chair. He took another cigarette from the pocket of his sweatshirt and lighted it. "Then perhaps in your mind, my belief in the reality of spirit seems at odds with my scientific education and my profession as a psychologist. Culturally, we try very hard to see religion and science as two distinct and separate paths. But the fact is, they can be reconciled. I believe those paths have merged quite convincingly here in Father Mosely's notes." He patted the Bible. "In our Roman Catholic belief system, we call evil spirit 'preternatural.' By that we mean that it is present here, with us, in our material world. Yet it is not *of* this material world."

Karen shook her head, "I don't understand."

"Okay. You, and I, and the world around us—we all have this in common: we are *material* things. Our actions are governed by natural law."

Karen nodded.

"Now," the priest continued, "see if you can imagine a preposterous situation in which all material things suddenly cease to exist. At that instant, you and I and our entire physical environment would no longer be. We are God's creations, true, but we are undeniably, at least in part, *material*. If the material world were suddenly to cease, spirit would continue to be. It was here before the world began; it'll be here after the world ends. But right now, it—like you and me—is present in this world. Yet it is not of this world. Do you see?"

"I'm not sure," said Karen. "What I think you're leading up to is that these . . . demons can influence our behavior. They can change us, maybe even possess us? Our physical bodies are not a barrier for them?"

"Right. But I didn't say 'demons.' I'm just talking about spirit. But let's back up. The Roman Catholic Church believes . . . I . . . believe, that there are invisible powers that we call *spirits*. Like us, spirits were made by God. He designed them to be in an intimate relationship with matter—place, objects, and humans. Spirits are bodiless, like God; but they are also creatures—like humans. God gave them functions we can only guess at.

"All spirits, good or evil, have these things in common: they are not fixed in time the way we are; they relate to matter in an entirely different way; and they apparently have the power to know without reasoning.

"Man is never in conflict with the spirit of good. But *evil* spirit, quite simply, is contrary to man. It's older, much more powerful, and far more cunning. It can—for reasons we cannot begin to fathom—influence the human environment. So you're right, Karen, spirit *can* interact with human beings. Occasionally, it can even take possession of them."

Karen felt herself growing strangely tense. "But as a clinician, as a practicing psychologist, don't you think—"

"—that what appears to be demonic possession is simply some form of mental or physical illness?"

Karen nodded her head vigorously, trying to restore the conversation to safer ground.

"Of course. But not in every case. That's the point. In the past, a victim of disseminated sclerosis might have been judged possessed. Same for Huntington's chorea, Parkinson's disease, even dyslexia. More recently, paranoia, MPD, and especially Tourette's syndrome were thought to manifest characteristics similar to demonic possession. Maybe we still don't know the organic causes of these afflictions, but we know they do not conform completely to legitimate symptoms of possession."

"Symptoms of possession?" Karen struggled to keep her features free of her building skepticism. For the first time she considered that coming here had been a big mistake. She had promised Jeff a reality-based, down-to-earth clergyman. Instead, they were getting a theological lecture in medieval demonology. Still, the man's earnestness was compelling, his sincerity convincing.

"Yes, Dr. Bradley, symptoms. Just like symptoms of a disease. There are observable signs of an evil presence. The most obvious can be mistaken for something we're far more comfortable discussing: psychic phenomena. Objects flying around, glass breaking, wallpaper peeling off the walls, dramatic drops in temperature, nauseating odors, noises that come from nowhere . . . All these fascinating effects can be the product of preternatural power intruding on our human fields of perception. But we have at least one power on which evil spirit cannot intrude: the power of the human will. They may be able to produce a pile of gold by any number of means—but they can't force a person to take it. . . ."

"But all those things, those symptoms—"

"Yes, Jeff, those *can* be the result of natural phenomena. Or they can exist as legitimate physical mysteries *without* the involvement of preternatural forces. The most important fact to remember about evil spirits is that *none* of their faculties are divine. This simple truth allows one surefire test: the most telling, in fact the only infallible indication of a demonic presence is its obvious repugnance to the touch, the sight—even the mention—of anything holy: signs, symbols, objects, even places, people, or ceremonies. For example—he held up the small silver vial—"a demonic presence cannot tolerate the tiniest drop of holy water. It's a fact."

"So you're saying that Father Mosely tried to exorcise a demon from this rectory?"

"No, Dr. Bradley. The application of holy water is how Father Mosely finally determined that the thing in his rectory *was not* a demon."

"Was *not* a demon?" Jeff stared in disbelief, his confusion obvious. "Then what was it?"

Father Sullivan shrugged and shook his head. "I spent most of this afternoon reading his notes and I still can't decide. He called it a demon as a matter of convenience, but he also made it clear that it did not conform to the laws of religious demonology. Father Mosely's tragedy is that he never found out what was attacking him. The final face-off apparently occurred in the church. You see, a demon could never have followed him there."

"What happened in the church?" Karen asked.

"We'll never know. Even after Father Mosely concluded it wasn't a demon, he fought it as he would fight a demon. What else could he do? And once begun, the exorcism can't be stopped. There is no making peace with evil, there is no compromise, no friendly coexistence. There must always be a victor. And a vanquished."

The three sat in silence for a few moments.

"Father Sullivan," Karen began slowly, "if multiple personality disorder can sometimes be misperceived as demonic possession, can the reverse also be true?"

"That legitimate possession is mistaken for MPD?"

"Right."

"Of course. But what mainstream therapist will say he believes in demons? That's why I'm afraid some dangerous cases of possession never come to the attention of the church. But I'll tell you this: while the church is trying to diagnose or verify possession, we do extremely thorough physical and psychological evaluations. We have to eliminate the natural before we can attack the preternatural. Why do you ask?"

"Because I'm beginning to see why Dr. Gudhausen wanted to discuss my patient with you. My gosh, looking back on it, I suspect he thought we had a case of possession on our hands."

"Stan was pretty open-minded that way—"

"So he believed in demonic possession?"

"He didn't *dis*believe it. He was unbiased, far more so than most of our colleagues."

"Did he ever come across a case of real possession?"

Sullivan tipped back in his chair. He squinted at the ceiling as if gazing through some invisible window into the past. "He considered it in at least one case I know of. A few years ago he talked to me about a man he was treating, a very complex case. One of the patient's several alters was decidedly satanic—physical features, vocabulary, knowledge of Satanism and occult belief, the whole works. You see, Stan thought people with a weakened sense of personal identity—and MPDs would be a perfect example—might be especially vulnerable to demonic possession."

Karen knew she was staring wide-eyed. "So he must have thought Lucy might really be possessed?"

"It's a possibility."

"Father Sullivan, I realize patient confidentially is an issue for both of us, but please, could you tell me the name of Dr. Gudhausen's patient?"

Sullivan leaned forward again. "Karen, I understand the urgency of the situation. And I have the utmost confidence that if you ask me a question like that, it must have an important bearing on this situation. But it was a long time ago; I simply can't remember the man's name."

"If I said it, would you remember?"

"Try me."

"I think the patient's name was Gold. Herbert Gold, from Andover, Massachusetts."

"That's it!" Sullivan smacked his desktop. "Herb Gold! Stan liked him a lot."

"I thought so," said Karen. "Now wait'll you hear this—!"

"*Damn it!*" Jeff sprang to his feet. "All this talk isn't getting us anywhere!" He stomped to the window and stared out at the dark main street.

Karen rose and went to him. She rested her hand on his arm. Looking at their reflections in the dark glass, she spoke. "Jeff—?"

"Casey's out there somewhere, and all we can do is sit here talking about magic and demons and MPD. This is crazy. We've got to *do* something."

"What, Jeff? What can we do?"

"I don't know! God, I've never felt so helpless in my life. I can't leave for fear of missing a phone call; if I sit still I'll go crazy."

He turned slowly to face Karen. She opened her arms and they embraced. She could feel Jeff's heart pounding against her chest. His breath was warm on her neck.

* * *

"At least I don't have to tie you up," the man said as he removed the blindfold from her eyes. "You aren't going to run off." He smiled at her expectantly, as if he'd made a joke that demanded appreciative laughter.

Casey Chandler stared at him, unresponsive, her icy fingers tightening on the tires of her wheelchair. Though fear knotted her stomach, she refused to let on. The man had seemed so nice at first. So normal. He still hadn't lost his congenial air, but now he seemed so . . . maniacal.

He turned away, started doing something with a black briefcase.

Casey looked around, trying to determine exactly where she was. The dull, peeling wallpaper, the faded nylon curtains covering dirty windows, the old bedroom furniture made her think they were in some deserted farmhouse. The bed itself was covered with a stained chenille bedspread. That one detail suggested the house wasn't truly abandoned.

How far could they have traveled? Blindfolded, direction had been impossible to determine, but they could be no more than thirty to forty-five minutes outside Burlington. Somewhere in the countryside. But where?

She recalled her terror when he'd abandoned her, handcuffed and unseeing, in the car. Waiting there, for hours it seemed, she'd heard the sharp crack of a gunshot—a sound she'd always recognize for sure.

Then he'd come back, pulled her from the car, put her in her chair, and bumped her up a set of stairs to this second-floor bedroom.

Now what was he doing? The briefcase held some kind of portable computer that he'd placed on top of the vanity.

Completely engrossed, he clicked his tongue as he worked. "Do you follow the afternoon soaps, Miss Chandler?" He looked at her as if he'd made another joke.

She glared at him.

"What say we tune in and see what your father and Karen Bradley are up to? Would you like that? Maybe we'll ask them to join us."

Casey turned away, biting her lower lip.

"Not going to talk to me, eh? Why's that? Your father tell you not to talk to strangers?"

Casey said nothing.

"Well, I'm hardly a stranger," he said. "In fact, I'm your father's boss. My name's McCurdy."

* * *

As Karen told Father Sullivan about Lucy, she watched Jeff become more withdrawn. He'd dropped out of the conversation. Worry dulled his eyes as he repeatedly glanced at the silent telephone. Karen knew his thoughts were only of Casey.

She had to draw Jeff out. "Why don't you tell Father Sullivan what you told me about the dates."

Jeff looked at her blankly. "What dates?"

"What you noticed about the opening day of hunting season."

"Oh, right." She could see his heart wasn't in it. "That was November twelfth, last year, the day that man in California was executed via computer. It was also the day Alton Barnes and his friend were in the woods hunting here in Hobston. I don't know exactly how the two events are related, but the coincidence seems odd to me. See, the man in California died and Mr. Barnes's friend vanished that same day. And roughly at the same time."

Jeff went on to explain how Stuart Dubois's footprints ended and how, under hypnosis, Alton recalled a white light that seemed to lift the old man off the ground and pull him into it.

"Here's what bothers me," Jeff said, "to the casual observer there could be no relationship between a computer in Boston and a man dying on the West Coast. But I know differently; I have the videotape to prove it.

"As I told Karen, Hobston keeps coming up in my research at the Academy. Strange things have always happened here. Not just UFOs but phantoms in the woods, Bigfoot sightings, odd noises with no apparent source. Supposedly there was even a rain of stones sometime toward the end of the last century. And your story about Father Mosely and his demon is a good case in point."

"Why Hobston?" the priest said.

"If what I suspect is true, if the Academy has actually managed to harness these . . . these magical powers by using the computer, then one thing we know about the laws of magic applies: Whatever is sent out, comes back. It's an occult variation of Newton's law of motion—for every action there is an equal and opposite reaction."

"Right," Sullivan said. "Medieval magicians protected themselves from recoil by constructing protective circles around the invocation area. They knew the psychic and physical dangers of crossing that circle! It's a cause and effect principle: energy used to create the effect had to be expended somewhere. It might come back in the form of a storm, a disease, an avalanche, a lightning bolt—"

Karen was surprised. "Jeez, Father Sullivan, how come you know so much about magic?"

He gave a short chuckle. "The fact is, Karen, I wrote a book about it—*Mania, Magic and Religion.* I've studied magic as both a psychological phenomenon and as a component of religious demonology."

As the priest paused to light another cigarette, Karen remembered! The book she had seen in Dr. Gudhausen's office. The smiling priest on the dust jacket, it was Father Sullivan! Odd, she thought. Odd I should end up sitting in his office like this. What a weird coincidence.

"Believe it or not," the priest went on, "both applications were essential to my work at St. Mark's College. Heavens, we had kids messing with Ouija boards, dabbling in the black arts, studying Satanism, witchcraft, voodoo, you name it. Most of them didn't know the dangers they were flirting with. I had to do what I could to keep ahead of them."

He cleared his throat. "You see, magic is not merely some kind of spontaneous physical reaction to uttered words, rituals, and burning candles—one doesn't say 'Presto!' and cause an enemy to vanish. There has to be an intermediary. One useful definition of magic is that it is the science of controlling the *secret* forces of nature. It is the harnessing of some unknown, but apparently very real power."

"This business about *spirit* that you were explaining before," Karen asked, "you mean magic can actually control spirit?"

"That's a terrifying notion, Karen. But it may be partially accurate. Maybe that's why the Church differentiates between good spirit and evil spirit. It would be theologically destructive if we believed human beings could manipulate the spirit of good. If magic works, then it works by the manipulation of evil.

"Like any power, magic requires a source, a battery. One explanation is that black magicians, through certain rituals—anything from chanting to sacrifice—can gain the cooperation of evil spirits, demons that exist in another dimension, outside our physical realm. If the magician wants wealth, the demons can bring it. If the magician wants to make someone ill, the demons can accomplish that as well. How? We don't really know."

"Do you really believe that, Father Sullivan? Do you believe these other dimensions can exist?"

Sullivan smiled at Karen, but not condescendingly. "Of course, I believe it. Anyone who believes in Heaven and Hell believes in other dimensions. In my line of work, we're just not in the habit of using the word 'dimension,' but that's what we're talking about just the same. I think what Jeff is suggesting—and please correct me if I'm wrong—is that every time a magical force is invoked, the barrier between our world and the next is somehow weakened. If the barrier is especially thin here in Hobston, then this is where the breakdown will be most obvious. Am I right, Jeff?"

"Yes, that's my best guess. It sounds off the wall, but I suspect every time they use that computer in Boston, they open the Hobston door a little wider."

"But, Jeff," Karen said, again experiencing that unfamiliar tension provoked by alien ideas, "what makes you believe there's a relationship?"

"Call it a hunch, Karen. I mean, who would have ever guessed a blast of Right Guard would lead to a hole in the ozone layer? McCurdy and his Academy boys just don't know what they're dealing with; they have no way of visualizing the consequence of their acts. And if they really are opening that interdimensional door, it's scary as hell to think about what they might be letting in."

* * *

Casey had to go to the bathroom very badly. She pressed her legs together using the added strength of her hands and arms. At the same time, she didn't want to voice this need to McCurdy.

He was still sitting in front of the computer. She'd watched his back for a long time. The freckled dome of his bald head was bright with perspiration. The ring of red hair was a rusty halo. He seemed totally engrossed in the changing patterns of color on the monitor. Now and then he'd click his tongue and nod his head as if he were reading information on the display. But Casey could see nothing there, nothing but the multicolored screen swirling and changing in meaningless motifs.

At length McCurdy turned around with an expression of great satisfaction on his face. "Well, my dear young lady, it's time to send for your father."

She could hold her silence no longer. "Why did you bring me here? What do you want?"

"Ah-ha, so you can speak!"

"What do you want with me? What about my father?"

"We have a meeting scheduled. We have important business to conduct."

"What business?"

"The Lord's work, my dear. You'll see soon enough. You kids today are all so terribly impatient. Can't sit still; can't concentrate. You must learn important things take time. The Lord works at his own pace, Miss Chandler, not yours."

Casey's anger mounted; now she was more angry than afraid. "Why won't you tell me what's going on?" Then, with sudden inspiration, she changed her tack. As a timid afterthought, she whispered, "I'm scared."

He stood up, walked over to her, and took a seat on the bed. With fewer than three feet between them, she could smell his body odor and his rancid cigarette breath. "There's nothing to be afraid of," he said gently, reaching over to pat her knee. "Soon everything is going to change. Improve. You're going to be able to walk again. Wouldn't you like that?"

Hope leapt inside her. She controlled it. Pushed it back out of sight where it belonged. Her head drew away from his stream of smelly exhalation.

"What do you mean?"

"Young lady, the Lord's work is just beginning. Some of us—you, me, your father—we are put here as His helpers. We all have missions. He has something important for each of us to do."

Dad had often talked about Dr. McCurdy's religious fundamentalism. "It's like he's got a Bible in one hand and a bomb in the other. But it doesn't seem to interfere with his work."

Casey wondered if Dad would feel the same if he saw Dr. McCurdy now.

Fear spread like a paralyzing drug. Casey dared say nothing more. Karen might know how to talk to this man, but Casey sure didn't. Something in his manner was more than frightening. Beneath his soft speech and eccentric behavior, Casey sensed something uncompromising, something totally dangerous.

She tried to sound sweetly demure. "But why would God want you to take me away from my father? Why would He want you to bring me here?"

"Very simple: you received a calling. When the Lord wants you, He calls. And you couldn't come on your own, now could you? So He asked me to help."

"I . . . I don't understand."

McCurdy exhaled loudly through his nose, a sound of impatience. "You will. Soon. Now you must be patient, my dear. There are great changes coming. We're entering an age of miracles. A *world* of miracles. There will be new prophets, new visions, new beginnings. Some of us have been chosen. We will be the shepherds of the New Light. The Lord talks to me, my dear. He tells me what is right. He tells me all the things to come."

McCurdy's eyes danced. They were alive with fire. "This is an age of great sin and corruption. God's earth is black with the stain of evil. People are born without souls. Darkness fills them, and they do the work of Satan. The Lord cleansed this earth before. He called down the purifying waters of a great flood. But now—" Excited tones softened to a coaxing calm. "You, my dear, are still innocent. You have nothing to fear. When you stand up it will be a sign to the others. When you walk, they will follow where you lead."

McCurdy fairly blazed with manic fervor. "I should kneel before you now. I should thank you for what you will do for God's children."

Casey gripped the arms of her wheelchair. She didn't want to see his eager grin and his blazing eyes. She was terrified of the forces that filled him.

"The Lord speaks to me," McCurdy said. "He tells me of the things to come. Shows me the great new world where the good will walk in the light and the corrupt will sink into the darkest bowels of the earth."

"I have to go to the bathroom," Casey told him.

* * *

When he heard footsteps coming down the stairs, Alton Barnes knew his capacity for terror was about to be tested. The image of his Korean interrogator, still vivid after forty years, jumped full force into his mind. Frantically, he tugged at the cords binding him to the kitchen chair. It did no good.

Things had been so crazy lately. They'd grown impossibly crazier when Dr. Bradley drove up with that terrible message about Jeffrey's daughter.

Missing.

Kidnapped. Now he was afraid there was no way out for any of them. If only he had left Daisy Dubois's farmhouse when he'd had the chance. If he'd just gone back to town with the young couple . . . If he'd returned straightaway to his car and driven off . . .

But then, how could he have refused when he thought Daisy was asking him for help? It was all so . . . inevitable. . . .

McCurdy walked into the room and took a seat across the table from Alton. He was all business. "We can do this in either of two ways," he said in calm, deceptively conversational tones. "In the end, one way or the other, you are going to see the wisdom of what I'm about to propose. You've been sent here to help us. But maybe you don't realize that yet."

Alton looked at the gore-splattered dead man on the floor, then at the bestial little girl watching him like a guard dog. He looked back at McCurdy, who appeared no more malevolent than an executive at a conference table.

The executive continued, "You were in the war, Mr. Barnes. So you've seen man at his worst. But you also understand something about loyalty and idealism—those are among the attributes of humankind at its best. Suppose I were to tell you there will be no more wars? That we are entering an age of peace, of ideals and loyalties? A better time is coming, Mr. Barnes. You can be part of it. You have seen the light. You know that it's real."

"I see a dead man, and a little girl that looks like she belongs in a hospital. I know you're keeping another little girl upstairs. And I *don't* see the woman whose house we're sitting in."

McCurdy cocked his head to one side, smiling wanly as if he were listening to some sweet music, faint and far away. "Things are not always as they appear, Mr. Barnes. But I don't have to tell you that. Now that you have seen the divine light in the forest, nothing will ever appear the same to you. You are growing under that light, Mr. Barnes, like a flower. For you it is the sun."

"Frankly, mister, I ain't got no idea what you're talkin' about." Again Alton flexed his arms. The cords bit into his wrists. "If what you got to tell me is so all-fired holy, how come you gotta tie me up to do it?"

"The light can be painful."

"What's this *light* you keep yakkin' about?"

"The light you saw in the woods. The light you try to understand in your dreams. Like any miracle, it's difficult to comprehend, but you may accept it on faith."

"How the hell you know what I seen?"

"I know the ones who are chosen. They're the ones who see the light. You were chosen. Your friend Mr. Dubois was called. Summoned."

"Then I suppose you can tell me where he was summoned *to!*"

McCurdy clicked his tongue, shaking his head as if Alton were impenetrably obtuse. "I can do better than that, my friend. I can *show* you. Think of the light as a gateway, Mr. Barnes, a golden gateway that shines like the sun."

* * *

Casey suspected McCurdy had been embarrassed to stay while she urinated; he'd left her alone with an old plastic dishpan.

Good! Now, she had some privacy. Yet she had no idea how to turn the situation to her advantage. Escape was out of the question. Simply getting down the stairs would be impossible. And since there was no electricity, it was unlikely there'd be a phone. Contacting the police was another impossibility.

What about the window? Opening it and crying for help would do no good. No one would hear in this wilderness.

The only thing she could do was arm herself. If she could find some sort of weapon . . . But there was a problem with that, too: even if she were able to knock McCurdy unconscious and crawl all the way out to his car, she still would not be able to drive.

Casey fought her growing sense of hopelessness. She had to be tough, determined. Hell, hadn't she recovered from the paralyzing bullet? Didn't she survive the devastation of her mother's death? By God she could handle this, too.

First, she knew she'd feel a little better if she were armed. That way if McCurdy tried anything she could fight back.

Casey wheeled herself around the bed, past the computer, and over to the window. Silent shadows filled the yard. Hundreds of fireflies blinked in the neighboring pasture.

Below the horizon, about halfway up the massive silhouette of a far-off mountain, she could see a hazy white light. She watched it burning among distant trees.

What could it be?

At first she hoped it was some kind of search party that had come looking for her. But no, that couldn't be right.

In a moment the light seemed to rise, then—like the single headlight of a fast-approaching train—it appeared to be speeding directly toward her!

It must be a UFO, Casey thought. *A real UFO. Dad was right about these things!*

In seconds it was in the yard below her window. There it stopped, hovering above the ground like a six-foot globe of pale fire. As she watched, it began to shrink like a balloon deflating, until, amazingly, it was no bigger than a firefly of incredible brilliance.

Bright as it was, the intense glow did not hurt her eyes; it wasn't like looking into a spotlight or photographer's flash. She wasn't trying to blink away afterimages.

Odd.

In motion again, it floated closer to the house where it vanished beneath the overhang of porch roof below her window.

She felt muscles tightening in her stomach as the fantastic realization took hold. A *UFO.* Something from another world. Something completely alien and strange. . . .

Her mind fought the notion, repelled it like a psychic magnet. She pushed back into the shadows of the bedroom where she sat trembling, her laced fingers pulled tightly to her chest.

* * *

In an upper corner of the kitchen, at the right angle where two walls met the ceiling, a point of light appeared as if moving through the wall. Disbelieving, Alton stared. The light pulsed, and spun, seemed to grow. Now it was the size of a golf ball, now a baseball.

The naked child cringed from it. She flattened herself against the kitchen floor like a dog expecting a beating. Alton could hear her whimpering, and the sound wrenched his heart.

The light grew, became round and perfect, like a radiant crystal ball. Yes, Alton thought, it *is* very like the sun.

It seemed to get closer. Alton strained his neck backward as it moved overhead. There it stopped, hovering directly above him.

Panic seized him with electrical fingers. He bucked and fought, pulling against his restraining cords, rocking the chair on its wooden feet. Yet he couldn't tear his eyes away. It was as if he were looking up into the round shade of a brilliant lamp. This time, as before in the woods, the intensity of the light didn't hurt his eyes.

Now—he was sure of it!—the light was descending. He closed his eyes as it got closer, squeezed them tighter as his head passed through the radiant sphere. A trillion electrical prickles danced across his skin as the circle of light settled over him, enveloping his whole body.

I have to fight this, he thought. *I have to be strong and fight this thing.*

Oddly, when he dared look, he found himself in utter darkness. The room was gone, the whimpering child was silent.

There was the sensation of cold wet flesh, like the side of a salmon, rubbing against his face. He tried to draw away, but the chair and ropes were unyielding. When he inhaled, he could smell an acrid odor, putrid as a corpse, and he felt his gorge rising. The air tasted of filth and decay. Nausea roiled in his stomach.

I've got to fight this.

He could almost make out the words of distant whispering. Almost. Or was it a mechanical humming? Or an insect buzzing? Or—? Before he knew for sure, all sounds were lost as a clammy breeze swept past him. And as the wind grew stronger he somehow knew its source: the beating of giant wings. He heard them, great leathery sheets flapping in the black void.

He wanted to scream, but a voice cut him off—

You're one with us, it seemed to say in his reeling mind. *Your will is our will. You are of us, and we are one.*

Alton felt the pressure of panic building. Heaving against his restraints, he felt his invisible chair rocking on the vanished floor.

A light flashed. He snapped his head to look.

Something slapped him.

Another flash jerked his attention to another bright point. Another slap.

He felt warm blood trickling over his lips.

His gut clenched like a fist, lungs fought the alien atmosphere.

Slap!

It's that hypnotism business, he thought. *It's some kinda trick or drug. . . .*

As the foul wind subsided, he heard whispers again, closer now:

Shall we take him?

Let's peel his skin.

Freeze his lungs, turn them to powder.

Snatch his soul!

Open him up! Let's see what this old man's made of. . . .

The words came faster, faster.

When Alton screamed, no sound came. Some invisible substance, slimy and moist, entered his mouth, pushed wetly against his eyes, his ears. He couldn't breathe.

Hot; he could feel his temperature soar.

A new sensation—some vast wet tongue lapping at him, dragging itself across the skin beneath his clothing.

A horrible dizziness . . . his head floating above his body. Separating at the neck. Drifting away.

Take his mind!

Take him now!

Rattling. Vibrating. Chair scraping the vanished floor . . .

We want you. . . .

We have use for you. . . .

We are your purpose. . . .

We are what you wish. . . .

We are what you are. . . .

. . . and suddenly Alton could see himself, far below. His body bound to the wooden chair. A tiny struggling man trapped in a circle of light.

We have him! There was triumph in the voice.

He is ours!

He is ours!

Alton knew something was pushing against him, pressing at his mind. It wanted him to scream, but—damn it—he would not scream. It wanted him to surrender, but he refused.

* * *

Alton Barnes had no idea how much time had passed before he came to in Daisy's kitchen.

He remembered the light and the terrible void as he might remember a dream. He had come through it. And he had been through hell before. So he had won; he knew he would be protected as long as he maintained his nerve, his independence of spirit. The realization gave him confidence.

He had also learned that the pain was much less when he pretended to go along with their demands. And pretending, he found, was easy enough.

He was all right. He hadn't surrendered. In the end he had been stronger than the thing that tried to enter him.

But there'd been a trade-off. Yes, some kind of tradeoff. He had agreed to do . . . something.

"Come on, Mr. Barnes," said McCurdy. "I'll drive you into town."

Following McCurdy, Alton stumbled from the farmhouse in a kind of weary daze.

As they drove down the hill he thought about the future. Thought about the Chandlers. And Dr. Bradley.

Thought about the light.

And within that light, he thought about the things he had seen. Oh my God, the things he had seen.

* * *

"This is amazing," Jeff said, closing Father Mosely's Bible.

"I know," Father Sullivan answered as he entered the room with three bottles of Miller's beer. "I admit it's pretty unbelievable."

"No," said Jeff, "that's not what I mean. This old man, this Father Mosely, he's speculating about many of the possibilities I was forced to consider while I was at the Academy. This is eye-opening stuff, but he was just pulling it out of the air, figuring it out all by himself with guesswork and intuition. He doesn't really reach a conclusion, but he comes close."

"Frightening, isn't it," Sullivan agreed.

"At the Academy, we were cobbling the same theory together from literally millions of pages of documentation from all over the world. And we had use of a multimillion-dollar computer!" Sullivan handed bottles to Karen and Jeff.

"What's Father Mosely say, Jeff?" Karen shifted her position, crossing her legs.

Jeff used the Bible's marker ribbon to find where he'd left off, then turned back a few of the delicate pages. "This part near the end, the part I was just reading, it really blew me away. Listen to this. . . ."

It is quiet now. The thing is at rest, or it has retreated to wherever it goes.

No. More precisely, it is I who retreat. I must. I need this precious respite. I need to think, to meditate. I pray for strength and guidance.

It is so terrifying to realize that it is me the thing wants—ME. Yet I still do not understand why. Nor do I understand what made it take notice of me in the first place. Why have I become its quarry and its prey? Even after all these days of torment, I still do not know what it requires of me.

It will not say.

I know one thing: if I try to escape, it will find me. If I leave St. Joe's for a trip to the store or to the library, it will follow. Even within the rooms of the church and rectory, it pursues me with a diabolical persistence. It whispers in my ear; it touches me at the most private of times, in the most personal of places. It inflicts pain and unprovoked terror. It keeps me from my sleep.

And now I am so tired, so worn, yet I dare not ask for help. Though it lies, I believe its promise: that it will humiliate and destroy all who offer comfort or assistance. I believe it can do that.

Alone against it, my only weapons are words and relics, prayers and faith. I have implored, beseeched, entreated, but I have not begged. As I reflect, I have come to understand that its apparent aversion to holy things is only a part of its pretense. I admonish it with holy water, and the water turns to blood. It taunts me in a nonsense language that is no more than the Roman Ritual recited in reverse. It mocks me; it mocks the Church and the sacraments.

I will not beg! (Is that my pride and thus my failing?)

But how am I to fight? Please, dear God, help me to know what I must do. Do not desert me, I pray. If it is Your will that I must fail, please let the one who finds this book have an understanding greater than my own.

The thing is demonic, but I am convinced it is not a demon. At first it feigned great fear when I took crucifix in hand. When I commanded it to leave in the name of Jesus Christ, it would vanish for hours, even days at a time.

And for a while I thought He had put an end to things.

Later, when it dropped its pretense, the wooden crucifix exploded in my fist. Upon opening the pyx, I saw it was seething with maggots. The name of the Savior evoked gales of hideous laughter. Each utterance brought the sensation of burning to my lips and tongue.

With God's help I would challenge a demon. But this is something else, as old, as cunning, but impervious to the very forces of light that should repel it.

But I will not beg!

I cannot leave the grounds. We are stranded together by a terrible bond. Sometimes I think it is trying to chase me away, so that by taking my leave I will allow it to follow. I cannot loose this thing into the community. I must contain it here, I must.

Young Barry brings my supplies and runs my errands. I fear for the boy; he has seen too much. I dread that by accepting his help, I have guaranteed his destruction. God help me. God forgive me. And please, dear Lord, I beg You—spare the boy.

Perhaps there is some small protection in that I have sworn him to secrecy. No one must discover what we have here. Young Barry understands this; he knows he must be strong.

As I must. As must we all.

It is my greatest sadness that the mass can no longer be celebrated publicly at St. Joe's.

My parishioners, whose good works I have seen as they struggle to nurture their young in a Christian environment, must learn nothing of this. I fear the consequence. It is not boastfully that I say I have heard some of them cite me as an example to their children. What if they discover their priest can be so easily undone by things preternatural? In their eyes would not the Church itself seem beaten? There would no longer be a sanctuary for them, as there is no sanctuary for me.

What am I saying? And to whom? I feel that madness is near. Fatigue and pain are all that I know, all that I trust. Is this a blasphemy? Or does it put these thoughts in my head?

I reflect—and I do little else now that I accept how helpless I am—I try to put the thing in a historical perspective. I am not the first. It has long been known within the Church that such events as these are not uncommon. Men have too often been tormented by evil things. And we have called them demons. Devils. Evil spirits.

But am I too cloistered in my thinking? Over the centuries, mankind has been visited by myriad unworldly creatures, and they have been known by many different names: the Titans were replaced by the Olympians. Then the Christian God arrived with His hierarchy of angels and their unholy counterparts. And what of the faerie faith? It is still with us though now the wee folk and their faerie mounds go by more modern names: extraterrestrials and their fantastic alien crafts. The spirits of the dead that spoke through nineteenth-century mediums now communicate through channels. They no longer claim to be our ancestors; some even claim they have never lived.

Is there a truth in all of this?

Things appear different but things do not change. New faces replace old, but the voice is always the same.

I have heard talk of other dimensions, other "levels" of reality outside the teachings of the church. I do not have the education to understand these notions as scientific concepts, yet they compel me to ask: Could this world be home to so many diverse supernatural residents? What of our poltergeists, our hairy man-beasts, water monsters, and ghostly visitations? What of all things supernatural and strange?

Could it be that they are one?

Could it be that they lie, as Satan is known to lie, and that all things that speak articulate but a single truth—that their name is in fact Legion?

I weaken; I fear my faith is at risk. I fear my mind is not my own. I cry for my immortal soul.

But these questions torture me. Could the voice that addressed Moses from the burning bush be of the Legion? Could the shining presence that made itself known to Bernadette be among them, too? Could the Ouija board, the tarot, and the crystal ball speak and deceive? Could all mystical utterances rise from a single unearthly tongue?

If so, then I am not damned. Nor are we all. But in that knowledge we cannot rejoice, for our true fate could be far more appalling than damnation.

* * *

"Absolutely terrifying," Karen whispered. "That poor man." Though her education and training argued against it, Karen found herself believing what the old priest had written. She looked at Jeff and at Father Sullivan, trying to gauge their responses, feeling a little embarrassed about her own.

"Sadly," Sullivan said, "it sounds like schizophrenia. A month ago I would have dismissed it just that simply. But now—"

Jeff closed the Bible and tossed it onto Sullivan's desk. "Sounds to me like Father Mosely came to pretty much the same conclusion we did at the Academy: that consistent with all sorts of religious, supernatural, and occult evidence, there *really is* a parallel dimension. And on certain occasions, under certain circumstances, we can interact with it."

"Yes," said Sullivan, "apparently your computer is the device that makes it possible."

Jeff nodded. "And if we can accept an unseen world, it's not too much of an imaginative leap to guess there are beings that inhabit it, whether they're angels, demons, or something completely unheard of."

"It's too weird," Karen said, denial and wonder warring in her mind.

"Yes," said Jeff. "but it's a notion as old as history. The Academy's data entry staff input hundreds of volumes of information from hundreds of cults and sects and mystical traditions dating back thousands of years. Certain traditions, *ancient* traditions, have elaborate explanations of different forms of matter. At first they sound like superstitious mumbo-jumbo because they're expressed in forgotten vocabularies and defunct jargons. But when the computer translates everything into a common language, what do we find? That many bygone teachings are concerned with advanced physics, nuclear energy, atomic structure, and other things our state-of-the-art science is only beginning to discover.

"The ancients also knew the human eye can only see a tiny part of the electromagnetic spectrum—from violet to red. So other worlds *could* exist, they just couldn't see them. But someone at the Academy made an interesting observation: many modern UFO sightings are described as going through color changes: first they appear as purple blobs, then descend the visible spectrum until they turn red—at that point they seem to get solid, just as if—"

"Something is passing from one dimension to another," Sullivan finished the thought.

Jeff nodded.

Karen felt herself holding back, as if resisting getting suckered into a paranoid's elaborate fantasy. "These supposed beings? What are they made of? Some alternate form of matter?"

"Who knows," Jeff replied. "Maybe Father Sullivan's term 'spirit' applies. My guess is they're not solid and physically stable. When they make themselves known in our three-dimensional world, they're probably nothing more than temporary manipulations of energy. That's how they can assume different forms, anything from a wolf to a ship to some iridescent god as big as Mount Mansfield."

"But it doesn't sound as if Father Mosely ever *saw* anything." Karen's mind wrestled with the alien ideas.

"Maybe not," Sullivan agreed, "but millions of people have. And thousands of books have been written about the encounters. I'm not talking about drug freaks, schizophrenics, and charlatans, either. I'm talking about a whole range of credible people: insurance salesmen, factory workers, elementary school teachers, government officials, and just plain folks by the thousands. They meet these creatures and their lives are changed forever. . . ."

"Like Father Mosely," Karen whispered.

"Right. Exactly," said Father Sullivan. "Think of the impact such encounters have had on my line of work. You know, most religions were founded as a result of encounters with angels and demons. Take Mohammed. Until he was forty years old, he was just an Arab tradesman. Then he started having visions and conversations with supernatural messengers. The experience led him to organize the Muslim religion and to write the Koran. Think about the Mormons and their golden tablets. The angel Moroni. The founders of the Seventh-Day Adventists and Jehovah's Witnesses claimed communication with supernatural beings who offered amazing prophecies. . . ."

"If it's all true," said Karen, "if *any* of it's true, what do you suppose these . . . these *creatures* want with us?"

Jeff shrugged his shoulders. "Based on what Father Mósely says, it seems they are . . . connected to us in some way we don't, or can't, understand. He calls it 'a terrible bond,' remember?"

"If this world is indeed God's creation," Sullivan said, "then all creatures—flesh or spirit—play a role in the grand design, even these—"

"Maybe," Jeff went on. "But even if we can't guess their motives, we know they try to confuse us. They mislead and misinform, and they play crazy head games with us. Over the centuries, in one disguise or another, they've taught us, and tormented us. They've influenced our religion and our philosophy. No doubt they watched our long hard climb from the mud all the way to the moon. Yet they never say why; they never tell the truth. All I know, all I *believe*, is that they're here, and we're here, and we seem to be inseparable."

Karen looked around, wondering if invisible creatures could be in the room with them now, watching, listening, maybe laughing at their conjecture? She hugged her shoulders as she spoke. "Why don't they just contact us and level with us?"

"A better question," said Jeff, "is why don't they leave us alone? Apparently—for whatever reason—they can't."

Karen felt a chill. Her mind wanted to wander to safer topics, but she forced herself to speak. "To me, the implications are more than terrifying. I . . . I mean *everything* we believe. Everything we know and possess and value might be . . . something else. Something . . . different. Science, religion, ethical humanitarian beliefs, the evolution of consciousness and conscience, everything could be . . . wrong."

"That's the notion that came to terrify Father Mosely," said Father Sullivan, lighting a cigarette. "It made him doubt his faith."

"Pretty sobering, isn't it." Jeff wasn't smiling. "It could be that the only thing we know for sure, the one and only reality, is that a parahuman race exists alongside us. Period. End of discussion."

"All of a sudden the idea of magic doesn't seem so farfetched," said Karen. "So how does the Academy and the computer fit into the picture?"

Jeff swigged the last of his beer and put the empty bottle down. "Just like this: Magicians seek to manipulate our world by influencing unknown forces. Perhaps these 'forces' are the invisible residents of a parallel dimension—what Father Sullivan calls spirits. Magic seeks to enslave them. Apparently, when these invisible residents enter our dimension they can manipulate energy in ways we don't understand.

That's how they assume physical form—any physical form they want to!"

"Right," said Father Sullivan. "And if they can control our perception, then they can control our reality. More than one political system—from the sun kings to the divine right monarchs to Adolf Hitler's Third Reich—has subscribed to the idea that not only do these invisible worlds exist, but mankind can either control, or be controlled by their invisible residents."

"I'm pretty sure that's what the Academy's up to," said Jeff. "Using McCurdy's computer as a weapon of war, we can control, possibly dominate the denizens of the parallel world. Think of it! Thanks to McCurdy, the United States may now be on the verge of commanding an infinite army of lethal, preternatural soldiers! Why, it's the most significant advance in warfare since we split the atom!"

"And by far the most terrifying," Sullivan said. "It could be uncontrollable. Irreversible. . . ."

Karen looked down at the empty beer bottle in her hand. A hush fell over the room.

She gave a quick cry of surprise.

Someone pounded on the door.

Jeff and Father Sullivan jumped to their feet at the same time.

Dread hardened Jeff's eyes as he stared at the door. "Oh Christ," he whispered, "this is it."

Karen glanced at her watch. 10:25. She took a deep breath, held it, ordered herself to be calm.

Pounding continued. Constantly, allowing no time to respond.

With Jeff and Karen in tow, Sullivan crossed to the entryway. He opened the door to the mudroom, then stepped to the outside door. With his hand on the key, he glanced over his shoulder. Was he as frightened as he looked?

Louder now, the pounding persisted.

Sullivan spoke in a tense whisper, "Jeff, Karen, maybe you'd better move back."

Neither argued. They stepped away from the cloak room and out of sight.

Then Karen heard the metallic grind of the lock turning, the screech of long disused hinges as Sullivan pulled open the outside door.

And a familiar voice said, "I come to explain."

Sullivan's reply was strict and demanding, "Who are you?"

"Name's Barnes. Dr. Bradley and Mr. Chandler're here, ain't they?"

Karen heard the priest hesitate. "Y-yes. . . .?"

Relieved, she stepped into view. "It's okay, Father." She smiled at Alton who stood under the outside light. Grinning nervously, he appeared pale, uneasy. Wringing his hands, he rocked from foot to foot.

"Mr. Barnes," she said, "I'm so glad it's you."

The older man stepped past Father Sullivan and into the living room.

"You look like you could use a drink," Sullivan told him.

"A drink? No. No, thank you. Can't do that. If you have a glass of water . . . ?"

"Yes. Certainly. Let me get it for you." Sullivan hurried toward the kitchen as Karen led Alton to the sofa. They sat side by side with Jeff across from them.

In a moment Sullivan returned with the water. Alton took it, chugged it greedily.

"Thank you," he said, wiping his mouth on his wrist.

"You obviously know these people, Mr. Barnes, but I don't think we've met. My name's Bill Sullivan. I'm the new Catholic priest in town."

Alton reached over, extending an unsteady hand. "Al Barnes." He nearly collapsed back onto the sofa pillow. Sullivan sat on the chair next to Jeff's.

"You look exhausted, Mr. Barnes. Is everything okay?" Karen noted streaks of dirt and scratches on Alton's face; his hands were filthy with black grime and a rusty stain that could have been paint.

"Oh gosh, yes. I'm all right, miss. It's about Jeffrey's daughter—"

"What about Casey?" Jeff was on his feet.

"She . . . she. . . ." It was as if Alton had forgotten what he was going to say. Confusion obscured his features; his eyes rolled skyward, squinting at the ceiling.

"What about her, Al?"

"Give him a minute, Jeff . . ." said Karen, ultra aware of Alton's every move. Something wasn't right, that was easy to see. But she couldn't put her finger on exactly what.

Sullivan took hold of Jeff's wrist. He coaxed the younger man back into his seat.

"I seen her. I seen your daughter. She's all right. They want me to tell you she's all right."

"Where is she? *Who* wants you to tell me?"

"Them people. She's back at the house with them people."

"What people? What do they want—?"

"That's what I'm tryin' to tell ya. Your daughter, she's a big part of it. Just like you and me and all of us is a big part of it."

"Of *what?*" Jeff pounded the leather arm of his chair. "Christ, Alton, talk sense! Karen, what's wrong with him?"

She reached over, touched Alton's forehead, his cheek. She looked into his eyes and picked up his wrist, counting pulse beats. He let her do it without protest.

"He's tired, Jeff. He's exhausted. Look at him. Sit back, Mr. Barnes. Try to relax."

Alton settled back. His chest expanded with a deep breath. Wheezing, he exhaled.

"Now," said Karen, "slowly, one thing at a time, okay? First, please tell us, where is Casey?"

"She's up the farm. Right where we was earlier 'saf noon. The Dubois place. If you'd've stayed put another minute you'd've seen her."

"How'd she—?" Sullivan quieted Jeff with a hand on the shoulder.

"Okay," said Karen. "Good. Now, is she all right? Is she hurt or sick?"

"Oh no, she's fine. Fact, she's getting better. They're gonna help her. They're gonna heal her up. Wait'll you see. It's gonna be the real thing, a miracle."

"Christ, Al, *who* are you talking about?" Jeff's face was tense and frightened. He looked as if he might erupt from pressure mounting inside him. Karen noticed how alert Father Sullivan seemed. He was ready to move quickly, if need be.

"There's a doc up there. McCurdy—"

"*McCurdy!*" Jeff sat ramrod-straight. "McCurdy's up there? What's he want? What's he—? God damn it, if he hurts her—"

Alton smiled up at Jeff. "Jeffrey," he said, "you got this whole thing sized up all wrong. Nobody wants to hurt nobody. Specially your girl. Somethin's happenin' here, somethin' important. Your daughter's part of it. We all are. It's strange, scary, maybe. But it's good, son. I promise you, it's good. I got my understandin' just this evenin'. I'm part of it, too."

"Part of *what?*"

Jeff was too agitated to see what Karen saw. As she listened to her patient, observed his unfamiliar mannerisms and odd speech patterns, she knew something extraordinary had occurred. Whatever it was had been powerful enough to influence Alton's behavior quite dramatically. He was more than simply tired, he was under the influence of *something*. When he spoke it was as if he were in some kind of trance. Was it drug-induced? Or a spontaneous flashback to the hypnotic state? She just couldn't judge. She had to learn more. A telling look from Father Sullivan said he could see it, too.

"Hold on, Jeff," the priest said. "Let Mr. Barnes tell his story."

"Hold on nothing! If Casey's up there with McCurdy, I'm going. You can't expect me to sit around here and—"

As Jeff rose and started to move toward the door, Alton jumped up as if he were on springs. "I can't let you do that, Jeffrey. Not yet."

Jeff started to detour around him. "Christ, Al, that son of a bitch *kidnapped* my daughter—"

Before Jeff took another step, Alton's right arm leapt with the force of a pneumatic hammer. His fist connected with the side of Jeff's head, and Jeff went down.

Karen screamed, "Jeff!" as Sullivan stepped between her and Alton. She grabbed the priest's arm, cowering behind him in terror and surprise. What this kindhearted man had done was completely out of character.

Alton's eyes darted back and forth in manic confusion. "I . . . I'm sorry," he said, looking at the unconscious man at his feet. "I . . . I didn't mean . . . I don't know what—"

"Please, just sit down, Mr. Barnes. Please." Sullivan spoke with calm authority.

Again Al returned to the sofa. "I never meant . . ."

"I know," Sullivan said. "Please, just take a deep breath and try to relax."

Karen knelt to examine Jeff. His pulse was fine. He was breathing normally. When she spoke, he groaned and started to come around.

She looked up at Alton. His sad eyes showed deep concern. His lower lip trembled. "Jeffrey, I'm sorry. I don't know what come over me."

Karen helped Jeff sit up. He appeared dizzy and disoriented. He shook his head, wincing in pain.

Alton's foot tapped, his hand massaged his thigh, his gaze flitted around the room. His tanned skin had paled to a sickly white. "I never done nothin' like that before. Can't tell you how sorry I am, how ashamed. . . ."

"Jeff's okay, Mr. Barnes," Karen soothed. "We know you didn't mean it. You're tired. Upset. We're all jumpy. This has been a horrible day for everybody."

"Can't understand what come over me. . . ."

"Mr. Barnes." Father Sullivan spoke in calm, steady tones. "You said you had come here to tell us something. You said you'd come here to explain . . . ?"

"Yessir." Alton drew his palm across his mouth. "What I come to say is it ain't chance and it ain't coincidence that brung us here tonight. All of it, every step of the way, was worked out a long, long time ago. Each of us is part of a plan, part of a design. We each got a role to play in the change that's comin'."

"Stu Dubois, he always tried to make a God-fearin' man of me, same as he was. Now I understand; ol' Stu was right all the time. Jes' tonight I got me a little glimpse of how the pieces fit together, how the whole world and every one of us in it is like a great big piece of machinery. It all fits together snug as can be. I seen it. I *seen* it all at once. An' now I understand it. Pretty quick, you'll see it, too. Ain't that right, Father?"

Sullivan reacted with a start. "Yes, perhaps it is." He cleared his throat. "I believe each of us has a role in God's plan. Is that what you mean?"

"Yep. And you believe in miracles, too, don't you, Father?" Karen could see Alton wasn't baiting the priest. He was talking to him as if they shared some secret understanding.

"Yes," Sullivan hesitated, "but the Church is pretty conservative about what we'll call a miracle. We believe they're possible, we believe they happen, but only by the will of God."

"Then you ain't gonna be as surprised as I was to learn what's goin' on right now."

"And this is what you've come here to tell us?"

"That's right. I'm gonna prepare you. That's my job. Always figgered somethin' big, important like this, would be up to somebody else. Somebody special. A fella who can lead other men. But no sir, it's my job this time. And after I prepare you, then, one at a time, each of us is gonna go up there and go through our change."

Our change? What could he mean? Karen studied the priest, wondering how he was assessing this. His expression didn't offer a clue.

Our change? Alton had sure changed. Had his fear been so great, his terror so deep-rooted? Had she underestimated the extent of his pain? Suddenly this kindly, down-to-earth Vermonter seemed dangerously disturbed. In fact, she thought he should be in a hospital. In just the course of the afternoon and evening, he had lost touch with reality. To some degree, she felt it was her fault. She felt she had failed him.

She was grateful to Father Sullivan for handling the situation; things had progressed well beyond her competence level.

"Our change?" said Sullivan.

"It's what ya call a 'spiritual miracle.' That's what you Cath'lics call 'em, anyways. It's when God comes down and He makes some kinda change in the human spirit and the human mind. Like in the Bible when St. Paul has his change of heart, what ya call his conversion. That's exactly what happened to me. *Exactly.* I never used to believe. Then I *saw.* . . ."

"Mr. Barnes, you referred specifically to a spiritual miracle. How many types of miracles are there?"

Sullivan seemed onto something.

"Miracles? Jest five."

"What are the others, do you know?"

"Sure. I guess. There's miracles that happen to things that ain't alive. You know, like one loaf of bread feedin' hundreds of people. Or like some statue bleedin' or cryin', maybe. And a'course there's miracles happenin' to livin' things that *ain't* human. Like in plagues. . . . You know, locusts, flies, beetles, frogs, stuff like that. And then there's miracles of faith, like what you call the Eucharist. You know, when Jesus shows up in the bread and wine.

"And—you wait and see, now—there's healing-type miracles. Miracles of the human body. Like what happens in them shrines you read about. Sick people get better. Cripples get up and walk. . . . That's all five, ain't it?"

"Yes. Yes, it is." Sullivan looked intensely wrapped up in this strange dialogue. "You sound like you've been to catechism."

Alton smiled shyly.

"How do you know about the classification of miracles, Mr. Barnes?"

"I jes' know."

"You just . . . ?" Sullivan broke concentration to look at Karen. It was a colleague-to-colleague appeal—what's going on here? Help me out, won't you?—but Karen had nothing to offer. She just sat beside Jeff, holding his hand, watching and wondering.

"Mr. Barnes," Sullivan began a new approach, "what are these changes that you say we'll be going through?"

"Oh, they're good ones, don't you worry. Each of us is gonna learn how to help when the time comes. Each of us has been picked, selected. We each have a special something to offer. Like Mr. Chandler's daughter, she's very lucky. She's gonna show the world a miracle of the human body."

Alton smiled at Jeff. "She's gonna get right up and walk, Jeffrey, and there'll be no question about it. You wait and see."

Karen felt Jeff's muscles tense. She massaged his shoulder, encouraging him to be patient.

"So, Al," Jeff sounded falsely calm, "are you saying Casey is still up to Daisy Dubois's house? That Skipp McCurdy is . . . keeping her up there?"

Father Sullivan reacted to the question. His reaction was identical to Karen's. Jeff had said the wrong thing and she knew exactly where it was heading. She strengthened her grip on Jeff's hand, knowing it would do no good.

"She was just the first of us to be summoned," Alton explained patiently. "We'll all have our turn. You'll see."

Jeff made as if to stand up. "There's no point sitting around here waiting to take turns. I'm going up there right now. I'm going to talk to McCurdy."

"No sir," Alton said. His fingers curled into a fist. His arms flexed, his eyes narrowed. Karen pulled on Jeff's arm, making it impossible for him to rise. If he stood up, she knew Alton would hit him again.

She saw Sullivan square off, ready to tackle Mr. Barnes.

Jeff kept his seat.

Karen had been holding her breath. When she breathed again, she was panting. She cleared her throat, everyone looked at her.

"Mr. Barnes?" she said.

He smiled, eyes twinkling merrily as if nothing had happened. "Yes, miss?"

"Has Dr. Sparker put you on any medications you didn't tell me about?"

He shook his head. "Medications? No, miss. I'd've told you. But this ain't comin' from no medication, don't you worry about that. I know it's tough for you to understand right now. But you'll see soon enough. And that's a promise."

Completely delusional.

A drug could have been administered without his knowing it, but that wasn't the whole problem. The way he'd kept reflexing to stop Jeff from leaving suggested something else. Maybe, she thought, maybe it's worth a try. . . .

She stepped directly in front of Alton and, with a finger under his chin, lifted his head so they were looking eye to eye.

"Mr. Barnes?"

"Yes, miss?"

"Are you relaxed?"

"Am I—? Why, yes, sure. . . ."

Without breaking eye contact, she said, "You're much sleepier than the last time, aren't you?"

Alton's eyes closed. His head sagged forward.

Jeff stared at the sleeping man in confusion. "W-what happened?"

"He's in a trance."

"How'd you—"

"Posthypnotic suggestion. When I hypnotized him for the therapy session in my office, I left him with a suggestion that would make it easier to invoke the trance at our next meeting. I figured, why not try it now? 'You're much sleepier than the last time, aren't you,' was my trigger phrase. Thank God, it worked."

"Thank God is right," Sullivan said. "And good thinking, Dr. Bradley."

Jeff still looked confused, "But what made you think—"

"The more I watched him, the more I began to suspect he might be responding to suggestions. Not mine, but somebody's. That's how he was acting, don't you think, Father Sullivan? Especially the way he'd tense up, ready to fight, every time you threatened to leave. It was as if he wasn't supposed to let us go. Then it occurred to me someone else might've used hypnosis on him, too. Luckily, I was the first to put him in a trance. If I hadn't been, I bet he wouldn't have responded this time."

Sullivan looked at the sleeping man. "You're right, Karen, he does act as if someone's been messing with his subconscious. Thanks to you, I think we're going to start getting to the bottom of things now. Would you like to question him, or should I?"

Karen shrugged. "I'm not sure what to ask. I don't have any idea what's going on."

"Join the club." Sullivan thought a moment. "Jeff, is it possible McCurdy and the Academy are involved in any brainwashing or mind manipulation experiments?"

Jeff shook his head. He didn't know. "He keeps talking about that light. It's what he saw in the woods last November. Apparently he saw it again this afternoon."

"Well," Sullivan said, "something powerful sure got to Mr. Barnes. Let's see if we can find out what it was."

* * *

In the darkness, parked across the street from the rectory, McCurdy observed the people inside the lighted rooms.

As he watched the house, he saw all things. The great globe of the world, slick with oceans, spinning in infinite space, its island continents dappled with cities, houses, people, animals, vegetation, individual grains of sand, all encased in a delicate membrane of atmosphere. And above, wrapping it again, the Light, its tiny golden beams shining down to each human soul. He saw all existence as an organized system, with everything interconnected.

He saw it all at once. Everything. There was no difference between one thing and another. The mitochondria in living cells converting oxygen to energy; tectonic masses of land moving minutely; interrelated societies changing vastly with each new birth or death. . . .

He visualized the perfect coalescence of myriad independent actions, each easily dismissed as insignificant, random, and unassociated. Some were taking place hundreds of years ago. Some thousands.

Others occurred only moments before.

An African moth flapped its wings; hurricane winds leveled an Indian village. The Maine tide feasted on sandy shore; the earth yawned on Pitcairn Island. An Arab child vanished in Israel. A pterodactyl streaked through the Texas skies.

For McCurdy it all was part of the great, bright, whirling, flowing truth. In his crystal vision, all diverse actions harmonized with elegant precision. He could see an ingenious master plan. No chance, no coincidence, had brought Jeffrey Chandler to the Academy three years ago. It was not some random act of violence that left Jeff's wife dead and his daughter helpless in a wheelchair. Each action was related, each reaction calculated, and McCurdy could see it all perfectly. He could see the ultrafine individual strands that made up the vast, elaborate tapestry of what's real.

He saw Dr. Karen Bradley mindlessly pursuing her profession with a compulsion she had never stopped to analyze or examine. She had no way of knowing she'd been selected to play an intricately choreographed role in the most important drama in the history of the world.

The priest, Father William J. Sullivan, a man of God—who knew nothing about man and less about God—applying his limited intellect and the pretense of his faith, hoping to comprehend that which he could never grasp nor expect to change.

And then there were the disposable people, the soulless ones: Alton Barnes, Lucy Washburn, Jerry Finny, Herbert Gold, Daisy Dubois, Beth Damon, and a billion billion others. They would burn like candles, lighting the pathway to the new day.

McCurdy laughed quietly in the dark vehicle. Staring at the door to the rectory, he knew it would open momentarily. Then the next act in the drama would begin.

* * *

Alton Barnes's eyes were open. He glared at the ceiling, cringing from something no one else could see.

Karen and Father Sullivan crowded closely beside the seated man. Jeff had faded into the background early in the hypnosis session.

"It's okay, Mr. Barnes," said Karen, watching him cower from the unseen light. "You're safe and comfortable. You're watching it on a television screen. Nothing can hurt you. Now, you're in the kitchen at the Dubois farmhouse. . . ."

Alton's lips trembled. "It's . . . it's above my head, coming down, coming closer. Oh! It . . . it's passin' right over me like some kinda mouth swallowin' me up! And inside . . . oh, it's dark in here. And there's voices, speakin', whisperin' right into my mind . . . !"

"Relax, Mr. Barnes. That's right. Now what are the voices saying?" Karen looked at Father Sullivan as she spoke. He shook his head, puzzled. Both moved closer to the seated man.

"Horrible things. Talkin' about horrible things they want to do to me, to hurt me . . . scare me. I try to hold on. I know they can't really hurt me because I'm tied up in a chair, and they're . . . they're just in my head, in my mind, like some kinda bad dream. But somehow—I know I ain't imaginin' it—they're talking' to me from *outside*. From somewhere far away. But I'm hearin' 'em in my mind. It's like they're tryin' to pull me away. Like somehow they can pull me right out of my body. And I'm scared they really can. If they do, what if I can't hold on? What if I can't get back?"

He gulped a few rapid breaths, his barrel chest heaving and falling. "And one of 'em tells me, this's what happens when you die. You fly out of your body and into this other place. A place that's all around us, but it's . . . *different.* And all of a sudden, I can see it! I can see that other place! The place beyond the light. And, oh, it's beautiful! There's so much color and shine, and the sky's just as clear as the glass on a pocket watch. And flowers, beautiful flowers like nothin' I ever seen before."

Alton's eyes narrowed; tears swelled at their corners. He smiled and his voice softened. "There's Stuart! He's smilin' and wavin' and he's all sorta glowin' like some kind of angel. 'Stuart!' I says. And he says to me, 'See there, Alton, didn't I tell ya it was gonna be fine? Didn't I promise?' And it *is* fine. That's the thing, it's jest as fine as can be.

"See, I'd passed right on by them bad ones that wanted to hurt me. And now I'm in— Well, I guess it's what you call Heaven. An' Stuart's tellin' me, 'See there, Alton, ain't it just as pretty as I always tried to tell ya?'

"And he says, 'Now you go on back, but keep listenin' to what I tell ya. 'Cause now you know I ain't lyin' about none of it. An' I'll be right there with ya, jest you wait and see. I'll tell ya what you gotta do every step of the way. It may seem wrong, and it may seem bad. But that's just how it'll *seem.* 'Cause now you seen where folks come to when they die. You know better'n anyone that none of it's bad or wrong, it's jest the road we gotta take to get from there to here. This here's the new beginnin', and you got yourself a job to do.' That's just what he says to me, 'You got yourself a job to do.'"

Alton Barnes fell silent. For a few moments no one spoke.

"Hal-lu-cin-a-tions?" Sullivan silently mouthed the word.

Karen shrugged. She didn't know. Maybe it was real. Maybe this was what happened when people had a vision. Maybe this was an honest-to-God religious experience?

"Mr. Barnes," she said, "when you came to join us here tonight, you wouldn't let Jeff leave. Why wouldn't you let him leave this house?"

"'Cause his daughter, she's got a job to do, too. So's Jeffrey. Right now they just ain't supposed to be doin' it together."

"I see. Can you tell me about these jobs they have to do?"

"I don't know no more about it than you do, miss. All I know's that each of us has a part to play. Beyond that, we all gotta wait an' see."

"Okay, Mr. Barnes," Karen said as she stood up. "You just rest now. Relax and rest."

Her eyes met those of Father Sullivan. He shook his head as if to say, I don't understand any of it, but it's sad. It's very, very sad.

The room seemed to shake as the grandfather clock began to strike midnight.

Karen looked around for Jeff. She wondered what he made of it all. But he was gone.

PART FIVE

Armageddon...

"The glacier knocks in the cupboard,
The desert sighs in the bed,
And a crack in the teacup opens
A lane to the land of the dead."

—W. H. Auden

Excerpt from
The Reality Conspiracy:
An Anecdotal Reconstruction of the Events at Hobston, Vermont

Ronald E. Boudreau's Scout died.

Just like that, it stopped. The engine didn't knock or fart or wheeze—it just quit without warning or protest. One second it was on, the next it was off. Simple as that.

"Jay-zus Christ, what now?" Ronald said and he didn't care who heard him.

He'd stopped on a slightly downhill grade, so it was easy to let the vehicle roll to the side of the road out of the way of oncoming traffic. Of course, there wasn't much traffic to worry about after midnight on this rutted and frost-heaved road back to his trailer.

It was the first hour of the first day of July. Ronald had worked second shift. He was tired as hell and eager to get home.

"Christ, I could set here all frikkin' night," he said to the tiny glow-in-the-dark plastic statue of St. Christopher that dangled from his rearview mirror.

Again he turned the key and the starter motor sang its whining, grating song. The engine didn't kick in; it didn't even attempt to fire.

"Looks like we got us a problem, m'friend," he said to the saint.

Ronald's oldest boy, Joe, often made fun of the St. Christopher statuette. "That's MISTER Christopher, Dad. Don't forget, he ain't a saint no more; he's been *DE*-moted!"

That Joe was a godless boy, worse than his mother, but Ronald knew he was right about St. Christopher. Still, he just couldn't figure out how a guy can be a saint one minute, then busted to civilian the next. If a fella's a saint to start with, how could he do the kind of sinning required to get his sainthood revoked? The bottom line, of course, was that the whole thing didn't make much sense. Far as Ronald was concerned, once a saint always a saint, so he left the statue swinging from his rearview mirror and he thought no more about it.

It was real dark. Thickening clouds blotted out the stars, but there was a little moonlight.

Ronald twisted the key again. The starter groaned, slowing ominously as the battery lost power. "Prob'ly the goddamn timin' chain. Always goddamn somethin' t'piss my money away on! An' jes' when a fella thinks he's gettin' ahead . . ."

Last month, Ronald had received a thirty-five-cent-an-hour raise. He and Betty were planning to put a little away so they could add a deck to the south side of their trailer.

And now this. Christ. One goddamn thing after another.

For a moment Ronald thought that maybe he was very much like St. Christopher. One minute he's a wealthy man, the next minute he's paying through the nose for some mechanical fucking at thirty christly dollars an hour. Not to mention the cost of the frikkin' tow!

"Well, sir, Mr. Christopher," Ronald said, "looks like we're gonna be hoofin' it."

The woods around him were filled with the silvery luster of cloud-filtered moonlight. Long as the moon stayed out he wouldn't have to walk home in the dark.

On either side of him towering thick-leafed trees merged their branches high above the road. It made him feel as if he were walking in a cathedral. Ahead, the road angled to the left and vanished from sight.

It was there he saw the glow.

A pale light moved through the forest as if someone were walking among the trees, carrying a lantern.

Goddamnedest thing . . . he thought.

He stopped, staring at the moving light as it came closer to him. He rubbed his eyes, took another look, and rubbed his eyes again. It was still there, only now it didn't seem to be a light at all. Instead, it was a glowing shape. Ronald's mind worked to reject the image. No fuckin' way! He simply could not be seeing a six-foot-tall glowing man striding through the trees.

Toward him!

Ronald blinked. Looked away. Looked back.

Rapid-fire, his mind pushed a confusion of theories at him: it's a ghost; a game warden in some glow-in-the-dark uniform; a luminous gas spurting from a fault line in the forest floor; a new kid's toy, a phosphorescent kite maybe. It's somebody—probably Joe—playing a frikkin' trick on me?

But it was none of those things and he knew it.

And the light wasn't shining *on* the thing like a spotlight or a flashlight beam. Instead, the glow was coming from the thing itself. No doubt about it, the thing was actually giving off the light.

Ronald stood rooted to his spot at the roadside.

Now the thing was close enough so he could make out facial features. It looked like . . . a man, a shining man. God, maybe it *was* a ghost after all! Ronald could distinguish a golden beard, and golden hair that hung to the man's shoulders. And he wore a long white robe secured at the waist with a golden cord. The man's gentle blue eyes were the kindest Ronald had ever seen. They too seemed to shine with an otherworldly intensity.

"Come closer and be welcome," the man said. The smiling lips never moved, but Ronald could hear the voice. It was gentle and sincere. Musical.

Ronald tried to move but he couldn't. He was frozen—paralyzed—transfixed like a deer in the headlights of his Scout.

The radiant apparition floated closer. Now Ronald could feel a warmth, like a gentle summer breeze. The warm light felt good, like sunshine on his skin.

"You know me," the figure said, "and you have always been loyal and true. I bring great news for you, and for the world."

"W-what news?"

"There is a new time close at hand. A change. Only the strong of heart will be prepared to meet what is to come."

"Ar-are y-you an . . . angel?" Ronald asked.

"I am *your* angel." When the figure smiled the light on Ronald's face seemed to warm him even more. "I am Mr. Christopher."

Still its lips didn't move. "You are the one I choose to bring my message to the world. You are like Noah. Like Bernadette. Like Joseph Smith and the children at Fatima. You are of the chosen."

"I . . . I . . ." Ronald's head whirled; doubt warred with his senses. "Whatcha want me to say? Whatcha want me to do?"

"Believe. Pray. Cleanse your spirit and seek forgiveness. Tell your priest he must come to the mountain."

"I . . . I . . ." Not knowing what to say or what to do, Ronald dropped to his knees.

The thing smiled down at him. Perfect teeth glistened like gemstones behind its motionless lips. "I will return to this place tomorrow night. Come back and tell me you have done what I ask."

"Naa . . . now, let me get this straight," said Ronald, his dry lips forming words with difficulty, "you want me to go talk to that new priest? You want me to go there right now?"

The smiling man nodded within his luminous cocoon.

"Which mountain you talkin' about?"

"He will know. He will understand. Go to him at once."

"But . . ."

The glowing figure faded a little, turned cloudy, then became a churning pillar of mist. It dimmed, it darkened, it was gone.

Ronald felt his heart pounding. He discovered he was breathing way too rapidly. Pains in his knees from kneeling on the roadside forced him to stand up. He brushed dust off his pants, all the time squinting into the trees for some sign of his unearthly visitor.

The angel was gone.

Glancing repeatedly over his shoulder, Ronald returned to his Scout.

As he opened the door and got in, he realized that he was sweating something wicked, even in the cool midnight air.

The key in the ignition felt cold between his fingers.

He turned it.

The starter groaned.

"Well, how the fuck am I s'posed to go *anywhere* if my christly Scout don't work?"

23

The Change That Is Coming

Casey had been alone for a long time.

Upstairs, directly under the slanting roof, the temperature had soared during the afternoon until the farmhouse bedroom felt like a steam bath. Now, after several hours of darkness, it had cooled off. It was almost comfortable.

Casey could smell her own body odor. Her shirt and slacks stuck to her limbs. The urine in the plastic dishpan was rancid, foul. She'd been tempted to dump it out onto the porch roof, but when she tried to open the window, she found it was stuck.

What time was it, anyway? She couldn't tell. She just knew it was late.

And it was so very dark. There were no electric lights to turn on, no lamps, candles, or matches. The only illumination was the faint neon glow of the computer screen, and outside the round white light of the moon.

For a long while Casey had stared at the moon. She imagined it too was a screen on which she envisioned pleasant scenes. Her mother's smiling face. Her dad laughing just the way he did after he made one of his corny jokes. Karen's pretty smile. Once Casey had even pictured Dad and Karen holding hands, two tiny images framed in the white circle of the moon, a bride and groom on a wedding cake. Maybe she should object to the thought of Dad and Karen together. But she didn't. She liked it.

She missed them both.

Casey gritted her teeth and pushed away a tear.

McCurdy had left the room hours ago and she'd been alone ever since.

She recalled the gunshot, the strange white light, and a terrifying commotion downstairs: loud voices, heavy feet. And the hysterical cries of a man who'd screamed and screamed.

Then everything was quiet.

After that, crying and cringing in the corner, Casey remained alert, expecting McCurdy to come back any minute. But he hadn't come. And the house had been silent for— She didn't know how long. Hours.

Okay, that must have been McCurdy she'd seen leaving with another man, driving off down the road. So he was gone. Maybe he'd never return. He'd left her alone in the house, trapped on the second floor, with no access to food or water and no way to send a message for help.

Again, like so many times before, she wheeled herself to the door and peeked out into the dark upstairs hall.

There was no motion. No sound.

For a while she had done something very like praying. Over and over in her mind she had said, "Let everything be all right. Please let me get out of here. Let everything be all right, please. Please."

But she had not addressed these thoughts to anyone in particular. No, she certainly wasn't praying.

Casey didn't understand why it was so difficult to pray. At a time like this it should be easy, even automatic. After all, it seemed only God could free her from this horrible old house.

But praying had never come naturally to her.

Her parents had never taken her to church; she'd had no formal religious education. Nonetheless, in a way she did believe in God. In fact, sometimes, back when she was a little girl, she recalled how she had timidly, experimentally, tried to talk to Him. But not understanding, she had always expected some kind of answer, some acknowledgment, and it had never come.

Three years ago, when she was in the hospital, Casey had tried praying again. Really praying. Trying to do it right this time. And again it hadn't worked. Her mom died anyway.

And Casey had lain, no, she'd actually *lived* in that hospital bed. For months. Refusing all the time to pray for herself. She learned then, for sure, that she *did* believe in God. She'd believed enough to be angry with Him for His rudeness and His silence. Although her own suffering had been great, she had refused to ask Him for anything ever again.

She was older now and she realized praying was just a way of talking to herself. It was positive thinking, a method of dealing with her fear in short affirmative instructions to herself. "Please let me get out of here. Please let Dad find me. Don't let this crazy man hurt me."

Prayer was a way of maintaining hope.

Well, if positive thinking had gotten her out of the hospital, it could get her out of here, too.

Casey set the brakes on both wheels of her chair. Leaning forward, she was able to grab the flat metal foot supports and lift them out of the way. With both hands firmly gripping the arms, she slid forward, swung herself off the seat, and began to lower herself to the floor.

Her arms vibrated with the exertion.

In a moment she was sitting on the coarse wooden floor. She wiped her hands on her pant legs, fighting the feeling of insecurity that always came when she was out of her chair.

She looked around in the darkness.

Summoning all her resolve, she permitted herself to topple sideways, supported by one hand. She lowered herself to her elbow, working her body all the way down in safe short increments. Soon she was lying on her stomach. In this position she could pull herself along with her elbows.

It was a quick painless crawl to the top of the stairs where she stopped to listen for noises below. Everything was quiet. Like her, the old house seemed to be holding its breath.

With no illumination, she could see very little in the darkness below. Nothing seemed to be moving. She was almost confident she was alone, except for maybe—and this hit her with all the force and clarity of a blow to the windpipe—the dead man! Casey was pretty sure someone had been shot, murdered on the floor below.

Was there a dead body down there waiting for her?

Was more than one person dead?

What about McCurdy? Had he left with another man? Would they come back?

It didn't matter. Nothing mattered but the straight as an arrow route between here and the outside door. She had to get out and the sooner the better.

But she had to be careful.

Her chin hovered inches above the top step. She studied the descent as best she could in the lightless hallway. The stairs might be a problem. It would certainly be dangerous to try to crawl down headfirst.

Before she'd been discharged from the hospital, physical therapists in the rehab unit had taught her what to do if she found herself in a situation like this. Grabbing the banister, she pulled her dead legs around, and sat up on the top step. With her legs stretched out in front, pointing down, she adjusted her spine so it was almost perpendicular with the floor.

Essentially, getting downstairs would be just like lowering herself from the wheelchair several times in a row.

Exploring with her hands, she discovered that the edge of each step was rounded, with a bit of an overhang. That was lucky; she could grip them securely. The whole staircase was covered by a filthy old carpet. Lucky, too. It was not as slippery as bare wood and would make the bumpy trip down softer and safer.

Carefully, slowly, one step at a time, she lowered herself. She could feel the edge of each carpeted step sliding up her spine. Each touchdown was a relief, each offered a feeling of progress.

There were twelve steps in all. Just twelve. That didn't seem too bad. But she knew she would have to be perfectly careful on every one. One slip, one lost grip, and she could slide downward like a child on a play yard chute. Without the use of her legs, she might not be able to stop herself. She could break a bone. Do more damage to her spine.

Halfway there!

She rested a moment. Her biceps, forearms, and hands were sore already. She flexed one fist at a time, holding on to the stair with the other.

The house below remained quiet. And full of shadows.

From here she could actually see her goal! Faintly, yes, but she was sure. A distance of thirty feet separated the bottom of the stairs and the front door. Even without her chair she could make thirty feet very quickly.

Then there would be the problem of what to do once she was outside.

No! Worry about one thing at a time. It was better not to think about outdoors yet.

She lowered herself another step.

From here she could look to the right and see a bit of the kitchen. Moonlight cast eerie shadows on the dark floor. Although she couldn't see much, just a couple table legs and the bottom of a chair, she thought she could make out a pair of shoes and white socks stretching from the cuffs of black pants.

Someone was lying on the kitchen floor.

The dead man!

Casey looked away.

She paused a moment to let her breathing calm, then lowered herself another step.

Just four to go!

A noise from the kitchen made her gasp. It sounded impossibly loud.

In her mind's eye she saw the dead man struggle to his feet and walk. He was coming after her. Unsteady, awkward, lurching sightlessly, he was coming! She didn't want to look. She *fought* the need to look. But a slapping, scampering sound on the kitchen floor made her gape involuntarily to the right.

Oh God! Something was moving in the shadows!

Something four-footed scurried from the kitchen, coming toward the stairs. It wove through the darkness like a fish through the depths. Swiftly it came, noisy on the floor. Breathing loudly, making growling sounds, as if its air passages were obstructed.

Was it a dog? It was too dark to see.

It was too big for a cat.

It looked white, animallike, and it came to rest at the foot of the stairs, its face no more than five feet from Casey's.

Casey tried hard not to scream when she saw it was a little girl. The horrid child was naked, filthy, her pallid skin streaked with grime. Something limp seemed to be dangling from her mouth.

What's *wrong* with her? Is she retarded? Or crazy, or what? Frightful stories about mentally defective children locked away in old houses jumped into Casey's mind.

The crouching child looked up with a demented savagery in her eyes. She fidgeted on her knees, rocked from side to side, rubbing her palms on the floor.

Fear grew along with revulsion. Without daring to lower herself another step, Casey tried to calm the child as she might try to calm a growling dog. "Hello there," Casey said. She wondered how the apprehension in her voice would affect the girl.

The girl tipped her head to the side. Dark eyes locked on Casey's.

What do I say to her? Casey realized the little girl had deliberately made herself an obstacle in the path to the front door. "Do you have a name? My name's Casey. What's yours? Can you tell me yours?"

An odor rose from the child. Dirt and feces and sweat.

Perhaps they were both captives in the old house? Why? For what purpose?

In time would Casey be reduced to a similar bestiality?

"Do you want to go with me? Do you want to get out of here?"

The girl sat on the floor. She made a muffled growling noise, rude, like air over flaccid skin. Now Casey could discern how grotesquely the child's mouth was deformed. Those were her thick black lips dangling obscenely, giving the impression she was holding something small and limp and dead in her mouth. The bubbling, flapping sound might be an attempt to speak. But Casey couldn't understand. She looked away as a long glistening tentacle of drool groped from the child's mouth toward the floor.

"Could you move out of my way, please?" Casey said, trying to smile.

The child squinted up at her, its eyeballs moving from side to side. Still, it didn't move. Perhaps it didn't understand.

When she caught herself thinking of the little girl as an *it*, she tried again to smile a kind of apology. So what if the child was retarded or crazy, she was still human. If she were treated decently, she should respond to kindness.

Gripping one of the banister's support posts, Casey reached out with her free hand, hoping to rest it on the child's cheek. "Don't be afraid," she said. "Let's be friends, you and I. Okay?"

The child pulled her head away and made an ugly sound through her deformed lips.

Casey didn't know what to do. Her arms and hands were tired. She didn't dare move down another step. Going back upstairs would be impossible. Even attempting to backup a step or two would be dangerous. She might slide, fall . . .

At least the child wasn't moving any closer. That gave her a moment to think.

"Do you have a name?" Casey asked, trying to sound gentle and unthreatening.

The child grunted. Her lips vibrated as if she were blowing air through them.

"If you could move out of my way, please . . . ? I can't walk, you know, and I'm afraid I might fall on you." A nervous laugh escaped Casey's throat. She immediately felt stupid for having done it. It was inappropriate and involuntary.

This time the girl inched closer. She lifted her hands to the bottom step and leaned forward, sniffing. Now her face hovered less than three feet from Casey's. Her hair was matted, wild in greasy disarray. Her animal scent was stronger now.

Cringing, Casey felt herself recoiling in disgust. Every muscle tensed. She tried to speak calmly, still not knowing what to say. "Are you all right, little girl? Are you sick? Can I do something for you? All I want is to get out of here, okay?"

A hand leapt at Casey like a pouncing crab. She couldn't feel the pressure as the girl's fingers tightened around her insensate ankle. She couldn't flex her leg to pull it away.

"No!" Casey cried.

As the girl squinted up at her, something in the dark cavities of her eyes glistened.

"No!"

Casey groped for the flimsy dowels that supported the banister as the girl began to tug.

"Oh no!" Her bottom slipped forward on the stair. She bounded down another step, letting out a shrill cry of surprise. The back of her head struck a stair. The jolt made her bite her tongue.

She clenched the dowel. If she didn't hold on, she feared her head would bang again. It could knock her out.

Hand over hand, as if the banister posts were the rungs of a ladder, Casey tried to slow the girl's efforts to pull her down the stairs.

On the floor now, she still tried to hold on. She wanted to lock her fingers around the newel post, but the girl was too quick and too strong.

In a moment she was sliding on her back across the pine flooring in the hall.

The girl dragged her toward the door.

Pausing, the naked girl dropped Casey's foot. Then she stretched her filthy hand up toward the door latch, lifted it, pushed open the door to freedom.

Before Casey could understand what was happening, the girl dragged her across the threshold and into the night.

* * *

He knew exactly where Jeff was going.

McCurdy would relax a moment before getting out of the car. Then he'd take his time, amble up the walk to the rectory. He had something to do there. Something that would involve the priest, the girl, and the old man.

Without thinking, he put his hand in the slack pocket of his suit coat. The automatic was cold as ice in his fingers.

Another minute passed.

McCurdy never stopped marveling at the way things worked. By forcing Jeff to remain at the rectory, Alton Barnes had sent him away. An exquisite paradox. Beautiful and pure.

Paradoxes made perfect sense to McCurdy. They were part of an infinite flawlessness that would be unfathomable to the uninspired mind. And anyone outside the Light. And anyone incapable of seeing with immaculate clarity.

Perhaps, McCurdy wondered, he was experiencing the coveted nirvana all those deluded Buddist monks fancied they could attain.

Ha! What did they know?

He chuckled. Smiled. Felt an excited tingling of great satisfaction. It was, he knew, the sensation of perfect grace, the Light in his mind and soul. Since it had revealed itself to him that night in the church— it seemed so very long ago—he had become . . . something else. Something more than a man. He had evolved.

His new spirit grew stronger with each passing minute.

When he touched the car's door handle, it hit him.

It was as if a slackened wire in his mind suddenly jerked tight.

A warning.

A summons.

Something was wrong!

At the house.

Something had willfully violated the plan.

McCurdy started the engine.

He didn't need to follow Jeff Chandler's car. He knew exactly where Jeff was going.

* * *

Casey lay on the flagstone walk in front of the farmhouse, resting after she had tumbled down the porch steps. She'd been banged up. Her hands were filthy, her clothing torn. She knew there were probably wounds, open and bleeding, in the skin of her unfeeling legs.

But there was no time to rest.

She tried to crawl, dragging herself along on her elbows and forearms. Air hissed through her nostrils.

Every part of her that had feeling ached.

Why bother? Why? Escape would be impossible. She was in the middle of the woods, miles from anywhere.

In the distance, parked on the side of the road, she could see a car. Even if she were able to crawl all that way, the keys were probably not in the ignition. And if they were, how could she drive a vehicle that wasn't equipped with special hand controls? There was no way she could work the gas pedal or brake. And what if there was a clutch? She had no idea how to drive a standard transmission.

As she crawled across the dark damp farmyard, she knew what she was doing was stupid. Futile.

The horrible little girl had pushed her down the front steps, then turned around and walked back into the house. Casey had been thrown out! Like a pet at bedtime. Like a bag of garbage.

At least the little monster hadn't hurt her. The child's strength had been great and there was an unbridled savagery about her. She'd made Casey feel she was in the presence of something not quite human.

Well, no matter. At least Casey was outside now. And though she was tired and scared, she seemed unharmed. That was something, at least.

Okay, so how unrealistic was it to think she could crawl all the way into town? In dangerous situations, people had done things far more difficult. At the very least, maybe she could make it to the first house with electric lights and a telephone. Perhaps someone nearby could help her, maybe phone her father.

So things were not as hopeless as they seemed.

Still, on some level she was aware of how she must look. If she were not wearing her torn and dirty clothing, she'd look like that horrid little girl. And the little girl looked like an animal.

A clattering startled her. An awful metallic banging came from inside the house, as if the little girl were in there throwing things around.

Casey tensed, sped up a little, hoping to crawl as far away as possible. She felt the bite of tiny stones and gravel as they pushed into the exposed flesh of her arms.

Behind her, the front door of the farmhouse crashed open.

Casey looked over her shoulder to see the little girl struggling with the wheelchair. She was tugging it down the steps and into the yard.

A fat raindrop hit Casey on the cheek. Another one.

Lightning flashed and thunder rolled heavily across the sky.

* * *

"We *know* where he's gone. Why don't we just go up there? Why don't we just—"

Karen heard her own voice, shrill, almost shrieking. Suddenly she knew exactly how Jeff must have felt when he learned Casey was missing. Just as suddenly, she realized how very much she cared about him.

It had been easy to comfort him about his daughter; it was completely consistent with her training, almost within the day-to-day routine of her job. But now things had changed. Professional became personal. This sense of desperation, this powerless panic was something she had never felt before. She was ready to do anything, smart or foolish, to insure Jeff's safety.

Father Sullivan paced back and forth, his hand on his chin. "Wait, Karen, wait. Let me think a minute."

"But we can't wait—"

"We've got to. It's too late to stop him before he gets to the farm. If we're going to go barging in there, we'd better plan it out and do it right. We'll only get one chance at it."

He walked to the window and stood beside her. "Frankly, I think we should call the police."

"But, Father—"

"Look, I understand all the reasons not to, but this is dangerous. I don't think we can pull it off on our own. Think about it. Apparently this McCurdy character is holding Casey up there. Now he's probably got Jeff, too. And it looks to me as if he's bright enough to guess we're likely to follow. I can't see the point of jumping right into the fire."

"Call them, then. We've got to do *something!* We've got to hurry!"

Sullivan walked to the desk in his study where he kept his telephone. He picked up the phone book, began flipping pages. Karen glanced at her watch.

As Sullivan ran his finger down a column of names, a deafening crack, like cannon fire, shattered the silence. Bright light flashed in the room.

Karen looked through the rain-splattered window. "That's all we need, a thunderstorm."

Sullivan tossed the phone book aside and began to rummage through the scattering of papers on his desk. "I just thought of something," he said. "Turns out I've met someone from the state police. I'm going to phone her." He picked up something from the desktop. "Ah, here's her card. Sergeant Shane. At least we've met, so maybe she won't think I'm a complete nut case."

He began to punch the buttons as another thunderclap shook the rectory. A blinding flash left the room lights flickering. Then they went out.

Everything went dark.

"Damn!" said Sullivan. "The phone just went dead in my hand." He slammed it into its cradle and reached for a cigarette. The match illuminated his face.

"That's too weird," Karen said in a whisper. "It's as if . . ."

"It's as if the phone circuits went out along with the lights. Come on, Karen, that's perfectly normal in an electrical storm. Let's not let our imaginations make this situation worse than it is."

"But is the thunderstorm normal? A little while ago it was nice outside. The sky was clear and there was a moon."

Sullivan looked as if he might say something. Instead, he took an aggressive drag on his cigarette. Air hissed. Smoke billowed from his mouth. "So we get in the car and we drive to the police station," he said.

"Do you think the car will work?"

He looked as if he were about to lose patience. "You're convinced now that we're dealing with magic, aren't you?"

"I *saw* the videotape, Father. You didn't. It was pretty convincing. More than Father Mosely's journal."

A series of thunderclaps rocked the sky. The glass shade of a table lamp rattled. Overhead, the cast-iron chandelier shook.

Sullivan's cigarette glowed like a red eye in the darkened room. It moved as he looked up. "We could use some light in here," he said, positioning a chair beneath the chandelier. He climbed up and lit the candles.

The room trembled with the next explosion of thunder. The chandelier quivered. Plaster dust snowed down. Sullivan jumped from the unsteady chair. "Whoa! That one felt like an earthquake!"

"Father, come here. Look at this!"

He joined Karen at the window. Rain pelted the glass. Together they watched a ball of light streak across the sky. Then another and another. They were like a premature barrage of Fourth of July fireworks, dramatic, beautiful.

"Are those meteors?" Karen asked.

"Comets? Meteors? I don't know. . . ."

Soon the black forms of pajama-clad people appeared at front doors on the other side of the street. Some were holding flashlights. Everyone looked upward, watching the white globes flash across the sky.

"Something's happening," Karen whispered.

"So it would appear. I know what you're thinking, Karen. Assuming you're right about this, the only one who might know what's going on is Mr. Barnes. Do you think you can . . . I want to say 'deprogram' him. Can you remove the suggestion that's affecting his behavior?"

Karen looked at the sleeping man in the chair. Head tipped forward, his chin rested on his chest.

"I don't know," she said, her voice flat with worry. "Let me give it a try."

* * *

Jeff stomped the brake pedal when his headlights washed over something in the driveway. Through the swishing windshield wipers, he recognized the reflective metal frame of Casey's wheelchair. Then he saw his daughter on the spattering ground.

And who was that crouching nearby? Some little kid? Had there been an accident here?

What the hell was going on?

"Casey!"

He fairly leapt from the car. Wind-driven water smacked him like an ocean wave as he ran toward the girl.

A fireball hissed overhead. Its stark white glare streaked across the field like a searchlight.

At first Jeff didn't know where the thick low growling was coming from. Before he could think about it, the naked child sprang at him.

She wailed like a cat, flinging her arms wildly as she flew through the air. Wet sinewy legs coiled around his waist, her arms encircled his neck. Still growling, she attacked with her head, bashing at him. He braced himself for an assault of teeth. Instead, a moist leathery suction attached itself to his cheek.

"Get off me!" he cried, trying to pull the convulsing child away. Her arms and legs tensed, coiled tighter. She pumped her bony pelvis against his abdomen. He felt his cheek swell and tear under the incredible suction of her mouth.

"Dad!" Casey screamed. "She's crazy, Dad. She's crazy."

Jeff lost his footing, tumbled to the muddy road. He felt the impossible sucking lips crawl across his face, widening their hold. He felt them touch his own lips and it disgusted him.

Jeff locked his hands between his neck and hers. Then, with all his strength, palms pressing her throat, he tried to push her away. She didn't budge, she was stuck to him like a parasite.

Adrenaline shot killing thoughts into his mind.

No! God! This is a kid, a little kid. I can't—

But she was strong, full of manic energy, and he had to do something to stop the attack.

Christ, this little kid could kill him!

In mounting panic instinct overcame conditioning—he hit her. Big fists pummeled her head, her neck, her shoulders.

She whined like a squalling feline, slamming her heels against his spine. One connected with the soft flesh covering his kidney.

Sharp pain turned to nausea.

Casey was working her way across the damp ground toward the struggling pair. Squinting into the rain, she grabbed a handful of the girl's greasy hair and pulled. "Leave him alone! Leave my father alone!"

Something happened.

The word "father" worked like a magic word. As if suddenly understanding that this man was not an enemy, the little girl stopped struggling. Her arms, legs, and those terrible lips released their powerful hold. On all fours she scampered away into the shadows.

Panting, Jeff touched his cheek. The skin was raw. His fingers came away damp, slick with a mixture of saliva, blood, and rain. The viscous liquid glistened in the white beam of his headlights.

As he tried to catch his breath, another car pulled up and ground to a halt.

Two sets of headlamps combined to make an illuminated island in the dark farmyard.

Rain battered the ground.

A car door opened and slammed. A shadow moved behind the headlights.

In a moment, Jeff recognized a familiar sound. "Tch, tch, tch."

McCurdy.

"Yes, Jeffrey, we are all together. But it is nothing like you imagine."

With new strength he'd been conserving for this confrontation, Jeff sprang to his feet. Rage pumped adrenaline to his muscles and his mind. His nerves were on fire. "You sick son of a bitch, McCurdy. You've really gone too far."

McCurdy seemed calm, as if the situation were civil and entirely under control. "I was just doing what I had to do, Jeff. Just like you do what you have to. But we're both working for the same thing. Don't you understand that?"

"I don't think we are. Not anymore. I know what you're working for and by God I'm going to put a stop to it. If anything happens to me, that videotape will go right into the hands of somebody who can do something about it."

McCurdy laughed. It was condescending, full of derision and superiority. "Tch, tch, tch. Jeffrey, you can't believe all this has anything to do with that videotape. Haven't you figured it out by now? Can't you understand anything on your own?" He clicked his tongue. "You're nowhere near as bright as I'd hoped, you and your priest and your girlfriend."

Jeff turned his back on McCurdy and went to help Casey into her chair.

"Stop!" McCurdy cried. "Leave her right where she is. You're working for me, Jeffrey, you must learn to obey."

Jeff turned on him. "I'm working for—? You really are sick, aren't you? I am *not* working for you or anyone else. But I am going to put you and that whole lunatic asylum you call the Academy out of business. You can be damn sure I'm not the only one who won't tolerate what's going on there."

McCurdy wiped rainwater from his eyes. "Jeffrey, listen to me. Listen. You'll have to sometime, it might as well be now."

"Like hell I will—"

"I told you the computer would work magic, remember? And that's what you think. That's what your videotape proves, am I right? But listen, it isn't magic, it's more than that. It's miracles, Jeff. That machine helps me do the work of God. I am God's Man, Jeffrey. And I can prove it. You'll believe it, too. Let me show you."

Jeff knelt beside Casey, his hands on her shoulders. Her eyes were wide with terror.

He remained highly alert as McCurdy walked through the lighted area toward the filthy, cowering beast-child. He grabbed the cringing creature by her hair and dragged her into the rain-softened glow of the four headlights.

"I had told my ratty little friend here to keep your daughter inside. That was her job. That was all I expected of her. Jeff, I promise you I never meant for Casey to leave the house and get into a situation as . . . uncomfortable as this. For that I must apologize to both of you."

Redirecting his attention, McCurdy spoke through clenched teeth, "The problem is here."

He shook the sobbing child by the hair and flung her into the mud where she curled into a tight, protective ball. Jeff could hear her whimpering.

"As always," McCurdy continued, "the fault is with the soulless ones. They're imperfect, incomplete. They don't *need* to perform good works for they have nothing to gain; salvation is beyond them." He kicked the child. "They're here to *serve* us. And in the case of completely defective ones, like *this*"—another kick—"they are ours to destroy. The power of the Light can make them— Well, let me show you."

McCurdy closed his eyes. His lips moved silently as if he were praying.

Lightning flashed. Another comet split the sky.

Jeff held Casey tighter. Her fingers dug into his arms. He felt her breathing rapidly, trembling. Gently, Jeff pulled her rain-soaked head to his chest.

And still he watched, fascinated, as a tiny bead of white light, intense as a laser, appeared about three feet above the whimpering child. It enlarged to the size of a golf ball, then flattened until it was the size of a dinner plate. It hissed and spat white sparks, as if it were burning the damp air through which it moved.

Thunder crashed overhead. The sky flared with lightning.

Casey buried her face against Jeff's arm, yet he watched in wonder. "What the hell's going on," he said, but not loud enough for anyone to hear.

A black spot appeared at the center of the fiery dinner plate. It broadened as the perimeter of the light expanded. Soon the thing had formed itself into a three-foot blazing circle. To Jeff, it looked for all the world like a white-hot hula hoop.

It started to descend around the little girl.

Casey looked up. Jeff saw the hoop's reflection, bright in her teary eyes.

The blazing ring dropped to the ground, surrounding the little girl, enclosing her like the magic circle of a satanic magician. She screamed.

"Stop it!" Casey cried. "Leave her alone. She tried to *help* me. She doesn't under*stand*—"

"QUIET!" McCurdy roared. "She's bad. She's useless."

Then the circle rose again, leaving a scorched ring in the wet gravel. As it passed over the little girl a second time, she seemed to catch fire. Searing threads of glowing silver encircled her body, wrapping her almost completely in a luminous cocoon. She screamed and bucked as the fiery strands sank, one after another, into her flesh. Her arms flattened against her sides, her fingers melted into her thighs as if she were made of molten wax. Her thrashing legs jerked straight, fused together. Jeff thought he could see motion beneath her rippling skin. Bones warping and re-forming. Muscles repositioning. The rigid line of her spine softened. Her shoulders slackened, her neck retracted into her torso.

Before his eyes, Jeffrey Chandler saw a little girl transformed into a four-foot white worm with a human head. The body twitched like a landed fish.

The light was gone.

Jeff sat on the ground beside his daughter. Rain beat around them. He felt empty of emotion; terror filled the void. He didn't know what to say or do. His mind threw useless explanations at him: a trick, a drug, hypnosis.

Something bright tore across the sky. A fireball of dazzling brilliance. Thunder crashed in its wake.

McCurdy didn't seem to notice. He spoke softly, sympathetically. "I know how you feel," he said. "You are overcome. There's no precedent for this in your experience. I understand that, Jeffrey. It is always this way when God reveals his power to man."

Jeff held his sobbing daughter. "Casey, Casey," he cooed. He didn't know what else to do. If he did nothing he would go mad. McCurdy's raving frightened him, but nowhere near as much as the demonstration he had just witnessed.

McCurdy went on. "Soon both of you will change, too. Oh, it'll be nothing quite so . . . physical. You'll be like me. You'll be one with the Light. Before, when I was merely a man, I could close my eyes and see a darkness blacker than any night. Now, I see nothing but the Light, everything is illuminated. At all times. Even when my eyes are closed.

"Soon, Jeffrey, soon the Light will be yours to control, to command. We can send it out to shine on whomever we please. We can use it to show people what no one else can see. We can use it to create. Or, when it's essential, we can destroy."

Jeff thought of Karen. Though he'd never wish her into this mad situation, she'd know how to deal with McCurdy's insanity.

Then a terrifying thought occurred to him: Was it really insanity?

The mind-numbing demonstration suggested part of McCurdy's ravings were on the level. God, he didn't know. He just didn't know. Fear immobilized him, made it impossible to think. Suddenly Jeff was thick-tongued; speaking was an effort.

"Ss-Skipp, listen. It's something about that computer. You're too involved with it. Too wrapped up. You believe it's capable of things it simply cannot do. You think—"

"It *can* do them! It can do what I tell it to do! Are you too feebleminded to believe your own eyes? Do I have to give you another demonstration?" McCurdy stomped over to them, towering above Casey and Jeff.

The sky brightened behind him with a slash of lightning.

In a moment McCurdy's angry face softened, he bent down to where he could look Jeff in the eye.

"Try to see it like this. The computer is for reference. Just that. It is no more magical than a library in a priest's home. It gives us access to more information than any one man could acquire in a hundred lifetimes. Somehow, through the goodness of the Lord, I am linked with that infinite body of knowledge." He chuckled. "You might say I'm a remote work station with a direct line to all the learning of the past. Think of it, Jeffrey! At no time in the past has man ever been able to come so close to God."

"But, Skipp, can't you see you're hurting people? Look what you did to that little girl. And Casey. Look at her! Would God want—"

"How dare you suggest what God wants? You don't *know* what God wants, Jeffrey. So you must believe me. That little girl was nothing. She was an animal without a soul. God doesn't care about her. The soulless ones are here to serve. To use and to serve. To become examples."

"No!"

"Jeffrey, accept it." Then in the most companionable of tones, "You are one of the select. And I must help you to understand that. Before today, man's lifetime has never been long enough to attain a true union with the divine. Think of all who have tried, think of the different pathways they took to discover the truth. Imagine the generations of psychics, occultists, magicians and mediums, Egyptian priests, African shamans, Indian medicine men. . .

"And think of our Christian holy men, the saints and martyrs of the Christian Church, each struggling through a lifetime of self-denial and discipline. And in the end, each gained no more than a fragment of the wisdom and the power. Maybe enough to tempt, but never enough to satisfy. Only enough to inspire other searchers, but that's all.

"Perhaps the lucky among them died possessing just one infinitesimal morsel of truth, a single tiny grain of sand out of all the beaches and deserts of the world."

Thunder crashed.

"But each did an important job, don't you see? Each played a minuscule but essential role in the acquisition of that boundless knowledge and awareness for which I am now the overseer.

"And that's my contribution, Jeffrey, you see? The computer. The synthesis. It was I who enabled, I made it all possible. So in a sense— although none of them ever came to know it—they were all working for me. For thousands of years they've been working for me. Exploring, meditating, searching, researching, all the time acquiring data that only now can be processed. They were working for me just as you are working for me. Just as everyone will happily work for a man who can perform miracles in the service of the Lord."

"But—"

"How? Is that what you want to know? I am in a psychic link with the computer. I control it from wherever I am. I no longer need the keyboard." McCurdy touched his index finger to his forehead. "It's all in here. My gift from God. It's *like* magic, Jeffrey, but it's miracles." McCurdy's lunatic expression was illuminated in a strobe of lightning.

Rain splattered down unrelenting. Bright comets zipped across the black sky.

Jeff felt a pressure behind his eyes. It made him fear he was going to cry. He looked down at his daughter's face as she hid her eyes, sobbing against his chest. He looked across the yard at the twitching white monstrosity that moments ago had been a little girl.

And he looked at McCurdy.

"Wh-what do you want with me, Skipp?"

* * *

Father Sullivan went into the church for a few minutes of prayer while Karen worked with Alton Barnes.

Alone, kneeling before the candlelit altar, the priest's thoughts kept returning to Father Mosely's journal, a journal written on the pages of a Bible, a journal that gave the only insight into horrors the old priest had endured during his final days in Hobston.

A maverick suspicion floated into Sullivan's mind: Was Father Mosely's confrontation with the preternatural a precursor to what was going on at this moment? Could it be that everything—including all the terrors of the last few days—had started right here in St. Joseph's Roman Catholic Church some ten years ago?

The church quaked under a new assault of thunder. The stained-glass windows glowed rainbow colors as lightning flashed and fireballs flew. Candles in red glass containers flickered, projecting dancing crimson phantoms against the plaster walls. Above Sullivan's head, timbers groaned.

Shifting his weight on his knees, Sullivan rested his forehead on his hand. Even as he concentrated, mouthing the words of a prayer, his mind persistently returned to the cycle of incredible events. And, damn it, he felt as if he'd been hurled right into the center of them. It was as if—he had to admit it—there was some pattern behind it all.

Had some grand design returned him to Mosely's church to battle Mosely's demon? Had he inadvertently followed that closely in the old man's footsteps?

Dear God, deliver us, he mouthed. *Dear God, protect us.*

A banging on the church door startled him. Five heavy thumps, then silence.

Sullivan stood, genuflected, and hurried down the central aisle to the double doors. They were not locked, he knew, and for a moment he wondered if he should lock them. Now.

BAM-BAM-BAM!

He touched the cold metal latch, pulled the heavy door open enough to see a short man in a glistening yellow slicker standing in the rain. Lightning lit the sky behind him.

Without waiting to be asked, the man slipped through the opening and into the church.

"Got a message for the priest," he said. His eyes were wide; he looked distressed.

"I . . . I'm Father Sullivan."

"Name's Boudreau." He ran his tongue around his lips. "Ah . . . fella told me to come in an' see you. . . . Christ, she's really pourin', ain't she?"

"It's an unbelievable storm. Why don't you come into the house, Mr. Boudreau. Take off those wet things and dry off. Can I get you something hot? Coffee, maybe?"

"I dunno." Furtive eyes explored the church interior. "Maybe we oughtta get our talking done first. Somethin' tells me I mighta waited too long as it is."

"Certainly, Mr. Boudreau. You say you have a message for me?"

A moment's hesitation. "Fella says you oughtta go to the mountain."

Sullivan shook his head. "W-what?"

"Don't mean nothin' to me," Mr. Boudreau said. He was slipping out of his wet slicker as he talked. Water dripped to the floor, pooling at the men's feet. "I kinda figured you'd know what it's all about."

Sullivan smiled uncertainly, not knowing what to make of his late-night caller. "Maybe you should start from the beginning, Mr. Boudreau. *Who* sent you to see me?"

"Think he mighta been an angel," Mr. Boudreau said, and proceeded with the story of Mr. Christopher, the shining man with the golden hair and beard.

Sullivan listened with rapt attention. Not long ago the same story would have sounded incredible to him. Now it had an uncomfortable ring of consistency, if not exactly truth. It was no more strange than the fantastic light show that was going on in the skies. In fact, something told Sullivan the two events might well be related.

"He says to me, 'Ronald, you're the one I want to bring my message to the world.' Says he's got good news and that there's a new time comin'. Then he says, 'Go to church, go find the priest'—musta meant you—'and tell the priest to come to the mountain.' That's just what he said. Weird, eh?"

"It is a bit . . . out of the ordinary. You actually saw him disappear? Vanish?"

"There one second. Gone the next. As God is my witness."

Sullivan searched the man's face for a hint of deceit, trickery, or madness. "Tell me something, Mr. Boudreau . . ."

"Yes sir?"

"Why did you come here at this hour? I mean, why here, to the church, rather than to the house? How did you know I was in here?"

"I just done what he told me to do."

"And then he said, 'Come to the mountain'?"

"Yup. Jes' like that."

"Did he say which mountain?"

"He said you'd know, you'd understand."

Sullivan dropped heavily into the nearest pew. Suddenly he realized how weary he was. He'd been watching passively as unbelievable event piled on top of unbelievable event like the performance of a magic show. Which events were true? Which were misleading? Which should he choose to believe?

He closed his eyes, uncertain. Was Mr Boudreau's message some kind of test of his faith?

Of course, such angelic visitations were known to happen. The church was still debating the recent events in Medjugorje, Yugoslavia, while other alleged holy visions were reported regularly in the Russian village of Grushevo and various places around the U.S. It sounded so fantastic! Could an angel really have appeared to this man?

An *angel* . . .?

If so, then Mr. Boudreau had delivered the answer Karen and Sullivan were searching for: they *should go* to the mountain where Jeff and his daughter were waiting.

But if the angel were imaginary, or the work of forces other than divine, then—

Then what?

Sullivan didn't know. A trap, maybe?

In all his years as a priest and as a psychologist, he had often encountered people with religious delusions, people who heard voices, saw visions, suffered intrusions both demonic and divine. In every case the visions had been psychological aberrations, not genuine religious experiences.

This, however, might be very different. There was no time to test or investigate, but he hoped he had not become too much of a skeptic to recognize the real thing when he saw it. It was a question of faith, after all. Tonight, moments ago, he had asked God for guidance. Mr. Boudreau's arrival was the most prompt answer to a prayer that Sullivan had ever experienced.

"So what're you gonna do, Father?" Mr. Boudreau prodded. "I mean, he's gonna want to know. Mr. Christopher, I mean. He told me to come back tomorrow night and tell him what happened. . . ."

Sullivan looked directly into his visitor's eyes. "We're going to go to the mountain, Mr. Boudreau."

"Good. I s'pect that's a good idea."

"And what about you? Will you be coming along?"

"Me? Hell no. I'm goin' home, take care of my fam'ly."

* * *

Downstairs in the Dubois farmhouse, Casey was free to roam around, but she didn't want to leave the living room. She was afraid of what she might find.

She recalled there was one room, just off the kitchen, that McCurdy had been careful not to let anyone see. He kept the door shut and Casey was pretty sure she'd seen him lock it. She suspected another prisoner might be in there. If so, who? Could it be someone who could help them? Should she go in there and try to open the door?

No!

No way was she going to wheel herself through the kitchen. That's where McCurdy kept the bodies. She'd glimpsed at least two corpses leaning against the cabinets on the floor: a poor old woman, badly burned, and the guy who'd been shot in the head.

Casey shuddered. A frigid knot grew in her stomach.

What kind of a crazy man would kill an old lady?

The thing that had happened to the little girl messed Casey up even more. Now, having witnessed the awesome power McCurdy controlled, the whole world had changed. No matter what happened, no matter where Casey and her dad went, things would never look the same again. She feared the dread she felt was now a permanent part of her character.

Dad ruined things. Worried as she was about him, Casey resented her father's intrusion. If he'd stayed away he might be safe now, and Casey might be free! Dad's arrival had stopped her escape attempt.

In her clumsy, brutish way, the little girl *had* tried to help and for a moment Casey's terror had turned to hope. Maybe the little girl could have pushed her down the hill to safety. But Dad had showed up and he'd brought crazy McCurdy with him. Now all of them were prisoners.

Still, she was comforted with Dad nearby, though if she could save him by wishing him away, she would do it gladly.

Where *is* Dad? Casey wondered. Was he still upstairs with McCurdy? What were they doing? What were they talking about?

She hoped Dad was just playing along, stalling for time. Or had he felt sufficiently intimidated by the horrible display to buy into McCurdy's plans, whatever they might be?

She didn't want to think about it.

Thunder crashed. The house vibrated. Rain beat heavily on the tin roof of the porch. The worsening storm made Casey feel even more nervous. She knew their situation wasn't likely to improve at all.

* * *

"Mmm-phh, ummm-ph. Mnnuh." The little girl was awake now. She twitched and made sounds from the sofa where McCurdy had dumped her.

Casey rolled the chair in that direction and stopped. She'd been grossed out enough by the way the child had looked *before* McCurdy went to work on her. Now, Casey didn't want to look at her at all! She felt sorry for the little girl, sure. But she had become so repellent, so disgustingly deformed that—

Stop it, Casey! She spoke angrily to herself. *Don't forget some people find you pretty hard to look at, too.* She'd seen it happen often enough; certain people averted their eyes to avoid looking at her. Once at the Chestnut Hill Mall she'd heard a cute boy say, "Nice face. Too bad she's a crip."

"Oh, I dunno," his companion replied with feigned interest, "might be nice, who knows? I hear epileptics are lots of fun. . . ."

Casey wheeled herself over to the couch, determined to look at the little girl. If she got grossed out, fine, then she'd be done with it. With that behind her, she might be able to offer some kind of help or comfort.

The girl's face was unchanged by the weird transformation. Now, taking the time to have a good look, Casey guessed the child might once have been pretty. It was only the lips that disfigured her face. What could have made them that way? They were like big floppy ears, elephant ears, the color of raw liver. No wonder the little girl couldn't talk with lips like those. It was a miracle she could eat or drink.

But the body, that was something else. It was completely altered. Impossibly, that weird light had done something awful to the child. It had changed her, melted her like wax, then reshaped her, blending arms and legs and hands and feet into a white, elongated, vein-streaked body that resembled a finless dolphin.

The little girl looked at Casey, and Casey tried to smile. "Hi," she said, "are you feeling okay?"

The girl blinked at her.

"Are you . . . are you thirsty or something?" She didn't know what else to say.

The little girl shook her head vigorously.

"Hungry?"

Her eyes widened as if in fear, as if the thought of eating or drinking terrified her.

Casey—with a great effort of will—reached out slowly, and touched the little girl's forehead.

There, that wasn't so bad.

The girl closed her eyes and tipped her head back against the seat cushion. Her facial features seemed to relax a little.

Casey stroked her gently and heard a soft sigh from deep in the child's throat. The body shivered; a tear glistened in her eye. "Hmmm-pffft. Hummmmmmm," she purred softly.

Casey continued to run her hand over the pale forehead, smoothing her greasy hair until the girl seemed to sleep.

Everything was fine while Casey looked at the child's face. But she didn't think she could stare at, much less actually touch, the ghastly body. How do doctors and nurses do it, Casey wondered, imagining crash victims and burn patients. And the birth abnormalities. . . . Oh God! How did they deal with it?

But medicine could work miracles of its own. Could surgeons somehow restore this girl?

Or would McCurdy's magic—if magic it was—eventually wear off as it did in storybooks? If everyone cooperated with him, could McCurdy reverse the process, return the child to normal now that he'd made his point?

Casey felt warm tears sliding down her cheeks.

The child snored, air bubbled grotesquely through her lips.

Delicately, Casey touched the place where the child's shoulder used to be. The flesh was soft, spongy. Not like it would feel if bone were underneath. It seemed more like the flexible cartilage of a nose.

She left her hand flattened there for a moment, trying to accustom herself to the odd sensation. She didn't want to break the contact that seemed to have such a calming effect on the child.

Gently, Casey rolled the girl toward the back of the sofa, hoping to free the blanket she was sleeping on. She would cover her, tuck her in, keep her warm against the cool rain that kept pouring down.

But in doing so, she saw the other side of the snakelike torso.

New terror flashed like the lightning outside the window. The orifices were gone! The body was smooth. Completely smooth. It was as if the child were a prisoner in a seamless sock of flesh.

And in that moment Casey understood the child's terror about eating and drinking.

Oh dear God, she thought, covering the girl with the blanket. She wept in silence as she stroked the little girl's head.

* * *

In the upstairs bedroom, Jeff and McCurdy sat in ladder-backed chairs before the empty computer screen. The monitor's neon glow was the only light in the room. Now and then the sky outside the window would light up like a flashbulb, blasting dense shadows against the bedroom walls.

A half-dozen fireballs whizzed by in rapid succession, like tracer bullets. "Looks like Pearl Harbor all over again, doesn't it, Jeffrey?"

Jeff tried to keep his voice clear of emotion. He wanted to answer in a businesslike way, in exactly the same matter-of-fact manner he normally used with McCurdy. He hoped a business as usual attitude would insure some level of safety. "What's going on, Skipp. What's happening here? Did you cause this somehow? The storm? The lightning?"

McCurdy laughed low in his throat, like a series of belches. "It's sure an attention getter. A good one, too, don't you think? Tomorrow it'll be in all the papers. It'll be on TV. I bet the networks will show up before morning. Miracles are big business, Jeffrey. Miracles are news."

"Miracles? Like what you did to that little girl?"

"The Lord permitted it. Don't forget that. The Lord permitted it so it can't be wrong."

"Can't be wr—!" Jeff got hold of his temper before it flared. *Calmly,* he thought, *calmly. . . .* "Okay. I understand. So what do you want with us? What do you want me to do?"

McCurdy's eyes widened, as if the answer to Jeff's question should be obvious. "Quite simply, you will be a spokesman. This, my friend, is the promotion I've been grooming you for. Your new assignment will be very much like . . . well . . . public relations." McCurdy smiled. "Hey, you're a good-looking guy, Jeff. You have an attractive way about you. You're quick-witted and bright. You've got charm, charisma. We need those qualities. This is a media age, you know. And, thanks to the

Academy, you've got the smarts to know the impossible can sometimes happen. Sometimes the unreal is real." McCurdy winked at him as if they were old friends.

Jeff hoped his fear didn't show. He had no choice but to believe McCurdy's weird science had somehow tapped into the secret forces of the universe. Had this new knowledge and power driven McCurdy into self-righteous megalomania? Did his madness control Jeff's fate and the fate of everyone he cared about?

"And what about Casey?" he asked.

McCurdy smiled warmly. "That's all part of the benefit package. In exchange for your cooperation, your daughter will get up and walk. People will see that. They'll see it and they'll believe. Maybe then you'll believe, too. Jeff, what's happening here is the work of the Lord."

"I . . . I . . ." Jeff cleared his throat. "Okay, Skipp, let's put our cards on the table. Suppose I refuse to cooperate, suppose I say I don't believe any of this, and I don't want anything to do with it?"

McCurdy shook his head sadly, clicking his tongue. He reached into the pocket of his pants, jingling the change there. Then he pulled out a handful of coins. After selecting a shiny twenty-five-cent piece, he held it up in front of Jeff.

"Remember the coin I showed you during our talk at the Academy? 'In God We Trust,' you recall?"

"Yes."

"Well, I recall something, too. According to your résumé, you have a special interest in magic tricks. It's your hobby, right?"

"Y-yes."

"Then you should know better than anyone the difference between deception and reality. Let me show you one of my own little tricks. Hold out your hand."

Slowly, Jeff offered his open hand. McCurdy placed the bright coin in the center of Jeff's palm.

"Close your hand," McCurdy instructed.

Jeff's fingers curled over the quarter, covering it completely. He felt its firm metal edge against his skin. Then immediately McCurdy commanded, "Now open it."

Jeff looked down at his palm in utter disbelief. The coin was gone!

"Th-that's impossible!" he said. He knew enough about sleight of hand and misdirection to know how the trick could be accomplished if the coin were in the *magician's* hand. But not like this; it was absolutely impossible for the coin to vanish from his own fist. It couldn't be done.

McCurdy smiled, pleased with himself. Then he was silent. Outside, the thunder and lightning stopped. The whole universe seemed to pause.

McCurdy's eyes were deadly earnest. He looked at Jeff with a terrible intensity. In a low voice, almost a growl, he said, "I wanted you to see that video, Jeffrey. I want you to remember it now. That coin could as easily be your heart."

* * *

The five-mile drive had been nerve-wracking.

They'd sped through a terrifying rainstorm. Fat heavy drops pelted the windshield with surprising fury. Wind picked up, whipping across the flatlands with hurricane force, battering Sullivan's car from one lane to the other.

The defrost motor hummed, fighting to clear the windshield. It was a losing battle. The air was so moist Father Sullivan joked that they were in a submarine.

Before them, above the deserted road, Karen could see mist-dulled flashes in the eastern sky.

"Some fireworks," Alton said from the back seat.

A few cars were parked at the roadside with their lights off. Driving past, Karen could see people inside, watching the sky.

At a turnoff near the road to Dubois's farmhouse, she saw a huge RV with Quebec plates. An elderly couple had set up aluminum armchairs under a fold-up metal awning. They were sipping drinks as they watched the sky show.

Sullivan clenched the wheel with both hands as his car ripped through thickening sheets of rain.

* * *

They left the car partway up the hill, off the road and partially hidden.

Karen and the priest crept through the rain and darkness, following Alton Barnes. They paused when the house came into view, a dense black rectangle in the night. When lightning flashed, the place looked haunted.

She saw Jeff's car parked near the driveway, with another vehicle beside it. Both sets of lights were on; now their beams had faded to a lifeless glow. The taillights of a third vehicle, a station wagon, reflected beyond the open door of the barn.

Candles or kerosene lamps burned upstairs and down. Karen guessed the lighted windows indicated which rooms were occupied. She suspected at least four people were inside: the owner, Jeff, Casey, and the frightening unknown in this equation—Dr. Ian "Skipp" McCurdy.

Standing there in the rain, the reality of what they were doing struck her like a sudden chill. Her body had prepared before her mind—teeth clenched, muscles tense and ready. But ready for what? She didn't know.

"My car's way over there," Alton whispered, nodding toward the dark distance. "I left it when McCurdy drove me to town. . . ."

The priest crouched beside Karen. She could see his eyes trained on the house. "I think I should try to get up close," he said, "maybe look in the windows."

"Oh, Father—"

"It's all right, Karen. One of us has to go. There's no point all of us taking a chance. I just want to make sure Casey and Jeff are in there. If they're not, we're wasting our time out here."

"Please be careful."

The priest crouched, flattening himself as best he could. He looked like a giant black toad in the tall grass. Impressions of raindrops caused a rippling effect on his clothing.

"Father?" Alton said.

Sullivan looked at him.

"Why don't you let me go? I been in there before, I know the layout."

The priest shook his head. Karen had a pretty good idea what he was thinking: If her hypnosis had failed, the suggestions governing Alton's behavior might still be in place. If so, he could be dangerous; he could betray them to McCurdy.

"The sketch you made for me is fine," Father Sullivan said. "I'd appreciate it if you stayed with Karen. Don't worry about me. I'm not planning any heroics. I'm just going to take a look and come right back."

"Father?"

"Yes, Mr. Barnes?"

"There's a pistol in my car. Want me to get it for you?"

"Is the car locked?"

"Nope. Never lock it."

"Then I'll get it on my way. If anything happens, you and Karen run for the car and get the hell out of here."

Karen wanted to say something to the priest, something comforting and encouraging, but she remained silent as he made his way through swaying wet stocks of timothy and rain-blasted buttercups. He quickly vanished from sight until a hissing fireball streaked across the sky.

"I hope they don't spot him," she whispered to no one.

"I feel it's me oughtta be goin' up there," Alton told her. "I know he don't trust me. But I'm okay now. I know I am. Besides, I been in combat; I can use a weapon. He's a priest; prob'ly can't handle himself if things get hairy."

"I'm not sure I agree with you, Mr. Barnes. Something tells me there's a lot about Father Sullivan we don't know."

"I hope you're right, miss. I sure hope you're right about that."

* * *

The pattern of lighted windows suggested someone was upstairs and someone was down. Okay, Sullivan could check the bottom floor easily enough, but he'd have to stand outside a while to see if anyone went up or down the stairs.

He moved in a wide circle around the house, keeping low to avoid being spotted in a flash of lightning. Certain rooms had no lights burning in them. Could he safely presume those rooms were empty?

Not necessarily.

The whole situation seemed to grow more complex as he thought about it. The impulse grew stronger to abandon this foolishness, to drive back and get the police.

Fine, but what, exactly, would he tell them?

Maybe Casey Chandler was abducted? *Maybe* her dad went looking for her. *Maybe* they were both inside this farmhouse, held against their will. *Maybe* the Academy was experimenting with magic and mind control.

Pretty lame.

Hopefully he'd have more to say once he'd established Jeff and Casey were inside.

Standing by the eastern wall of the house, he found himself beneath an icy waterfall—rain pouring off the roof. He'd have to endure it; this was the only place from which he could watch the living room.

Yes. . . . Someone was in there. Someone seated and almost invisible in the faint orange light. Someone in . . .

The wheelchair suggested the young woman was Casey Chandler. And she was not alone. Someone else was lying on the couch under a blanket. Jeff? Mrs. Dubois? Sullivan couldn't make out any facial features among the shadows.

Casey was stroking the unknown person's hair.

It must be Jeff. Who else could it be? But why was he lying down? Had he been hurt? There was no way to tell. Also—Sullivan had to admit it—there was no visible evidence that these people were being held against their will. They weren't tied; they weren't under guard. . . .

Fearing he'd make some telltale noise, Sullivan avoided the porch, inching his way to a dark window at the rear of the house. According to Alton's sketch, this would be the kitchen.

The soggy weight of his saturated clothing and the freezing rivulets of water dribbling down his neck made him shiver in discomfort. Wind assailed the shrubbery around him. More than anything, he could use a drink right now, a shot of bourbon to warm his insides and steady his nerves.

But there was no time for such thoughts. He crept through a muddy flower bed and stretched up to the windowpane. Thorny rosebushes scratched at his pants.

Carefully, ever so carefully, he peered in. Weak light spilled in from the living room and spread among the solid shapes of kitchen furniture. Sullivan groped under his jacket and removed a yellow disposable flashlight from his shirt pocket. When he was sure no one was there, he flashed the light into the room and turned it off quickly.

Dear God!

He thought—he couldn't be sure, but he thought—he saw bodies on the floor! Two of them. A wave of dread left him short winded—what if Jeff were among them? He tried the light again but couldn't discern the faces.

Rounding the corner, Sullivan crept along the back wall until he came to the next window. This should be Mrs. Dubois's bedroom.

Before he could ready his flashlight, another fireball split the sky. Emerald-leafed trees, vivid green grass, the house itself, lit up with three-dimensional brilliance. In the dazzling flash he caught a glimpse of the drawn shade beyond the windowpane. For now, the contents of this room would remain a mystery.

Reflected in the glass, another blazing globe soared off and vanished behind Stattler Mountain. Funny, he thought, so many comets. And all of them moving *toward* that mountain. It's as if it attracts them, as if they're trying to draw attention to . . . something.

But that was speculation; he had other things to concentrate on, like how little he'd accomplished here. And he'd been at it so long! All he could report with certainty was that Casey Chandler, and someone, were in the house.

He hoped Karen was all right with Alton Barnes. He'd better get back and find out.

But what of Jeff? What of Ian McCurdy? What of Daisy Dubois herself?

Sullivan decided to go back to the living room window and watch awhile longer. Anyone moving around inside should eventually pass through there.

* * *

"There it is again! Oh my Christ, there it is again! *Look!*"

Alton Barnes pointed at the black mass of mountain that rose behind the Dubois farmhouse.

Karen looked up, following the direction of his trembling finger. There she saw a bright light among the distant trees. It looked as if one of the shooting stars had landed on the mountainside where it continued to burn like a hazy beacon.

But this was no shooting star; this was something *new*. It resembled a pale white sun rising from within the mountainside, a luminous mushroom sprouting from the earth.

"That's what I seen, miss. Right up there, same place. That's the thing I told you about!"

Karen squinted through the rain. The light's perimeter appeared misty and ill-defined. Nonetheless, she could see how bright it was. Spindly black silhouettes of trees obstructed her line of sight, but she could still sense its general shape—round, and its approximate size: big. Very big.

Curiosity tempted her to run up there and examine it. A stronger urge said *no*. More than ever, she wished Jeff were with her. He might have some idea what it was. Theories ping-ponged in her mind: a UFO, methane, some kind of searchlight or rescue flare, some variety of—

Of what?

What else *could* it be?

She felt Alton grasping her arm. "Don't you feel it, miss? Don't you feel that scary feeling inside you? Don't you know what we're lookin' at just ain't right?"

Karen put her hand on Alton's. "I'm sure there's an explanation, Mr. Barnes." Even to herself, the words sounded empty and deceitful. How could she be sure of anything?

Perhaps fear *was* the appropriate emotion just now. Perhaps the instinct to flee should be taken seriously. They could be in terrible danger.

Karen's knees felt wobbly. Waves of light-headedness weakened her, made her feel as if she were about to faint. Alton still held her hand, and his firm grip was suddenly the only real thing in the world.

The next clap of thunder was so near it shook the earth below her feet. The rock she leaned on vibrated. Her very bones seemed to rattle.

"H-how far away is it?" she asked.

"Mile. Mile an' a half, maybe. Not far."

"That's the same spot where you saw it with Stuart Dubois?"

"Yes, ma'am. Same place. You b'lieve me now, don't you?"

"I always believed you, Mr. Barnes."

"See there, it's just like I told you, ain't it?"

"Yes. I see it, too. It's just like you described."

As she stared, the light seemed to get bigger. Brighter.

Again the sky split with a fissure of lightning. The bolt touched down in the field beyond the house. Sparks erupted like a flaming geyser. Thunder cracked like a whip.

Another light attracted Karen's attention: the sweep of headlights. A lone vehicle—a pickup truck—made its way up the hill, its bright twin beams diffused, softened by the rain.

Mr. Barnes pulled her down and out of sight. Side by side they knelt in the soggy earth behind a protective outcropping of shale that buttressed a stone wall.

"Sightseers, I betcha," Alton whispered.

The headlights blinked out. Karen watched a boy and a girl jump out of the Toyota pickup. Holding hands, the teenagers stood at the roadside, looking up Stattler Mountain at the misty dome of light.

"I hope they ain't plannin' on headin' up there," Alton whispered. "I don't think I can let 'em do that."

Something alarmed Karen at his choice of words.

"Dangerous up there," Alton added, apparently noticing her reaction. "'Member what happened to Stuart when he met up with that light."

Karen spoke with hesitation, "Do you think we should warn them?" She didn't want to reveal their hiding place, especially if McCurdy were inside the house. At the same time, she couldn't stay still and let the young couple put themselves in danger.

"I'll keep an eye on 'em, miss. You keep an eye on the house."

* * *

When Jeff saw headlights moving up the hill, he feared Father Sullivan and Karen were coming after him.

Christ, not now! He'd just gotten McCurdy calmed down and speaking somewhat rationally. But if the madman noticed those lights, who could tell what he might do?

But McCurdy did see the lights.

"Ha!" he said, dashing to the front window for a better look. "It's happening! It's begun! The first witnesses are here!"

Jeff joined him at the window to see a second vehicle making its way up the hill. It was followed by another. And another.

McCurdy slapped Jeff's shoulder. "It's in motion now, Jeffrey. It's on automatic pilot. We can just sit back and watch the whole thing take its course."

* * *

Karen watched about a dozen people gather in the field between Daisy Dubois's farmhouse and the slope of Stattler Mountain. They stood like dark statues in the rain; all facing the glowing mist on the distant mountainside.

A fireball whooshed by. Wind whipped the dark trees bordering the property. They swayed and danced as if performing some mystic ritual.

Undetected in their hiding place, Karen studied the strange scene. Crouching beside her, Alton whispered, "Bet we could just step out and join them folks. Nobody inside's gonna notice a couple more sightseers. Can't see much sense stayin' cooped up here."

"But don't you think we should wait for Father Sullivan?"

The observers stood strangely close together, like a tightly packed congregation at a prayer meeting. Karen guessed they felt exactly as she did: curious about the thing on the mountain, but not daring to venture too far.

"I hope to Christ they stay put," Alton said. "I don't want nothin' happenin' to 'em. Why cripes, I *know* some of them folks. That's Gary Laymon's little girl over there with the Rellings boy. And that's Chick McNaughton and his wife. . . ."

Karen couldn't decide what to do. She wished Father Sullivan would get back. What was taking him so long? What if she and Alton were hiding out, drenched and shivering, for no good reason? Maybe Jeff and Casey weren't even in the house. Maybe they'd gone up the mountain. Or maybe McCurdy had carted them off somewhere else. Or maybe—

Darn it all! Where was Father Sullivan?

* * *

"I was hoping for a bigger crowd," McCurdy said, peering from the upstairs window. "But maybe this is it. Takes a lot to drag people away from their beds and TV sets." Then, turning back to Jeff, "Well, no matter. I'd say we've got a dozen out there. Don't forget, the first time word got out fast enough with only twelve men spreading it."

McCurdy laughed a misplaced, maniacal laugh. Again he slapped Jeff on the back. "Okay, Jeffrey, we're on. What say we go show these fine people their first miracle?"

* * *

Concealed behind a wind-lashed cedar that swished like a paintbrush against the front of the house, Father Sullivan wiped his eyes with a saturated handkerchief. Through the window he saw the girl in the wheelchair stroking the forehead of someone lying on the sofa.

From this vantage point, he could also see the stairs to the second story. If anyone went up or down, he'd know.

Should he chance tapping on the window? If he could talk to Casey she could tell him everything he needed to know.

Hand in his pocket, he touched the cold metal of Alton's revolver. Would he dare use it on a human being?

Did he *dare* tap the window? Did he *dare* use a gun? What was he going to do, sit in the rain all night like some indecisive simpleton?

Dear God he *had* to do something.

Forcing himself to be calm, he silently recited an Our Father until loud clattering noises from inside interrupted him.

A disheveled man with flyaway tufts of red hair led Jeff Chandler down the stairs. The man—it must be McCurdy—was smiling. But Jeff looked troubled; he seemed to be shouting at the man, possibly pleading.

At least there were no weapons in sight. And no one was tied up. In fact, nothing seemed especially menacing. This wasn't the tense hostage situation Sullivan had expected.

But he couldn't forget those bodies in the kitchen. Not for a minute.

Sullivan slipped the weapon from his pocket.

Inside, the girl's glance ping-ponged from one man to the other. Her mouth moved, her hands gestured frantically.

Sullivan checked the position of the revolver's hammer, preparing to act quickly if he had to.

Now the redheaded man grabbed the handles of the wheelchair and began to push it toward the door. The girl seemed to protest. Jeff dashed ahead.

When Jeff opened the door, Sullivan flattened himself into the mud and shadows beside the porch. Finally he could hear what they were saying.

"Jeff, lift the front end of this thing and help me get it off the porch. We may have to carry her through the field; I don't think I can push her over the wet ground."

"Skipp, please, this is dangerous. What if it doesn't work? What if—"

"Jeff, you have to have faith. That's what this is all about—faith. You'll see. I should think you'd rejoice that your daughter won't have to use this contraption after tonight."

Jeff helped lift Casey and her chair down the outside steps. Through the latticework below the porch floor, Sullivan watched them move off in the direction of the crowd.

He waited a few minutes wondering if the person on the couch was going to follow. Apparently not.

More uncertain than ever, Sullivan made up his mind to check the house's interior. He'd do it quickly, then get back to Karen and Mr. Barnes. He'd kept them waiting long enough.

* * *

As quickly as Jeff and McCurdy moved Casey out of sight, Father Sullivan crept out of the shadows, climbed over the railing and onto the porch. He moved as silently as possible, knowing at least one more person remained inside.

There was no way to determine who was lying on the sofa, no way to say if it was friend or enemy. Sullivan guessed it was Mrs. Dubois and he suspected she was alone in the house.

Now he had to find out for sure.

With the revolver in his right hand, and the doorknob in his left, Sullivan made his move. He twisted the knob, pushed open the door to the kitchen, and quickly stepped inside, crouching combat style, his weapon ready.

Nothing moved. He heard no sound but rain on the roof and a far-off growl of thunder.

Waiting a tense moment, he determined he was alone in the room. Still, his sweaty fingers clutched the revolver as he turned on his flashlight. All other details escaped him when he saw bodies on the floor. Two of them, a woman and a man. Someone had propped them against the cabinets like cast-off mannequins in a storeroom.

The man wore soiled wrinkled work clothes. His concave forehead was split nearly in half; his gory face unrecognizable. Sullivan flicked the light away.

The woman had been burned beyond recognition. He guessed it was Daisy Dubois, but if so, who was on the couch in the other room?

Sullivan moved closer, knelt on one knee beside them. Still alert, holding the gun like a lifeline, he said a quick prayer for their souls.

In a moment he tiptoed to the living-room door. Slowly, carefully, he looked in. From here, the back of the sofa hid its occupant.

Who can it be?

Arm extended, gun clenched in his fist, the priest moved silently as a shadow toward the sofa. After six steps he could peer over its back. Long dirty hair—a woman's?—was visible outside the woolen blanket. The sleeper was fully covered, her face turned away, half-sunken in a pillow.

With his weapon pointed at her skull, Sullivan spoke. "Who are you?"

The sleeper groaned as if in a dream.

Sullivan reached down and tore the blanket away.

"Oh dear God!"

The small naked body was grotesque. Muscles rippled like convulsing worms beneath translucent skin. Nerves twitched. Blood pulsed through swollen arteries. Sullivan fought the disgust that made him want to look away. He had seen the product of multiple birth defects often enough, but this poor child, she had no arms, no legs, her body was featureless as a fleshy football. He dropped the blanket back in place, then gently rolled her toward him in order to see her face.

The distended lips made him wince, but he prayed his revulsion didn't show. They could fix that, he thought, at least the surgeons could do something about *that.*

"Can you talk, child?" he whispered, trying to smile.

"Mmmph. Ppppft." Her answer was evident in her distressed eyes. She might have shaken her head, but she had no neck. Instead, she gaped at him.

"Can you understand me, sweetheart?"

"Fffff."

"Blink if you understand me."

She blinked.

"Once for yes, twice for no."

She blinked.

"Are you in pain?"

Blink.

"Have they done something to hurt you?"

Blink.

"Do you want me to take you out of here? We can go to a doctor or to the hospital?"

She just stared at him, looking fearful and lost. Sullivan saw tiny crystal tears blooming in her eyes. Then, slowly, blink-blink.

"Okay, sweetheart." He reached down and put his hand on her forehead. She was hot. Running a fever. "I'm going to get you out of here just as quickly as I can. But first you've got to help me. Can you tell me if you are alone in the house."

Blink. Blink-blink. Blink.

"I don't understand. Blink once for—"

Blink. Blink-blink. Blink.

"You don't know? Is that what you mean?"

Blink.

"Jeff and his daughter are gone?"

Blink.

"And McCurdy, he's gone, too?"

Blink.

"You know that for sure?"

Blink.

"And someone else is here?"

Blink.

"Yes? A woman?"

Blink-blink.

"A man?"

Blink-blink.

"It's not a man or a woman, is that what you mean?"

Blink.

"What is it, then? An animal?"

Blink-blink.

"Not an animal, not a man, and not a woman? What else could it be then, child?"

Blink. Blink-blink. Blink.

* * *

"That's Jeff! Look! And Casey!" Karen dug her fingers into Alton's arm. She watched Jeff and the other man slogging through the rain over saturated ground. They carried Casey between them in her wheelchair. Obviously they were heading toward the crowd of watchers.

"Who's the man with them, Mr. Barnes?"

"McCurdy. That's McCurdy." There was something tense in Alton's voice, a coldness she wasn't used to. But Karen was too agitated to analyze it.

"Oh thank God, they're all right." She wanted to run to them, but before she could stand up, dread seized her; its fist clenched in her stomach. "But where's Father Sullivan?" She started to move out from behind the rock, mindless of being spotted. "I don't see him, Mr. Barnes. Do you think something's happened to him? Why are they going out in the field?"

Alton pulled her down beside him. He grabbed her by the upper arms and stared into her eyes. "Listen," he said, "maybe we don't need to worry about Jeff and Casey for a minute. They're out in the open, right where everybody can see 'em. Nothin's gonna happen to 'em in front of all them people. You understand?"

Karen nodded.

"Okay then, you stay here and stay quiet. I'll go up to the house and check on Father."

"I'm coming with you."

"NO!" Mr. Barnes shook her. Hard. "You stay put. None of us knows what the hell's goin' on around here. I ain't riskin' your neck by lettin' you follow me to the house. Besides, I gotta move quick and sure, and I gotta stay outta sight. Ain't no way you can help me with any of that. You understand?"

"But . . . No. I mean I can't stay here. What if something's happened to Father Sullivan? What if something happens to you . . . ? I'll . . . I'll be alone. I won't know what to do."

Karen hated herself as those loathsome words tumbled out on their own. She had confessed to her weakness, flaunted her fear, admitted how ineffectual she was. She knew this was a life or death situation, and she was terrified.

What should she do? She wasn't armed, she didn't know how to fight or defend herself, and she had no clear sense of what was happening around her. Fear intensified like rising heat in a closed room. Sweating, trembling, Karen knew what was coming next.

She froze.

Her limbs locked. Paralyzed. Just as she had been so very long ago on that busy Boston street corner.

But Jeff had come to her rescue then.

If only she could rescue him now.

"Dr. Bradley! Karen. What's wrong?" Alton shook her again, very gently this time. He spoke like a concerned grandfather. "What's the matter? What's happened?"

This was a bad one. Maybe the worst ever. She couldn't talk. Couldn't move.

"Karen!"

They'd *never* lasted this long. She struggled without moving, couldn't find her voice, couldn't even shake her head.

"What's happening to you? Are you sick?" First the old man looked concerned, then desperate. Rain slid in rivulets down his face. "Please, miss. Please . . ."

She wanted to tell him she was okay, that everything would be back to normal in a minute or two. But no. She couldn't even protest as he gently positioned her against the rock. She couldn't stop him as he struggled out of his jacket and put it over her like a blanket. Its outside was saturated, but the inside was warm. She could feel the heat from his body; she smelled his Old Spice cologne. Like her dad's.

"Listen," he said, "I'll come right back, I promise. I won't waste no time. I just gotta check on Father Sullivan. I'll come straight out and tell you what's going on. Then I'll get you outta here. You just sit tight and stay quiet. And please don't be scared, I ain't gonna let nothin' happen to you."

She couldn't turn her head to watch him go.

* * *

A blazing white comet streaked across the sky.

* * *

As Father Sullivan recalled Alton's sketch, the closed door off the kitchen led to Mrs. Dubois's bedroom. That was the room he'd tried to look into but the shade prevented it.

Now he could just walk in, but he paused.

Labored communication with the tragically deformed child had made it clear that no one was upstairs in the house. The only other presence—neither man nor woman nor animal—was right down here, in that bedroom.

When he'd pieced that much together, the girl had become excited. Her eyes flashed, she made disgusting sounds with her mouth. Sullivan couldn't understand what she wanted to tell him. Did she want him to stay out of the bedroom? Stay clear of that closed door?

No matter what she meant, he had to look.

Strange thoughts tore at his courage, making him hesitate. Thoughts of Father Mosely battling the demon in the church. Of the remote assassination recorded on videotape. Stuart Dubois's disappearance and the dramatic light show in the sky.

Again he looked at the sprawled bodies on the kitchen floor. Shot in the face, the poor man must have died instantly. But the old woman must have known real terror. Had she been tortured? Burned alive?

Good God, what had happened in this house?

Sullivan shook his head. Grasping the cold knob in his hand, he prepared to yank the door open.

. . . *neither man, nor woman, nor animal* . . .

Why did he hesitate?

Why did his heart pound so furiously?

He had a gun; there was no reason to be afraid. Nonetheless, he paused a moment to pray. When he braced himself to open the door, he saw motion outside the window.

Who?

McCurdy and Jeff coming back?

He dropped to the floor, then crawled through waxy blotches of blood, until he could crouch below the windowsill. A man stood on the porch. He'd pressed himself tightly against the outside. Sullivan couldn't get a look at him.

The porch door opened slowly.

Hinges groaned.

Using both hands to steady his aim, Sullivan pointed the revolver at the widening opening. His hands were so slick with sweat he feared his finger might slip from the trigger.

Then he saw. "Alton!"

The newcomer dropped to the floor. He looked up at the priest, half smiling. "Jeez, Father, you gonna shoot me or scare me to death?"

* * *

The people in the field were oddly silent.

Motionless, they stared at the faraway light as if it were hypnotizing them. When Jeff and McCurdy carried Casey into their midst, they hardly paid attention.

McCurdy lowered the chair's small front wheels to the ground. Jeff put down the back. The bottoms of the thin rubber tires vanished into the grass and muck.

Jeff's muscles ached from the weight. Massaging his lower back, he wished McCurdy would move out of earshot so he could talk to Casey. Even if they could speak freely, he had little to offer but empty comforts. This whole situation was out of his control, had been since he saw the destruction that ghastly light could cause. Two vivid images held him at bay like twin barrels of a shotgun: the convulsing man whose heart had vanished, and the horrible little girl who'd been transformed into a—into a— God! His mind could not accept what his eyes had witnessed!

And if McCurdy could actually control that hideous light, then Jeff and Casey and all these people were at his mercy. Literally, at his mercy.

Just how benevolent was the mercy of a madman?

The only thing Jeff could hope to do was exactly what he had done back at the farmhouse: bide his time until an opportunity—and he had no idea what that opportunity might look like—presented itself. Till then he could only watch and plan and think and try to figure some way out of this.

Apparently McCurdy had achieved a sort of mind-link with his computer in Boston. It seemed impossible, but he'd learned to bypass the keyboard and operate the machine through concentration and force of will. Staggering enough by itself. But when Jeff reminded himself that McCurdy had harnessed the product of over four thousand years of magical practice and tradition, he realized just how powerful his adversary really was.

In effect, Ian McCurdy was the most powerful black magician who had ever lived.

Christ, what could Jeff do?

Could he compete for control of the machine by using the remote terminal in the farmhouse? Maybe. But as yet he'd had no such opportunity. Besides, he wasn't a skilled operator, not like McCurdy.

And how would he get McCurdy out of the way long enough to experiment with the thing?

Perhaps their only real hope was to put McCurdy out of commission. But that was dangerous. McCurdy could utter a fatal phrase or direct his lethal thoughts faster than Jeff could jump him or wield a weapon.

"Stand behind your daughter, Jeffrey," McCurdy said pleasantly, motioning like a preacher at a wedding and beaming his idiotic smile. "We're just three more sightseers, that's all. Just three curious people out to see what gives. . . ."

* * *

"Holy jumpin' Jesus, she sure wasn't in that condition when I left here!"

Color drained from Alton's face as he stared down at the little girl on the sofa. "Merciful Christ, I never seen nothing like this in my life!"

Father Sullivan put his hand on Alton's shoulder. He could feel the man trembling. When Alton lifted his eyes, Sullivan saw a kind of fear he'd never before witnessed. "Her lips was messed up jest the same," Alton whispered, "but her arms and her legs was just fine. Fact is, she was the one tied me up! Oh good God, Father, what could do somethin' like this to her?"

"She can't talk, Al. She can't tell us."

Alton dropped his gaze, then turned to face the priest again. Tears sparkled in the subdued light. "I know they can get inside my head and fuck it all up. And they can do somethin' like . . . like *this* to a little kid. What's happenin' here, Father? What kind of stuff is this? How the Christ can we fight it?"

Sullivan shook his head.

"Can't we do anything to help her, Father? Isn't there somethin' we can do?"

Sullivan nodded. All he knew for sure was what he had to do. He had to protect these people. "Yes, I think so. You can take her to your car and then drive her to the hospital in Burlington."

"But I can't leave you alone—"

"Yes you can. You've got to. And take Karen with you, if she'll go."

"But what about you?"

"I'll be all right here. I have your gun, remember? I want to look around some more. I also want to keep an eye on Jeff and his daughter."

"I . . . I—"

"It'll be all right, Al. This child needs medical attention. And frankly, I'm old-fashioned enough to want Karen out of harm's way.

The best thing you can do is get them both out of here. Then go ahead and call the police."

"They ain't gonna believe—"

"It doesn't matter what they believe. Their job is to protect people. I think those people out there—all of us—need some protection right now. Please, Al, don't argue about it. Just go."

Al folded the quivering child in the woolen blanket and picked her up. The lower part of her body drooped over his arm like a sleeping snake. "It's okay, honey," Al said, "we're gonna get you out of here."

The little girl blinked and blinked and blinked.

* * *

In the distance Jeff saw the incandescent cloud glowing on the mountainside.

The sky was black now, undisturbed by the flash and whoosh of fireballs. Heavy rain pelted the ground and onlookers, as if the heavens had sprung a leak.

Nearby, two teenaged boys, their denim jackets worn over their heads like monks' cowls, were going through a familiar adolescent ritual of courage-building. Jeff could hear every word.

"How the fuck should I know, man. Maybe it's a UFO or something. Bet the army shows up any minute. Sure wish I had my fuckin' camera."

"The army? Shit no, man; they'd be here by now if it was somethin' dangerous. You don't see no cops or firemen do you?"

"You think they know what it is? The army, I mean?"

"Hell yes, 'course they do. They got computers and stuff, right? You know, aerial surveillance, radar, stuff like that. They probably checked it out long time ago; now they're home in bed porkin' their wives."

"So why don't they tell us what it is then?"

"Probably did. You got a fuckin' radio?"

The more fearful boy shrugged.

"Tell ya what, man. I'm sick of standin' around here jerkin' off. I'm goin' up and have a look at that thing. You comin'?"

Jeff didn't hear the answer. He was too caught up in watching McCurdy, who was pacing around looking at the other people, introducing himself, smiling his crazed and saintly smile.

"We are the chosen ones," Jeff heard him say. "We are the witnesses, the selected servants who'll see this great event."

Long ago, McCurdy's religious mania had gotten under Jeff's skin. At the Academy, at least McCurdy held it in check. But now, with the awesome force of magic behind him, it had grown untethered, becoming monstrous.

Magic? Miracles? Jeff had come to accept massive doses of unreality. Still, he couldn't agree the driving force behind all this was purity and goodness. No, craziness and brutality simply were not part of any Christian tradition he had ever considered.

Then again, what did he know? He had always rejected the notion of God even when presented in far more palatable forms. McCurdy's God was tougher to reject and impossible to ignore.

Jeff shook his head. Standing behind her wheelchair, he massaged Casey's shoulders. Surely McCurdy realized Jeff wouldn't try anything violent with his daughter near enough to suffer. If this were a cosmic game of chess, Jeff had just lost to McCurdy's checkmate: he couldn't attack, he couldn't move, he couldn't escape.

"Stay calm, sweetie," he whispered. "Somehow we're going to get out of this. Somehow everything will be all right."

It was all he could say, and it was nothing.

When he looked down at her he almost cried. Wet and bedraggled, she'd been sitting in that same position for, it seemed, hours. Her fingers were snugly interlaced, her palms pressed together, her forearms pulled tightly against her chest. Shivering and pale, she'd sometimes rock back and forth and her chair would squeak. She seemed locked away in self-protective catatonia. Maybe the best thing was to leave her there.

McCurdy took a position in front of the crowd. He placed himself between the light and the observers. Now he was holding up his arms for attention.

Jeff's hands tightened on Casey's shoulders. Her right hand moved up and covered his left.

"Ladies and gentlemen . . . friends . . . we have been summoned to this place by a power far greater than we can imagine."

People looked at each other, trading puzzled, skeptical glances. McCurdy continued, "We have been chosen and we have been summoned; we are the ones brought here to witness a sign."

"Who the hell is he?" the boy whispered to his companion.

"Beats the shit outta me. Think he's with the army?'

The first boy giggled into his fist.

"What you will witness here tonight is the beginning of a change, a change that will swiftly circle the globe. I ask only that you watch, and believe, then go and tell what you have seen. You there—!"

McCurdy pointed at a man and a woman who were crossing the field. They were carrying video equipment. Jeff saw the Channel 21 logo on the woman's raincoat—a TV crew.

"—bring your camera and get ready for the biggest story of your life. You, young woman, have been chosen to record the changing of the world. *LOOK!*"

With a dramatic half turn and a sweep of the arm, McCurdy pointed to the mountain behind him. The strange light hovered and pulsed.

"Watch and believe." McCurdy fairly screamed, *"Witness now the Light of the Lord!"*

Beyond bent pasture grasses heavy with rain, beyond the stone wall and the acres of forest that dipped and climbed and became Stattler Mountain, beyond the slopes where the path ended and trees grew wild and tall, the light began to move.

Jeff saw it rise like a translucent hot-air balloon. It rose slowly until it was no longer visible against the mountain, but against the sky.

Casey's hand tightened over Jeff's. Murmurs and whispers raced through the crowd.

"Those who are faithful shall be rewarded," McCurdy chanted, "those who have lost faith shall have faith renewed. Those who've never known faith shall find it in the Light."

The light was moving closer now, traveling toward them like a glowing discus in the sky.

Unbelieving, Jeff saw that it did not illuminate the ground below as it passed.

"Holy Jesus," somebody said.

A boy and girl who had been holding hands at the edge of the crowd about-faced and started to run for their car.

"Look!" McCurdy cried. "LOOK AT THE *LIGHT!*"

* * *

The constant intrusion of a man's voice brought Karen around. She realized whoever was shouting was addressing the crowd, but she couldn't understand his words above the droning rain.

This is stupid, she thought, I can't keep freezing up like this. I could get someone hurt; I could get hurt myself. She stretched her fingers, clenched both hands into fists. Her arms and legs tingled as the paralysis dissipated.

Whoa, she thought, this was the worst attack ever! What's happening to me, anyway?

Supported by the rock, she worked her way to her feet. Her legs felt like leaden weights, her arms numb as fence posts.

From where she stood she had a perfect view of the pale brilliance of the floating light. It moved slowly from the mountainside toward the gathering of spectators.

Heart pounding, she asked over and over, *What can it be?*

Her first impulse was to run, join the circle of observers in order to be with Jeff and Casey. Maybe they could tell her what was going on. But she couldn't ignore the potential danger in such an act. Instead, perhaps she should go to the house? That could be dangerous, too, but at least she could do it covertly.

With a mounting sense of dread, Karen realized she was absolutely alone.

She glanced at the house, hoping to see Alton returning. *He said he'd be right back,* she thought, *so where is he?*

How long had he been gone? She couldn't tell. She couldn't even guess the length of time she'd waited, locked in her terrified trance.

What should she do now?

The old place appeared dark, lifeless. Something must be going on in there. Something bad. First Father Sullivan had entered, then Alton Barnes had followed. Neither had returned.

A cold spring of fear wound tightly in Karen's stomach.

She *had* to do something. She couldn't stay here. Not alone, not with that thing in the sky getting closer and closer.

Another moment of indecision held her in place.

* * *

Jeff watched the incandescence move with the lighter than air grace of a zeppelin—silent, smooth, slow, and steady.

As it got closer, it became less obscured by the damp air and rain. Now the amorphous cloud had taken on shape. It looked solid, a floating disk moving silently beneath black clouds.

He guessed it was halfway between the mountain and the crowd.

Jeff realized he hadn't been breathing. Tense throat muscles had locked it shut. He gulped in air, felt his heart pounding like a tom-tom.

So great was his rising terror that he might have turned, run away, abandoned his daughter and the crowd, his mind and heart and spirit empty of everything but the frenzy of escape. He might have done that were it not for the warm reality of Casey's hand on his own.

"Good God, Casey, what's happening?"

His eyes, her eyes, and every eye in that dark field locked on the circle of light as it came closer and closer.

A few moments and it would be above their heads.

* * *

Karen thought of the scene from *Close Encounters* when the giant spacecraft appeared in the desert. That's exactly what this looks like, she thought, it must be a hundred feet across!

Then she noticed an odd detail far more unsettling than the vision itself: why didn't something as big and as bright project its light on the earth below? The assembly of onlookers appeared as three-dimensional shadows when the light passed over them.

That didn't make sense!

Could all this be an illusion? Could it be some kind of spotlight or a movie projected on the screen of clouds? Was it an ingenious magician's trick that looked real but wasn't there at all, like the holographic flames in Dr. Gudhausen's fireplace?

Then Karen observed something else: it wasn't raining beneath the light.

That means it's solid!

Holy cow! This was no vision, no optical illusion. The thing was large and round and silent. It sheltered the crowd from the rain like a giant umbrella.

It's gotta be a UFO, she thought. *Holy Jeez, something's making contact!*

"Feel it!" The ranting man went on, "Feel the warmth and power of the Light."

Three members of the crowd dropped to their knees. Karen spotted Jeff and Casey. Oddly, Casey's head was down, her hand covered her eyes as if she were praying.

Karen checked to insure that no one in the crowd was looking in her direction, then she ran through the rain toward the porch of the farmhouse.

* * *

The moment Alton left with the child, Father Sullivan moved to a rain-spattered window from which he could see Jeff and Casey in the flashing distance.

When he identified them in the crowd, breath snagged in his throat. His lungs and heart seemed to suffer the icy grip of an alien force as he studied the strange drama playing out before him. The whole sky was awash with illuminated haze as if some powerful celestial spotlight were piercing the thick storm clouds from above. Silhouetted trees, wind-thrashed and tall, danced maniacally as if the forest were alive.

In the field, shadowy shapes cowered on their knees, or stared skyward, transfixed, dumbfounded. As if on cue, a trio of shadows broke away from the cluster and ran toward parked cars at the roadside.

Sullivan's mind confirmed what his soul knew: this was not the work of the Lord. Something fierce, maybe unstoppable, was taking its course.

Urgency seized him—he had to protect Jeff and Casey, he had to save them. For reasons he did not completely understand, he would willingly risk his life to get them out of here before . . .

Before what?

He took a breath, tried to concentrate.

What was *really* happening out there?

He'd often remarked that in an institution as fraught with mysteries as the Roman Catholic Church, it was tempting to stop searching for solutions. Much easier to abandon the questing mind for the comfortable complacency of blind faith. If voluntarily lobotomized, it might be possible to accept this travesty as some kind of revelation, some kind of miracle.

No!

His mind and soul and spirit screamed that this had nothing to do with the church, or God, or even Ronald Boudreau's angelic visitation.

That was no angel in the woods.

This was no miracle.

It was a dumb show, a gaudy deception. Instinct told him it had something to do with the demonic presence Father Mosely had battled in the church.

Yes, this too was a manifestation of evil. Real. Tangible. Deadly and absolutely corrupt. Sullivan watched evil operating before his disbelieving eyes. In all his life, nothing had prepared him for anything like this. No one ever told him he'd someday meet evil face-to-face.

He took a deep breath, trying to focus his thoughts. Was he the only one who recognized this malignancy for what it was? Was he the only one who could fight it?

Sullivan's heart pounded like a frenzied fist. So this is what it's all about. This is the culmination of a lifetime in the priesthood. This is the battle for which we all prepare, but so few of us undertake. Today is the day I've been training for all my life.

But he had one more piece of information to gather before he launched any sort of an attack. Almost immobile in the clutch of mounting terror, Father Sullivan once more turned his gaze to the last locked door in the farmhouse kitchen.

* * *

Karen stopped in the middle of the dooryard when she saw Alton Barnes leave the house. He carried something bulky in his arms. Thank God he was all right!

He ran down the steps toward her, making no attempt to conceal himself as she hurried to meet him.

"Father Sullivan's okay," he blurted as soon as he was within hearing distance. "He's gonna keep an eye on Jeff and Casey. Come on, miss, we're gettin' out of here. We gotta get this girl to the hospital and we gotta call the police."

Karen fell in step behind him, rushing toward Alton's car. "Who's this?" Karen asked.

"Some kid we found in the house. Something awful's happened to her. We gotta get her to a doctor."

"Is she all right? Hold on a minute, let me have a look."

"I'm not so sure you wanna, miss."

Without pausing, Alton hugged the child tightly and hurried on his way.

* * *

From the doorway of the dark bedroom, Father Sullivan studied the nearly invisible form on the bed. It didn't move; there was no sound of breathing. Was this another murder victim like those in the kitchen?

Holding his breath, he stepped closer, sensing a rapid temperature change. Odd, it was so much colder in the bedroom. When he finally inhaled, the air was ripe with a feculent odor. The body on the bed must be a corpse; *had* to be.

Squinting into the gloom, Sullivan stepped slowly to the foot of the bed. The corpse was a spidery old man lying beneath a sheet. His skin appeared brown, leathery. His face and upper body were crisscrossed with deep wrinkles like bloodless cuts.

Sullivan was about to utter a prayer when something moved!

The head turned almost invisibly on the pillow. One eye opened. Just a bit. It seemed to glow in the shadow-shrouded face.

And there was a whispered growl, "Father Sullivan, pray for me." Then a wheezing chuckle.

Sullivan's muscles locked. Somehow the voice sounded vaguely familiar.

"Come in, William, I've been waiting for you."

He stepped closer, walking along the side of the bed. It was too dark to recognize the man beneath the sheet.

He realized his flashlight was in his hand, but it was off. When he pushed the switch nothing happened.

The air became fouler with each step. He swallowed rapidly, an effort to short-circuit his reflex to vomit.

As he neared the reclining man, he experienced a sensation of inexplicable dread, as if he had touched something completely unclean and totally unhuman. The feeling rippled in nauseating waves through his stomach. His hands shook; his legs felt weak. It was nearly impossible to find his voice. "W-who is it?" he asked tentatively. "Do I know you?"

The voice came from far away. "You will recognize me, but you do not know me." A hint of delicate laughter rumbled from the dark man in the bed. "Strike a match, William. I'm best seen in firelight."

* * *

The cold sting of rain had stopped. Jeff's skin tingled as he looked up. The thing was directly overhead.

He squinted needlessly against light that did not hurt his eyes. As he watched, every muscle tensed; his blood froze in his veins. His own voice spoke clearly in his mind, *Hold on, don't move, don't panic.*

In spite of numbing cold and damp discomfort, a feeling of misplaced tranquillity passed through him. It was akin to the relaxing sensation of sinking slowly into a warm pool.

Still staring, the light seemed different now!

Though it had not changed, perhaps *he* had: his vision had improved, his mind seemed oddly sharper. It was as if he were not looking at a *thing* at all, but at a lighted emptiness, an illuminated passageway. He saw a bright tunnel that ran, not through earth and rock, but through time and space, and on to an infinitely distant world.

Jeff might have closed his eyes, basked in that tranquilizing light, but his mind said, *No! Don't buy it; you're not thinking clearly. Hold back. Look away. . . .*

But he could not look away.

All the while, in some barely functioning pocket of rational consciousness, Jeff knew the hypnotic thing in the air was soothing him, influencing his thoughts as it was influencing those around him. He fought, trying to concentrate, trying to understand, to analyze. *Resist,* he told himself. *Resist. . . .*

Images from his research moved in and out of focus. He recalled that bright tunnel of light sometimes perceived by dying people. He remembered their reports that a comforting contentment beckoned from the unseen end of the luminous passageway. It lulled them with infinite gentility until they were called back, rudely, only to waken with a profound sense of peace and no more fear of death. . . .

Don't move. Hold on. . . .

Jeff imagined the circular hole in the sky that Alton Barnes had described, a hole through which his friend Stuart had been pulled, kicking and screaming. . . .

Don't move. Don't speak. . . .

And there were the lights, the fiery globes that had zipped through the skies since before the time of Ezekiel, continuing their celestial light show unabated until . . . tonight . . . when the air above Hobston was thick with them.

Spacecraft? Witchcraft? The glowing eyes of demons peering hungrily from the heavens?

If he stared long enough, he knew, the light would pull him to it and he would understand everything.

Hold on. Please. Don't let go.

* * *

Sullivan patted the pockets of his jacket and pants until he found a butane lighter. He flicked it on. Light flared. His hand trembled and he almost dropped it. "N-no. Oh no! This is impossible."

The chuckle again.

"Impossible, William? Hardly. Even if you were exceptionally dull-witted, the events of today would have taught you that nothing is . . . impossible. You *do* recognize me, don't you, son?"

Son? The word was uttered with a chilling contempt.

Orange light played on the man's face as Sullivan stared aghast. The butane lighter grew strangely heavy, as if every reserve of strength had drained from him.

"F-Father Mosely! You're . . . you're . . . But . . . what's happened to you?"

He could step no closer to the old priest.

Pencil-thin lips twisted into a tight smile exposing gray toothless gums. The eyes were beady dots, glistening black marbles embedded in wrinkled sockets. The pale skin of the forehead stretched tightly, transforming the old man's face into a grinning skull.

Sullivan let the flame go out. Oddly, he could still see clearly in the dark bedroom. Shadowy shapes of wooden furniture—chairs, bureaus, benches—stood like alien watchmen at the periphery of the room. A round mirror above a vanity was covered with a dark blanket.

"I've waited a long time for this day, William."

Sullivan stared dumbly, trying to blink away the strangeness.

"I grow stronger . . . stronger."

Father Mosely had awakened from a decade-long coma but he had changed. Though recognizable, something essential about him had . . . altered.

"Strength comes and the power grows . . ." he whispered.

Beneath the folds of the lightweight sheet, the delicate outline of his twisted limbs completed the image of a living skeleton.

Whatever he was sensing, Father Sullivan knew this was unnatural. Maybe ungodly. He lacked the joy he should feel as he stared into the aged eyes of his beloved friend. "Y-you know what's going on here, don't you, Father Mosely. You know what . . . all this is about." Sullivan took a step closer.

"Of course. And each of us has a role to play. I know that, too; I wrote the parts long before you were born."

Something slipped; it heaved and shifted in Sullivan's mind. Bombarded with an infinity of impossibilities, how could anything ever again strike him as strange? But this, this was truth. This was reality. And it was flexing. Contorting. Changing shape before he could understand any of it.

As Sullivan wrestled with this deviant reality, fragments of his body and his mind responded in unfamiliar ways to alien sensations. He was in the presence of something totally foreign, something otherworldly, cunning, and profoundly evil.

In his jacket pocket, Sullivan's hand tightened around Alton Barnes's revolver.

* * *

McCurdy's sing song sermon droned in Jeff's ears, disrupting his euphoria like the howling of a dog. "Now you'll see that the Light is good and true. Now you'll see what it has to offer. Now you'll see a miracle of the Lord!"

As the crowd looked on, Jeff witnessed fear and wonder in a dozen upturned faces.

"Look at that!" somebody cried.

"Oh, it's so beautiful!"

The fascinating unreality that held him began to loosen its hypnotic grip as the one-hundred-foot expanse of light began to shrink, to draw itself together. Jeff watched its circumference pulling toward its middle, contracting like a gargantuan amoeba wriggling in the sky. It became smaller, brighter, like a spotlight adjusted to a crisp, sharp focus.

"This girl cannot *walk!*" McCurdy screamed, crossing the ground directly toward Casey. "Just look at her!" He waved his hand at Casey, as if she were an exhibit in a courtroom. "For *years* she has been paralyzed from the waist down. See there; her legs are as useless as empty sleeves.

"But in the Light she can walk! She can stand and walk and do the work of the Lord. Help me. Pray with me! Let the Light that heals perform its holy work!"

McCurdy reached out for her—

"NOOO!" Casey cried, turning terrified eyes toward Jeff.

—and grabbed her under the arms. Seemingly weightless in his hands, McCurdy snatched her from the wheelchair. "You don't *need* this mechanical abomination," he said, spinning her away from the chair toward the open mouthed spectators. "God gave you those legs to *walk.*"

Casey's legs dangled like ribbons, her toes skimming the ground.

"Pray with me now," McCurdy bellowed. "Everyone, pray to the Light. Give this girl the strength she needs to do Your holy work. Let the Light shine and strengthen. Let it return the warmth to these cold and useless limbs."

"Daaad! Help me!"

Jeff couldn't move. Fear of that horrid light held him immobile. Even the screams of his daughter could not animate him. It was he who was paralyzed. Helpless. Useless.

"Let Your warmth fill these dead limbs! Walk now. Arise and walk!"

McCurdy let go of her and she collapsed to the ground like a wet rag. Casey hid her face in her arms; her body quaked with silent sobbing.

"Up now, girl! On your feet. Be cured! Do as the Light commands!"

You're crazy, McCurdy. You're crazy as hell! Jeff couldn't push the words out. All he could do was stand there, a brainless scarecrow, watching his daughter suffer relentless humiliation at the hands of a madman.

"Stand up and walk. Now. Up. Do as I tell you, you weak ungrateful child."

"I can't."

"You *can,* damn it. You can!" Veins bulged like blue blisters on McCurdy's forehead. His cheeks burned livid red. Tufts of red hair shot out from his scalp as if they were electrified.

* * *

Quickly, like slides on a screen, Sullivan's years in the priesthood flashed through his mind. He searched his memory for some point of reference, some precedent, some particle of information to help him analyze what he was experiencing in this simple farmhouse bedroom.

He wanted an explanation beyond the obvious, the one he was trying to deny.

If this was not a demon, what could it be?

Over the years he had fought evil on many battlegrounds: in the classroom, in the confessional, and in the comfortable chairs of his consulting room. More recently he'd fought it from the altar of St. Joseph's Church. And long ago, in the military, he'd witnessed firsthand the damage evil can do. He'd seen the scars it left in the form of hollow-eyed skeletons stumbling, liberated, from among piles of stinking corpses at Nazi concentration camps. Then, and ever after, he'd known the enemy.

But, now, in this room, he realized he had been mistaken. He had not been fighting evil itself, only the product of evil. The weapons he'd used—intellect, knowledge, and faith—were useless to him now.

He shuddered, and the motion shook him like an earthquake. He hoped his fear did not show. Yet somehow he knew that the man on the bed saw everything, and sensed what he did not see.

Invisibly, Sullivan released the gun. It would not protect him. This unholy presence *filled* the room; it was not confined to the fragile figure on the bed.

The ancient body laughed. It was a muted, sharp-edged sound, the product of unpracticed lungs.

Until this moment, Sullivan had spent his life and career without looking evil in the face. He—and most of his colleagues—had squandered their years preparing to fight an enemy most would never meet. How many truly believed there could be such an enemy? And if they'd known, how many would have continued in the priesthood?

Most of Sullivan's colleagues would snigger at the idea they might one day come face-to-face with Satan. But *all* would laugh at the suggestion there could be something far worse than the devil.

"You're not Father Mosely," Sullivan whispered. "W-who are you?"

Again Sullivan endured that low, growling chuckle as it corrupted the darkness. "Who am I, Father Sullivan? I thought you were beginning to understand." The thin-lipped smile was the sneer of a serpent. "Look at me. Do you see nothing at all? Am I not the soul of those who died at Salem? The death cry of all who perished in Torquemada's fire? The stain of blood spilled by the swords of Christian crusaders?

"No?

"Then I am a whisper in Jeanne d'Arc's ear. A homeless child asleep against the walls of the Vatican. The terror-prodded pittance tithed to televised salvation."

The creature laughed and his words took on speed. "I am the bite of the Spaniard's lash. An Indian's blistered back, the poison cup of the holy power-seeker, the ash of the banned and burning book. I am all hypocrisy and lies. I am all good Christian works done in the name of God and in the celebration of Satan.

"And I grow stronger as we speak. With each death my power grows."

Sullivan felt feverish. Hot bolts of terror seared through him. Again his clumsy, sweat-slick fingers fumbled inside his pocket. This time he was not looking for the gun. This time he groped for his rosary.

For now he understood: Father Mosely's demon—or whatever this obscenity was—had won. It had possessed the old man completely, lived within him for a decade, dormant, infinitely patient, waiting for whatever evil rite would set it free.

And Sullivan grappled for the only weapon that might save him. Even as his fist closed around the rosary beads, part of him rejected what was undeniably happening. He wanted to turn and run from the unearthly atmosphere in the dark, cold, foul-smelling bedroom.

Possession was not the conceit of medieval demonologists. The Church still trained exorcists. And, rarely, the exorcists were called upon to challenge the fiend. Within the last year New York's Cardinal O'Connor had authorized at least three exorcisms. Three out of how many possessions?

But if this were not a demon . . . ? If this were something else, something impervious to the Church's holy arsenal . . . ?

No! He had to control himself. He had to remember that whatever evil this was, it was his responsibility to oppose it. He had to fight it, fight the only way he knew how.

The beads were in his fist.

Mere human power, he knew, was always useless against the preternatural. To challenge a demon without divine aid would be to invite personal disaster.

Sullivan removed his fist from his pocket. He extended his arm toward Mosely, let the rosary dangle from his thumb and forefinger. "In the name of Jesus Christ, I command you to identify yourself."

The old man pulled back, sucking air with a wheezing snarl. Turning his head away from the swinging crucifix, a frightened look distorted the time-scarred face. But Sullivan immediately realized the reaction was insincere, an expression of mock-terror. The demonic impostor laughed again. "We have taught you to defy us with your baubles and trinkets. Now I'll show you how completely you've been deceived. Now you'll see the folly of worshiping your humiliated god on his popsicle stick."

The dangling silver crucifix twitched in Sullivan's hand. It leapt, tugged, coiled around his right wrist like a metallic snake. Stumbling backward, Sullivan reached out with his left hand to untangle himself. The chain of beads flexed again. It jumped, twisted, curled itself around both wrists, binding him as if he were handcuffed. He struggled, knowing that to free himself he would have to destroy the sacred beads.

Evil laughed.

"Your symbol is now my symbol, William. And we are presented with an interesting paradox, don't you think? You are bound by your beliefs, aren't you? Would you destroy your precious symbol of good to escape the proximity of evil? Would you burn your church to save your parishioners? Would you press the button to demolish this world for the promise of a better world to come?"

The shackles tightened. Sharp-edged beads nipped at his wrists.

"Let's talk, William, shall we?"

A cane-backed chair from the corner scraped noisily across the floor and stopped behind the struggling priest.

"Sit down, why don't you?"

The pressure of phantom hands drove Sullivan into the chair. He struck it solidly, almost toppled.

Uncontrollable physical responses began to hammer him: sweat oozed from every pore, his heart pounded like a timpani, adrenaline surged, provoking a desperate, mindless panic. He resisted as best he could, commanding his mind to focus on a Hail Mary. His bleeding wrists flexed and squirmed, trying to free themselves from their tether of beaded chain.

* * *

Fear rushed through Jeff like lava flooding stone. Immobile, he watched a pulsing tentacle of light descend, a radiant octopus arm groping from within the shining circle.

In his mind he saw that poor naked child, changing, mutating . . . . With his eyes he saw the river of light settle over Casey. It flowed across her body like liquid, painting her with sunshine.

Then it was gone.

Above, the ten-foot circle darkened, went out like a light bulb. Now it appeared as an ink spot on the ebony sky, visible only because it was blacker than the surrounding night. Jeff saw it as an unholy tunnel in an ethereal mountainside, leading nowhere.

McCurdy's voice boomed in the new darkness. "Rise, child. Rise and give thanks. The Light is in you!"

Jeff wanted to take McCurdy by the throat, choke him into silence, force him to stop badgering the terrified girl. But his muscles were insensible stones beneath his flesh.

With a single phrase McCurdy taunted them both, "You can *do* it . . . !"

But Jeff couldn't. He couldn't do anything. He just watched the spectators form a tighter ring around his cowering daughter.

"Stand!" McCurdy commanded.

"*Stand,*" the crowd echoed.

Casey's body shook with the effort.

"STAND!"

She was struggling, using the strength in her arms to pry her torso from the sodden ground. Now Jeff could see her face. Tears streamed down her cheeks. Her eyes darted madly as the human circle closed around her.

Was that motion Jeff saw? Had Casey's foot twitched? Had her leg flexed just a bit at the knee?

Yes, his mind cried, *yes, honey, stand! STAND!*

But he heard Father Sullivan's voice, too. It echoed clearly in his memory:

The demon can bring you gold . . .

Supporting herself with trembling arms, Casey somehow pulled her legs under her, poised in a lopsided kneeling position. Ready.

. . . but can never force you to take it.

"Stand! Stand! Stand! Stand!"

My God, she's going to get up!

"Praise the Lord," someone said.

McCurdy extended a hand. Casey reached to take it.

Awkwardly, unsteadily, she started to pull herself up.

"NO, CASEY! *STOP!*"

The crowd fell silent. Jeff's own voice echoed in his ears. As Casey fell back, McCurdy glared. The crowd redirected their attention toward Jeff.

* * *

"Let's talk about free will, Father Sullivan." The evil's eyes glowed red again, as if a light behind them were increasing in power. "I'm going to ask for your help. But before I do, let me assure you that I will have it, either against your will, or with your complete consent. To me, of course, it makes little difference, for the outcome will be the same."

Sullivan stared, he hoped impassively; the words of his Hail Mary were foremost in his mind.

Again the evil laughed its weak, windy laugh. "'Pray for us sinners. Pray for us, sinners. Prey for us sinners . . . .' Oh, William, how well I understand your retreat into faith. It's a reasonable choice, after all. You haven't anything else just now, have you?

"And of course I know better than anyone how faith is built upon your arrogant belief in free will and personal choice. So now you *choose* to pray, right? But isn't your faith tainted with the absurd promise of reward in the afterlife? Let me see if I've got this straight: to earn your reward all you have to do is choose good over evil, is that it?"

Sullivan glared at him.

"Doesn't that strike you as simplistic? Sophomoric? Even idiotic? It should, to a man of your intellect. But here's truth from the lips of a liar: there is no reward, William, just as there is no good and no evil. They are lies, and they come from the source of all lies. We have created them for you just as a farmer creates a fence around his cattle—the lies contain and control. It is as simple as that."

* * *

Alton's car still wouldn't start.

He'd laid the bundled child on the back seat, tucked her in, and, whispering soft encouragements, tried to make her comfortable.

Then, with Karen behind the wheel, he'd pushed the vehicle far enough to get it rolling down the hill.

The key was switched on, the car was in gear, and Karen had repeatedly jumped the clutch. The engine just wouldn't fire.

"It's that damn *light*," he told her. "I've read about it time and again. Nothin' works right when them UFOs are around."

* * *

Jeff screamed, "Don't do it, Casey. Don't get up. If you stand up, you'll be in its debt. It'll *own* you."

Casey flattened herself against the ground.

McCurdy's tongue clicked loudly. His eyes sizzled with hatred. The crowd of spectators parted, forming a corridor in which Jeff and McCurdy stood face-to-face. "I warned you, Jeffrey. I offered you so much."

Stalking toward Jeff, McCurdy continued speaking through clenched teeth. "All I asked was that you have faith and stay silent until you had witnessed the truth. *Damn you,* you could have saved your daughter. Can't you see it's your selfishness that cripples her? Can't you see it's you who stands in her way?"

His voice rose, sped up, took on the fire and brimstone strength of a Chautaugua tent preacher's. "You block the Light, Jeffrey. You and the other soulless shadows keep the Light from the world. But no one can hide within the Light; it has shown you as you are. I have seen, we all have seen that you are *not* of the chosen."

Now McCurdy stood so close that Jeff could smell his acrid breath. Eye to eye, McCurdy spat venomous words in his face. "I was wrong about you, but that's *your* mistake, not mine. The Light can heal, but it can cripple and destroy. It illuminates the worthy as it blasts the soulless into endless realms of unimaginable torment."

He raised his arms.

Jeff tensed, preparing for an assault of terrible unknown pain like nothing he'd ever experienced.

Behind McCurdy, a webwork of electrical arcs danced and crackled within the black airborne opening. Frigid mist blasted out like a smoke from a cannon.

The vapor split when it hit McCurdy's back, forked into a two-pronged cloud that passed on either side of Jeff. It never touched him yet he felt its arctic bite. In a moment the gathering was shrouded in a freezing, putrid fog.

Jeff shivered, looking around, hoping someone would step forward to help him. Instead, everyone stood still as statues, their faces frozen masks. Each was an individual pillar of stone; together, they formed a mist-filled cage in which McCurdy and Jeff faced one another.

Jeff fought the urge to plead. Damn it, he wouldn't!

Rain began anew. It pelted Jeff, stung his face and hands. Drops smacked the ground like tiny bursting balloons. As the downpour covered McCurdy, Jeff saw its color. Deep crimson, the color of blood.

Roiling clouds of icy mist billowed past Jeff on either side. He held his ground, shivering, suffering the nauseating odor, wiping the blood rain from his eyes, thinking, thinking . . .

If McCurdy controlled the light with the power of will, then Jeff's only hope was to challenge that will, weaken it, destroy it if he could. If he could break McCurdy's concentration . . . If he could make him doubt his power, he might lose it.

"The light is gone, Skipp. It's in Casey now. It's for her to control, not you."

"Dad . . . Dad, I feel funny." Casey's voice was wracked with sobs as she cried out against the wind and rain. She looked up at him, her eyes glassy, her mouth twisted in pain. Crimson rain covered her like blood.

"Stay still, baby. Try not to move."

Ignoring Jeff, McCurdy shouted at the girl. "Yes, you feel it, don't you! You feel the Light inside you. The warmth, the power. It's mending you, isn't it? It's cleansing your blood, repairing your nerves, pumping new life into your crippled limbs. You can stand now, girl. You can walk. Get up! Don't just lie there like a lizard in the mud. Stand! Show these people the power of the Light."

"The light is *gone*, Skipp," Jeff cried. "You thought you controlled it, but it controlled you. You were its puppet. It used you, now it's discarded you. It has moved on to someone more worthy."

"*NO!*" Smoke coiled around McCurdy's head. Bloody water ran down his face, wind tugged at his rain-slick tufts of hair.

"You thought you contacted God on that computer of yours, didn't you? But you were wrong. You were tricked by some terrible power that would destroy you and me and millions of others to gain access to this world. Think about it, Skipp. You're the soulless one, aren't you? You're the one who let the devil into God's world."

"Blasphemer!" McCurdy looked to the people surrounding him, face after face. Mist rose from their features like swirling ghosts. Again fixing his deadly eyes on Jeff, he pointed and cried, "You'll burn like the sinner you are. . . ."

Words locked in Jeff's throat. The wind died; the rain stopped. The whole world fell into silence, as if waiting for the next atrocity to come.

"*Damn you!*" McCurdy pointed at Jeff. "I'll crush your heart in my hand! And the fire of the Light will strike you from God's earth—"

The fatal pronouncement was halted by a heart-stopping scream.

* * *

"She's breathing funny," Alton said. "I think maybe she's dying."

"Let me take a look." Karen ran around to the back of the car, pulled open the rear door, and knelt in the rain. "I've had some medical training. Maybe I can help her. Let me check her pulse. . . ."

The dome light revealed the child's face.

Wide eyes stared up in confusion. Karen watched perplexity change to tentative recall.

At first Karen didn't recognize the distorted face. She struggled to tear her gaze from those ugly distended lips.

"Pretty bad, ain't it, miss?"

Examining the rain-matted hair, the shape of the skull, the distinct set of the eyes, Karen began to realize who this child really was.

"L-Lucy . . . ?" she whispered.

Tears welled in the girl's eyes.

"You *know* her?" Alton said.

"I . . . I think it's . . . Lucy Washburn. She's my patient, she's . . ."

Karen climbed into the car and took Lucy's head on her lap. "There, honey, it's going to be okay."

With trembling hands, she peeled the saturated blanket from the naked child. "Let's just have a look and see what's wrong."

When she saw what the blanket concealed, she screamed.

* * *

The loud cry tore McCurdy's attention from Jeff.

For the first time his lunatic expression was tinged with fear. Mechanically, he shouted into unresponsive faces, "This man speaks with a viper's tongue. He lies! He deceives! He'll say anything to make you look away from the Light. Don't listen to him. Don't believe. His false words are the route to darkness."

"Dad . . . !" Casey rolled on the ground, clutching her stomach.

"It's all right, Casey."

"No, Dad, I'm sick. I feel awful. . . ."

"Look at him," McCurdy continued, "he would shade his own daughter, his own flesh and blood from the healing power of the Light. Think, brothers and sisters, is this the man who can lead you to salvation?"

"You're alone, McCurdy. Your power is gone. The light is out."

"NO!" McCurdy's voice resonated with false confidence. "*You* are the soulless one; *you* must be removed. Take him, people. *Take him!*"

No one moved. McCurdy looked around expectantly. Not one person returned his gaze. "Can't you recognize the voice of the damned? For God's sake grab him! Tie him."

McCurdy shook the nearest person. Then shoved the unresponsive man toward Jeff. But instead of obeying, the man toppled, shattered on the ground with a sound like ice breaking. Jeff cried out as the man separated into a half-dozen pieces. Each severed fleshy chunk glistened with blood.

Unbelieving, Jeff looked at his daughter. Casey was vomiting onto the ground.

McCurdy's scream was demented and painful, the anguished wail of a man who'd lost everything. He pushed person after person. Each tumbled like bowling pins and shattered as if made of glass.

They're frozen, Jeff thought. They've turned to ice!

A teenager in a tank top broke in half as she fell across the body of a man in gray coveralls. McCurdy shoved a woman holding a video camera. She toppled against the old man standing beside her. Both split into sharp-edged fragments. The cold damp air filled with the stench of vomit and excrement.

"See what your light has done, McCurdy? See what your god thinks of you and your misguided apostles? My God, look what's happening!"

McCurdy dropped to his knees, sobbing, hyperventilating.

"Is this the miracle you promised?" Jeff stepped toward him. McCurdy, gasping, looked up with plaintive eyes.

Propelled by the strength of tension and terror, Jeff lifted a foot that caught McCurdy solidly under the chin. McCurdy's head snapped backward and he sprawled on top of a frozen pile of human remains.

* * *

A change came over the old man in the bed. As Sullivan watched, the old man somehow looked . . . younger. His drab flesh seemed to catch fire and glow. Closing his eyes, he smiled with tremendous satisfaction.

Father Sullivan lowered his gaze. He had stopped trying to disentangle himself from the rosary. His wrists were bleeding where the sharp-edged beads had scraped and cut him. Undaunted, he held the tiny silver crucifix between his fingers. And he prayed; with his head bowed and his eyes squeezed tight, he prayed.

Still the unhuman voiced droned, creating an inaudible hissing in his brain.

"It is done . . . done . . . done."

The old man took a deep breath that rattled in his lungs.

"Tell me, Father William," he asked pleasantly, "do you think about your death? Do you hypothesize that it might be scant moments away? Are you praying now for your life? Or for your soul?"

May your will be done on Earth as it is in Heaven.

"There are many ways to destroy a man, Father William. Perhaps the most humane is to completely and instantly extinguish his physical body—a boot upon an ant. At least this permits a sense of . . . hope. For if he has faith, the doomed man ends with his cherished beliefs unviolated."

. . . as we forgive those who offend against us.

"Less charitable but perhaps far more honest is to destroy the man by destroying the beliefs. Destruction yes, but not necessarily death. Do you understand what I mean, Father?" The voice was clearer now. Stronger. More youthful and familiar. "Suppose I were to tell you that every principle for which you've lived your long and painful life is bogus, a contrivance, a system of lies and illusions aimed at seeking your cooperation in the advancement of abstract and incomprehensible ends, ends you can never understand the first thing about?"

And lead us not into temptation. . . .

"From the human viewpoint, of course, either notion is ugly, ultimately undesirable, it would seem to me. But I propose a compromise. Suppose I were to offer you an *alternate* system of beliefs? One based on observable phenomena, signs and events that shine as great truth within the muddle, murk, and mud of the human mind? In other words, William, suppose I were to cut through the crap and tell you what life is all about?"

. . . deliver us . . .

"Believe me, Father William, I can show you the reason you are here. I can tell you where you are going and what will happen to you the instant immediately following the moment of your physical death. I can tell you the meaning of all the institutions and political systems that have arisen and fallen, and I can show you the tangible ends of religions, arts, and philosophical thought. In short—and with a very few words—I can teach you the indisputable meaning of life. And I can offer what your church cannot. William, I can offer proof. Would you like that?"

. . . from Evil.

Father Sullivan's mind was so paralyzed that his only defense was to fall back into ritual. The words of the Pater Noster played in his brain like an endless loop on a tape recorder. This effort of faith seemed to shield a deeper level of mind where rational thought continued unimpaired. There was no denying that he was a prisoner. If he got up from the chair, that same invisible force would propel him back down again. But more than that, he suspected he was in that chair for a reason, according to the irresistible demand of some infernal designer. This reunion with his childhood mentor must have been planned. It was too utterly fantastic to be total coincidence. He had replaced Father Mosely in Hobston at St. Joseph's parish. Now he faced the diabolical facade of his precursor in some kind of withering good-against-evil confrontation.

How had he been manipulated like this?

How could he hope to stop it?

Had his years of education, devotion, and professional experience prepared him to offer no better resistance than the parrotlike uttering of prayer? Sullivan pinched his eyes tightly together, pleading for guidance.

Was it humility or hubris that made him think he had been the one—the only one—divinely selected to parry this satanic assault?

I must do what I can, he thought. *I must meet this challenge of my own free will, but in the name and by the authority of Jesus Christ and His Church.*

If Sullivan could hold his faith intact, perhaps his wits would contrive some sort of defense. He lifted his head, opened his eyes to meet sparkling black orbs that bore viciously into him, probing toward his soul.

"What do you want with me?" he asked.

* * *

When McCurdy came to, he was on the soggy ground. Though the rain had stopped, he was soaked to the skin. And he was cold, shivering. Bone-deep pain permeated his face, radiated down his spine as he remembered the kick Jeff had delivered to his chin.

He broke my jaw, he thought. A dry sob wracked his aching chest. Breath felt like sandpaper in his throat.

Before he was able to open his eyes, he smelled carrion and offal.

Reluctantly, he willed his eyelids to open. His hands and his clothing were smeared with streaks of the bloody rain.

Looking around, he saw Jeff and his daughter were gone.

Carnage surrounded him, as if he were the sole survivor waking on a battlefield. Pieces of bleeding bodies had turned the mud red. The smell was appalling. He gagged. Retched. Vomit spewed across his knees and splashed against a severed hand that clutched a Bible.

The agony of the violent expulsion filled his head with new pain.

Chunks of bodies. Heads. Split torsos. Intestines. Legs so cleanly detached they appeared the work of a butcher's cleaver. These were his apostles.

These were the witnesses who would have sung the glory of the new day. As he painfully contorted to a sitting position he saw the bloody fragments of the TV newswoman and her shattered video camera. Videotape spread from a cracked cassette like entrails extruding from a wound.

He grabbed a handful of his magnetically recorded miracle, then cast it down into the mud.

Worse, as his fuzzy thoughts cleared he knew the connection was broken. The voice no longer whispered in his head. His psychic link with the computer was severed like a nerve.

Why have you forsaken me?

McCurdy tried to get to his feet, but he was too heavy. He fell, rolled onto his back, and looked up at the sky.

He had been duped. Deceived. Now, with a fresh clarity of thought, he began to realize what he had done.

It was a sin too great to be forgiven. It was a realization no mind was strong enough to bear.

He wanted to repent, but to whom?

He felt moisture on his cheeks.

Was it raining again?

In the distance, he saw three people running toward the farmhouse.

* * *

"What do I *want* from you?" The creature's words carried images and meaning directly into Father Sullivan's mind. "This is not a matter of *I* and *you*, William."

Father Mosely's mouth wasn't moving. Sullivan wasn't listening. But communication occurred just the same. Sullivan could feel it humming in his brain.

The alien presence in the room had increased tremendously. Its power made it almost visible in the darkness. It was all around him like a nauseating vapor.

"You are far too provincial, William. You must learn to think grandly. Not just globally, but universally, cosmically. It will soon be within your power to make things better, easier, for many people on many different levels."

By now there was no more room in Sullivan's mind for prayer or independent thought. The onslaught of demonic ideas overloaded the strength of his mental resources. He was enduring a kind of psychic brainwashing. Everything registered as true; he found himself believing every word.

"First I want you to consider the near-fanatical capacity your race has for destruction. While boasting that you strive for order, you destroy with intent. You destroy with abandon and from innocence. Destruction is in your nature—and by design, that's exactly as it should be.

"Most of what you do is of little consequence to us. If you seek to befoul life-sustaining waters with your waste and excrement, that's fine and good. If you want to annihilate a companion species or two—a bird or animal or fish—so much the better. If you prefer to engage in warfare for politics, principal, economics, or even population control, we have no quarrel with that. In fact, over the eons we have done our share to encourage you along all those lines. We *enjoy* your antics until they begin to affect our well-being. The truth is, your antics bring death. And death is . . . of great value to us.

"That's right, William, we . . . encourage certain of mankind's delusions because they provide us with . . . merriment. Your struggle to the stars is a favorite comedy. What can you possibly hope to gain from such frivolity? Your efforts are akin to those of a mite on a carnival wheel.

"But while your puffery and pride may entertain us, they must be controlled and directed, for—after millions of years—you are starting to become dangerous. Even when you act out in ignorance you often perpetrate far greater damage than you have the capacity to understand. Universal damage. Cosmic damage.

"The balance of nature is something your kind can never understand. Why? Because nature extends too far beyond you. You cannot fathom the simplest cause and effect relationships, so any concept of totality is impossible.

"Let me give you an example: you have the wisdom to recognize how your destruction of forests endangers the creatures residing there. Yet you selfishly continue, though ultimately that same destruction is a far greater danger to your own oxygen supply. You can't muster the will nor the wisdom to stop. Headstrong you violate nature's precision: you kill, you damage, you destroy. But individually you are protected; your trivially short life span exempts you from suffering any immediate personal consequences of your actions.

"By dismissing us as *supernatural* what you have failed to understand is that we too are a part of nature. We may not be accessible to your telescopes, microscopes, or electronic equipment, for we exist outside the confines of space and time. Yet—along with birds and fish and animals—we are a companion to your species.

"As one trained in Roman Catholic theology, William, you are better equipped than any scientist to understand the nature of our existence. You understand *spirit*. You accept its reality. Do you understand?"

Yes, Sullivan understood perfectly. The colloquial phrasing, the familiar, almost companionable mode of address, the ecological examples, the overall logic of the presentation—all of it might have been articulated by a friend or colleague. Mosely's demon knew how to speak to him, how to convince him. Sullivan was beyond resistance, yet the creature continued. . . .

"Unlike your kind, we have existed since the beginning of time. Symbiotically, we are linked to you like an older brother who has been with you since the moment of your birth. Throughout the ages we have played a critical role in your upbringing by creating your myths, your folklore, and . . . your religion."

Sullivan closed his eyes. He had expected that final revelation, but didn't want to hear it. Protesting, he knew, would do no good. Defending his faith was impossible. Though he tried to form a prayer in his mind, he could not. He wasn't in control. All that filled him was the creature's words.

"Unlike you, we are not bound in the evolutionary manacles of brief birth-death cycles. We have watched your mistakes, have watched you repeat them, and regret them, and repeat them again, until your blunders grow and evolve beyond your ability to correct. All the while each of you is restricted to a lifetime of a scant seven decades; your blunders evolve while you do not.

"Know this, William: mankind is an imperfect animal. In each of you, from the most primitive cave dweller to the most advanced humanistic thinker, each of you holds within himself the capacity to destroy all things. You are held in check only by the vague and vanishing concept of conscience.

"And who created conscience?

"We did.

"Then we taught you how to acquire and instill it."

Father Sullivan groaned, slumped in his chair. The rosary beads were hot coals against his wrists. His skin seemed to vibrate like the head of a drum pounded by the creature's words.

"For thousands of years we have revealed ourselves to you by accident and by design. We present ourselves as angels, spirits, fairies, monsters. Even demons. We are your UFOs and the UFO occupants. And whatever form we take, our purpose is to guide, instruct, and ultimately to keep mankind confused, ideologically at odds with itself. We see to it that your religion, your scientific research, your political philosophies, are fragmented into myriad conflicting and nonuniform disciplines. Thereby, we render all your institutions ineffective.

"Our tools—or weapons, if you prefer—appear to you as magic, supernatural intervention, and individual inspiration. I'm talking about lies, jokes, coincidences, and metaphysical theatrics. I'm talking about cosmic minstrel shows like the one occurring around you right now. By forming and reinforcing human experience, we help to perpetuate your most primitive beliefs. Thus, exactly like the farmer who fences his livestock, we control you."

Father Sullivan felt himself shivering. He wanted to pass out but the creature's words burned like a fire in his mind.

"We are like you, but we are your antithesis. Where human beings boast of their instinctive quest for order, logic, and fulfillment, our goals are quite different. Different, and I'm afraid completely beyond your capacity to understand.

"That's why we have the right to command and direct you. And this relationship has worked well for millions of years. But now something has happened.

"Unfortunately, we've never completely controlled the channels of communication between our dominions. Some of you, through accident, instinct, or imaginative persistence, have *almost* come to know us. Some have even initiated communication using magical rites, spiritualism, channeling, and religion. Those, you see, are the languages of communication between our realms. Sometimes when you call, we answer. Sometimes we do not.

"What do I *want* from you, Father Sullivan? Only what is best for all of us.

"A short half century ago you stumbled onto something essential. You learned to manipulate the most fundamental particles of matter and nonmatter, and, in doing so, came very close to the source of creation. Immediately, you used this knowledge for destruction. Yet even today only a minuscule portion of the devastation you caused in Japan is known to you. Typically, what you do not perceive is of no concern.

"Make no mistake, William, it is not the residual damage to you and your world that concerns us. It is the damage to us. You have discovered the means to kill the undying. You have learned to eradicate spirit, to destroy soul.

"And now, with your mindless enthusiasm and wide-eyed blindness, you have stumbled onto something vastly more dangerous. As usual, you were looking for a weapon but you found a key. It is the key that will unlock the door to our domain.

"Quite simply, Father William, we will not allow you to control that key.

"We have begun a new era of expanded intervention and . . ." the creature laughed, "unrestrained contempt. We will no longer laugh as you annihilate each other. From now on we will relieve you of that pleasure. We will torture and destroy you ourselves.

"Today, on this hilltop, it begins. It cannot be stopped. It cannot be reversed. As the deluded Dr. McCurdy asserted: a new time has come. It's in motion right now. And unimaginable changes will follow.

"For you and your kind, life will become far more difficult but . . . mercifully less abstract. Certain religious zealots will believe the devil is at the helm. At first everyone will look for sanctuary in their churches—but to no avail.

"As demons and angels, we have taught you that your religion is effective against us. But as you have seen, we lied. And thinking you were safe, you have squandered the eons. In all the time you've existed you have built no defense to repel us.

"Many of us are here already. When we come en masse, there'll be nothing you can do.

"What can you *do* for us, Father Sullivan? We will require of you no more than we asked of Hamilton Mosely a decade ago. As you can see, his physical state has degenerated terribly. This body hasn't the strength to rise from this bed. So it can be of no use to us. . . .

"What do we ask of *you?* Nothing, William, nothing at all. We already have you. Come closer to me now."

Eyes pinched closed, Sullivan lurched forward, propelled by invisible hands. The sound of laughter echoed in his ears.

* * *

"Look! There's Jeff and Casey!" Karen pointed toward the front porch of the Dubois farmhouse as she led Alton along the dark muddy road. She watched a grotesque shadow approaching the house—Jeff carrying Casey in his arms.

He mounted the steps and lowered his daughter into a wooden Adirondack chair. Then he stood up straight, massaging the muscles of his lower back.

Casey cried, "Dad, look!" She pointed into the darkness directly at Karen.

Waving, Karen ran ahead. She saw how haggard Jeff appeared.

His face was painted with grime and rusty-colored stains. His clothing was so filthy he appeared to be sculpted from mud.

"Oh, Jeff. . . ."

They embraced in front of the steps. Karen smiled and cried at the same time.

"Thank God you're all right," Jeff said hoarsely. He hugged her so hard it hurt. Alton threw a big arm around both of them.

"Jeff, Jeff." All at once Karen redirected her gaze. "Oh, Jeff, is Casey . . . ?"

"She's fine. She's been through hell and she's exhausted, but—"

"Let's just get *away* from here," Casey said.

"What about Father Sullivan?" Alton asked. "He was inside last I seen him."

Jeff shook his head, looking confused. "I don't know; I haven't checked." He fell back onto the steps and put his face in his hands.

"And McCurdy?" Alton pressed.

"I knocked him out. Whatever power he had, I think he lost it. After the massacre—"

"Massacre!" Karen and Alton spoke in unison.

"They're dead. All those people in the field, dead. I don't know what happened. There was a blast of wind. Cold. Freezing wind. People started falling. Shattering, li-like statues made of ice." Jeff rubbed his eyes with his fingertips.

Karen turned, facing the empty field. "The whole crowd? All of them?"

Jeff nodded.

She didn't know what to say. The men stood silent. Everyone traded frightened, disbelieving glances.

"Oh my God," Karen finally said, "I still can't believe any of this. What's going on here, Jeff? How can s-something like that be happening?"

Jeff blinked at her several times as if trying to get his eyes to focus. "That damn computer. It's just as we figured: McCurdy somehow tapped into another . . . realm, another dimension or whatever you want to call it. And they're coming through. I think they're . . . attacking us."

"Holy shit!" Alton grabbed Jeff's arm. "Then that's what happened to Stuart, ain't it? Somethin' from the other side . . . it pulled him in?"

"That's about the size of it. They used Skipp McCurdy's religious beliefs to manipulate him. Made him think he was leading the way to the world's salvation. They gave him a taste of power, then they took it away. But the gate, the passageway's still open. And I don't know what's going to happen now . . . ."

"You make it sound like . . . I mean is it really . . . an *invasion?*"

"Christ, I don't know, Karen. I think that's just what it is. Unless . . ."

"Unless what?" Alton leaned forward. "You figger there's somethin' we can do?"

"I don't know. That's what I've been trying to figure out. Christ, I'm so tired my mind's hardly working."

"Can we . . . close the door, somehow?" Karen asked.

"Maybe. If McCurdy opened it with the computer, maybe we can use the computer to close it."

"But that's in Boston! Do we have time to drive—?"

"McCurdy's got a terminal upstairs in the bedroom. I saw it when I was up there. He wasn't using it. Apparently he had some sort of telepathic connection with the CPU in Boston. But now McCurdy's done his job so he's become obsolete. His mental connection's broken. So maybe, if I can just get to that terminal . . ."

Jeff stood up. Karen watched his glance shift from the house back to the dark field and the slopes beyond.

The terrifying circle of light was gone now; the whole panorama was beginning to brighten. A wavy red ribbon of morning rested on the mountains to the east.

"Al," Jeff said, "why don't you see if you can find a car, then get the women out of here."

Al nodded. "Mine ain't workin', but maybe I can get one of 'em started. Looks to me like things have settled down some. . . ."

"But wait! What about *you?*" Karen clutched Jeff's filthy shirtfront.

"I'm going to get to that terminal and see if I can put the CPU out of commission. Whatever door McCurdy's opened, I've got to close the sonuvabitch and bar it forever. If I don't, we'll be getting all sorts of unwanted visitors."

"No! You come with us. Just grab the terminal and let's get out of here." Karen looked him directly in the eyes.

"I'll find us a car." Al carried Lucy up the steps where he placed her on the cushions of the old porch swing. "You take care now, sweetie," Karen heard him whisper.

Then he about-faced.

As he walked off the porch and away, he said, "You folks round up whatever you need. I'll be back in a jiffy."

* * *

McCurdy dragged himself through the mud.

He was too weak to get to his feet. Even if he did, he was afraid he wouldn't be able to walk. He slapped the wet ground as he pulled himself forward. Foul water splashed his face and he spat it back at the soggy grass.

Though the sharp pain in his jaw continued its electric jolts, the tears had dried in his eyes. More than anything else he wanted to pray, but he feared the wrong deity might hear him.

Mumbling to himself, he crawled.

He knew he was alone. Completely, totally alone. There was no one else to hear him.

He had something to do. Something important. But he had to keep that to himself. It was for him to know. Just him.

He tried to click his tongue, but pain stabbed at his mouth like shards of glass.

The house seemed such a long way off. He wasn't sure he could make the distance without passing out. Determined, he kept inching along like a snake in the mud.

A clear perfect thought shone brightly in his mind.

* * *

Karen followed Jeff through the front door of the farmhouse. Just inside, they stood together in the dark hall, looking around.

The air was foul. The whole placed reeked with a terrible nauseating stench Karen could not identify.

She peered into the gloom, not wanting to get too far from Jeff. Downstairs, the rooms seemed empty. A kerosene lamp burned beside the couch in the living room. Two candles flickered atop a drop-leaf table near the bottom of the stairs. To the left, the unlighted kitchen seemed cavernous. Its furnishings were buried in shadows.

"You wait right here," Jeff whispered. "Keep an eye on Casey and Lucy. I'll go upstairs and grab the terminal."

"Okay, but hurry."

She watched him poke his head through the living room door. "Father Sullivan!" Jeff called.

When no one answered, he walked straight toward the stairway at the back of the house. There he hesitated, looking up. "Are you here, Father?" Jeff's voice seemed uncomfortably loud in the quiet house.

He began to climb the stairs.

"Stop right there, please." The voice seemed to come from nowhere. Father Sullivan's voice.

"Wha . . . ? Where *are* you, Father?" Jeff said again. Karen saw Jeff's puzzled face as he turned and walked back toward her.

"Karen, Jeffrey, please stay where you are. I want to talk to you."

"But, where—?"

"PLEASE!"

Karen stood twenty feet from Jeff. Both looked around, trying to determine the source of the words.

"If you have a flashlight, leave it off, please."

Karen's eyes met Jeff's. He shrugged and held up his empty hands. "No light, Father."

As candles flickered, Karen saw movement deep within the kitchen. A door opening. Hinges squealed.

"Jeff!" she called as he joined her at the threshold.

A door in the kitchen opened. Father Sullivan stepped into its frame. There he paused, leaning against the vertical woodwork, staring at them from across the room. He appeared profoundly tired. Drained. His skin seemed bleached, his sunken eyes rimmed with black. His thick gray hair was wild in disarray.

"Jeffrey, you're on a fool's errand, I'm afraid," the priest said with hollow tones.

Sullivan seemed so weary that he could not stand without the support of the door frame. Karen wanted to go to him, but for some reason hesitated. "Father, you don't look well. Can I help you? Why don't you let me—"

"STAY BACK, DAMN IT!"

The force of his words held her in place.

Now more softly, "Please stay where you are. It's better you don't come near me. I may be . . . sick."

"Then let us help. You look exhausted, Father. What's happened?"

Sullivan shook his head, slowly, sadly.

Muddled with fatigue, Karen couldn't trust her judgment or her instincts, yet both insisted Father Sullivan was behaving strangely.

"We're going to get out of here," Jeff said. "Alton's gone for a car. We can take you to the hospital. . . ." He glanced at Karen, then back at the priest.

"No. I . . . I have something to tell you." Sullivan's eyes closed, as if he had passed out against the door frame. "It's going to be . . . unpleasant. But please listen. Then all of us will know what must be done."

With his right arm and shoulder pressed firmly against the wood, Sullivan appeared as a white-masked shadow in the dim light. His image upset Karen, but she didn't know exactly why.

"Of course, Father. Please go on," said Jeff.

"Tonight I have suffered a great blow to my faith." His voice was a hoarse whisper. "Moments ago, I was convinced I had come face-to-face with the devil. As a priest, I know the devil wears many masks.

But tonight . . . tonight I looked into the face of the devil, only to discover that it too is a mask."

"Oh, Father. . . ." Karen took another step, but Jeff grabbed her.

"Tonight I have learned, with no doubt whatsoever, that our speculation was correct. There *is* another world existing synchronously with our own. It is here now, all around us. It is not Heaven or Hell. It is not the Kingdom, the Spirit World, Magonia, the astral plane, or any of the myriad names we have contrived for it. It is so carefully disguised that its' true nature has remained undiscovered for centuries.

"But tonight I have glimpsed that world. I have understood enough to perceive answers to . . . ultimate questions. I have attained an . . . imperfect enlightenment."

Jeff and Karen exchanged glances.

"The riddle of the ages has an answer. I have learned why we are here, what life means, what happens when we die, and why our death is essential to the workings of the universe."

Karen thought she heard a series of quiet sobs coming from the priest. When he continued to speak, his voice was less steady. "For thousands of years mankind has lived an illusion. We have regaled ourselves with the notion that we are the highest form of life on this planet. That the beasts of the field, the fowl, the very earth itself, are there for us to control, to exploit, and to dominate."

He took a deep asthmatic breath. "But we have been . . . wrong.

"Tonight things have . . . changed. Call it Armageddon, Judgment Day, call it whatever you like. The simple truth is that a new order is about to assert itself. And there is n-nothing we can do to oppose it. They . . . the creatures we'll soon confront . . . are as different from us as we are from . . . worms or roaches. They can present themselves as visions. Or invisibly. They can speak directly into our ears or into our minds. And our only action, the only thing we can do, is to let it happen."

"Father," Jeff said gently, "I'm afraid I don't understand. Maybe you're too tired . . . Maybe we shouldn't be talking right now. . . ." He inched forward.

"NO! Stay there. Let me finish. You have to know. Everyone has to know. I have to make you understand. . . .

"The Otherworlders, they can come here, but they can't remain for long. To remain, they have to . . . inhabit one of us, they have to possess a human being.

"Ten years ago one such entity tried to inhabit Father Mosely. Its intent was to remain as a gatekeeper, to facilitate the passage from their world to ours. But when it completed the possession, Father Mosely's paralyzing stroke made the body useless. The intruder was forced to remain dormant, trapped in a state much like physical death, until it could be freed.

"McCurdy and his experiments at the Academy inadvertently provided the rituals necessary to give the entity new strength. Eventually it became strong enough to exert its influence on specific individuals, people with a diminished sense of personal identity.

"That's why it could manipulate Lucy Washburn and Herbert Gold. That's why both externalized the same alternate personality, the one who facetiously identified himself as Mr. Splitfoot. By controlling Lucy and Herbert, the entity forced them to kidnap the shell in which it was prisoner: Father Mosely's body.

"At the same time it learned to manipulate the Academy's computer. McCurdy's machine is constructed with experimental substances nearly identical to human flesh—the flesh of our brain matter. The substance is human enough so it could be . . . acquired by the entity. Gradually, through processes we may never understand, it used the computer to continue building its own strength and to, in effect, seduce the system's designer, Dr. McCurdy.

"Now, with all its forces in place, the entity brought Father Mosely's body here to Hobston. Here the forces of its alien domain are most powerful, because here there's an actual entry point to the other realm. And McCurdy summoned a handful of people to be used in the ritual necessary to free it."

"The . . . the dead people," said Karen. "The people who were massacred out there in the field?"

"Yes. But not massacred, Karen, sacrificed. They require deaths to gain strength."

Jeff looked at Karen, then back at the priest. "This entity sacrificed a group of people so it could free itself?"

"Yes. It needed their strength. The combined strength of all of them. And it needs more still."

"S-so, you're saying that now the spirit that possessed Father Mosely is free?"

Father Sullivan didn't respond.

"So why isn't it over?" Karen's voice rose. "If the darn thing is free, how come this . . . this craziness is still going on?"

"It has to keep the gate open. It's going to provide its kin with free access to our world. And to us."

"Christ, how many of these . . . entities are there?"

"I don't know. There could be fewer than a dozen. There could be billions upon billions. It's entirely possible there is one for each person living on this earth. . . ."

"But, Father, please, how do you know? How can you be sure about this?"

The priest chuckled weakly. "Ah, Karen, you are such a child. Even when you know something, you continue to deny it."

Without moving her eyes from the priest, Karen reached out and took Jeff's hand. Squeezing it hard, she watched Father Sullivan step away from the door frame. He staggered toward the table at the center of the kitchen.

Then she saw a pale white cable behind him.

He's tied up, she thought.

A rope appeared to be wrapped around his neck like a noose.

When Sullivan took two more halting steps, Karen realized someone was standing behind him. What she had mistaken for a rope was in reality the arm of an impossibly fragile-looking man. He had a hand on Sullivan's back, apparently to steady himself.

He moved along with the priest, one tottering step at a time, approaching them with a painful slowness.

Who was it? She couldn't tell for sure.

Was it McCurdy? No way! The man was too old and delicate. His body seemed twisted, impossibly thin. He hardly seemed alive.

Then Karen saw his hand wasn't on Sullivan's back. Not exactly. It was as if this frail naked corpse had its hand clamped to the back of Sullivan's neck. But as Sullivan drew nearer, Karen perceived something she wanted to deny: the corpse was not *holding* Sullivan's neck at all; its long, skeletal fingers were actually embedded in the back of the priest's skull.

A scream locked in her throat. She dug her fingers into Jeff's arm.

When the old man's shadowy form met the hall's dull light, he seemed to glow. A luminescence molded itself to him, forming a kind of aura. With great difficulty he raised his arm, stretching his free hand skyward.

The heavens split with a magnificent crash of thunder; the concussion rattled the house. Dishes clattered. Timbers groaned. Lightning blasted the hall into momentary brilliance.

But instead of vanishing, the white electrical glare seemed to swirl within the room. Karen had never seen light behave so strangely. Impossibly, it rotated counterclockwise like shining water in a drain, whirling until it flowed into the tottering old man.

His laugh was a booming demonic howl, a chilling hybrid of triumph and madness.

"Holy shit," Jeff whispered, "I've got to get to that computer!"

He pushed Karen toward the outside door as he turned and bolted for the stairs.

But Karen caught herself. She watched in fascination as the ancient man lifted the priest with one hand and hurled him toward the wall. Sullivan crumbled near Karen's feet.

"Another broken puppet," the skeleton laughed, shaking gore from his fingertips.

Karen felt as if she were being torn in half. Should she run away? Or kneel to help the fallen priest?

What should she do? She didn't know. She couldn't move.

* * *

Father Sullivan could not open his eyes. He couldn't feel the floor under him; he no longer sensed temperature in the room. Even his olfactory functions had shut down. His single sensation was that he was hovering weightlessly in the infinite blackness of space. The only thing he'd ever experienced remotely like it was a brief period immersed in the warm liquid of a sensory deprivation tank at St. Mark's College.

But he was not uncomfortable.

Somehow he knew Karen was nearby. He sensed her. And he was sure if he waited, rested a minute, he would be able to speak. He had to warn her. Had to tell her the truth.

But what should he say?

On some diminishing level of functioning intellect, the dying priest realized what had happened to him. The demon-thing had pulled the strength from him, had filled his mind with horrific thoughts, and in so doing, had pushed out his . . .

His what? His essence? His life force? His immortal soul?

Thoughts continued, so he knew he was still alive. More than anything, he wanted to pray, but what good would it do?

If he could just summon the strength to speak to Karen. He could tell her. He could explain what he had just learned about the order and reason of the universe.

He reviewed it in his mind, hoping to discover a flaw in the creature's logic.

Was what he had learned really part of the undisclosed secret of Fatima, as the beast had insisted?

Oh my dear God! Sullivan would have wept if it were possible. But no. He had to think. He had to disprove this ugly revelation before he . . .

Died.

He thought: The human body is home for the soul. Also its protector. And its incubator. The soul matures as the body ages. Mankind's strongest instinct, the will to live, insures the soul's continuation for as many years as possible. Survival is a powerful instinct, genetically encoded, programmed into us long before we are born. It is human nature to allow the soul decades to strengthen, to . . . ripen.

An equally potent instinct is the urge to reproduce. But, the demon-thing had communicated, humankind's function is reproducing soul, not progeny. It is our mission, our purpose, to keep the supply plentiful.

And when we die there is no personal transcendence into Heaven or Hell, our soul merely makes its exit and takes its place in the universe. There it nourishes the things that depend on it for their own sustenance and survival.

The cycles of nature.

The end of the food chain.

It was contrary to everything Sullivan had ever believed.

Could it be true? Was this the hidden revelation of Fatima? If so, perhaps Sullivan should hold his tongue. As the Pope had held his, preserving an illusion designed to make reality endurable.

Or was this another demonic fabrication?

He *had* to know, *had* to discover the flaw in the creature's logic. But there was no time!

I . . . can't do it, Father. Please, I can't.

"You *can* do it. Concentrate, William. *Concentrate!*" It was Father Mosely's voice. Again Sullivan was a small boy on a chinning bar, not rising, not falling, hanging like a plump apple on a bough. Would he be able to pull himself up and ascend into Heaven? Or drop forever into the black bowels of Hell?

Or—dear God help me!—would he literally be consumed by malignant forces he had just recently come to know?

As consciousness waned, Father Sullivan realized one thing for certain: in a moment he'd learn which it was to be.

* * *

Jeff Chandler ran up the stairs toward the bedroom. When he had almost reached the second floor, he faltered. His head began to spin, his vision darkened.

A shadow materialized before him on the stair. A shadow blacker than the night that filled the old house. It loomed directly in his path, filling the entire top of the stairway. He couldn't step around it, though he knew the entrance to the bedroom was directly on the other side, a scant five feet away. He would have to plunge into that concentration of darkness, pass through it. That was the only way to reach McCurdy's terminal.

Uncertain, he turned, looked downstairs.

Karen was assisting the skeletal man. Together they moved toward the foot of the stairs. She looked as if she were in a trance.

Christ, what now? Jeff wondered, watching the strange couple moving closer. Were they coming up to get him?

It was too late. He had no alternative but to press forward, cross that preternatural darkness, and enter the bedroom.

Of course I can pass through it, he thought. *It's an illusion, a trick to scare me away!*

It would be no worse than jumping over a puddle.

Battling a crippling fear, Jeff faced the shadow. He thought of himself as a sky diver, petrified before jumping.

He took a deep breath, braced himself, and plunged.

Then he screamed!

* * *

When Casey heard her father's cry, she wanted to jump up and run to him.

"Stay here," he had told her. "No matter what, stay here till I come back for you."

But now he was screaming.

Casey *knew* she could do it. She could get up and walk. She could run to him if she had to. But her father's other warning held her in place. "If you get up it'll own you. You'll be in its debt."

Could that be true? If she'd really regained the use of her legs, wouldn't it be wrong to remain seated at a time like this? Wouldn't it be a sin not to assist her father if he was in trouble?

She remembered the bullet shattering her mother's forehead, fast and final. There was nothing she could have done, yet she'd felt guilty just the same. But now . . . maybe this time . . .

The little girl beside her made a hissing sound, blinking her eyes frantically.

What was she trying to say? That if Casey got up, something awful would happen to her, too? Something worse than what happened to this pitiful child?

Oh my God, what should I do?

And then she knew.

Casey Chandler did something she had not done since her mother died. She prayed.

* * *

At first the slight bulk of the old man's body made Karen feel as if she were carrying an impossible load. His weight, she knew, was not just physical, it was in some way incorporeal. Somehow, he was adding the density of his spirit, his essence, to her own. Before they'd made it halfway to the bottom of the stairs, the demon was seeing through her eyes, moving with the strength of her muscles, tottering forward propelled by her life energy, rather than his own.

It was a perfect sharing. It felt right. Complete.

Although he was not speaking, he was communicating with her. She could feel his thoughts and her thoughts as a single mind. He was telling her what he wanted. What he had always wanted.

Her.

Not the old priest, not Father Sullivan. Not Jeff or Casey, not Alton Barnes or any of the others. They were all expendable parts of the plan.

The demon wanted Karen. Just Karen. For she was unmarred and uncorrupt. She was unspoiled, youthful, perfect, and powerful. And with those persuasive words ringing in her mind, Karen began to feel beautiful, dynamic. Supremely confident, perhaps for the first time in her life.

It was wonderful!

Though she knew she was seeing herself as the demon saw her, their visions were starting to mesh, blend, become a single perception. And she welcomed this new outlook, loving these strong and unfamiliar feelings about herself. She *was* lovely, vital, glowing with feminine charisma. She felt an ecstasy moving in waves along her spine, splashing between her thighs, lapping at the two perfect points where her nipples met the fabric of her bra. Her face was a beautiful persuader, her body a potent sexual tool. She could do anything. Influence anyone.

Her clothes fell away and pooled at her feet. She stepped over them, another shackle gone forever. Standing elegant and free, her naked body shone with a fierce sexual radiance. She sighed deeply, her muscles rippled and flowed beneath a steaming glaze of sweat.

Now she could actually *feel* the demon's will coupling with hers. He would command her to take another step, and she would move forward. Step after step until she needed no more commands, progressing toward the stairway and toward Jeffrey Chandler.

Yes. She would stop him. Now. Forever.

"Jeffrey," she said. "Wait, Jeffrey. . . ."

* * *

The darkness was complete. It was as if his eyes had suddenly vanished from his head.

Blinded, Jeff suffered a profound disorientation. No up or down. No floor beneath his feet. Oddly, he stood in a slippery, sloshing liquid. And he could walk on it! He took another tentative step, fearing that if he acknowledged this impossibility he'd sink and drown in a bottomless sea.

Another cautious step. The waves he caused rippled in concentric circles to the ends of the universe. Then back. Flooding over him as an invisible tide.

He felt things that might have been fish brushing against his flesh as they swam by. Their touch was cold, clammy, impossibly foreign. He pulled away in disgust.

Someone called from all around, "Jeffrey, wait. Jeffrey . . ."

When he turned he saw his wife Jessica. His dead wife. Grinning at him from Casey's wheelchair.

Her face exploded, just as it had a million times in his mind. The assassin's bullet blasted it to pieces.

There was another face underneath. It exploded, too.

And another . . .

Jeff turned away, screaming. All the time knowing that if he escaped into hysteria, something would jump into his mind and take hold of him.

But he didn't care.

He heard the sound of another explosion. Another.

He screamed again.

Then something grabbed him.

* * *

Lying flat on the porch floor, McCurdy tried to open the screen door without making any noise.

He allowed the spring to tug the door's weight against him, forcing it to close a little at a time as he dragged himself through.

When he was fully into the kitchen, he let the door shut quietly against its frame. Then he exhaled with great relief.

The first thing he saw was the priest's body, a new addition to the farmhouse morgue. Seeing it shriveled against the wall inspired a momentary stab of hopelessness. The priest had been God's man. Did this mean all faith was powerless against the accursed thing?

Because McCurdy had been deluded, was he also to be damned?

Had salvation and a lifetime of prayers been . . . wasted?

No matter. God or devil, the thing had betrayed him.

The remnants of his pride demanded revenge. With a motivator stronger than love, McCurdy propelled himself forward. Arm over arm, he slid across the gritty floor toward the hall. Beside the doorway, he used a chair to help himself get to his feet. There was no way he'd meet the fiend lying on his belly, groveling on the floor.

Leaning against the door frame now, McCurdy reached into his pocket for the pistol.

Then he stepped into the hall, took aim.
And fired!

* * *

Alton Barnes pulled Jeff into the bedroom. Jeff's face was brilliant red. Veins stood out in his forehead and neck as he screamed and screamed.

"Jeff, *stop it!*"

Jeff's body was rigid, almost convulsing. His hands were balled, locked against his chin.

"Jeff, it's okay, you're all right."

Al slapped him gently. Slapped him again, harder. "Jeff, come on. Snap out of it, for Christ's sake. You're *okay.*"

Tension released and Jeff slumped into Alton's arms. The old man supported him with ease, dragging him into the bedroom.

"You was so dazed up I thought you was gonna walk straight into that christly wall out there. What they doin', messin' with your mind, Jeffrey?"

Jeff shook his head as if trying to wake up. "Alton? Christ? What . . . ? Where'd you . . . ? How'd you get up here?"

"I come back with the car and seen what's goin' on in here. Figgered I'd better get the computer for ya. So I climbed up that maple by the porch roof and come in the window. Hurry up now, grab the sonuvabitch and let's get the hell out of here."

"There's no time. I've got to do it here. Now. Stay by the door, will you? See to it nobody bothers me."

"You got it."

The liquid crystal screen was still lighted, glowing its eerie neon purple glow. Jeff hit the *enter* button to activate the program. When the outline of a left hand with a truncated little figure appeared, he knew he was beaten.

* * *

McCurdy's bullet smacked the old man in the shoulder, spinning him away from Karen.

Instead of falling, the ghastly body spun slow motion into the air as if it were no longer subject to gravity. With arms spread, the old man hovered between floor and ceiling like a wrinkled helium balloon.

McCurdy aimed, preparing to fire another round.

Karen turned, ready to attack the intruder.

Sneering, the old man pointed a gnarled finger at McCurdy. With a voice that seemed impossibly loud, he commanded, *"Disarm him!"*

McCurdy's arms snapped straight out to the sides as if yanked by invisible ropes. The gun flew from his hand and vanished in the darkness.

It was as if the old man's unseen bodyguards were holding McCurdy in place while brutally pulling his arms at right angles to his body. And those invisible protectors were impossibly strong.

McCurdy screamed in agony, his body lurched this way and that, caught in an impossible tug-of-war. He issued a lunatic scream as both arms ripped from their sockets and thumped to the floor. Blood spurted like a fountain as McCurdy's body started to spin.

On their way downstairs, Jeff and Al watched McCurdy collapse, crying and moaning.

"Al—" Jeff began.

"I know," Al assured him and ran down the stairway.

* * *

In her peripheral vision, Karen saw everything go crazy.

Alton Barnes scooted by her like a furtive animal and disappeared from sight; McCurdy twitched and cried on the floor; the walls seemed to fade and the candlelit hallway became part of some endless emptiness that was far too alien to register coherently on what remained of her human senses. She saw tiny beings composed entirely of light skittering around her feet. They emitted high-pitched birdlike giggles as they scampered and swarmed. She heard leathery wings flapping like sodden sheets somewhere behind her. Vaguely human voices whispered, "It is done." She saw stars blinking out one by one in the vast celestial dome she used to call the sky.

Even while these impossible things happened around her, she could not move her eyes to see them directly, to try to understand. Instead, her gaze was welded to the eyes of the old man who floated before her, suspended horizontally in the blackness of space.

As Karen stared, his eyes glowed like two penlights, boring laser beams directly into her mind. What looked like fine silver strands extruded from the many orifices of the old man's body. They reached out from his ears, his nostrils, his tiny pores, millions of them, stretching toward her like the threadlike tentacles of a gigantic jellyfish. And when they touched her, they tunneled like worms into her skin.

Words from her profession popped to mind and fell away like dry, dead leaves: delusion, hallucination, dementia.

Reality had changed, shifted. Then it too fell away with the obsolete jargon of her career.

I can kill and destroy, she thought. *I can bring this whole house to the ground with the flex of a finger.*

Spiderweb strands continued to flow as the old man emptied himself into her. It was a preternatural copulation that would bring about the birth of a new god on the earth. A god of metamorphosis and transmutation. Because Karen herself was mutating, becoming. The demon spirit, the god spirit, the soul of Splitfoot poured into her, its essence surging, its will filling her to the bursting point.

And when what she saw as silver cords stopped moving from the withered body into hers, she watched the once-human thing shrivel and fall away.

Like a snake shedding its skin.

Like a chrysalis discarded.

Like an insect sucked dry.

It flashed and streaked and vanished like lightning from Heaven.

And a will that was almost her own commanded, *End this now. Finish them! We've toyed with these puppets long enough.*

She turned on Alton Barnes who was moving past her like a fish, swimming in slow motion against a night-black tide. His aura glowed rainbow patterns and she found them irritating.

She watched as he clutched at something. He picked it up, threw it into the void. She saw the alien object catapult from his hand. Flying toward the stairs.

Turning end over end, the thing vanished into oblivion.

Finish him!

Karen flexed incorporeal muscles. Air moved around her in response, swirling, gathering speed and density, growing to whirlwind force. It smashed Alton. He flew off his feet. His back smacked an invisible wall and he crumbled to an invisible floor.

Tides of electrical pleasure coursed through Karen; the workout was invigorating.

Good, her instincts assured her. *Now stop Jeffrey. Stop him, kill him!*

Yes, her mind hissed. *Yesss.*

She turned to face the invisible stairs.

* * *

When she suspected Lucy was no longer breathing, Casey knew what to do. Mindless of the insanity around her, she flopped from the chair and crawled across the porch to the little girl's side.

Lucy's chest wasn't moving. Her lips and nostrils were still.

How to help? The child's deformity made mouth-to-mouth impossible.

Fighting growing revulsion, Casey folded the rubbery lips against the child's chin and held them there with her hand. Then, reluctantly, she lowered her mouth over Lucy's nose and exhaled. She breathed and exhaled, just like they taught her in school. She kept this up until she realized it was no use. The child's body had swollen to twice its former size, and mean as it sounded in the privacy of her own thoughts, Casey guessed death might be the best thing for her.

Should she call for help? Maybe someone would come out and look at Lucy. But Casey didn't dare risk shouting.

She dragged herself to the door and looked inside.

What she saw made no sense.

Karen was standing in the middle of the hall, naked, grinning like a madwoman. There were two bodies on the floor: the priest and McCurdy. Where'd he come from?

And old Mr. Barnes was standing near Karen. He shrank from her as if she frightened him. All at once Mr. Barnes heaved something to Dad. It was white and bent. Before she could tell what it was, Dad snatched it from the air.

Then Karen flicked her wrist. It was a quick, tight motion, as if she were trying to shake a drop of water from her fingertip. Though she never touched him, Mr. Barnes flew off his feet and slammed into the wall!

And when he crumbled to the floor, Karen laughed. Then she turned her whole body toward the steps that led to the upstairs room where Dad had just disappeared.

* * *

Holding the severed arm, Jeff flattened McCurdy's left palm against the computer screen. It flashed:

MCCURDY VERIFIED

Then he typed frantically. Part of his mind tried to ignore the slow steady pounding of feet coming up the stairs.

But it was impossible to ignore the unfamiliar female voice that called to him. "Say your prayers, Jeffrey. And if you want to save yourself, you'd better say them to me."

No, not now. He needed time. Time!

* * *

Alton Barnes picked himself up off the floor. I'm okay, he thought. Nothing broken this time. Shaking his head, he looked around.

He saw Karen, heavy-footed and awkward, walking up the steps toward the bedroom.

Somethin's got her, he thought.

Alton knew what Karen was experiencing. The thing was inside her. Fucking with her mind, eroding her values, battering her principles, mocking everything she loved with irresistible temptations. It wanted to tear down everything good, replace it with sickness.

"Wait, Karen. Stop! Don't go up there."

* * *

Jeff hit the REPEAT command. He hit it again and again.

Any minute someone would burst in the door and force him to quit what he was doing.

What if he couldn't finish?

And if he did, what if his plan didn't work?

But damn it, he had to try.

All he needed was a little more time.

* * *

The loudest voice was the one in her head.

It said, *Move faster! Get up the stairs!*

She took another step.

"Karen. Dr. Bradley. Try to stop. I know what's inside you, but you gotta fight it. Come on, you gotta . . ."

She glanced over her shoulder. Alton was looking up at her, his eyes imploring. She wouldn't stop.

With a wave of your hand, with a nod and a wink, you can blast Jeffrey and that damn machine back to atoms.

She took another step.

When the machine is gone, your place in this world is assured. The greatest musicians will play for you. They'll write you operas and symphonies. The most charming, the most powerful men—politicians, entertainers, power brokers—will be yours for playthings.

Fire erupted on the stairs around her.

Flames jumped and danced around her legs. Fiery tongues climbed her torso, lapped at her breasts. It didn't burn. No. In fact it felt cool, soothing. Its radiation caressed her skin. Surrounded her. She wore it like a garment. It moved along with her like a protective barrier. And when she commanded, it would leap forth and destroy.

As she took another step she saw the wallpaper turn brown and peel from the plaster like scorched parchment.

Although she wasn't looking at him, she could see Alton Barnes behind her at the foot of the stairs. He held his hands before his face, shielding himself from the heat. He wouldn't be able to come any nearer.

"Can't you see what it's doing?" he cried. "That's fire, miss, that's the devil's tool. You can't let that sonavabitch do this to you."

The devil's tool? She'd let him play with the devil's tool. She'd fuck him with it! When she laughed a column of flame leapt toward Alton like a blazing attack dog. Scorching wind whizzed past his face, turning his cheeks red, making him screech in pain.

Hurry now, hurry. When the computer is down all the world will be yours!

One more step and she'd be in the upstairs hall.

In spite of the heat, Alton pursued her up the stairs. His shirt burst into flame. The skin of his face blackened. "Wait, Karen, please wait. Let me help you like you done for me. Don't go up there. Don't go in that room. *Please!*"

He was only able to make three more steps before intense heat stopped him. His face blistered. His hair fell away as gray ashen powder.

Fire poured down the stairs, cascading over the steps like a flaming waterfall. It flooded over Alton and he vanished, screaming, under thick smoke and a fiery tide.

* * *

Casey saw it all.

Saw it, and still she did nothing. She hated herself for her indecision. She *never* knew what to do. Never acted quickly enough.

Okay, she thought, I have to stand.

Yes, she had to run in there and offer whatever help she could.

She tried to calculate the risk: if she stood up, she'd be accepting the demon's healing gift. And if Dad was right, the moment she accepted the gift, she'd belong to the demon.

But if the effort of standing and walking made the demon abandon Karen and come to claim Casey, that would be okay. Karen would be safe, and Dad would have extra time to finish what he was doing. Maybe the two of them could even get away.

Prayers came easier now. She offered one more, confiding what she was going to do, asking for God's help.

Casey gritted her teeth, concentrating, forcing long-unused flesh to obey forgotten commands.

Muscles stretched. Tendons pulled like steel cables. Dormant nerves shrieked painful messages of distress.

It hurt like hell, but it was working. Casey was standing up!

She walked inside, her legs stiff as crutches. "Karen," she cried. "It's me, Casey. Please stop. Don't hurt Dad, Karen. Please. He loves you!"

* * *

Almost, Jeff thought. Almost. Just another second . . .

His fingers flew over the keys. In triumph, he hit the ENTER button for the last time.

"Now we just wait and see," he said it to no one. In his profound concentration, he'd been oblivious to the shouts and noise filling the air around him.

Words danced across the computer screen. He smelled smoke and the sweet scent of burning flesh. His strength vanished and he wilted in his chair.

It was over. One way or another, it was over.

* * *

The tiny dying part of her mind that was still Karen Bradley heard the terrified child—*he loves you*—and she stopped.

Indecision held her in place. Fear locked her muscles. Fear for what she had done. Fear for what she might still do.

She had felt this paralysis many times. But it was new to the alien presence that tried to propel her onward.

MOVE, you damn surly cow!

Yet as she stood there, still as a statue, the evil words sounded farther and farther away until they were a faint echo on the threshold of vanishing forever.

The ring of flames around her lowered like a gas burner going out. In a moment they were gone.

Casey. Jeff. Mr. Barnes. Lucy. She couldn't speak their names, but they were the clearest thoughts in her mind.

And suddenly the world changed one more time for Karen Bradley. The air in the old house clarified. Sounds once again began to resonate properly. The oppressive weight of an alien presence lightened until it departed altogether.

The first rays of morning sunshine poured in the windows and through the open door at the bottom of the stairs.

Karen heard Casey's footsteps coming up the stairs behind her.

She wanted to turn, to smile at the girl and hug her for saying the wonderful magic words that had broken the demon's spell.

But she was still immobile, rooted to the spot. Paralyzed.

A haggard-looking Jeffrey Chandler appeared in the bedroom door directly in front of Karen. Though he was filthy and seemed exhausted, he somehow managed to smile at her.

With five steps he was at her side. Jeff took Karen's arm and looked into her eyes. "Here," he said, smiling, "let me help you.", His voice lacked some of the depth and confidence of the first time he had uttered those words.

But they sounded like music to Karen.

24

The Name of the Father

After a twenty-minute drive they arrived at the Medical Center Hospital in Burlington. Two flashing ambulances blocked the emergency-room doors. Two more had passed them en route. Jeff suspected the emergency vehicles were attending the pileup of cars and trucks he'd seen while speeding down the hill from the Dubois farmhouse.

Two police cruisers, a fire engine, and about a half-dozen passenger cars had gone off either side of Bingham Creek Road.

As they drove by, Jeff saw the unmoving forms of people inside the dark vehicles. Apparently the forces that were active on the hilltop had made it impossible for anyone to approach. Were the occupants of the derelict vehicles dead or just out of commission? Jeff didn't know; he hadn't stopped to find out.

He pulled the car as close as he could get to the entrance, parked, and carried Casey into the emergency room. Two orderlies with a stretcher hurried out to help Karen, who had passed out in the back seat.

Doctors and nurses moved in well-rehearsed patterns around Casey. In what Jeff guessed was a major violation of hospital protocol, the emergency team rushed his daughter off for X rays before any paperwork was done.

Shortly, an urgent-voiced woman with a clipboard summoned him to the admitting desk. Fighting tears, he supplied information on Casey and Karen. Again he insisted an ambulance be sent for Alton. "He was alive when we left," Jeff said, "but he was burned. I couldn't risk moving him."

A harried young doctor appeared, interrupting the intake process. She shouted a confusion of questions. Jeff could answer none of them. "I don't *know* what happened to Casey. I don't *know* what happened to any of us!"

* * *

"Your daughter is fine," another white-smocked doctor told Jeff. "She's resting; I gave her a sedative. We've gotta say one thing for her: she's a very strong young woman. You must be very proud of her."

Jeff nodded dumbly, searching for words. Glancing at the doctor's name tag, he saw he was talking to B. Bernstein, M.D., Resident.

"Th-thank . . ."

"It's okay, Mr. Chandler. That's what we're here for."

The young doctor seemed tired, yet his puffy, dark-rimmed eyes were compassionate. He'd probably been up for hours, maybe longer than Jeff. "More police are on their way. They're going to want to question her. You, too, of course. Why don't you go down to the cafeteria and get some coffee? Maybe something to eat?"

The young doctor smiled and put his hand on Jeff's shoulder. Jeff wanted to thank him. Instead he said, "Can I see her?"

"Sure. But I'd like you to wait awhile, okay? She needs to rest. The best thing for her is to rest. I can find a bed for you, too, if you like. Bet you could use some sleep."

Jeff shook his head. "Doctor . . . ?"

The doctor raised his eyebrows.

"What about her legs?"

"That's the strangest part of all this. Her legs seem to be fine, just as you said. The reflexes are there; she can move her toes a little. She has sensation. It's probably best she doesn't try to walk again for a while, though. I suspect they're too weak to support her weight for very long."

The doctor shook his head as if puzzled. "I mean I've heard of people doing astounding things in emergency situations, but never anything like this. It's not a term people in my profession use very readily, but it certainly appears to be a miracle. A neurologist wants to check in on her later this morning. We don't get situations like this every day. . . ."

"No, not every day," said Jeff.

"Frankly, I think she's a little scared of her recovery."

"What do you mean?"

The weary young doctor scratched curly hair. "As I was examining her she kept saying, 'I'm never going to walk again. Never.' I guess she just couldn't believe it, you know?"

"I guess not," said Jeff. He turned and started toward the elevator. Yes, a cup of coffee sounded like just the thing.

*   *   *

Thank God, Karen thought when she spied Jeff through the glass doors to the hospital cafeteria. Now everything seemed all right.

He sat alone at a rectangular table, staring straight ahead as if he were asleep with his eyes open. A plasticfoam cup and an untouched sandwich on a paper plate sat abandoned in front of him.

Only three other people occupied the dining area at this midmorning hour: two white-garbed men and a woman in surgical green. The trio huddled around a circular table smoking cigarettes and laughing.

As Karen opened the door, she saw how haggard Jeff appeared. Apparently he had made some effort to freshen up. His face was so clean the black stubble of his beard stood out prominently. His hair was wet and freshly combed. But his clothing was more filthy than a mud wrestler's.

When he noticed her he stood up. She rushed to him and they embraced, transferring some of his powdery dirt to her clean clothing.

"Well, look at you!" Jeff said hoarsely, trying to smile.

"A nurse loaned me this lab coat," Karen said. "How do I look in white?"

"Like an angel."

Her smile faded as Karen took the seat across from Jeff's. "Have you heard anything about Casey?" she asked.

"Fine. She's just fine. Sleeping. And how are you?"

She reached across the table and took his hand. "Oh, as well as can be expected. I'm ambulating, taking nourishment, receiving visitors . . . All thanks to you."

Jeff squeezed her hand, smiling weakly.

"Jeff . . . ?"

His eyes fastened on hers.

Karen bit her lower lip. Her gaze dropped to the tabletop, rested there a moment, then rose to look Jeff full in the face. "Mr. Barnes didn't make it."

Jeff appeared to be staring at his untouched sandwich. He remained that way for a long time.

After a while, Karen took a sip of Jeff's coffee. "They want me back upstairs. More tests. I told them I had to talk to you first. I had to tell you myself. Want to walk up with me?"

"Sure."

They stood up.

"Jeff?"

"Yes?"

"Is it really over? Do you think it's really over?"

They walked toward the door. Jeff opened it for Karen. "I don't know. I honestly don't. I guess all we can do is pray."

"But you did something with the computer, didn't you?"

"I tried."

"What did you do?"

That boyish, slightly mischievous grin tugged at the corners of Jeff's eyes and mouth. "I poisoned it."

The elevator doors slid open. Karen led Jeff inside where they were alone.

"Poisoned it? What do you mean?"

"You've heard of computer viruses?" he asked.

"Yeah. I guess . . ."

"I input a few names of God. You know, Yahweh, Jehovah, Adonai, Elohim, Shaddai, Allah—all the ones I could think of, anyway. I told it to find every possible translation from every known language. Then I instructed the machine to replace its entire memory with those names. To repeat them over and over, continuously, deleting everything else, replacing everything in storage with all the names of God. It was the only thing I could think to do."

He laughed a quick quiet laugh. "It's probably still at work.

Deleting words, replacing words. Might take days. Weeks, maybe. That machine's memory is bigger than the Library of Congress."

The elevator doors opened and Karen led Jeff toward her room.

"So what do you think," she asked, "did the names of God kill the demon?"

"No. Not if it really *was* a demon. Demons don't die, remember? But if we're lucky, those words banished it for a while."

"And if it wasn't a demon? I mean Father Mosely and Father Sullivan both suspected it wasn't a demon. *It* even said it wasn't a demon. . . ."

Jeff shrugged his shoulders. "Maybe it lied."

"Then it really could be over!"

"Yup, it could. For this time. For now."

Karen and Jeff paused in front of her room.

"Jeff, I have to ask you one more question, okay?"

"Shoot."

"W-was it really true. I mean what Casey said . . . ?"

"You mean the thing about me loving you?"

Karen looked down. Her face grew warm; she knew she was blushing.

Jeff touched her cheek, then took her in his arms. "More than anything else in the world. Even if I were a demon, I couldn't lie about that. In fact," he whispered softly into her ear, "when you've rested up a bit, I'm going to try to talk you into marrying me."

Excerpt from
The Reality Conspiracy:
An Anecdotal Reconstruction of the Events at Hobston, Vermont

You are reading the next-to-last chapter. The final installment is yet to be written. When it appears, it will detail a history that has not yet come to pass.

Already we know it will be inaccurate.

No event can be described with precision until the Reality Conspirators, those orthodox defenders of the paradigm, have learned one simple truth: dexterous as they are with their string, it's not long enough to tie all the loose ends.

Military involvement in the events at Hobston was quick and decisive. Since no one could reach the hilltop, no one witnessed McCurdy's destruction, the preternatural slaughter, or the horror at the Dubois farm. By midmorning the area was cordoned off and secured. Outgoing information was easily controlled.

Newspapers announced the greatest shower of comets in a hundred years. Network television broadcast indistinct videos of a dramatic sky show. All media reports mentioned the tragic deaths of a handful of overeager sightseers who'd stood too close to the meteor's point of impact.

A priest, a janitor, and a farmer's widow were killed in the resulting fire at a nearby farmhouse. Their obituaries ran in the Burlington papers. Two unidentified bodies were found in the rubble: "a grossly deformed individual and a man with a severe head injury." Lucy Washburn and Herbert Gold. Both burned beyond recognition. Father Mosely's remains were never accounted for.

Ironically, tabloids with garish headlines got closer to the truth. As usual, they were discounted.

Any citizen voicing a conflicting claim, accurate or fanciful, was dealt with as a rumormonger, sensationalist, or lunatic. Many endured systematic ridicule or a campaign of disinformation that eclipsed those that disguised the Manhattan Project, Watergate, and the release of Iran's hostages.

The three survivors—in some ways hostages ourselves—were visited by stone-faced officials in severe black suits. On July second they advised us that any disclosure would win harsh and immediate retribution. I could be imprisoned, they reminded, for violating my oath of secrecy. But prison was not an option, they told me with Jack Webb earnestness, because they dispensed justice far swifter than the court system.

I believe them.

I marvel that we are alive, that we did not "vanish" from our hospital rooms.

If I had not run once, I might not have tried it again. This time we did it right. By chance we left Burlington the night Karen's condo exploded. A gas leak. We escaped by less than one hour, and never smelled the fumes. . . .

At the time of our marriage we all changed our names. We are in hiding. Copies of this manuscript are with my publisher, my lawyer, and with a friend at *The New York Times*. None of them knows where to find us.

Casey still does not walk. She can, but she refuses, fearing the return of dangerous visitors.

Karen doesn't freeze anymore. She had spent a lifetime apologizing for an embarrassing personal imperfection that, quite possibly, saved the world.

I ponder the inevitable. To me it seems that all of it was planned, choreographed, plotted long ago in that unwritten text that will become history.

New irony has entered our lives.

Now, months later, we watch shadows with heightened alertness. Darkness takes on new meaning. Whispers unnerve us. A bird glimpsed in our peripheral vision has the potential to terrify. A flower grows; a mountain moves. . . .

Each of us—Karen, Casey, and myself—sees the world in an unfamiliar way. And what we see is incomplete.

We have new knowledge: We, everyone, holds duel citizenship in two separate realities. One, the known, is the construct of rational thinkers, those degree-waving ortho-docs who pound their gavel of conviction and scream with judicial authority

> that frogs don't rain from the skies,
> and men don't fly without wires,
> red-eyed man-beasts don't shamble in the forest,
> people don't spontaneously combust,
> statues don't cry,
> children never issue from virgin wombs,
> and no one ever walks off the face of the earth forever.

Yet, like it or not, from the moment of our birth, and always thereafter, regardless of our level of personal enlightenment, we cannot avoid participation in a conspiracy to deny what we cannot, or will not understand.

And with each new heartbeat the string that ties all truth together tightens like a noose.

—Jeffrey Chandler, 1993

Amber Sulick

Author's Note

DEUS-X: The Reality Conspiracy is perhaps my darkest book. This time the menace is not only physical but also philosophical.

The idea evolved from my interest in anomalous phenomena. I remember thinking about all the strange things that actually occur, not only in Vermont, but all over this world, from fish falls to spontaneous human combustion. Such outbreaks of high strangeness seem random and totally unrelated.

Crackpots and courageous scientists study UFOs, Bigfoots, ghosts, aquatic monsters, and myriad other mysteries and marvels, all just a bit outside the spotlight of conventional science. Yet these maverick researchers often demonstrate a certain territorialism. Those investigating UFOs ignore, sometimes scoff at, the Bigfoot hunters. Bigfoot hunters question the credibility of people who see ghosts. And ghost hunters might mock anyone who sees the Lake Champlain Monster. Four phenomena, four separate sets of investigators. Everyone looking in different directions.

I started to wonder, What if the various supernatural and semi-supernatural phenomena were not different? What if they—Bigfoot, Champ, ghosts, and UFOs—were generated by the same source? What if they are elaborate distractions designed to keep our attention away from the true source?

If so, what might that source look like?

Considering our own condition and the state of our world, it would have to be something highly unconventional and truly terrifying.

With that in mind, the rest of the book almost wrote itself, colored, of course, by my personal paranoia about big government and my distrust of commercial religion.

Thematically, I am reminded of that old Firesign Theatre comedy album titled "Everything You Know is Wrong." To me there was never anything comic about that idea. It's a horrific notion and seems to be at the root of *DEUS-X*.

Though this may be a dark and pessimistic work, it is optimistic about the value and strength of human beings and the bonds they form. And in that sense, the book comes very close to what I truly believe.